An Illustrated Guide to the
Secrets of Finding a Home
That Fits You

RIGHT WHERE YOU LIVE

Constance Brady, A.I.A.

Celestial Arts
Millbrae, California

To Faith Nash, my mother

Celestial Arts
231 Adrian Road
Millbrae, California 94030

First Printing, September, 1979

Made in the United States of America

Cover Design: Bill Yenne
Cover and Interior Illustrations by Constance Brady

Library of Congress Cataloging in Publication Data

Brady, Constance.
    Right where you live.

    1.   Architecture, Domestic—Psychological
aspects.   2.   Architecture—Environmental aspects.
3.   Architecture—Human factors.   I.   Title
NA7125.B66   643   78-73550
ISBN 0-89087-242-2

1 2 3 4 5 6 7—85 84 83 82 81 80 79

Contents

STEP ONE

Will the Shoe Fit?

*"There was an old woman who lived in a shoe,
She had so many children she didn't know what to do;
She gave them some broth without any bread;
She whipped them all soundly and put them to bed."*
Mother Goose

That's not exactly a funny story. When I was a child, I thought this family must be very poor and this was why they had no bread; but I never understood why the old woman whipped the children, nor why she was *old* and had *little* children. I think I've got it figured out now.

Their *shoe,* or house, did not fit them! I think the shoe was so crowded (and weirdly shaped) that the children had no place of their own in which to play and therefore were under the feet of the woman all day. By supper time she was too nervous and impatient and tired to even get the bread out, cut it up, or clean up the crumbs afterward. The children's hunger pangs made them impatient and tired. Then they probably started to whine and cry and to get into spats with one another. This must have surely pushed the old woman over the brink;

she lost her self-control and whipped the children so that they would go to bed and leave her alone. Thus the whole family ended their day in misery. The children were miserable because they were hungry and felt unloved. The old woman was miserable because she felt guilty for being so mean to the children and because she had aged *another year in one day.*

This Mother Goose interpretation may sound absurd but it vividly describes how an ill-fitting and insensitive environment can affect our peace of mind, our relationships with others, our feelings about ourselves, and general ease and enjoyment of life and living.

Your home can make you sick or it can help you to be well. And that is what this book is all about. It is not another decorating book or "How to Buy a Home" book or a book about making money on the resale of your home. It is about how to buy or rent, on any budget, a home that will enhance your mental and physical well-being.

You deserve all the delight, satisfaction and rightness you can get from your home. People are

1

much more important than dwellings, so before you start to consider the type of shelter it will be, architecture, or location, you need to find what makes you feel good and function best. This book covers almost everything else about your home but the questions and answers that are unique to you. You must find for yourself the picture or image of what you really want your home to be and do for you. Frequently the picture in your mind is very distinct with favorite colors and decorative features which are not as important as some other characteristics and often can wrongly influence your judgment. It is imperative to learn the effects on your picture of critical and unalterable components, such as location, orientation, structure and the effects of light, noise and nature, as opposed to relatively cosmetic items which are inexpensive and easy to change. This book will help you apply the architectural principles necessary to achieve what is closest to your ideal. Many people actually cripple their potential by saying, "I can't afford the picture I have!" I believe that you can! It's affordable if you look for it in the right places, with wisdom, and recognize what will make the picture possible.

At the bottom end of the economic spectrum, I've seen some wonderful shacks, or fleabag hotel rooms for that matter, that provided the framework for the inhabitant to turn them into warm, wonderful places that offered sanctuary and reflected the creativity of that person. Another disabling phrase is "I'm not creative either." Everyone is. Just having your own needs and wishes will lead to creativity if you will pay attention to them and work towards satisfying them.

I've also seen expensive homes that were cold, unpleasant, uncreative, and not built in accord with good architectural principles. It is not a matter of money. If you will get your picture together, (Step One) the other six steps will help you get the rest right, so it is entirely within the realm of possibility for you to find more fulfillment in your home than a rich person could. I guarantee you'll get a much better home for the money you have to spend than you would otherwise.

This book outlines an architectural procedure to follow when shopping for a home, and programming, including picturemaking, is the first step. Architecturally, programming has to do with how many baths you need, how many bedrooms, and whether you want a kitchen geared to serve one person, a couple, or an army.

Much more important are the intangible things that can make you feel good or terrible. If you can find what these are you can program all the things that make you feel good *in* and all the things that make you feel terrible *out*. Your home, large or small, is often your only sanctuary in this nervous world, and you need one that affirms and lifts and comforts you—not one that will pull you further off balance, and down, and add more discord to your life.

First you must sort out what these good and bad things are, thinking about the things that turn you on and things that turn you off. For instance, the uplifted feeling you get when shafts of light cascade into a room, when moonlight beams across your room at night, when firelight and cooking aromas mingle, when chimes ring across the neighborhood in the early evening, or when the sun warms you while you read the paper on a winter morning. Or oppositely, how you feel on a sunless, gray day, when you hear sirens on your street and neighbors can look in your windows.

Even if you've never had your own home, you can remember times when someone else's environment felt right to you or you were in a public space that you found exciting. Perhaps eating breakfast in a restaurant that had indoor plants, and where you were seated at a table near a window in the sun and you felt warm and good and full and peaceful. The *feeling* of that is not expensive to duplicate on a small scale in your own home or apartment if you know how to choose the one that will allow you to do it.

Or perhaps you remember a really fine day when you and your friends had a picnic in the park next to the rose garden. You felt full of the scent and sight of roses and greenery and sun. Wouldn't it enhance your life to gather that up and recreate it in your own environment? You could capture that feeling in even a tiny patch of garden, or on a balcony, if you choose a home with the kind of sun input that roses need and that won't cost you any more money. The important thing at this point is to not allow yourself to limit your desires and dreams because of your budget.

Speaking of roses and shacks, I happen to be very fond of both. When I began college to study architecture, I had a choice of living in the federally-designed concrete dorms, a rented room in a tract house, or a single-room shack in someone's back yard. The shack was very tiny, but was covered with climbing roses, had a wild, overgrown garden around it, a claw-footed bathtub, and I could afford to rent it without a roommate. I chose the shack because it gave me a joy and privacy which the other two choices, which were more substantial structures (and probably warmer) did not. Incidentally, it was the least expensive choice.

We shouldn't all have to live in the same type of housing any more than we should have matching wardrobes. We are treated much the same by the builders but there are still many choices in the sameness. True, housing has reached a point where it is stamped out like clothes and cars, but just as people buy vans and customize them afterward, we can do the same with housing if we choose a unit that will adapt itself to our needs. So the first thing to do is choose (whether buying or renting) a unit that can be turned into our picture.

Step One leaves it up to you to determine your particular needs. Just make the greatest picture you can and hopefully the other six Steps will show you how to get as close to it as possible.

When I work with clients in this phase of design, I follow them about in their present home to see how they use it, what they don't or do like about it, and how it makes them feel. I don't pretend to be a psychoanalyst, but I do try to find out what does or doesn't make them happy.

It is a creative-delving process to get all the positives out in the open and to recognize, in order to avoid, the negatives. Usually, the architect and the client spend many hours working together at this stage, but there's rarely as much time available as I would desire to be sure that the optimum result is achieved. However, we almost always discover something so important to my client's way of life that they can't believe they could have ever lived without it!

MAYBE YOU'D LIKE A WINDOW OF YOUR OWN TO LOOK THROUGH!

You need to do this for yourself! To keep the process simple and get it into a form you can deal with easily later, start by writing things down. Carry a notepad with you and add items as they come up. Since you don't have an architect with you, and don't have to worry about what it is costing you, you can spend as much time as you feel you need in this phase and do an even better job of it than you could with me. But you must go slowly, carefully, and really look for the honest answers.

The following is a suggested process to follow but since there may be other areas or ways to proceed that occur to you, follow your own leads too. What's really important is to be absolutely certain at this point that you are thinking only about *you, your* feelings, *your* desires and *your* dreams, and that you are not thinking about *others,* except as to how they may relate to *you.* Be totally selfish for now because if you are not, you may suppress some desire for the sake of others which later may affect you and the whole family adversely.

3

Each person moving into the new home should make their own list, including children. (You can interview them if they can't write.) We will discuss the kinds of things that might be included but urge you to try to think of the activities unique to each individual. The important thing is for each person to become aware of what conditions affect them in the most positive way. Items concerning one's own private space should be noted as well as for rooms that will be shared. All the needs of each member of the household, young and old, should be recorded. Later ways will be found to integrate them so everyone will get the greatest personal benefit.

It is important, in compiling this information to pay close attention to everything you do, how you are doing it, and how you'd rather do it. What activities are hard for you, or annoying, or pleasant, or easy? What occurs during the day or evening that makes you feel especially good, or bad? What would you rather see out of your window than what you see now? Why is some aspect of housework really unpleasant, and what would make it better? Is there some activity you want to pursue that there is no room for in your present home? Where do you go when you're distressed, want peace, or feel nervous? Where do you go when you want to share, and be with others? The large things are fairly easy but small problems often have a bigger impact on your life. Background noise, bending over every five minutes to accomplish some chore, stepping over things, cleaning dirt out of cracks, carrying things too often and too far can drive you absolutely mad. They are so minor individually you don't notice them, and wonder why you feel tired and tense at the end of the day. Similarly, if a lot of *small things* are right, although you won't be consciously aware of that either, you'll feel considerably better at the end of your day.

Observe *every aspect of your present environment,* also everywhere you go, and whomever you are with. This includes your neighborhood, your yard, your house, your family, your pets, and your friends. Put everything on your list whether it seems relevant or not, even if it involves fantasy!

Your list may begin to look very disorganized but don't worry about it. After you have spent a couple of weeks on it and get all your thoughts on paper you can reorganize and rewrite it. The pattern of what you need and want will start becoming very apparent. Figure 1 shows what a list might look like in its disorganized state.

FIGURE 1.

PRELIMINARY PROGRAM
(LIST OF LIKES, DISLIKES, WANTS, NEEDS DREAMS AND PICTURES)

1. THE HALF OF MY HOUSEPLANTS THAT HAVEN'T DIED LOOK AS IF THEY'RE GOING TO.

2. THE BEDROOM I HAD AS A CHILD HAD A HUGE TREE OUTSIDE THE WINDOW. ALL I COULD SEE WERE LEAVES AND BRANCHES. LIKE LIVING IN A TREE HOUSE. I WOULD LOVE TO GET THAT FEELING BACK.

3. IT REALLY IRKS ME TO HAVE TO GET ONTO MY HANDS AND KNEES TO SEE INTO THE BROILER.

4. THE CHILDREN NEVER PUT THEIR TOYS AWAY. THEY'RE ALL OVER THE HOUSE.

5. MY BEDROOM HAS TOO MUCH LIGHT IN IT AT NIGHT. IT IS DISTURBING TO ME.

6. THERE'S NO PLACE IN THIS HOUSE WHERE I CAN HAVE SOLITUDE.

7. I MUST GO UP AND DOWN THE STAIRS 50 TIMES A DAY. GREAT EXERCISE BUT IT WASTES TIME.

8. I'D LIKE A BATHTUB I COULD SOAK IN WITHOUT GETTING A BACKACHE AND FROZEN KNEES.

9. I SAW A KITCHEN IN A MAGAZINE THAT HAD FRENCH DOORS OPENING ONTO A SUNNY DECK. ONE COULD EAT OUTSIDE IN GOOD WEATHER WITHOUT EXTRA WORK. I'D LIKE TO DO THAT.

10. WHEN I ENTERTAIN IN MY PRESENT LIVING ROOM THERE'S A STIFFNESS THAT I DON'T LIKE OR UNDERSTAND. I WANT PEOPLE, INCLUDING ME, TO FEEL COMFORTABLE.

———> AND SO ON

Following are some of the major areas and examples of the type of things you should think about. You'll think of many others that apply to your own lifestyle, so add them to your list.

THE INTANGIBLES

The King of The Mountain Syndrome

Remembering our childhood is a good place to start finding out some of the reasons for our preferences. The basic emotionalism of *I love* this and *I hate* that is important. If you can look at an emotion analytically and find the reason for it, you can better deal with what it is that you really love or hate.

That's why I started with King of the Mountain, a child's game. Some people have to have the house at the very top of the hill. They will choose it no matter what the view is, good or bad, and often without special concern for the house itself, whether it works or not, whether the weather is rotten up there or anything else. I wonder if perhaps they have waited all this time to have their desire for invincibility satisfied. It may also be because they won all the time and can't get used to not being on top of the mountain. If the desire to be on top outweighs all others, then the mountain top (or the penthouse) is the best answer. On the other hand, perhaps it would feel better to give up this position. It's possible that continuing to play this game will only leave the king person tense and wary. What if someone builds on a nearby hill that is higher than his? Will he feel suddenly threatened and inferior and have to run off and find a still higher mountain?

If you know why you're doing anything, then you'll be able to figure out whether it is making you feel better or worse.

In recent years I've thought about this and discovered the reasons for some strong likes and dislikes that I have. I grew up in the desert, which was nice in the winter but boring because the weather was always good. The summers were terribly hot, 110° to 120° F usually, although I don't remember minding the heat as much as I minded the restrictions. It was so hot we had to play in the air-conditioned indoors until the evening when it became cool enough to go outside. This has left me with a kind of claustrophobia, or starvation for natural conditions. I feel uneasy in air-conditioned space, or any space where the windows can't be opened. Even in a cold climate that necessitates shutting oneself off from nature to keep warm, I get de-

CHILDHOOD GAMES

pressed. Wherever I work or live, if I can't have natural breezes wafting by me from an open window I become totally miserable. I'm disagreeable, abrupt, discontent and even rude to others. It took me years to realize why I *hated* some spaces and *loved* others. Now that I know, I can avoid the buildings and the climates that make me feel bad.

The desert upbringing also leaves me with a distinct aversion to tan and treeless landscapes. I need green ground and green trees and green hills. Although in my case I want opposites from what I have known, other people feel better if they can duplicate their childhood surroundings.

What were your childhood dreams? Did you dream of a perfect room or house or garden in your play? Or was something already perfect and when you remember it, it makes you feel good? Maybe it was the room you stayed in when you visited your grandmother, or maybe it was her kitchen (cookies and pies). If you can draw upon any of the good feelings and bring them into your life now, it will increase your pleasure and well-being in a new home. Don't ignore these dreams and force yourself back into stiff adulthood.

Perhaps you had family problems that you may not even remember, but you might remember hiding in a closet often for whatever reason and feeling really safe there. If you had a place like that now to go to when you feel distress, would you feel better there, would you be able to think your problems through more calmly? There's nothing wrong with recreating anything that soothed you in your childhood if it would make you feel good now.

When I was little, we always drove by a certain landscape when we went to visit relatives. It was on the way to and from the desert I spoke of. It was a beautiful green grassy meadow, dotted with giant oak trees. I had many reveries that included walking or riding a horse through it wearing the sort of dress that Queen Elizabeth I wore. That dream has stayed with me through the years. Due to lack of money, it never occurred to me that I could ever have such a meadow and actually physically walk in it, so that has always been my impossible dream. Then, by accident it came true. A few years ago, we happened to move next door to such a meadow. The field has an absentee owner, so I am free to walk through it to my delight. It shouldn't have been accidental. Had I been more aware it would have been deliberate.

Private or Public Property?

Are you basically a private person? Do you need to be alone a certain portion of the day to keep yourself centered? Do you like to read, meditate, walk in solitude or just sit quietly and watch a beautiful leaf pattern shadow appear on the wall? If you need this, it can be disorienting not to have the peace or the place for it. If you live alone, this will take care of itself, unless you mistakenly choose a home in an apartment complex or a neighborhood where people have a habit of dropping in on one another. Personally, I want to visit when I'm in the mood for it, not when others are. Unexpected callers or unwanted conversations across the back fence disturb *my* pattern.

Perhaps you are a social creature by nature. Do you love everyone, enjoy lots of company, and want all types of people around you, day or night? I have friends like this and I love them. They complement my kind very well, because when I want companionship, I know where to go to get it. On a scale of one to ten, which type are you? The

twenty-four hour open house type or the happily sequestered recluse?

Not everyone in a family will always feel the same about this, nor will you always feel the same, so you should think about how your new home can be adapted to serve you best. Is it planned in such a way that part of the home can be a *retreat* area and another a *public* area, so that everyone will have a choice and can move back and forth as the need or a mood changes?

Are You An Indoors Person or An Outdoors Person?

This is another measure of the kind of place where you'll be happiest. Some people feel better indoors, while others feel better outside. Some have horrible allergies to the sun, pollen, grass, animals or other natural outdoor phenomena. Some want their house to stay clean and don't want dusty tables, flies, spider webs, or the open windows that allow these annoyances. If any of the above apply, you won't want a home that lets the outdoors come in. Do you really want a house with a yard that is surrounded by plants, insects and dust? Perhaps you would be happier in an apartment

THE GREAT OUTDOORS

with a great but distant view of nature and air conditioning inside to filter out the things you are allergic to. If you want or need to avoid intimate contact with the outdoors, maybe you shouldn't spend money to buy a piece of it that will cause you trouble or that you won't use. Your money might buy you more satisfaction if you spent it on interior space.

If you love the breeze blowing through your house even if it's dusty, hate the furnace in the winter, and would rather snuggle in front of the fireplace with a blanket, and generally need to know what nature is doing at any given moment, then you are an outdoor person. You'll want a home with lots of windows that *open!* You'll really use the outdoor space you buy (even if it's only a balcony) as an extension of your living space.

An Open or Shut Case?

Some people feel insecure about their personal safety and that of their possessions while others go through life never locking a door or looking over their shoulder and feeling totally secure. The question is not which group has more burglaries but how you personally feel, and what fears you have about this aspect of your life. If you can't sleep at night because every noise is an imminent threat, can't open the door without first knowing who is outside, or constantly hear suspicious noises in another part of the house, your fears are obviously going to make a large part of your life very unpleasant.

There is probably no perfect solution to this, but you can make certain that your next home will minimize the problem. You can have locks, naturally, but locks do not help everyone feel secure. Oftentimes these feelings go deeper and you have to discover what kind of situation will make you feel safer than another might. There are choices that are probably not apparent on the surface. A home in the country will be dark and so quiet at night that every rustle of grass can be heard, and if you are nervous about this it could drive you wild.

On the other hand, the same situation might make you feel very secure. You might feel that if you can hear every *little* noise, you can surely hear that *big* foreign noise! The choice should be one that will make you personally feel at ease.

A house in the suburbs or the city may have a higher incidence of burglary, but there will be street lights and closer neighbors which might help you to feel safer. If you are really a worrier, you may still wonder who might be climbing over the back fence, or if the sound of traffic from a nearby street is covering the sound of someone breaking the lock on the back door. A high-rise apartment might be the solution for you, as there is usually only one door to worry about.

I have always been afraid when I am alone at night, whether I lived in the city or the country. In fact, I was a chronic and sleepless worrier. Now I live on a houseboat. Surprisingly, I have discovered that I am never nervous or wakeful when I am alone at night there. If anyone steps on the boat while I'm asleep, it causes a movement that is very different from the one the waves and wind make, and I wake up immediately. Also, if anyone were to come on board, I still have the option of jumping into the water and swimming to safety. Now I feel secure without even locking the door. I may not *be* safer, but I *feel* safer and that frees one whole worry circuit. Just try to imagine a situation where you will feel at ease. Sometimes the answer to the security problem is very surprising, as it was with me.

Then there is the other extreme. Some people feel safe leaving their homes unlocked and the windows open night and day wherever they are. I really envy this lack of timidity. If you're like this, be sure that you are moving into a neighborhood where you can get away with it. If you've had no trouble in the past and you trust everyone, face the fact that things might be different in a new neighborhood. Burglary doesn't always occur in what looks like a bad neighborhood. It sometimes happens more frequently in what appears to be a good neighborhood. Be certain to ask the new neighbors or the police whether the neighborhood in question has major problems with burglary and other crimes.

WHAT FORM DOES YOUR
SOCIAL LIFE TAKE?

THE SEMI-TANGIBLES

Your Social Life

When you entertain, the object is, of course, for everyone to have a great time. This means that you, as host or hostess, should have a good time too! You shouldn't be overworked, nervous, or end up looking and feeling like a scullery maid. Try to remember your best party or dinner. What were the reasons it was so successful? Remember the occasion that made you feel best, the most at ease and was the least work. On the contrary, remember your worst experience and try to find the reason for that. Sort out the positives and put them on your list.

An example might be that you had a cookout on your patio and had room to put out a buffet, which had been prepared ahead of time. There was nothing left for you to do, so you were able to sit and talk just like the guests, without watching the clock to see when the souffle should come out of the oven. Maybe your new home should have a place indoors where you could duplicate the positive aspects of that party: room for a good size buffet and enough refrigeration and oven space to allow you to prepare all the food ahead of time and have it just waiting to be served when your guests arrive.

Perhaps you discover, when you analyze it, that at sit-down dinners you have to get up and down all the time to take things to and from the kitchen. You miss half of the evening and disturb the entire table. You might solve this by having a dining room large enough for an extra small table or chest near your chair so that you can keep warming appliances, a coffee pot, and a chafing dish near and never have to leave at all. Try to think of anything that pleased or bothered you in the past and think of a way to capture it or eliminate it for all time. If you take care of yourself first, it will be easier to take care of your guests later.

First of all, try to get the emphasis on entertaining into the right perspective for the way you live. Think of how much you like to entertain and how often you actually do it, or if, in fact, you seldom do it at all. Would you want to if it were easier for you? Perhaps you'd rather not do it at home but prefer to take people to a restaurant when it's your turn to entertain. When you do entertain at home, would you rather do it formally, keeping the guests in the living and dining rooms with the kitchen operation out of sight? Or do you like to serve food and drink in an informal way and have the guests mingle with you while you are preparing things? If you find that you don't entertain often, perhaps you won't want to devote a large portion of your house to this kind of space, but rather to another type that will give you more pleasure.

Often, people use their living and dining rooms only once or twice a year and this means that a large portion of their housing money is spent for rooms that offer little value to them. A friend of mine furnished his large living room very elegantly, but no matter how many people were over, they all crowded into the family room and the kitchen. Perhaps the living room was too perfect, and no one felt comfortable in it. Maybe they were afraid they'd get it dirty. Anyway, my friend discovered that it was a great place to take a nap when he didn't want to be disturbed.

If your children entertain friends often, perhaps you'll want a space for them that is separate from your adult place, but still in a location where you can supervise. Or you may want them right with you, because you like to play too!

Whatever it is you feel you need for your way of life, concentrate on getting it.

Your Creative Space

Consider your hobby, craft or any other creative priorities. If you have something of this nature that you love to work at frequently, it's very important that you have a space where you can do it. It should be in a place where you can leave the work in progress so that when you find time for it, you won't have to get it out, set it up, and put it away afterwards. Working on the dining table can become such a bother that you may choose not to do it at all. Be good to yourself. It would be great to have a separate room for your work, but if you can't afford that, find a place that has a large enough room somewhere to accommodate a built-in work area on one wall that can be shut off by folding doors when not in use. Or, to give up a guest room that gets little use to get a work room that would make your life more fulfilling would certainly be worthwhile. If you don't examine and define your priorities, you'll have no chance to satisfy them.

What about the creativity of others intruding on your senses? Is there someone in your family whose creativity involves repairing or rebuilding automobiles? This could turn your driveway and your yard into a blot on the landscape. Neither you nor your neighbors are going to enjoy looking at fenders, wheels and old engine blocks strewn on the lawn unless the mechanic has a great sculptural ability. Even if the work and car parts can be contained in the garage, the other cars will be forced onto the driveway or the street and your guests will have no place to park, except in front of the neighbor's house, or worse yet, his driveway. If unsightly clutter upsets you, try to eliminate the problem. Don't shoot the mechanic, just make sure he has a place to do what he wants where you won't have to look at it. If working on cars is important for someone in your family, try to get a three-car garage or a site large enough for a fenced yard with gates to contain all the repair activity.

IF YOU WANT TO PAINT - YOU SHOULD HAVE A PLACE TO DO IT.

Playing Around

What do you like to do most for recreation and entertainment? Whatever it is, your new home should allow you to have what you want and make it easy for you to get it.

If you enjoy live theater, concerts, films or disco dancing you want to be near an urban or semi-urban area. If you move too far from a city that offers this type of entertainment, you may find it takes more time and trouble to go there than you can manage conveniently. Often people move to the suburbs or the country, not because they really want to, but to give the children a better place to grow up in. If you, as a parent, begin to suffer from the lack of doing what you like, the total family harmony may be lessened. Try to find the compromise that everyone will be happy with. A house, closer in, but near a good park might offer you the best of both worlds. An apartment house with exceptional recreation facilities might be ideal.

THE HOME ENTERTAINMENT CENTER

If you prefer some form of home entertainment, you'll want to be sure that your new home will accommodate it well. Television, the radio and the stereo are the most popular home entertainment choices. Ownership has almost reached a one to one ratio. Although this gives each person the choice of listening to or watching his favorite, it can lead to problems. Sounds travel from a viewer in one place to a listener in another to nonparticipants elsewhere. It will take special care and thought to separate these areas so that different machines do not intrude on one another or on you.

The open family room/kitchen is a good example of where different uses might conflict. This type of space might seem to be what you want in terms of togetherness and openess, but don't forget the noise. Not every cook is going to be thrilled with the rest of the family watching and cheering a western on the television at the other end of the room while he's preparing dinner. The din of horses' hooves, the sounds of gunfire and war whoops can be very nerve-wracking when you are trying to read a recipe. If you'd rather cook to the strains of mood music on the radio, you're in trouble! You may end up serving dinner full of resentment at being left out of the group, or with worn nerves because you have been bombarded with unwanted noise for an hour, which caused you to put too much salt in the salad! If this is the way you might react in such a situation, it will be better if the television is far removed from the kitchen area. Then you'll be able to serve dinner with a smile on your face and calmness in your heart.

These sound conflicts can become very serious. I have a friend who is thirteen, whose father just bought her stereo equipment which she has eagerly looked forward to. That was good of him, but I think he didn't realize to the full extent what sort of music she would play on it. He likes classical music and she likes rock! They are in such conflict about her music that it's making their home scene totally miserable. She's ready to leave over this. Just think, a nice and useful birthday present turned out to be a unpleasant source of discord and alienation. The reason I give this example is that we all need to think about the results of our actions ahead of time.

Reading is a quiet activity which can very easily be intruded upon by the noise machines. True, you can always retreat to your bedroom, but it might be much more comfortable for you to have a special place where you can read. If you read a lot, you deserve a place that's out of reach of all sound tracts that might bother you.

There is another recurring scene from *Blondie's* Dagwood Bumstead. It's about men who have to sneak about the neighborhood to each other's basements, garages, or trash yards to find a safe and secret place to play poker. Their mates probably don't like them to play because they lose money, but it might be that they can't stand the cigar smoke or the bad jokes. If there is someone in your family who loves poker and you love him, try to find a place for him to pursue the game, where it won't disturb you. Maybe you need a room that is sound proofed, will vent the smoke outside, and has a refrigerator and sink so the card sharks don't have to come out for any reason. They will adore you for sparing them the indignities of Dagwood and Herb and you will have retained your peace and quiet. The preceding also applies to football game parties and the World Series.

The important thing is to get all possible activities and conflicts on your lists so that you'll be ready to look for ways to accommodate them.

Cooking and Other Maintenance Work

Cooking is love work for some people, but others hate anything beyond warming a TV dinner. If there is an avid cook in your family you probably already know it, and he knows it, and he is the person who should have all the say about the kitchen because the wrong one is going to make him miserable. If you have someone who hates cooking, you already know who that is too. If there is no one in the family who likes to cook, there is no need for anything but a minimal kitchen. A big one will only get dusty.

Aside from these two extremes of love/hate, there are borderline cases, and you may need to do some soul searching. I am going to tell what happened to me as a good example of really being off the track. For years I paid no attention to my real feelings, and I made myself very unhappy without realizing why. After fifteen years as an architect, and about the same number in the kitchen thinking I liked cooking and earning the praise of friends and family, I discovered that I really detest cooking! One day I realized that what I really loved was eating good food, and I wanted my family and friends to enjoy it also. I was only cooking because there was no one else who would do it. I love my

(MY KITCHEN GETS DUSTY A LOT)

food, but I hate being the cook! For me, it's pain to work in the kitchen, and it's not worth the product.

Having a chef would be the best solution but, since I can't afford that, the next best thing is to have a small and extremely efficient kitchen, so I can get out of it faster. I do not want an elaborate gourmet facility because I would feel obliged to use it. This would entangle me even more in doing something I don't like. The subtle realizations about ourselves come only from within, and it takes a careful searching to bring them out.

Gardening is another activity to think about. A garden (or yard) is *work,* so before you decide to take one on, try to be very sure it's what you really want. Having a garden sounds great, especially if you have always lived in apartments and never had one before. A garden brings images of blooming flowers, sunning on the patio, and green shady trees. It can also bring weeds, worms, bugs, snakes, and Texas root rot, and require constant attention.

I NEVER PROMISED YOU A ROSE GARDEN.

If you're planning to buy a new house that is not landscaped, find out ahead of time if your budget will bear the cost of new lawn, shrubs, trees and necessary walks and paving. And if you can't afford to have someone put it in for you, it's going to be an extreme amount of work.

After it's in, you'll be faced with the maintenance work a garden needs. What will you really feel like doing on Saturday mornings? Sleeping in, playing tennis, or doing stoop labor in the garden? You may decide that you really don't want to do the work it demands. On the other hand, you might decide that you'll get such a dose of peace, fulfillment and satisfaction from it that even the work in itself is fun. If you find your feelings somewhere between, you'll need an in-between garden, one with a lot of deck and very little dirt.

Try to picture yourself in respect to other maintenance chores, like painting the house every couple of years, fixing a fence that the dogs knocked down or, when it rains, trying to find the source of the water dripping on your bed. If these activities don't thrill you perhaps you should consider renting or buying a condominium someone else will maintain and repair.

THE ALMOST TANGIBLES

When you feel you've exhausted all avenues of your self-exploration, sort your list into some orderly form. Study it to see if it reminds you of more things. See what overall patterns appear that give you clues to what you really need. If there are any contradictory items, try to find the reason so you can see what is the real truth. Then after each item, write down what you think will furnish your needs! Figure 2 shows how the list might look now. When you and everyone else in the family has done this, you're ready to have a family conference. The purpose for such a conference is to gain insight from each other and find some common grounds. If you are single, you might ask a close friend or relative to help you.

One person might say, "Do you really want or need a den in our new home? You rarely use the one we have." Talk this over to find out what the

PROGRAM LIST (ORGANIZED)
FROM ROUGH LIST ON PAGE 4.

THINGS I WANT	WHAT'S NEEDED TO GET WHAT I WANT
GENERAL:	
ITEM 1. HAPPY HOUSEPLANTS	NEEDED? (SOME ANSWERS ARE IN STEP 2 AND STEP 3)
ITEM 4. NO TOYS UNDERFOOT	MORE STORAGE OR A PLAY AREA TO WHICH TOYS COULD BE CONFINED.
ITEM 6. SOLITUDE	NEED BEDROOM OR STUDY REMOTELY LOCATED FROM POPULATED NOISY PARTS OF THE HOME. (STEP 4 DISCUSSES THIS)
ITEM 7. FEWER TRIPS UPSTAIRS	A ONE STORY HOUSE OR A HOME ZONED TO REQUIRE AS FEW TRIPS AS POSSIBLE. (THIS IS ALSO DISCUSSED IN STEP 4)
LIVING ROOM:	
ITEM 10. TO FEEL COMFORTABLE IN IT	NEEDED? (STEP 5 SHOULD GIVE YOU THE ANSWER)
KITCHEN:	
ITEM 3. A BROILER I CAN SEE INTO FROM AN ERECT POSITION	A WALL OVEN OR A RANGE WITH AN OVERHEAD OVEN. (STEP 5 SAYS MORE ABOUT THIS)
ITEM 9. KITCHEN OPENING TO SUNNY DECK	FIND ONE OR GET A KITCHEN ON THE SUNNY SIDE WITH SPACE TO ADD DECK AND INSTALL DOORS. (STEPS 2 AND 5 WILL GIVE MORE INFORMATION)
MY BEDROOM:	
ITEM 4. TREES AND BIRDS OUTSIDE	ENOUGH ROOM OUTSIDE TO PLANT TREES OR BIG SHRUBS (OR A BALCONY LARGE ENOUGH FOR BIG PLANTS).
ITEM 5. MY BEDROOM TO BE DARK AT NIGHT	A BEDROOM LOCATED AWAY FROM STREETLIGHT OR A NEIGHBOR'S PORCH LIGHT.
BATHROOM:	
ITEM 8. A COMFORTABLE BATHTUB	AN EXTRA LONG TUB WITH BACK-SLOPE THAT FITS MY BACK.

———⟩ AND SO ON

FIGURE 2.

den person needs that he doesn't seem to be getting. Perhaps he doesn't feel at ease in the present den because it is dark or for some reason depresses him. Perhaps someone else has been using the den for a sewing room and he can't get through the mess to get to his own things, which would lead to the conclusion that the other person really needs a sewing room. If you can afford the space, maybe you need two rooms. If you can't afford it, try to think of a way to organize a den/sewing room so that one activity won't infringe on the other. When you get to the shopping phase, you'll be looking at that extra room in the light of whether it will do a double duty for you. You'll know whether it is large enough and can be arranged so it will work to make two, or more, people happy.

The friend of someone who lives alone might say, "Ann, this really troubles me, and it has for a long time. You give a lot of dinner parties, but this apartment doesn't really have enough space for it. People have to practically sit on one another or on the floor at your dinners. Your food is great, but the hassle and inconvenience spoil it." Ann hadn't realized that her parties were lacking in grace, but even so, her budget wouldn't allow for a larger apartment. After she and her friend thought about this and discussed it at length, they discovered that there was a way to solve this problem. Since entertaining mattered more to Ann than having a separate bedroom, what she needed was to find a studio apartment. It could have the same square footage as her old one bedroom apartment, and therefore cost about the same, but it would have one big room that she could entertain in. It wouldn't be important to her guests that there was no bedroom, and when she was alone she would have just as much privacy as she had before. It wouldn't actually cost more but she would be richer in terms of usable space, and could give more gracious dinner parties.

Your lists will probably show areas where your impact on each other is not pleasant. Talk out these problems to find a way the friction can be avoided in your next home. For instance, is there a person in the family who has to be nagged all week and every week before he will mow the lawn because he really hates to do it? Is anyone else willing and happy to take the job? If no one wants to do it, look for other options. Could you afford a gar-

dener? Maybe you need a yard that has low maintenance ground cover. You might consider moving into some sort of cooperative where someone else does the lawn. You can avoid most dissension by planning it out of your lives. Is a piece of green, trimmed grass in front of your house really worth the weekly fights?

Here's a very common source of friction. Is there someone in your family who monopolizes the bathroom to the annoyance of others? Maybe they could change their habits, but it is my experience that the bathroom people never change. And maybe they shouldn't have to. Now is the time to figure out how to avoid this problem in your new home. How many bathrooms will you need? Maybe it will be worth sacrificing space elsewhere so you can afford more baths. Perhaps you should shop for a house where the bathrooms are compartmentalized (divided into closeable sections), or could be remodeled to do this, so that more than one person can use them at the same time.

These are only a few examples of the type of things that cause conflict within a family, but there are an infinite number of other situations. You'll find your own sore spots when you have your conference but, remember, if you all get together and talk about it, there is a peaceful solution.

Due to budget or convenience or preference, you've probably already decided whether you want to live in the city, the country or the suburbs. No matter which it is, everyone should look his list over again very thoughtfully to see where his heart really lies. For example, if the majority say it's the country, do all the signs point to that being true? What if you have one person who is a sleepless trembler alone at night in the country? Then you see that often the rest of the family is away at night. Your country choice won't lead to any serenity for the person who can't stay alone. Is this worth the trade-off of being out in the woods?

If you do choose the country or the suburbs, requiring a long commute every day to work, very little time will be left for you to enjoy your home or be with your family. Maybe having more time with you will be more valuable to them than rural life. A house in the city with a safe yard to play in or a location in the near suburbs with a fast commute might work better for the well-being of the whole family.

If you plan to live in a city, try to visit the neighborhood ahead of time, at various hours of the day or night, to get an idea of how you'll feel when you live there. Will you feel secure walking your dog at night, or coming home late from a movie?

The last thing to think about is the future and how your needs might change, so that you can accommodate the changes now, rather than having to move again later. Do you think there will be more of you or fewer? Are you planning to start a family or increase it? Is a parent moving in with you in the future?

If you have a teenager who will be old enough to move away in the next few years, do you really need to buy a room just for him? Perhaps you have a craft that you're really into and you need space for it. If you choose a room mainly on the basis of how it works for the craft activity, even if you have to forego using it for now, you'll get more value from it in the long run. The teenager can use it for a bedroom until he leaves and then it will be yours. For instance, if you weave, the room should have good daytime light, be large enough for your loom, and have adequate storage facilities for your materials.

If you do expect a parent, everyone will be much happier if you can find a house that offers a separate apartment, whether it is connected to the house or not. In the meantime, give it to your rock music freak so he can play as loud as he wants to without bothering the rest of you.

Now it's time to choose someone who's willing, able, and the one that's most interested to take all the lists, put them together and bring them to order. The master list will still be loosely organized. It may have contradictions or highlight some problems that you don't know how to solve yet, but don't worry about it now. The first step is only to find all the things that affect your head, heart and soul. The following steps deal with the physical and technical aspects of a home and show you how you can get what you need.

Right here I want to caution you about your lists. They could and should be the outline of the home of your dreams. Any hardheaded person will start fussing over whether the spaces and vistas you find in your head are in reality much larger than your pocketbook or in other ways unavailable. The fact is that if you worry about reality at this point, you won't even begin to get in touch with your soul. If you can get close to all the things that would make you feel good at this point, that's all I want you to worry about. The other chapters will show how to get most of what you need, even if the space you can afford is minimal, or how to get twice the space from any ordinary site or room!

As you read, more you-related thoughts may occur to you, so keep adding them to what you already have on your list. If there are still some contradictions, you may discover the way you really want things to be. Or you may find the answer to a problem that you thought you couldn't solve.

Each step will also have a general checklist outlining the major items that need to be considered. You can add your individual needs to those or modify them so that they apply exactly to you.

CHECKLIST:

THINGS TO LOOK FOR:

_____

_____

_____

_____

_____

_____

_____

_____

_____

The Natural Environment

In the beginning humans were naked and had no shelter. Since they were probably living in the warmest part of the earth, near the equator, there was no need for either clothes or houses to shelter them from the elements. Then things changed. Perhaps the climatic paradise was altered by natural phenomena, or it became too crowded, or maybe there was one tribe that got selfish and wouldn't share the warm place. Something made it necessary for people to move to places that weren't perfect, and some ended up where it was too cold, or too hot, or both. At first, when people's bare bodies had no protection from the elements, it must have been very uncomfortable! Unlike the song in "Midnight Cowboy" about going "where the climate suits my clothes," they had to invent some clothes to suit the climate. And then, when clothes weren't enough, they moved into the nearest cave to protect their bodies from cold wind, rain, snow, and the hot summer sun.

Since there is a limit on the number of caves in the world, people were forced to create, or build, shelter for themselves. Since early human beings were in tune with the earth, and hadn't invented any machines yet, they knew how to use nature to help heat and cool their homes. Many who still live in the same type of early shelter are quite comfortable, because these structures were designed to work with the local climate. Where it was hot, dwellings were built to shelter them from the sun, with thick walls to keep the heat out. Other houses were designed to scoop breezes inside and vent hot air out naturally. In colder climates people faced the open side of their hut toward the sun. In very cold places they turned their igloo entrance away from the cold winds. By being close to nature, and the character of the site and surroundings, people knew what they had to do to get along with nature and how to make their shelter work with it.

Today we've invented all the tools and machines needed to make, or force, our interior climate to be what we want it to be, no matter what's happening outside. Most of our buildings are designed with little regard for the way nature works. The machines that allow us to do this are valuable inventions, or were when we had a lot of inexpensive energy to burn. But why use energy unnecessarily? Having a home that provides as much natural

17

heating, lighting, and cooling as possible is going to save money and add to our independence from existing sources of energy.

Nature can be our friend or our enemy and the choice is ours. If we were discussing building a new house, this chapter would show how it should be designed to take full advantage of nature. Since we're concerned with ready-made housing we need to look at each particular building to see if it has been designed, inadvertently or not, to do this also. The first step in choosing a home is to learn how nature works in the area, and how it will affect the particular building you are interested in. If you choose a home from what's available with the basic patterns of nature firmly in mind, you'll be able to select the house or apartment within an already developed complex or mobile homesite that takes the best advantage of nature. You will also know how to recognize and reject the units that interact poorly with natural forces. This chapter deals with all the ways you can use nature and prevent it from using you.

ORIENTATION

Orientation in architecture means the positioning of a building in a way that relates to and is in harmony with the existing environment, and especially so that it gets along with the weather. Unfortunately, most housing has been built with no thought given to this. Often the only orientation effort that has been made is to face the front door to the street, regardless of where north, south, east and west are, the plan of the rooms, or which way the wind blows. It's of utmost importance to consider orientation to nature and the elements because that will greatly affect the heat, light, and air inside.

The most important physical need our shelter must satisfy is keeping our body comfortable. If we are too hot or too cold, most of us just turn the furnace or the air conditioning up or down. Then we are shocked at the cost and start cursing nature and the power company. A home that takes advantage of all the natural heat and coolness available results in a harmonious relation with nature and

lower fuel costs. Bad orientation results in unpleasant confrontations with nature and unnecessarily high fuel costs.

In addition to free heat the sun also provides natural light, and good orientation will assure that you'll get all the free light possible too. A bad orientation might mean that you'll get too much light, and be forced to keep the drapes drawn all day or not enough and have to leave the lights on in the daytime. The way a building orients to wind and air can make a big difference also. Air can move fast and become wind, which usually doesn't feel pleasant on our bodies. Air that moves slowly, a breeze, can cool us when it's hot. It is important to learn how to encourage the good breeze to cool, and to discourage "wind."

The presence of water can help cool the air, or sometimes make pleasant sounds, which make you feel cooler even if you are not. But storms can beat at your home and the elements can find their way in. Good orientation to storms means having a home that turns its back to them! Proper orientation to all these natural phenomena will mean that you'll be twice as comfortable in your new dwelling place. Bad orientation will assure a certain amount of unnecessary misery!

CLIMATE

The best way for a house to be turned, or oriented, can vary widely, depending on the climate, where in the world the dwelling is located, and also on the latitude. When the sun is straight above, it will provide the maximum amount of heat. When it is at its lowest angle, the amount we receive is much less. You don't have to be concerned with what's happening in space, but it's very important to understand the effect it will have on your home.

Figure 1 shows how the sun moves back and forth with the seasons. Between the two tropic latitudes is the torrid zone, and this is the only zone that ever gets vertical rays. Here the year around temperatures will be fairly constant and usually hot. The temperate zones get seasons, because the sun is almost vertical at one time of the year and at a lower angle the rest of the time. The design of a

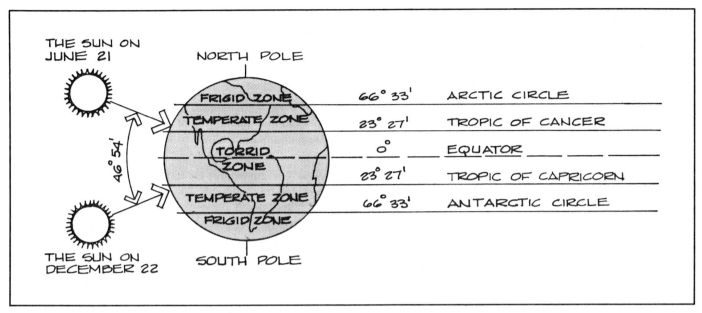

FIGURE 1. THE SUN'S SEASONAL PATH

structure in the temperate zones is more complicated than in the torrid zone, because two different conditions of nature, winter and summer, have to be dealt with. The weak winter sun needs to be invited in and the hot summer sun kept out. Since the temperate zones range from the tropics to the arctic, keep in mind that the design requirements within these zones vary widely. The frigid zones, the arctic and antarctic, demand that the designer think only about one thing, keeping people warm! The climate is only going to be cold and colder, since the sun only reaches this zone at a low angle if it reaches it at all.

The movement and nearness of the sun are only part of the reason for a particular climate. There are subclimates within any zone that are caused by other natural phenomena.

Regional architecture takes the climate and subclimate into consideration and therefore is (or was) very different from the architecture in another area, with good reason. Today we often confuse a regional design with a *style* and forget the fact that a particular style is not going to work well with the climate of our *region*. For example, the Cape Cod cottage doesn't take full advantage of a warm climate because its purpose was to keep the cold weather and wind out, not to encourage the warmth of the sun to come in. The southern colonial was designed with shaded verandahs to cool the hot air before it entered the large open windows of the house, an efficient natural air conditioning system. The same style in a cold region would not work with nature.

Nearness to a large body of water will affect the climate. Water absorbs heat more slowly than land masses do, and then gives it up more slowly. This has the effect of cooling the air when it is hot, and warming it when it is cold, with the overall result of making the climate more temperate. Mountainous areas, vast plains, river valleys and many other configurations of the land cause different subclimates.

Winds also affect climate. They can make the climate warmer or colder, depending on how strong they are, and what temperature they are. Knowing exactly how they work where you live will let you take advantage of their good effects and eliminate their bad ones.

Humidity has an effect on the climate and how our bodies react to it. Our natural body cooling system works by pushing internal heat out to the skin surface in the form of perspiration. When the outside air is dry, the perspiration evaporates, and this cools us. When outside air contains a lot of moisture, perspiration can't evaporate and our bodies cannot cool themselves naturally. If an environment is too humid and hot, it won't be comfortable unless the air can be dried or kept moving. Or the air may be too dry, and the addition of some moisture will cool the air and make it more comfortable.

There are also local climates, or microclimates, within any major climatic area. The existence of these is generally due to variations in the immediate land form. One particular site may be very cold, windy, or foggy, while just around the corner another site will be calm, sunny, and warm. Naturally, you'll want to choose the latter so we will discuss how you can recognize it.

Since all conditions will vary some, the best way to know how nature affects the site you're consid-

ering would be to spend several days there each season, prior to making a choice. Obviously this is time consuming, and assumes that you have a year to spend camped out on a prospective site. In the case of an apartment building, it assumes that the manager would let you camp in the parking lot. But it isn't necessary to resort to these measures. There are simpler methods by which you can predict the year around climatic conditions at any location without spending much time there at all. Regardless of which month you look at your prospective home, you will be able to predict fairly well what it will be like the other months of the year.

The rest of this chapter deals with the beneficial and detrimental aspects of nature's elements, and how to control them to give *you* the advantage.

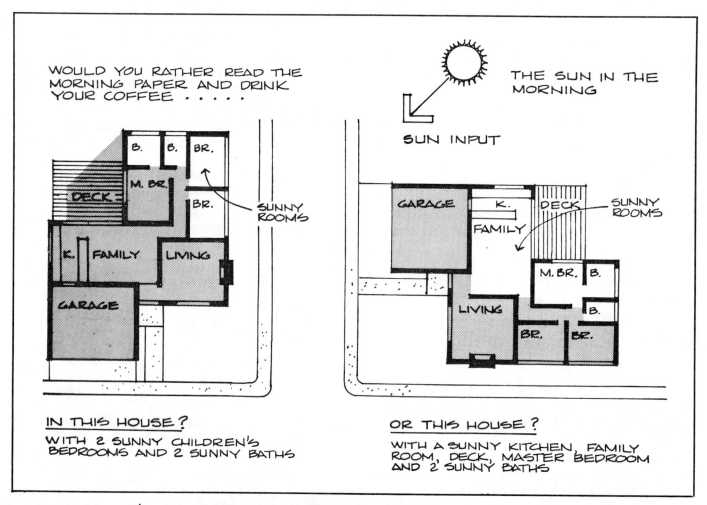

FIGURE 2.   IT'S THE SAME FLOOR PLAN

THE SUN

The sun keeps us warm and is absolutely necessary to life, but its effects are indiscriminate. It can give you a sunburn or a nice tan. It provides vitamin D to humans and solar energy to plants so they can grow and make our food, but it can also cause skin allergies and burn houseplants. The sun gives light as well as heat, but there is a line between what is too much and what is too little.

We saw the general effects of the sun on different zones of the earth. Now it is important to learn how the sun is going to affect a particular location and immediate environment.

Since most of the world's population lives north of the equator, this will be discussed in terms of the northern hemisphere. I apologize to the southerners, but I suppose, as with left-handed people, you are used to this kind of treatment. You'll have to reverse north and south and winter and summer, but it all works the same.

Where, When, and How the Sun's Rays Will Reach You

It's really important to know this in advance. If you do, you can have a natural passive solar home without starting from scratch. You'll want to know if the sun will reach far enough into the house in the winter to help heat it and to be sure that the building next door will not block it out entirely in December. Then you'll want to be sure that the sunlight will stay out of your house in the summer if you live where it gets hot. You'll also want to know if you'll have sun or shade when and where you need it.

The following is a good example of what might occur if this isn't considered. I have some friends who, in winter, have to gather their coffee and newspapers together on Sunday mornings and take themselves and their paraphernalia into their children's rooms. The children have the only two rooms in the house that get southern (and southeastern) sun in the winter. It is too dark and cold in the rest of the house in the morning to be pleasant or comfortable. All the houseplants live in the children's rooms, too. They had a choice of several houses in the development, but they didn't consider this aspect at all when making their choice. Other houses with the very same floor plan, in the same tract, for the same money, are turned differently and would not have presented this problem. Stop and think of where you like to have sun and what time of day you want it, and add this to your checklist to make sure you will have it.

Look at the overall view of the planet earth again (Figure 1). It shows that the sun moves back and forth a maximum of 46°54' and generally it behaves as Figure 3 indicates for the different zones of the earth. In the temperate and frigid

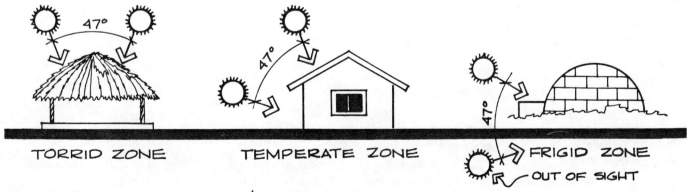

TORRID ZONE   TEMPERATE ZONE   FRIGID ZONE
                                          OUT OF SIGHT

FIGURE 3. THE SUN ISN'T <u>ALWAYS</u> OVERHEAD

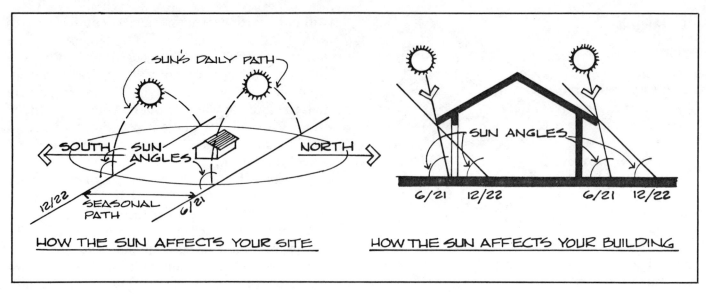

FIGURE 4. THE SEASONAL "PATH OF SUN" AND THE "SUN ANGLES"

zones, it is nearest to an overhead position in the summer and reaches its lowest angle in the winter. In the torrid zone it is almost straight overhead all the time.

Solar heat can enter a home from the east and west, but the best year-round orientation for maximum sun input is to the south in the temperate and frigid zones. More specifically, Figure 4 shows how the sun's behavior will affect any particular site and building. The site drawing illustrates how the daily path of the sun across the sky changes its position throughout the year along a seasonal path. The drawing of the building in section (the architectural term for a drawing which shows the cross section of a building as though it has been sliced in half) illustrates how the sun angles govern the way the sun will enter a south facing window, and where it will cast a shadow. Now we need to find what the sun angles are in your location (or latitude) so you will have them to work with.

There are ways to calculate these angles exactly so that it is possible to find where the sun's rays reach every hour of the day, every day of the year, and any place in the world. There is also a way to find the approximate sun angles, using only simple arithmetic, which is accurate enough for most purposes. If you are planning a local move, you can do this at your present home and then just keep your angle findings for later use when you do

move. Otherwise, try to be at any prospective home site around the twenty first of any month so you'll have the right reference angle to work with.

This is the stick trick for finding the sun angles and "Trick" angles:

Equipment:

1 stick 8'' to 12'' long (available in most Chinese restaurants or use a fireplace match or dowel).

Steel measuring tape (you'll use this for a lot of other things when you shop, so you might as well buy one if you don't have one).

1 plastic protractor to measure angles.

Play dough, clay or chewing gum.

18'' square (at least) of poster board or cardboard.

Small hand level (you'll use this for other things too).

Paper (graph paper will be easier).

12'' ruler.

Valuable Information:

Sun angles change from June 21 to December 22 and back to June 21 again, a distance of 46°54', which we'll round off and call 47°. Divided by 6 months that is approximately 7.8° per month.

FOUR THINGS YOU NEED TO KNOW

(A) THE LENGTH OF THE STICK

(B) MONTH READING TAKEN

(C) THE LENGTH OF THE SHADOW

(D) THE ANGLE IN DEGREES THAT THE BUILDING LIES OFF DUE SOUTH

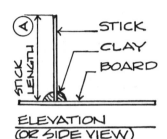

ELEVATION
(OR SIDE VIEW)

STICK
CLAY
BOARD

STICK LENGTH

FIRST

RECORD LENGTH OF STICK (A) AND THE MONTH (B).

PLACE BOARD ON GROUND OR FLOOR WITH EDGES PARALLEL TO SOUTH WALL AS SHOWN AT RIGHT. BOARD MUST BE LEVEL.

STAND STICK STRAIGHT UP ON BOARD AS SHOWN AT LEFT.

OUTSIDE POSITION

INSIDE POSITION

EDGES PARALLEL TO SOUTH WALL OF THE BUILDING

SET THE BOARD UP LIKE THIS

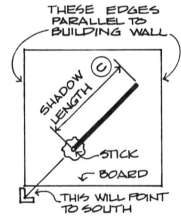

THESE EDGES PARALLEL TO BUILDING WALL

SHADOW LENGTH (C)

STICK
BOARD

THIS WILL POINT TO SOUTH

PLAN
(LOOKING DOWN)

SECOND

MEASURE LENGTH OF SHADOW (C) AS SHOWN AT LEFT AND RECORD IT.

DRAW PENCIL LINE ALONG SHADOW USING RULER EDGE

NOW REMOVE THE STICK BUT DON'T MOVE THE BOARD.

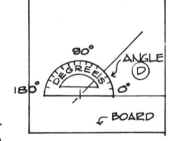

PLAN

FOURTH

PLACE PROTRACTOR OVER POINT WHERE LINES MEET AND READ THE NUMBER OF DEGREES IN THE ANGLE BETWEEN THEM, ANGLE (D).

WRITE THIS ANGLE DOWN WITH YOUR OTHER READINGS. NOW YOU CAN MOVE THE BOARD.

SHADOW LINE
INTER-SECTION
BOARD
PERPENDICULAR LINE

PLAN

THIRD

DRAW A LINE PERPENDICULAR TO HOUSE WALL AND INTERSECTING PENCIL LINE OF SHADOW.

THESE EDGES ARE STILL PARALLEL TO WALL

THE VALUES FOR (A), (B), (C) AND (D) SHOULD BE WRITTEN DOWN AND SAVED. YOU WILL WANT THEM LATER TO MAKE DRAWINGS TO GET MORE INFORMATION.

FIGURE 5. THE STICK TRICK

READINGS TO MAKE ON OR NEAR THE 21ST DAY OF ANY MONTH, AT NOON, WHEN THE SUN IS SHINING

INFORMATION YOU FOUND IN THE
SUNLIGHT (EXAMPLE VALUES):

(A) STICK LENGTH: 8"

(B) MONTH: FEB. 21

(C) SHADOW LENGTH: 6¾"

(D) ANGLE OFF SOUTH: 32°

SUN INPUT

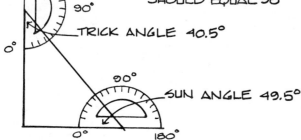

8" STICK LENGTH

6¾" SHADOW LENGTH

DRAWING OF STICK SIDE VIEW

STEP 1

DRAW A TRIANGLE USING LENGTHS (A) & (C). THIS DRAWING REPRESENTS THE STICK AND BOARD SIDE VIEW IN FIGURE 5.

THE LINE CONNECTING THE TWO LENGTHS IS THE LINE OF SUN INPUT.

STEP 2

MEASURE BOTTOM ANGLE, "SUN ANGLE" AND TOP ANGLE, "TRICK ANGLE" TO CHECK - BOTH ANGLES ADDED SHOULD EQUAL 90°

180°

90°

0°

TRICK ANGLE 40.5°

90°

0° 180°

SUN ANGLE 49.5°

STEP 3

WE HAVE THE TRICK ANGLE FOR FEBRUARY 21. NOW WE NEED TO FIND WHAT THE TRICK ANGLE WILL BE ON DECEMBER 22 AND ON JUNE 21 (OR ANY MONTH YOU WANT). TO DO THIS ADD 7.8° PER MONTH (OR 7.8 x 2) TO GET THE DECEMBER ANGLE AND SUBTRACT 7.8° PER MONTH (OR 7.8 x 4) TO GET THE JUNE ANGLE. USE THE PROTRACTOR TO MARK THESE OFF.

STEP 4

MEASURE BOTH ANGLES WITH PROTRACTOR (PLACE AS IN STEP 2 TO MEASURE TRICK ANGLE).
READ JUNE ANGLE, 9.5° (E) AND DECEMBER ANGLE, 56.1° (F)

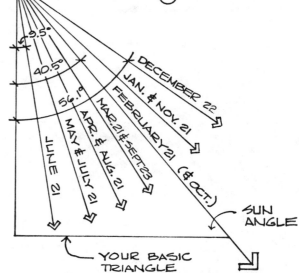

TRICK ANGLE

9.5°

40.5°

56.1°

DECEMBER 22

JAN. & NOV. 21

FEBRUARY 21 (& OCT.)

MAR. 21 & SEPT. 23

APR. & AUG. 21

MAY & JULY 21

JUNE 21

SUN ANGLE

YOUR BASIC TRIANGLE

NOW YOU HAVE ALL THE INFORMATION YOU NEED TO PREDICT HOW THE SUN WILL COME INTO YOUR ROOM, YOUR BUILDING OR YOUR YARD; OR IF THE SUN WILL COME IN AT ALL.

THE THREE FACTS YOU NEED ARE:

(D) ANGLE OFF SOUTH 32°

(E) JUNE TRICK ANGLE 9.5°

(F) DECEMBER TRICK ANGLE 56.1°

FIGURE 6. THE STICK TRICK CONTINUED

DRAWINGS TO MAKE SO YOU CAN FIND THE "SUN ANGLE" AND "TRICK ANGLE"

Auspicious Dates and Times for Performing the Trick:

Any month on or near the 21st (nearer to the 23rd in September and nearer the 22nd in December but on the average it is the 21st).

At noon when the sun is highest in the sky (or 11:00 if on daylight savings time).

Directions:

Follow the steps in Figure 5. First stand the stick up vertically on a level surface (check with the hand level). You can do this inside or outside, just as long as the board and the stick are in the sun. Make sure the stick is placed so that the whole shadow falls on the board and that the edge of the board is parallel to the wall of the building. Follow steps 1 through 4 of Figure 5. You can erase the lines you've drawn so you can use the board again after you know "four things" at the end of Figure 5 and write them down.

If you're doing this at your present home for use later on another building, find south with a compass. Lay the board down facing south and the sun and record only the shadow length. Then when you check prospective homes later, check which way they face with the compass to find the horizontal angle or the number of degrees the house lies off due south. The only problem with this method is that it adds some inaccuracy because magnetic north is always a few degrees different than true north, because magnetic fields deflect the compass. You can redo the trick later when you find your actual home and just use the compass information to get the first rough estimate of what the effects of the sun will be.

After you've taken your outdoor readings and when you get home, make a drawing of the stick length and the length of the shadow to exact size and scale as shown in Figure 6, but using your own measurements and your own month and follow the steps to find your sun angle. The sun angle would be all we would need if we were designing a new building, because one would project this angle to find out where overhangs and window tops should be to allow the sun in or keep it out. Since we are concerned with the way things already are, it will be easier to use the angle at the top of the triangle.

This angle will show in one step where the sun or shadow will extend from already existing structures by casting just one line. So we'll call this the "trick" angle (from "stick trick").

When you have the trick angle for any month, you can find it for all the rest of the months too. Figure 6 shows how to do this. Since the angle changes on the average of 7.8° a month, it is easy to add or subtract this amount of degrees from the angle for the month you know and find the angle for every other month. While June and December are the most extreme months, there are other considerations that will vary with where you live. If you live in an area that's hot in the summer, you'll be more concerned with the angles for July and August when it's hottest to be sure the sun will stay out. In the winter, you'll probably want to be sure that the sun will shine in your house not only in December, but January and February as well when it's usually the coldest. Again, if you're only moving locally you can do all this in your present home and save the information to apply it later to any house you look at.

Now to find out what will actually happen in any building, make a drawing to scale of the house wall that the sun is going to shine on, the window heights, the overhang and whatever else occurs, and the wall that will cast shade in both plan (top view) and section (cut view) as shown in Figure 7. Mark your angles with the protractor and extend the line of sun input to the floor or ground as shown. Then following Step 2 of Figure 7, you'll be able to see where the sun and the shade will be in and around your new home.

You can draw any part of a prospective home, anything next door, or adjacent trees to scale, and find out what will be in the sun or shade in the middle of the day, any month of the year.

Figure 8 shows all the ways you can use the trick angle to find how the situation as it exists will affect your home, and how you can use it to know the extent and type of sun control you will need to add to control sun input.

This stick trick enables us to find the sun or shadows that will extend from direct south at noon. Shadow readings could be made to calculate the angles at times other than noon, but this would be more complicated and it's really not necessary.

FIRST, DRAW YOUR BUILDING TO SCALE
IN PLAN AND IN SECTION, USING THE
VALUES OF FIGURE 6. WE'LL FIND THE
ACTUAL SUN INPUT FOR JUNE. USE
THE SAME METHOD TO FIND ANY MONTH.

VALUES: (D) 32° ANGLE OFF SOUTH
(E) 9.5° 6/21 TRICK ANGLE

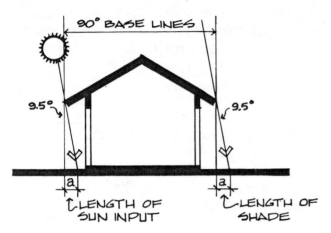

SECTION OR CUT VIEW

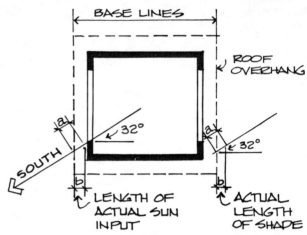

PLAN OR LOOKING DOWN

STEP 1.

ON YOUR SECTION DRAW TRICK ANGLES
AND PROJECT LINES OF SUN
INPUT TO GROUND OR FLOOR.
MEASURE LENGTH a, WHICH IS
THE LENGTH OF BOTH SUN
AND SHADE, AS ON ABOVE SECTION.

NOW, IF THE HOME FACES DUE
NORTH/SOUTH, LENGTH a WILL BE THE
ACTUAL EXTENT OF THE SUN AND
YOU CAN GO ON TO STEP 3. IF
THE BUILDING IS AT AN ANGLE OFF
OF DUE SOUTH DO STEP 2.

STEP 2.

ON THE PLAN DRAW THE ANGLE
OFF SOUTH AND MEASURE OFF
DISTANCE a FROM THE LINE OF
THE ROOF OVERHANG (THE TOP OF
A WINDOW OR THE WALL IF THERE'S
NO OVERHANG) AS SHOWN ABOVE.
CAST LINES STRAIGHT DOWN FROM
THESE MEASUREMENTS TO GET
DISTANCE b, THE ACTUAL JUNE 21
SUN INTRUSION. USE THIS SAME
PROCEDURE FOR ANY MONTH
YOU WANT.

STEP 3.

THIS IS TO FIND WHERE THE SUN AND
SHADE WILL BE AT NOON ON JUNE
21. AS ON THE PLAN BELOW, ON
YOUR PLAN DRAW LINES FROM
THE CORNER OF THE OVERHANG
AT THE ANGLE OFF SOUTH, 32°,
UNTIL IT REACHES DISTANCE b.
THEN DRAW SHADOW AS SHOWN.

IF THE BUILDING FACES DUE SOUTH,
USE DISTANCE a AND CAST THE
LINES TO DUE NORTH.

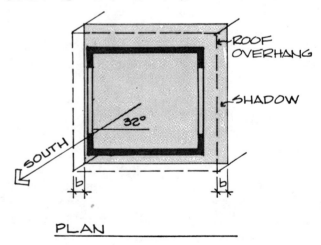

PLAN

FIGURE 7. HOW TO FIND OUT HOW MUCH SUN WILL COME
INTO YOUR HOME AND HOW MUCH WILL STAY OUT

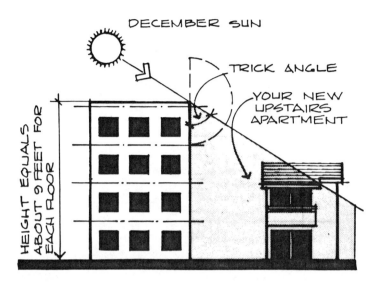

DECEMBER SUN

TRICK ANGLE

YOUR NEW UPSTAIRS APARTMENT

HEIGHT EQUALS ABOUT 9 FEET FOR EACH FLOOR

① TO SEE IF YOUR NEW APARTMENT WILL BE A DISASTER IN DECEMBER

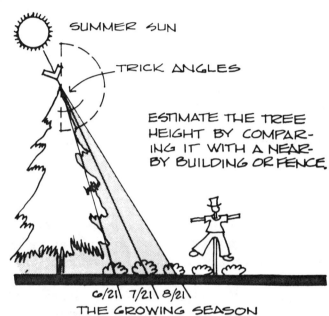

SUMMER SUN

TRICK ANGLES

ESTIMATE THE TREE HEIGHT BY COMPARING IT WITH A NEARBY BUILDING OR FENCE.

6/21 7/21 8/21
THE GROWING SEASON

② TO SEE IF, AND WHEN, YOUR VEGETABLE GARDEN WILL BE IN THE SUN

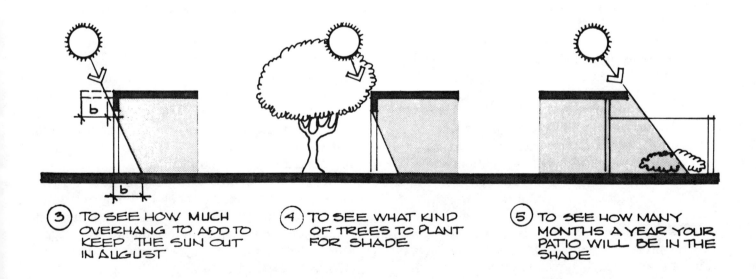

③ TO SEE HOW MUCH OVERHANG TO ADD TO KEEP THE SUN OUT IN AUGUST

④ TO SEE WHAT KIND OF TREES TO PLANT FOR SHADE

⑤ TO SEE HOW MANY MONTHS A YEAR YOUR PATIO WILL BE IN THE SHADE

FIGURE 8. SOME OTHER WAYS TO USE THE TRICK ANGLE

If you know how things will be at noon, you can cast an educated eye at your surroundings and estimate what other things might happen at various times of the day. If there is a building or a tree to the southeast or southwest that would, if due south, block the sun at noon when the sun is highest, you can be sure that it will block the morning or afternoon sun which is lower in the sky. If there is a building or tree directly east or west that is much higher than your building, it will shut out the sun in the early morning or late afternoon, but this might be a blessing in summer. Look around and be aware of what surrounds the place you're considering, and imagine what its effect is going to be.

Now that you know how to find where, and/or if, the sun is going to shine, let's look at some further things you can do with this information.

The Sun As Heat

The sun radiates heat and we want to capture and use all of this energy we can to warm us when the weather is cold, and to repel it naturally when the weather is hot. Figures vary, but an approximate estimate of the energy that can be saved by orienting a structure properly is somewhere around 30 percent summer and winter depending also upon location. The approximate sun angles for various zones show why people in the tropics are generally going to want to keep the sun out of their houses all year. Those who live very far to the north aren't going to have enough sun to worry about and will want to lose as little heated air as possible through their windows and walls. In the north, glass should be limited to the smallest area that will allow you to "feel good" psychologically. When we talk about inviting the sun's radiation indoors, it is mainly the temperate zones where this is desirable.

We've seen, from looking at the path of sun and the sun angles, that it will automatically shine in a south facing window when we need it for heat, and decrease its intrusion into the building in the summer when we don't want it. Nature really works with the properly oriented building. You can see, if you look again at Figure 4, that in the summer when the sun is hottest it will be striking the east and west walls of the building for long periods of

the day. This is more critical on the west wall because it will add to the heat that has been building up within the structure all day. The east and west walls get very little sun in the winter, due to the low sun angle and the extreme southerliness of the sun's path, so these walls cannot be counted on to contribute much heat to the interior at that time of the year. If you want to take advantage of the natural heating aspects of the sun in the winter and repel heat where you know it to be maximum in the summer, the ideal orientation of a structure would be with major walls of glass facing south, and with as many rooms facing south as possible. The best situation for both winter and summer would be to have the smallest expanse of wall possible facing east or west so that the heat gain in the summer and the heat loss in the winter will be minimal. The north wall should have small openings, and very few of them, to prevent loss of the heat being gained on the south side. It would be even better if rooms you don't use in the daytime were located on the north side to act as insulation. Rooms that face north always seem colder than they really are in the daytime, so from a psychological point of view only, they are not desirable to be in during the winter months. The next best orientation would be with the glass wall facing the southeast where you would pick up winter sun, but shut out the west sun in the summer.

Figure 9 illustrates the best orientation for most areas in the temperate zones. It's obvious that the ideal is not always possible to obtain but you should be aware of what it is so that you will know what problems you can expect, and what, if anything, you can do to remedy them. An apartment or home might have a great view, or be so perfect for you in some other way that you may want it no matter how the windows face the elements. And that's fine, as long as you know what's happening and can anticipate the consequences.

There are other ways to cope with the sun if you can't get ideal orientation or building exposure. The main living rooms can be protected from heat buildup on the west wall in the summer if garages, storage areas, or other rooms that are not used often are located in this area to act as buffers. If you are looking at apartments or row houses, don't pick the one at the west end of any group.

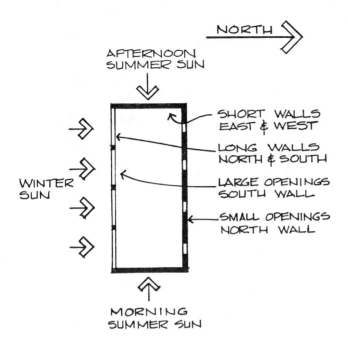

FIGURE 9. ORIENTATION THAT WORKS WITH THE SUN

Although end apartments give you many advantages an interior apartment won't, the western ones should be avoided. A possible compromise would be to have the bedrooms along the west wall. Hopefully, by bedtime they will have cooled off. Both of the above solutions will also work to isolate and insulate the living areas from cold winds in the winter. In any case, never have a kitchen on the west wall unless it is protected from the sun, because this is where the heat buildup and retention is going to be greatest just at the time when you need to cook dinner. On the other hand, if you don't want to cook, this will make a great excuse not to cook all summer!

Again, I want to say that the odds are against finding a house with perfect orientation to nature, but some are very much better than others. If you do keep the sun in mind when you shop, you can at least avoid the home that is asking for trouble. Furthermore, you'll get a better house than a lot of people who build custom homes without thinking of this at all.

Recently I saw something that made me very sad (I was driving around looking at houses again). I noticed a new, large, and obviously expensive custom home that was not quite finished. It was on a five-acre site. Since I'm always amazed, and a little jealous, when I see that some people can afford to spend that much on a home, I stopped to take a closer look at it. Then I noticed that it was an orientation disaster! The living, dining, family room and the kitchen were in one large, fairly open space under a high cathedral ceiling. The glass walls of this area were about sixteen feet high, and they all faced due west. It gets very hot in the summer where this house is located, and the western sun doesn't disappear behind a mountain early. In the summer this whole section of the house will be unbearable all afternoon and most of the evening. In the winter, this space will be cold because the sun won't ever shine into it. The good south side of the house was taken up with a three car garage. These people built an air conditioning and heating nightmare! Even if they can afford the energy bills, I doubt they can ever buy enough energy to be really comfortable in that house. The site was large enough to face the house in any direction and the plan lent itself to being properly oriented to the south, but sadly, no one seemed to have known enough to do this.

If the sun's radiated heat can come into a building, it can also escape from it, and you won't want to lose any heat to the outside that your furnaces and fireplaces have supplied. If your major glass areas face south, another of nature's magical phenomena will work to your advantage in winter, helping you to keep most of the heat inside. This is called the "greenhouse effect," and it works like this. Heat rays have lengths, and when they come directly from the sun the lengths are short and pass through glass easily. When the rays enter a room, the objects in the room absorb the heat and become warm. Then all the warm objects in the room (walls, furniture, carpet, people) re-radiate the heat. Now the heat rays from the warmed objects are longer rays than come from the sun. The glass will not allow long rays to pass through as readily as short rays. This means that in daylight hours more heat will come in and stay in than will pass out, and you'll get a net gain of heat. At night, when the house is not receiving rays, the stored heat can be kept inside by creating an insulated space of dead air across the glass. The simplest way to do this is to merely draw the drapes. Other more efficient ways to keep the heat in are to install double, or insulated, glass or to have a system of insulated sliding panels to pull across the glass.

If you can't find a home you like that is oriented ideally toward the sun, you can trap extra sunlight by installing skylights where they can face a southerly direction. These could be on the southern slope of a pitched roof or, if on a flat roof, the skylights themselves can be tilted toward the south and the sun. Skylights can be a problem in the summer when they catch unwanted sun. Light-diffusing glass will alleviate this problem somewhat, but you may have to devise some way to shade the skylights in the summer.

Orientation toward or away from the sun will also have an effect on how your yard or outdoor living areas will function. A deck or balcony needs warmth in the winter and coolness in the summer, so your outdoor spaces can be used the most days possible. You won't want to have a cookout on a summer evening on a deck that's facing west or sit out on it in the winter in the shade. Sun is also needed for garden plants, swimming pools, and solar heating equipment. You may not have or want these amenities now, but you may in the future. Having a sunny space for them will also increase the desirability and the resale value of a home. These particular outdoor functions depend on having a maximum number of sunlight hours per day, so a large portion of the yard should have southern exposure.

Figure 10 shows identical site plans, but they are reversed to show some of the problems that can occur when orientation is faulty. You'll want to be aware of these differences, because if you are considering a choice of one home over the other, why pick the one with problems? Use the trick angle and the height of the house wall to find the length of the shadow the house will cast.

Keeping the sun out of the house or off an outdoor living space when it is too hot or bright is as important as inviting it in when it is welcome. Overhangs and patio roofs can be used to do this for southern exposures, and you'll know by using the trick angle how far they should extend to block the sun in the summer. Sun control devices can be

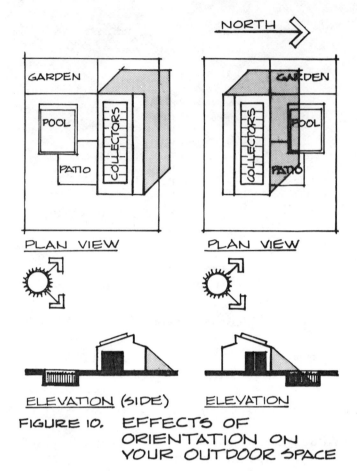

FIGURE 10. EFFECTS OF ORIENTATION ON YOUR OUTDOOR SPACE

designed in many ways to do many different jobs. They can be solid or made of louvers which can be inclined to match your local sun angles so that they let the winter sun pass through and block the summer sun, as shown in Figure 11. Louvers also let more light into the adjoining interior space than solid overhangs do. So if you need light use louvers, and if you have too much light, use a solid overhang or canopy. Louvers can also be used vertically to stop heat and glare, but the disadvantage is that you cannot see through them. If you need vertical louvers at times, it would be best if they were designed to slide back from the window when they were not needed. Louvers also have the advantage of letting air circulate freely while still shutting out the sun.

South facing glass also receives some east and west sun in the summer, and you may want to block it from the window. A good way to solve this

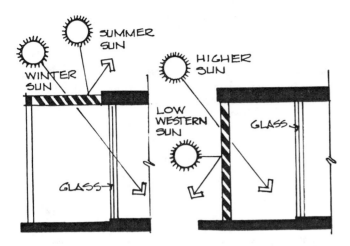

FIGURE 11. LOUVERS LET SUN AND LIGHT IN WHEN YOU WANT IT AND SHUT IT OUT WHEN YOU DON'T

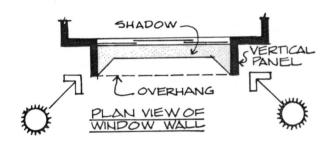

FIGURE 12. VERTICAL SIDE PANELS KEEP EAST AND WEST SUN OFF A SOUTH FACING WINDOW WALL

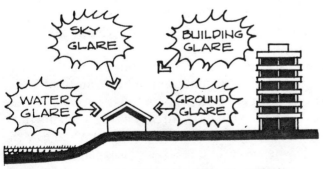

FIGURE 13. SOURCES OF GLARE

problem is to have solid panels installed vertically at each side of the window or window wall, which will keep the sun from entering sideways. East and west facing windows can never be protected totally from the sun by an overhang, because the sun's angle is almost horizontal morning and evening.

Vertical louver panels will stop the low rays, but again, they should be moveable so the light isn't kept out at other times. If you have room for landscaping outside the windows, then you can use plants and trees for sun protection, and we'll discuss these methods later in this chapter.

Since the entire structure of a building absorbs heat from the sun, you'll want to consider this also. There are many things that can be done to discourage the heat from entering when you don't want it and to encourage it when you do. Light colors on the exterior will reflect a portion of the sun's rays, while dark colors absorb them. In hot climates, white roofs and light colored walls will cut down heat absorption. In very cold climates, dark colors on your house and roof will absorb the sun's heat and help you with the heating bills. Here again, heavier materials will help keep heat inside.

The Sun As Light

The sun gives free light, and you'll want to get and use as much of that natural lighting power as possible. The sun's light comes to us in two forms, the direct rays, or sunlight; and the light reflected from the sky, other buildings, the ground or water, which is called glare. The largest source of reflected light, or glare, is from the sky, so the more uninterrupted sky view outside, the more light you will receive.

The rooms you'll use the most in the daytime are the ones you want to be sure have good light. These rooms should have windows large enough to let in good light, and they should not be shaded by other buildings or trees in the winter. Too often one sees houses or apartments that have lights on in the daytime in the winter months. This not only wastes energy but is psychologically depressing for the occupant.

If you work in the daytime and go house or apartment hunting in the evening, you won't know exactly how much light there will be in the daytime or in the winter. It would be best to go back in the daytime to check it, but you may think you have made a rare find and want to snap it up. If so, check the orientation factors with respect to the daytime rooms, take note of possible exterior obstructions, and you can make a very good estimate. If the rooms are very deep with windows only on one wall, it is doubtful that the room will be very bright except near the window. If the room faces east, west, or north, it will have to rely at least partially on artificial light in winter. Figure 14 shows two fairly typical apartment plans. One will get the maximum amount of daylight and the other will cost you extra to light. There is a good reason for the arrangement of rooms in Plan 1. The long, deep rooms allow the developer to keep costs down by getting more apartments per foot of exterior wall. In this plan, however, the dining area, the kitchen, and the bath-dressing area will not have adequate natural light. Plan 2 is arranged so that each room has a good exposure to daylight. The hall will be dark, but that's only a minor problem.

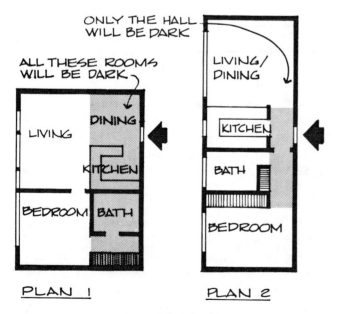

FIGURE 14. HOW MUCH NATURAL LIGHT WILL YOU HAVE?

What is too much light? It is not easy to determine the point at which too much light occurs, but when it does your eyes will tell you! They'll feel uncomfortable or you'll start squinting. If you find your space is receiving too much indirect light or glare, it can be discouraged in much the same way as the sun's direct rays. Shading and screening devices will minimize it. Glare reducing glass will also accomplish this if you own your own home and can afford to install it.

While too much glare is to be avoided, too little sky glare can leave you with underlit rooms. You may find a home that is otherwise perfect, but it's in a forest, there's a tall building next door, or it may have windows that are too small to let the reflected light from the sky enter. If you're going to rent the home, there is probably no way to correct this. If you're planning to buy, there are several ways to modify the structure to let light in or encourage sky glare. Following are several devices that will do this, as shown in figure 15.

Skylight: A skylight can be used to trap heat as we discussed previously, but in a foggy climate or where there are a lot of trees it is also good for trapping light. A skylight can be made of clear glass if you want to see the trees and stars. If there are ugly things outside or there is a privacy problem, diffusing glass will work better. A skylight does its work best in cooler climates.

Clerestory: This is a high window with a roof overhanging it. It should be used when you want to keep direct sunlight out and works well in hot, sunny climates.

Roof monitor: This works the same as a clerestory but has glass on two sides, so twice as much light can come in. It is like a small house on top of the roof and is also very good in hot climates.

All three of the above devices will work even better if they can be opened to vent hot air out of the house in warm weather. A skylight, clerestory, or roof monitor can miraculously transform the whole mood of your home. You can put them over a dark stairway, bath, or dim corners of other rooms such as the dining and living rooms. Where before you had a dark, dreary cave, suddenly there will be a bright and happy solarium! Check the roof when you shop to see if construction of any of these is structurally possible.

ALL OF THESE SYSTEMS
MAY BE OPENABLE TO
IMPROVE NATURAL VENTILATION

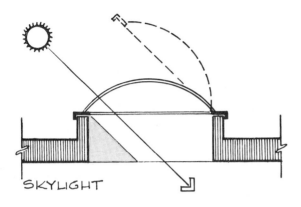

SKYLIGHT

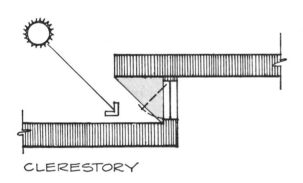

CLERESTORY

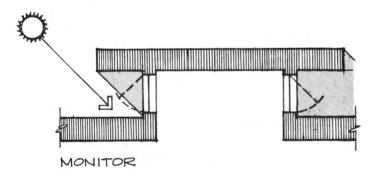

MONITOR

FIGURE 15.   WAYS TO GET LIGHT
THROUGH THE ROOF

THE WIND (AND OTHER MOVING AIR)

There are two major types of wind, *storm* and *prevailing*. Storm winds are usually, but not always, winter winds. Prevailing winds, as the word infers, occur with greater frequency and in some areas they are constant. Storm winds are intermittent and seasonal. Both types of wind come from a predictable direction in any particular locale because they are the result of major atmospheric patterns. In some areas storm winds and prevailing winds come from the same direction, but most often they come from different directions entirely.

If you don't already know how the wind strikes your area, or if you're a new arrival, the local weather bureau will be able to give the wind directions, and also the average and the maximum velocities at which they blow. Following is a brief outline of what certain velocities mean in terms of physical impact. If you are a sailor you already know this, but perhaps are used to thinking of it only when you want to know if you should take your boat out. It's even more important that you consider it when choosing a home.

1–10	miles per hour	light airs to gentle breezes
10–27	miles per hour	moderate to strong breezes
		(At this point the Coast Guard puts up flags of warning for sailors!)
28–40	miles per hour	gale winds—moderate
41–55	miles per hour	gale winds—strong
55 and up		storm (and worse)

Since gale and storm winds blow hardest and are the most destructive, a home that turns away from them or deflects them will be more pleasant to live in. If the prevailing winds are over ten miles per hour, they should be deflected from an outdoor living area so you can use it comfortably. Under the speed of ten miles, especially in a hot climate, the breeze should be captured or enticed into your garden and home for free cooling and ventilation.

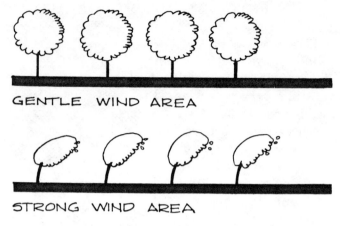

GENTLE WIND AREA

STRONG WIND AREA

FIGURE 16. TREES WILL TELL YOU WHICH WAY THE WIND BLOWS, IF IT'S REALLY <u>SERIOUS</u>

Even if the wind directions and velocities are known, when you visit a particular site *be sure* to look at the nearby trees. They will tell you some things about the winds in that particular area that the weather bureau may not know. If they are all growing *up,* the wind is not likely to be a problem; but if the trees are all leaning in the same direction

and it isn't up, it becomes obvious that you'll have to contend with some very strong prevailing winds, and you will know the exact direction from which they come.

Wind patterns and velocities can be altered drastically by man-made structures. One example of this is seen with high-rise buildings. The buildings are too tall for the wind to go over, so it compresses to pass around and between the buildings, and this compression increases the wind speed. Since this also is a condition local only to the particular building or group of buildings, you'll need to look for evidence of this phenomenon at each site. Figure 17 shows this in diagram. Notice that between two tall buildings the amount of compressed air is doubled, which increases wind velocity even more. There is a low pressure area on the warm side and the cooler air created by the shadow of the building pushes out and replaces the warm high-pressure air, making a local wind. Even a highrise standing alone can create a wind.

If you want to enjoy your balcony or the plaza below, you should determine in advance how the winds work around the building in which you plan to live. The best apartments would be on the lee-

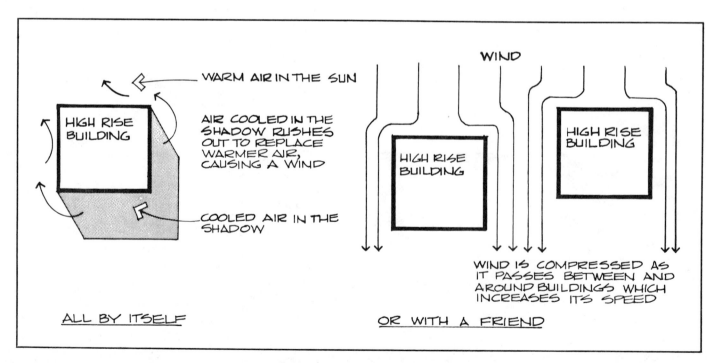

FIGURE 17. TWO WAYS HIGH RISES CAN MAKE MORE WIND THAN THERE REALLY IS

ward side of the building, out of the wind. However, if the leeward side is not facing south, there may be other problems with the apartment, so you'll have to consider the options. If you are in doubt about the effects or impact of localized wind, look at the landscaped areas around the base of the building to see if the vegetation is healthy. Plants whipped by wind do not thrive, and like wind-bent trees, tend to crouch low to the ground and grow away from the wind. Twiggy, weak plants could be the fault of an unskilled gardener, but it could also be that the wind is making it difficult for them to survive. Look in windward corners or at any other obstructions for piles of blown leaves, candy wrappers, and other litter which will also identify a wind problem (and incidentally a maintenance problem).

After you find the direction the wind comes from and approximately how fast or slowly it blows, then let's look at all the ways this knowledge can be used to your advantage. We'll see how to control the moving air if it needs to be avoided or blocked, and how to encourage it to help temper the climate of your home.

The Wind—How It Affects Heat Loss and Heat Gain

Wind, or moving air, doesn't just affect outdoor living; it also has a lot to do with how much heat loss or gain occurs within the building. Cold air moving along the outside surfaces of a building will convect heat away, or pull interior heat out through the walls and transfer it to the air. In the summer when you want the heat out of a building, a cool breeze is welcome, but when it's cold and the heat needs to be stored inside, a cold wind will steal some of it away. Knowing which way the wind comes from at any site in both warm and cold seasons will let you determine how it can affect the heat loss and gain in your home.

Ideal orientation to wind and air is seldom possible, but the main thing is to find a situatiion that will handle it reasonably. Figure 18A shows a fairly satisfactory orientation to the winds. The storm winds are from the northwest and strike the smallest portion of house wall, so the heat loss is minimized. Again, if garages or other rooms that don't have to be heated were on the windward side, they

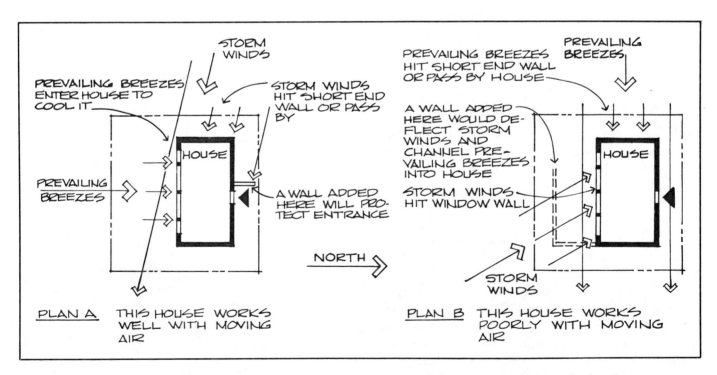

FIGURE 18. TWO EXAMPLES OF ORIENTATION TO MOVING AIR

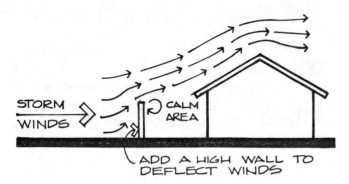

FIGURE 19. DEFLECTING WIND

they bounce up and over the wall, pass on over the roof and leave a pocket of calm warm air in the patio and in front of the windows. This one solution takes care of *two* problems.

Although I've used a single-family dwelling to illustrate how winds can affect the building and the garden, all the same factors apply to every other type of housing as well. Whether you're buying a mobile home or renting an apartment, this is something very important to analyze. It is especially important to get the right orientation to wind for your apartment balcony or patio, because there is almost nothing you can do to correct a faulty situation.

If you are buying a house, you can plan and plant to control wind and we'll discuss that later in this chapter. If you are going to rent, and can't use landscaping, look for the presence of other buildings, fences, walls, or existing landscaping that will shelter your patio or balcony from the wind.

would buffer the rest of the house from the winds and prevent heat loss also. The major window openings and the patio are on the sheltered side of the house, away from direct wind contact. The prevailing winds or summer breezes which come from the south blow across the patio and cool it. They also enter the major window openings to cool the house. The only flaw in this orientation is that the entry will be on the storm side of the house and will need to have a protective screen or wall to keep winter wind and rain away, but that's a very minor construction job compared to the free temperature control gained—both winter and summer.

Figure 18B shows a situation which is less than ideal, so we can look at what the problems will be and see what can be done to correct them. The prevailing breezes pass by the house and are not encouraged to come in. The storm winds hit the window wall and will cause a very large heat loss as well as rattling the windows. This house will have too much wind when and where it isn't wanted, and not enough at other times. However, there are ways to deflect wind or turn it around so that it will behave more desirably. The wind problems at this particular house could be solved by constructing a six- foot wall along the east and south sides of the patio. This could be a solid wall if it can be placed far enough out so it won't block the sun, or of a transparent material if space is limited or you want to keep a view. This L-shaped wall will scoop up the prevailing breezes in the summer and turn them into the house. It will also deflect the storm winds in the winter. Figure 19 shows how the patio wall will deflect storm winds just enough so that

PLAN A   THIS HOUSE WON'T CATCH ANY

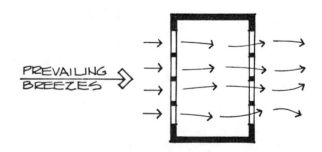

PLAN B. THIS HOUSE WILL HAVE FREE AIR CONDITIONING, OR "CROSS VENTILATION"

FIGURE 20. CATCHING BREEZES

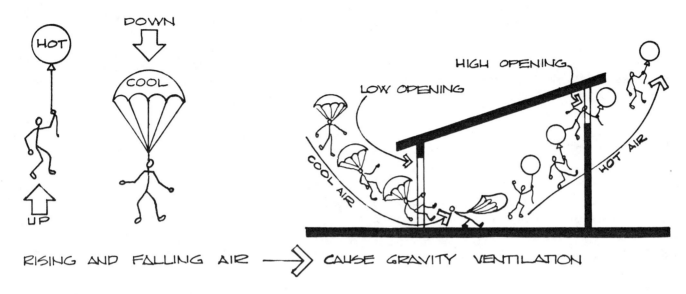

RISING AND FALLING AIR ——▷ CAUSE GRAVITY VENTILATION

FIGURE 21. GRAVITY VENTILATION

The Wind As Ventilation

Natural movement of air can help cool and ventilate your home. There are two ways the air moves naturally within a building that accomplishes this. One is "gravity" ventilation, and the other is "cross" ventilation. If you can get either of these working, you can, in many cases, eliminate the need for air conditioning. Even if you have a mechanical cooling system, good ventilation will result in using it less. You will save money if you can find a home that lets nature help with your cooling bills.

Cross ventilation can be accomplished by having windows or vents which open on opposite or nearly opposite walls. If there is a prevailing breeze, one side of the building should open toward it to let in the moving air. Figure 20 shows an orientation that will get maximum natural ventilation, and a poor one that benefits very little from the breeze. Of course, any cross ventilation is better than none.

It is much harder to find an apartment that is built to take advantage of cross ventilation since they are usually backed on one side to a common hallway or another apartment. Corner apartments offer some cross, or diagonal, ventilation. If you can find a corner apartment where the majority of

windows face the prevailing breeze, it should work quite adequately. The only other apartment situation I can think of would be one in a single bank of units having windows on both sides. Window openings on the entry side will let in noise also, so this may not be a completely satisfactory situation.

Gravity ventilation works another way. Hot air rises while cool air is heavier and tends to fall. If there is an opening in a room at a high level where the hot air can escape, cooler air from a lower opening can replace it. This will cause a natural cool breeze to move within the space. The cold air *parachutes* in Figure 21 fall and are pulled inside, while the hot air *balloons* float out and away. The high escape hatch could be an open skylight, clerestory window, roof monitor, or just louvered vents. A fan placed at the highest part of the ceiling and vented to the outside will do the same job. This can be a gravity fan which instead of electricity is set in motion by the pressure of the warm air passing through it. In a hot climate, it is best to have the intake or low windows on the north or shady side of the house, where the coolest outside air is found.

The older Spanish houses, early California houses and southern houses in hot areas had wide overhangs over verandas to create the shade needed to cool the air and cause ventilation within the house. Shade trees cool the air below them and have the same effect. The more we can deal with the heat as our forefathers did, or with more natural methods, the less we'll have to resort to air conditioning.

A house in the tropics, where a prevailing breeze is almost always available, should make use of that breeze to keep temperatures down. In these areas windows, doors, or solid walls are often completely unnecessary. The only barriers needed are for privacy, and often this can be achieved by the landscaping alone. If breezes are blocked, then what nature provides will be completely thwarted. Blocking the breezes may mean that an air conditioner would be required where none was needed before. Floors should be raised above the ground in these regions so that the air can flow under the house as well as through and over it to convect heat away.

WATER

Water comes to us in the form of rain or snow, and is usually accompanied by the storm winds. These winds blow precipitation, and cause it to hit a building at a partially horizontal angle. This is another reason to have a home that turns away from the storm winds. If windows are on the leeward side, the rain cannot beat against them and snow drifts will not cover them. If the major glass areas face the direction the storms come from, the same principles that work to deflect the winds themselves will also lessen the impact of rain and snow on the house. Figure 24 shows how a wind deflecting wall will also help keep drifts away from the house wall and cause a good deal of the rain or snow to blow on over the roof.

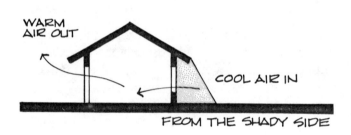

FROM THE SHADY SIDE

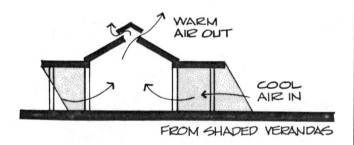

FROM SHADED VERANDAS

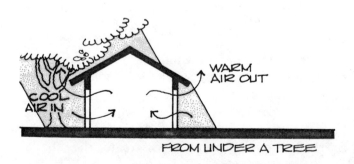

FROM UNDER A TREE

FIGURE 22. WAYS TO GET COOL AIR

FIGURE 23. NATURAL VENTILATION IN HOT CLIMATES WITH PREVAILING BREEZES

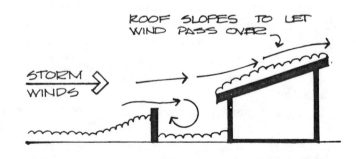

FIGURE 24. KEEPING THE FULL FORCE OF STORM-DRIVEN RAIN AND SNOW FROM YOUR HOUSE

Flooding is probably the most damaging of nature's water acts! You can never be sure you won't be a flood victim (unless you're a "king of the mountain") but you can lessen the chances. It takes an awareness of the possibility that flooding might occur and a prognosis of what might occur on your site. It is predictable that any given creek or river will at some time in the future overflow, but it is hard to know just how high the water may rise. Sometimes big storms are so many years apart that the evidence of the last one has disappeared. If the joy of being near a river, creek, or even a dry gully outweighs the possible dangers, then the thing to do is try to minimize the possible peril. Choose a home that is as far back from the creek as the oldest house or largest tree in the area. If an old object is there, it probably was above the last high water, or at least not located where the flood was bad enough to wash things away. If you want to be near a water course, try to find a house built on pilings, as at the seashore, rather than on standard concrete footings. Even if the home gets wet, it would be more likely to stay where it is if on pilings. Concrete footings can be undermined and washed away.

It's easy to see a stream that still exists, but in a heavily developed neighborhood or subdivision the natural water courses have been covered or diverted, and all evidence of where they used to be is obliterated. Usually a drainage system has been engineered to take care of the estimated water runoff, but there is no guarantee that the *big* storm won't be too much for it. Also, the system could become blocked and allow the water to back up and flood the neighborhood. Future developments on higher surrounding land may force extra water through your development that the drainage system was not designed to handle. It's just good insurance not to choose a home in the lowest area of any development. Flood problems may never occur, but if you have a choice, pick the site that's least likely to be affected.

Another location to avoid is any site below a dam and reservoir, or in its flood plain. All the assurances that it has been engineered to be totally safe are not enough to cover the fact that dams *do* break occasionally.

The same principle by which large bodies of water, such as oceans and seas, can moderate the

IF THE DEVELOPMENT IS LIKE THIS — CHOOSE ONE OF THE HIGHER SITES

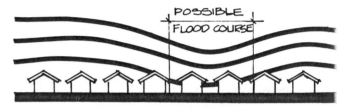

OR IF THE HILLS BEHIND LOOK LIKE THIS, TRY NOT TO BE DOWNHILL FROM THE LOW SPOT.

FIGURE 25. THINK ABOUT WHAT MIGHT HAPPEN IF THERE WERE A FLOOD

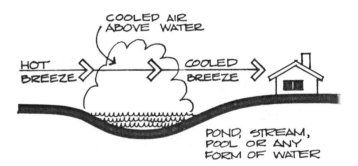

FIGURE 26. WATER CAN COOL AIR

climate is a phenomenon that to a smaller extent is performed by lakes, ponds and pools, especially if they are located between your site and the direction the breezes come from. As air passes across the water, it is cooled by the evaporation of the water. This is more free air conditioning, so take advantage of it when you can.

If there is no body of water near your site, surprisingly just the addition of a small fountain and the sound of running water can help make you *feel* cooler, even if you are not. With the small, self-contained, recirculating types available now, it is a simple matter to have a fountain even on a small apartment balcony.

TERRAIN

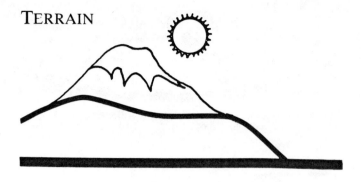

The shape of the land has a great deal to do with what the weather or the climate will be at any particular site. When the land is flat for a long distance, the effects of weather locally will be fairly uniform and predictable. When the land begins to rise and form hills and valleys, many different phenomena can occur that will change the immediate climate. These changes can vary almost from site to site; hence the word *microclimate* is used to denote a miniclimatic area. The terrain and its orientation to the elements can affect almost all of the natural occurrences we have discussed: sun input, wind, water, humidity, and the general climate.

Figures 27 and 28 illustrate some of the things that can happen at different types of sites in the summer months, and others that will occur at the same sites in the winter. What happens will apply to any structure at similar locations, so if you are considering multiple housing, you should still look for these variations.

First let's look at Figure 27, the composite site for the winter months. The drawings show steep slopes and narrow valleys. If the slopes are less steep and the valleys wider, the impacts shown will not be as severe, but there will still be effects of a similar nature.

The storm winds hit Site 1 with force because there is nothing to deflect them. The winds will be even stronger at Site 2 because the air has to crowd together, or compress, to pass over the hill, and that will cause it to move much faster. Passing over the hill, the wind slows again and passes over the house at Site 3, which is protected by the hill. Site 3, however, has another type of problem. The sun angle in deep winter is so low that the sun won't shine on Site 3 at all! This problem will also occur at least half of the day in the winter on any hilly site with an eastern or western orientation.

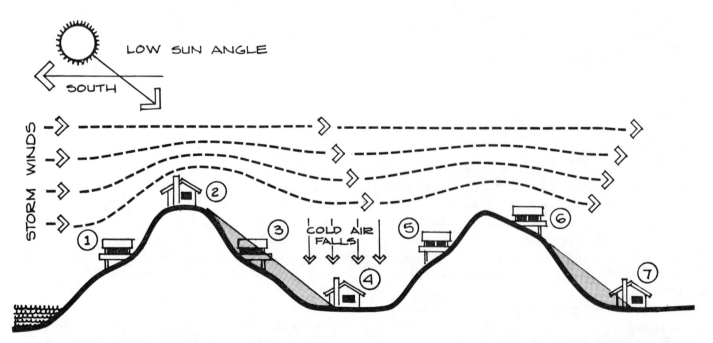

FIGURE 27. COMPOSITE SITE - WINTER

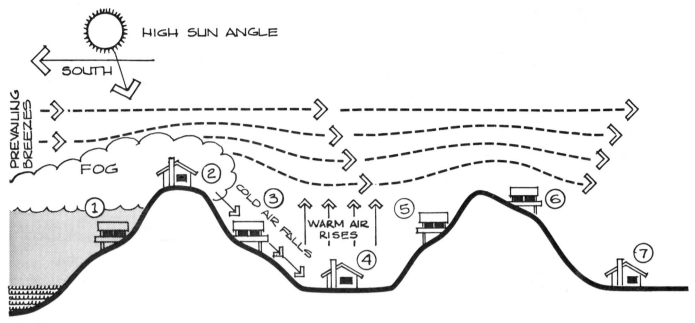

FIGURE 28. COMPOSITE SITE ▫ SUMMER

Site 4 is out of the wind and in the sun, but since cold air falls and seeks the lowest level, the floor of the valley at night, when it's not being warmed by the sun, will be colder than the surrounding higher land.

Site 5 is low enough on its hill to be out of the major force of the wind, high enough to avoid the cold temperatures of the valley floor and possible floods, and it is on the sun gathering side of the valley. Site 6 is just below the crest of the hill, just out of the full force of the wind, but high enough on the shady slope to gather sunlight all winter. Site 7 will have a similar climate to Site 4. If a protected site with a lot of winter sun input is desired, Sites 5 and 6 will offer the most benefits in winter.

In the summer, the warm air of the land condenses the cooler, moist air above the sea and causes a fog bank to form over the coast. This does not occur where the seas and the land are of fairly equal temperature, whether cold or warm, but it does when the temperatures are very different. Site 1 is below the fog in the summer and Site 2 is right in the fog layer, therefore sunless and very wet.

Site 3 is out of the fog, but since the valley air is hot and therefore rising, the colder air rushes down the hillside to fill the low pressure area and causes a very local, and very strong, cold wind. Site 4 has good weather and if the air here does get too hot, the cooler air falling down the slopes of the coastal hill will cool it.

Site 5 will pick up some of the prevailing breezes, while Site 6 will receive even more of them, but it will not be a cold and windy site, as Site 3 is, because the variation in air temperature will be less. Site 7, depending on what the general climate is in the area, may not have a breeze to cool it when the weather is hot. The best sites in the summer are Sites 4, 5, 6, and perhaps 7. Since Sites 5 and 6 are the best two winter locations, and are among the best summer locations, they will be winners, offering the most constant good weather and the fewest problems.

The factors that affect weather patterns and cause microclimates can vary widely. Figures 27 and 28 show just a few of the general variations to illustrate the type of thing to look for when choosing a home and site. If the microclimate of any particular site isn't immediately obvious, ask others already living in the neighborhood to share inside information with you.

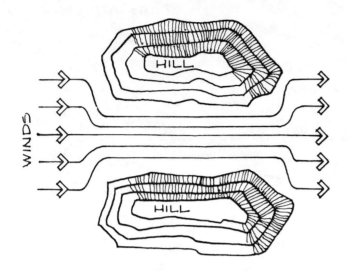

FIGURE 29. WIND VELOCITY INCREASES WHEN CHANNELED BY HILLS

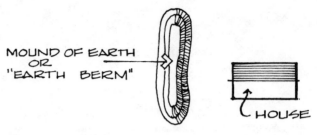

PLAN VIEW

ELEVATION

FIGURE 31. EARTH BERMS WILL DEFLECT STREET NOISE

MORE ROAD NOISE GOES UP

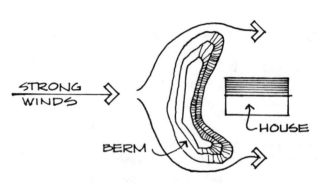

EARTH BERMS CAN DEFLECT WIND

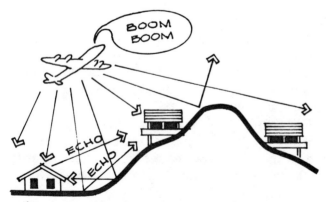

IT'S ONLY SAFE BEHIND THE HILL

FIGURE 30. NOISE AND REVERBERATION

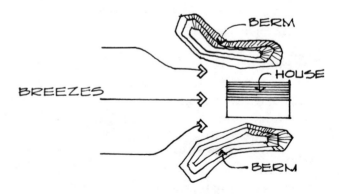

OR CHANNEL BREEZES INTO YOUR HOME

FIGURE 32. CONTROLLING MOVING AIR WITH EARTH BERMS

42

Another land form situation that can cause an uncomfortable microclimate (as shown in Figure 29) is a valley that runs in the same direction as the wind. The wind has to constrict to pass between the hills, which will accelerate its speed. In an area that has strong winds, this can make the area undesirable.

The shape of the land can deflect noise or magnify it. It's possible for two sites in the very same neighborhood to have vastly different noise levels. We inure to noise until after a while we are not conscious of it; however it still affects our physical and psychological comfort, so it's better to avoid as much of it as possible. Heavy traffic noise will have twice the intensity at a site above the road than at one below it. Above, the sound will strike the walls and windows, while below most of it will hit the roof, which has no opening to let the sound in. An upslope site will also receive all the sounds that echo back from the road and the roofs of the houses below. When you are shopping, stop and really listen to the noise level, not only the neighboring noises, but the total background sound. Watch out for airports! It has always amazed me that so many houses are built, and bought, right under the takeoff and landing patterns of an airport. If you have to live near an airport, try to choose a home that is not under the flight pattern, and preferably one that has a piece of high ground between you and the airport to block the sound.

If you've found a flat site that has a noise problem, use the lesson of Figure 30 and the airplane. Build your own small hill. A mound of earth, called an "earth berm," doesn't have to be more than three to four feet high to deflect a majority of the sound. Berms are practical on a city lot to deflect street noise, and they can also help deflect wind or encourage breezes. In addition, earth berms can be used to cut off a bad view.

PLANTS

Plants and trees can play a major role in climate control at your site. Many problems caused by imperfect orientation can be improved or alleviated entirely by trees and plants. Even if you find a home with good orientation, proper landscaping can make it even better.

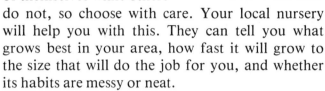

Some plants take care of themselves while others do not, so choose with care. Your local nursery will help you with this. They can tell you what grows best in your area, how fast it will grow to the size that will do the job for you, and whether its habits are messy or neat.

Landscaping can hold a slope, keep the summer sun off the house or yard, stop reflected heat and glare, direct wind where you want it, and generally enhance the environment of your house and garden. First let's look at what landscaping offers as a protection from the elements.

Nature has two basic tree designs, deciduous and evergreen. Deciduous trees drop their leaves in the fall and grow them again each spring. Trees automatically do the right thing at the right time, and if you know how to use that to your advantage, there are many benefits. Since deciduous trees shed their leaves when the sun angles are low, they let the sunshine through in the winter when you need it. Then they grow them back again in the summer when the sun angles are high and it is hot, to help keep the sun out. Evergreens can be counted on to always give shade, so you won't want to plant them between your home and the winter sun; but they make excellent year around windbreaks and are helpful in blocking low east and west summer sun.

Closely planted vertically growing trees, either evergreen or deciduous, are the most effective control for the low sun angles at the east and west sides of a building in the summer. To the south, southeast, and southwest, deciduous trees are needed so the sun's winter rays can penetrate the site through the bare branches.

To determine how tall a grown tree should be to extend shade where you'll need it, use the trick angle or the sun angle, as in the sample shown in Figure 34 and then ask the nurseryman for a tree that will grow to the right height. If you are concerned about the impact of an existing tree, estimate how tall it is in relation to a fence, a house, or

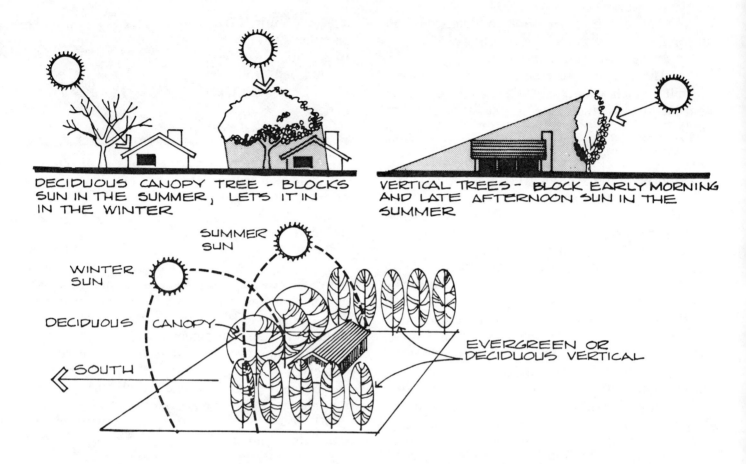

DECIDUOUS CANOPY TREE - BLOCKS SUN IN THE SUMMER, LETS IT IN IN THE WINTER

VERTICAL TREES - BLOCK EARLY MORNING AND LATE AFTERNOON SUN IN THE SUMMER

SUMMER SUN

WINTER SUN

DECIDUOUS CANOPY

SOUTH

EVERGREEN OR DECIDUOUS VERTICAL

FIGURE 33. USING TREES FOR SUN CONTROL

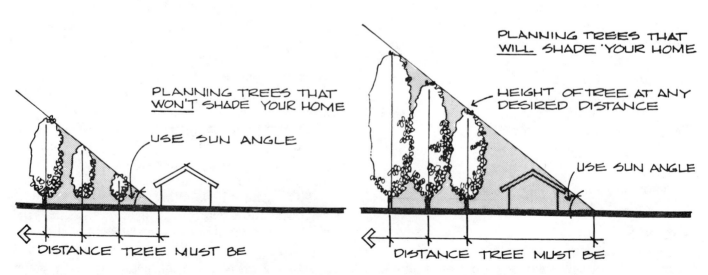

PLANNING TREES THAT WILL SHADE YOUR HOME

PLANNING TREES THAT WON'T SHADE YOUR HOME

USE SUN ANGLE

HEIGHT OF TREE AT ANY DESIRED DISTANCE

USE SUN ANGLE

DISTANCE TREE MUST BE

DISTANCE TREE MUST BE

FIGURE 34. PLANNING TREES TO DO THE JOB YOU NEED

a power pole, so that you can make a drawing and project the length of the shadow with the trick angle to see what its effect will be.

If you don't have room for a tree or trees large enough to shade your home in the summer, heat can be kept off your home by growing vines up the walls of the building itself. This is not the best solution since, if the vines are evergreen, they will keep the sun off the walls in the winter as well, and if the vines are deciduous, they will look unsightly in the winter, but it is a better solution than no shade at all. If you have room for a trellis that extends horizontally, grow a deciduous vine on that, because when it is dormant the bare branches will be overhead and won't be so noticeable.

A really great idea, especially if you don't own the building, is to plant an annual vine and train it to grow up strings extending from the ground to the eaves in front of a wall or a window that gets too much sun. The vines could be planted in the ground or in planter boxes. They could be a flowering type, such as sweet peas or morning glories, or you could plant vegetables, such as peas, pole beans or sweet potatoes. When the annual plants die back naturally in the fall, just tear them out and you are ready to capture the winter sun again. The exciting thing about the sweet pea or pole bean idea is that it will work on an apartment balcony also! Put planter boxes out at the railing and string your trellis with staples to the underside of the overhang or balcony above. This will make a cool, shady, and private place in the summer, and you can use it all day, even if the balcony gets the wicked west sun.

Trees can be used as wind control to channel breezes or deflect strong winds. Strong winds are forced up and over a windbreak, and a calm area is created in their lee. Trees can also channel strong winds away from your home and cool breezes into it. Figure 36 shows two examples of how to control or change wind patterns with trees. These trees are planned to protect the building from the wind and work with the sun input to solve as many problems as possible at different times of the year. Again, be aware that we cannot always solve a problem completely, but if a site can be tempered to some degree it will be to your benefit.

Trees have other attributes beyond changing the

RINGS OR STAPLES

STRING

PLANTER BOXES

FIGURE 35. USING VINES TO SHADE AN APARTMENT BALCONY

immediate climate. They filter air, and therefore decrease air pollution. Trees cool the air passing through them. They absorb sound, so plant them between you and quarreling neighbors or a noisy street. Trees outside a large glass area will cut down the amount of reflected light coming from the sky. Ground cover or lawn will reduce the glare and heat that is reflected from the ground. Avoid a place with a lot of paving or concrete on a sunny side (east, south or west) because these materials will reflect huge amounts of heat and glare. Especially in considering an apartment, try to stay away from the parking lots and driveways.

Trees can give you privacy. If a house looks down on your patio, the view can be blocked by some well-placed trees of the right height. But be careful not to block *their* view of the view, if they have one! It will lead to hard feelings. An apartment house next door that has windows looking into your backyard can be handled similarly. If your outdoor living area is on the street side, trees can be used to make a privacy screen.

Trees offer many benefits, but they can at times cause problems. They can make *too much* shade.

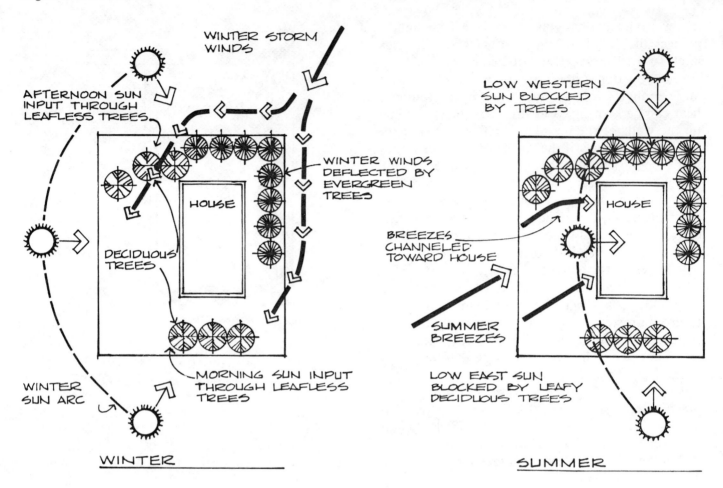

WINTER

SUMMER

FIGURE 36. LANDSCAPING PLANNED FOR WIND AND SUN CONTROL

If you've found a house on a heavily wooded site and it's too dark, and you don't want to cut the trees down because you love them (that's why you want it), there are a couple of ways to increase sun input. If you're lucky enough to have found a house with the daytime use areas on the top level, they'll get more light than they would if they were on a lower floor. If you're renting take an upstairs apartment. If you can't find a plan with the daytime use areas above, the branches of the trees can be thinned to let in more light. This process is called "daylighting," which is a shaping and thinning operation. Daylighting can even make the trees more attractive. Read up on pruning to avoid wrecking the trees, or, better yet, hire a reputable tree expert who will do a sensitive job.

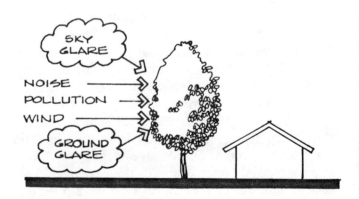

FIGURE 37 TREES CAN KEEP A LOT OF THINGS AWAY FROM YOUR HOME

TO GAIN PRIVACY FROM NEIGHBORS
- ABOVE OR BELOW

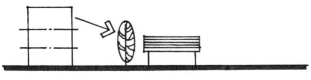

TO GAIN PRIVACY FROM THE
APARTMENT HOUSE NEXT DOOR

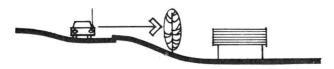

TO GAIN PRIVACY FROM THE STREET

FIGURE 38. TREES AS PRIVACY
SCREENS

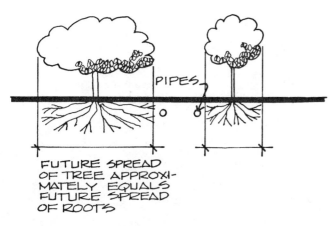

FUTURE SPREAD
OF TREE APPROXI-
MATELY EQUALS
FUTURE SPREAD
OF ROOTS

FIGURE 39. PLAN AHEAD AND
YOU CAN KEEP ROOTS
OUT OF YOUR PIPES

All trees drop leaves and needles, which can make a mess of the yard and pool, or stop up rain gutters and down spouts. Weigh the contributions they will make to the climate of your site, the resultant savings in energy, against the maintenance factor. If you choose trees and shrubs that don't have particularly messy habits, you'll probably find that it will be worth raking and cleaning up leaves occasionally.

Many people dislike trees because the roots break up concrete walks, patios, and building foundations, foul drainage and sewer pipes, and get into septic tanks. All these disasters will happen, of course, if you are not careful where you plant the trees. Make sure you know where all underground lines are located before planting, so you can stay away from them. If you check the nature of the root systems of any proposed trees with your nurseryman, you'll be able to determine how far away from any mechanical or structural item to plant them so they won't cause damage. A general rule to remember is that the spread of the root system usually equals the spread of the branch system. If you know the projected spread of a tree, you'll know where the roots will grow.

ANALYZING THE NATURAL INPUT FOR VARIOUS SITES

Now that we have seen the many ways nature can affect a home, let's do an exercise to show how you might use this knowledge to select a home, from among others, with an orientation to nature that will give the most advantages and the fewest problems. The practice problem is a block of buildings that could be subdivision houses, apartment houses, or mobile homes, all oriented differently. The same principles apply, no matter what type of housing you're considering. Assuming that these homes are otherwise equal in plan, size, and other amenities, which would you choose?

Some of these buildings pose problems that are solvable, while others have problems which are not. If you are looking at types of housing other

FIGURE 40. CHOOSING A HOME THAT HAS THE BEST ORIENTATION TO NATURE

ASSUME ALL THESE BUILDINGS ARE OTHERWISE EQUAL (PLAN, DESIGN, MATERIALS, ETC.). THEY COULD BE HOUSES, APARTMENT BUILDINGS OR MOBILE HOMES.

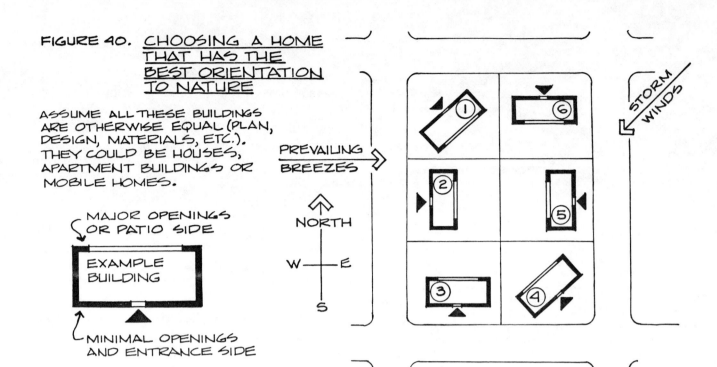

GRADING COMPARISON:

BUILDING ①

1. STORM WINDS HIT SHORT END WALL	GOOD
2. SOUTHEAST OPENING ORIENTATION	GOOD
3. BREEZES BLOCKED FROM REAR YARD	POOR
4. CROSS VENTILATION	FAIR

BUILDING ②

1. STORM WINDS HIT OPENING WALL BUT A WINDBREAK WOULD HELP	FAIR
2. OPENING WALL FACES EAST	FAIR
3. BREEZES BLOCKED FROM REAR YARD	POOR
4. CROSS VENTILATION	GOOD

BUILDING ③

1. STORM WINDS HIT OPENING WALL BUT A WINDBREAK WOULD HELP	FAIR
2. OPENING WALL FACES NORTH	TERRIBLE
3. BREEZES REACH REAR YARD	GOOD
4. CROSS VENTILATION POOR, BUT BREEZES COULD BE CHANNELED INTO HOUSE WITH FENCE OR LANDSCAPING	FAIR

BUILDING ④

1. STORM WINDS HIT SHORT END WALL	GOOD
2. OPENING WALL FACES NORTHWEST	TERRIBLE
3. BREEZES ENTER REAR YARD	GOOD
4. CROSS VENTILATION IS FAIR BUT CHANNELING WITH LANDSCAPING WOULD MAKE IT BETTER	GOOD

BUILDING ⑤

1. STORM WINDS HIT WALL THAT HAS MINIMAL OPENINGS	GOOD
2. OPENING WALL FACES WEST. LANDSCAPING WOULD HELP BUT IT WILL STILL BE TERRIBLE	TERRIBLE
3. BREEZES ENTER YARD	GOOD
4. CROSS VENTILATION	GOOD

BUILDING ⑥

1. STORM WINDS HIT WALL THAT HAS MINIMAL OPENINGS	GOOD
2. OPENING WALL FACES SOUTH	GREAT
3. BREEZES ENTER REAR YARD	GOOD
4. CROSS VENTILATION POOR, BUT BREEZES COULD BE CHANNELED INTO HOUSE WITH FENCE OR LANDSCAPING	FAIR

TO GRADE:

FIRST— THROW OUT EVERY BUILDING THAT HAS A "TERRIBLE", SO BUILDINGS ③, ④, AND ⑤ ARE OUT.

NEXT— BUILDING ② HAS ONLY ONE "GOOD" WHILE ① AND ⑥ HAVE TWO "GOODS" SO ELIMINATE ②.

NOW— WE HAVE ① AND ⑥ ON TOP TO CHOOSE FROM. ① HAS A "POOR" WHICH ⑥ DOESN'T. ⑥ HAS A "GREAT", SO IT IS THE WINNER AND WILL OFFER MORE TO WHOEVER LIVES IN IT. BUILDING ① IS A VERY GOOD SECOND CHOICE.

than single family detached or at a rental property, the orientation problems will be the same, but the landscaping solutions probably won't be in the realm of possibility. So, if this is the case, look for places that, accidentally or not, already have landscaping where it's needed.

Again, this is not an exact science, but let's try to grade each structure on the basis of its strong points versus its shortcomings. Anything that is very important to you and is perfect gets a "great"; if it is very important and all wrong, it gets a "terrible"; and if it's in between, give it a "good," "fair" or "poor." Any situation where the problems are solvable (by you) should only get a maximum score of fair because it will cost you work and/or money to correct it, and therefore it can't be good or great. The building with the best all around average is going to stand out when you add up the scores. Even if it is still not a perfect score, you will know it is the home, out of the available choices that will, from an environmental standpoint, give the most for your money.

CHECKLIST

THE SUN:

Find: North
 Trick Angle and/or Sun Angle

Will it shine into the rooms you want it in?

Will it stay out of the house when it's too hot?

If there are obstructions to the sun will they be to your advantage or disadvantage?

Will the areas of the yard which need sun have it?

Will the rooms that are used in the daytime have good natural heat and light?

Is it possible to correct any faults simply and inexpensively?

THE WIND:

Find: Wind directions and velocities for both
 Storm and Prevailing.

Will the building work well with the wind directions and speeds that affect the area?

If not, can the situation be corrected easily and inexpensively?

Will the natural ventilation be good?

WATER:

Does the building buffer the snow and rain well?

If not, can it be deflected without major expense?

Is the possibility of flooding unlikely?

TERRAIN:

Will the form of the land foster a good microclimate rather than a bad one?

Will the land form deflect noise, rather than channel it to your site?

If the site is noisy, can it be corrected with earth berms or landscaping?

LANDSCAPING:

Does the landscaping work with nature (to shade from sun, break the winds, etc.)?

If not, is there space to add landscaping so that the home and site will work with nature?

Is there enough landscaping, or room for enough to control heat and glare?

If privacy is a problem, can it be corrected with landscaping?

If trees cut out too much light, can this be remedied without cutting very many of them down?

Are the existing trees, or the spaces where you need new ones, not going to damage underground utilities or adjacent structures?

WORKING WITH NATURE ANALYSIS SCORE FROM FIGURE 40.

The Man Made Environment

We have seen the ways nature and the elements affect our environment and now we are going to look at the environment created by the building itself. The sum of all the parts, and the spaces created and served by them, will affect your mind, your spirit, and your body. Remember, you are looking for the shoe that will fit your own unique life and nature. Keeping in mind that perfection is not possible with a ready-made home, or even a custom home, it is important to shop with your mind open to the possibilities of making a space more perfect than it already is without spending a lot of money. You will want to determine how the total man-made enviroment will affect you and all aspects of your daily life.

DESIGN—WHAT IS IT?

All buildings are "designed," and I don't believe defining the word and all that it means is possible. Webster's dictionary defines it as "a plan or sketch to work from, as a design for a house." That is true as far as it goes, but it leaves us with no assurance that a design is necessarily good or beautiful; it is just a plan to work from. It could be a well-designed plan or a poor one. So how do we distinguish a good design from a bad one? A good architectural critic (they're like drama critics) can put the distinction into words, but often it is difficult to understand what the words *mean*. Words like scale and proportion, simplicity and restraint, esthetics and expression, may not mean the same thing to all of us. I feel that I know a good or bad design, and I am probably a good judge because of my training, but still what is good to me may not be to someone else. All we know so far is what "design" is not, and that is that it's not necessarily good or bad. This at least tells you that when an advertisement says "designer home," or "architect designed home," you shouldn't assume automatically that it is well designed. It may be better than most, but don't put your trust in advertising phrases.

Start thinking in terms of what pleases you, so design becomes a word you can *use*. A good design for you is one that makes you feel *at* home *in*

51

your home. The important thing is to make certain that you personally are turned on by a design instead of choosing one because other people say it is a great design.

Design Is More Than Meets the Eye

Design is not just in the eye of the beholder; it should be in the mind and heart as well. We are, each one of us, moved with delight by something. It could be a painting, a piece of music, or a beautiful sunset. The building or space that we live in should move us too! Unfortunately, most people only consider the practical things like the location, the number of rooms, the double oven, or the storage, or whether it's a "good investment." A design, if it's right for you, should give you a real high.

Many who are looking at ready-made housing, feel they have to settle for less. I disagree. I believe that with a little extra knowledge, a bit more patience, and some determination the particular house, apartment, condominium or mobile home that will give you daily inspiration is waiting.

The feelings a design engenders are intangible, very personal, and vary with each individual. It should maximize the things you enjoy and minimize what makes you feel uncomfortable.

Design Should Be Exciting

A good design will bring some excitement to you every day, even if you are not constantly aware of it. This could and should occur within the dwelling as well as outside in the space surrounding it. Most of us would love to have a view of valleys, mountains, the sea, or be surrounded by a forest, or any other expansive view of nature. Most of us, to be realistic, won't be able to find or afford this kind of outlook, but we don't have to do without it totally. It might be just as exciting to look out at a short view of nature, simulated in your garden, and closed away from the outside world. The Japanese have contributed greatly to this kind of mini-landscape planning. They may have a home in the city on a noisy street, but when you enter the yard and the home, you feel as if you are all alone

in a country setting. Seeing a fruit tree in seasonal bloom, birds sharing the quiet of the garden, and the sun changing on leaves as the hours pass are small daily delights. Even the tiniest garden space can often give you more excitement than a ten-mile view. This type of miniature garden can be enjoyed, through windows, from the inside too.

A good design will have a meaningful contact with the outdoors even if it is only a small side yard or a balcony. When you are shopping, look out of each room to see if there is anything with which you can work.

Outside, a good design will create a change of space as you walk around it. Long, straight walls are not interesting, although they are cheaper to build. A traditional home usually is built this way, but is done in a way that has meaning, looks organized, and has charm and dignity. A contemporary building, home or apartment house usually is more interesting if it is designed to create changing spaces as you move around it.

Think of what the space will be like to live in. Does the light enter in an interesting way? Is the color attractive? Try to think beyond "I don't like it" when shopping, to see what it is that you don't like or what bores you, and what you do like and what excites you.

A lot of excitement can be created with furnishings and color in a space that is not too scintillating otherwise. It is important when house hunting to determine if you can save it this way. A lot of excitement can be gained by having the things about you that please you personally. If you have favorite paintings, is there a place to hang them that will show them off? If you have a collection, such as old bottles, coins, or dolls, is there going to be a place to display them well? If you love to read and have many books, is there a place for them? All these things speak of the excitement of you, the individual, to yourself and to others.

Good Design Is Uplifting

There are enough things to get depressed about every day, if you let yourself, without your home adding to it further. In fact, the main job your home should be doing for you is to be so uplifting

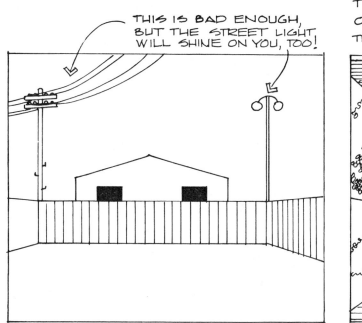

FIGURE 1. A REAR YARD OUTLOOK
NOT VERY EXCITING BUT FIXABLE

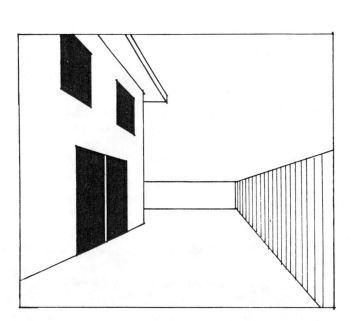

FIGURE 2. A TOO LONG, TOO NARROW, TOO TALL, AND
TOO STRAIGHT SPACE - BUT FIXABLE

WHEN I NEED TO BE
IN A CAVE, ALL I HAVE
IS THE LINEN CLOSET

to you that you will forget your depressions entirely! Try to find out what does depress you about rooms or homes so you won't inadvertently move into one that pulls you down. Start analyzing this. Visit friends to see what rooms make you feel happy and which ones are depressing. It is strictly an individual matter, nothing an expert can tell you. When you sort this out you'll be able to choose a space that's going to make you feel good.

An example of something that might depress you would be a small room with a low ceiling, painted a dark color. It might make you feel trapped, too tightly enclosed, cut off from the freedom of the outside, or just dreary. Another person might feel wonderful in the same room. It might feel like a cozy cave, a haven in which to curl up with a book, or just be with one's thoughts. And we don't always feel the same way all of the time. You may need to be in one type of space at one time, and another at other times. There may be a place for spaces to feel both ways.

Good Design Should Offer Serenity

Is there a place you can sit and be at peace inside or outside and contemplate nature and the earth and

yourself? Sometimes, you need to retreat for a while to get your perspectives sorted out. You need some distance from time to time to get along with your family.

Good Design is the Style That Suits You

Just good looks won't assure that a particular design is one that everyone could live with. Something that is acceptable to some, or a certain style, may not turn you on at all. Victorians and brownstones and old row houses are very popular right now because people are seeking nostalgia and because older buildings are usually more substantial than contemporary housing. On the other hand, if you feel good in a modern glass and steel house, obviously you're not going to be happy in something *old fashioned*. But some people can go from one style to another and enjoy them all. The most important thing is to have the self-confidence to choose something different if you want it.

Good Design Should Be Honest

A building should be what it is and not put on phony airs. Ornate moldings on the eaves and flower boxes under the windows will not make a tract house or a mobile home into a Cape Cod cottage. They just make the poor building look silly!

Recently I saw a new house that was designed to look like a colonial mansion. When I looked around the corner of the house, or at the end of elevation, I saw that behind two of the front windows there was a garage. First, this is dishonest because no colonial mansion ever had cars parked inside, or even a carriage. Secondly, no garage needs curtains, which this one had! And also, who wants to keep frilly curtains clean and ironed just to hang in the garage.

Often one sees houses that have one material on the front and another on the side and back walls. This probably looked great on the drawings, but a house is not just one dimension, or two, but three. When you move around so that you can see the sides of the house, you can see that the brick stops at the corner. This may not seem important, but subconsciously (consciously, in my case) you will

FIGURE 3. A HOUSE WITH
TWO FACES

Good Design Should Be Useful

Everything on a building should have a purpose. Materials should be chosen for their ability to handle weather, ease of maintenance and long life. An example of uselessness is what the building business calls *plant-ons*. These are design features of wood, tile, or any other material that are applied to wall surfaces, garage doors, or anywhere else someone decides they'll look good. These decorations deteriorate quickly in the weather and will need to be repaired, replaced, or removed sooner than the rest of the house. There are better ways to spend that money. A really good pair of front doors, a private entry court, or some landscaping would give more value. Some developers will change the color or shape of these decorations from house to house to try to give each house an individual look. If the houses are so similar you need a trick to tell which one is yours, you might start really wondering if it is a good development in the first place. Or you may wonder why the builder is trying to catch your eye with decoration. Is there something else that he doesn't want you to notice?

Good Design Should Be Ecologically Harmonious

A building should complement nature and fit with it. It can either blend with nature by being made of natural materials of local origin, by landscaping, or sit on its site in such a way that it seems to be-

feel uncomfortable with it. The material should continue all around, stop at a reasonable place, or not be there at all. This is spending extra money to put up a facade which will convince no one that the owner has a brick house. Sometimes a harder material is put along the base of the wall to keep muddy rain spatters from staining it. If it's only in the front, which is often the case, does this mean that it doesn't rain on the other sides of the house? A house is a total unit, not just a front. The back and the sides matter just as much as the front.

Arches were invented to hold up heavy materials, such as stone or brick, before builders got smart enough to use light materials in simpler ways. Now I see a lot of Spanish-style houses being built with arches cut from plywood or made from wood studs and covered with plaster. To try to duplicate or imitate traditional arches, which of necessity were very thick, with 3/4'' plywood or 2 x 4 studs, looks dishonest and is meaningless. To build a thicker wall just to get the right effect wastes material, but this is what should be done to make it at least look honest, even if it isn't, which is still cheating.

On the other hand, the VW bug with the Rolls Royce grill is fetchingly amusing and so obviously phony and whimsical that it is great fun. If you find a home that is phony with a flair, and you love it, great!

FIGURE 4. "PLANTED ON"
DECORATION

55

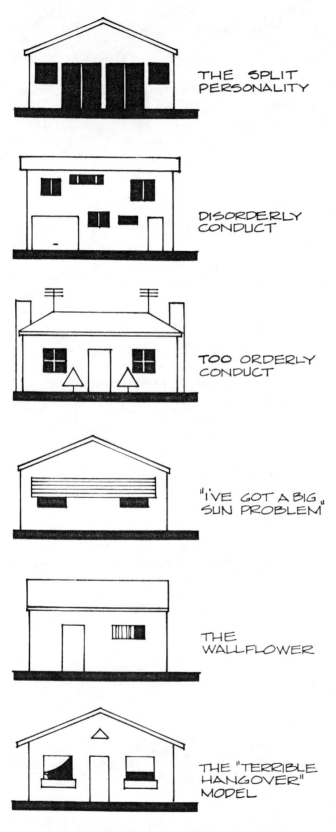

THE SPLIT PERSONALITY

DISORDERLY CONDUCT

TOO ORDERLY CONDUCT

"I'VE GOT A BIG SUN PROBLEM"

THE WALLFLOWER

THE "TERRIBLE HANGOVER" MODEL

FIGURE 5. SOME FUNNY FACES

long. This aspect of design is not nebulous or hard to understand. Think of a beautiful meadow with trees and wildflowers. Picture an aluminum mobile home parked in the middle of it. The whole feeling of the naturalness of the site is destroyed—a machine sitting in a meadow. Compare that to the feeling of a clean white farmhouse or a simply designed redwood house in the meadow. It's easy to see which is right. Or in an urban scene, think of a street lined with houses of muted colors, and one house among them that has been painted hot pink. This would be a discordant note on an otherwise peaceful street.

A Good Design Should Have a Nice Face, Not Frown Or Look At You Crosseyed

The well-designed building will look organized, have good shape and proportions, and appear attractive. To me, houses have faces just like people. If you look at a house as if each wall were a face, you'll start to see that there are some pretty funny ones and some handsome ones. If we think in terms of faces, it will be easier to see which are well designed. Some are orderly and in tune with themselves, and others are wearing too much makeup (useless decoration), weird hairdos (too many roofs in too many places), exorbitant false eyelashes (phony showiness), and broken noses (disorganization). Look at Figure 5. I'm exaggerating, but don't these houses really show the differences? When you choose a place to live, find a face that you'll want to love and be with for a long time.

SITING

Siting, or how a building integrates with and rests on the land, is an important part of the design. If it fits on the land well and works with it, it will be a better design than one that is forced on the land and fights with it.

Siting a house on flat land is not difficult and I can think of only one problem that it might present, and that problem can also occur on a hilly site. If there are big trees that took years to grow, it's very sad to see them removed. A building should be placed on a wooded site in a way that will save as many trees as possible and ideally all of them. That's good siting. Many times a developer will buy a wooded site, cut all the trees down because they are in the way of the buildings he wants to erect and then call the project "Willow Forest" or some other reference to what had been there. It takes more care, thought, and money to work around trees than to destroy them. If you choose a home in a development where the old trees have been saved it will probably be a better looking neighborhood in the future.

A sloping or hilly site should be cared for too. Flat houses are for flat sites and sloping houses are for sloping sites. Sites on a hill are all too often cut and filled to leave a flat area on which to put a flat house. This is not working with nature either. Cut and fill in moderation doesn't do too much harm because eventually landscaping will hide the scars. Extreme cuts are never going to heal because bedrock has been uncovered and nothing but moss will ever grow there again, at least not for several centuries. Not only is the scar of the cut visible for miles, but I've never understood how people who live on such sites can bear to look at the cut from their rear room windows.

Where it's impossible to cut and fill a site due to the terrain or local laws, a builder will often use his standard flat house plan and put it on stilts. This isn't a design with nature in mind either. It doesn't even necessarily protect the site because it usually puts most of it in shade so that plants can't grow. But stilts or pilings at least leave some openness. Many building codes require that the underpinnings be enclosed to protect the underside of the house from brush fires or for other reasons. This can mean that a wall three or four stories in height has to rise from below before even reaching the usable part of the house. This design solution may look small from above but from below it's a gargantuan mass; in addition to that, three or four stories of walls that aren't used inside cost a lot of money that will return no benefit to the occupant.

A well-designed hillside home will move up or down with the slope and of necessity be split or

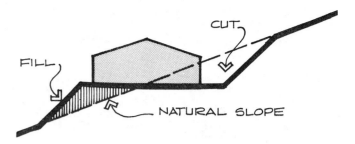

FIGURE 6. "CUT AND FILL" SITE

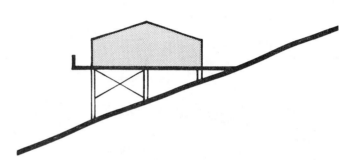

FIGURE 7. HOUSE ON PLATFORM

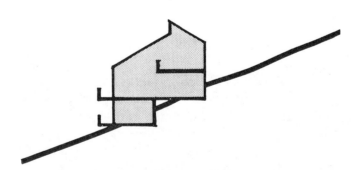

FIGURE 8. HOUSE CONFORMING TO THE NATURAL SLOPE

multilevel. This means climbing stairs but that's what hills are all about.

Another example of poor siting is a split- or two-level house placed on a flat or only slightly sloping site in such a way that one has to climb stairs to get to the entrance and then when inside go downstairs

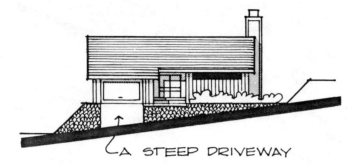

A STEEP DRIVEWAY

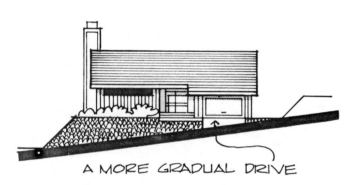

A MORE GRADUAL DRIVE

FIGURE 9. THE SLOPE AFFECTS YOUR CAR, TOO!

to get to the lower level. I have a friend who is a sculptor and an architect. He was remodeling his home and built a deck extending from his old front entrance. He had planned to build a new entrance at the side of the house so the entry traffic would stop passing through the living room. Then he found that there was no way a side entrance would work without going up steps and then back down steps again to the first floor level. He's a purist, and rightly so, and he will not tolerate what he calls an "up and down." It's an impasse that isn't solved yet. In the interim, to enter we all have to climb onto the new front deck which is three feet off the ground and has no steps. Everyone cheerfully enters his house like second-story artists while we wait for the solution to come to him.

Siting also affects driveways. If a sloping site has the driveway and garage on the downslope side, the driveway will be steep. There is a chance of losing a car if the brakes fail. Try to choose the

home in a sloped situation where the driveway is on the upslope end of the lot so it will be more level. It will be easier to drive into and out of, safer to park on, and maybe save you the deductible on your insurance.

MAJOR COMPONENTS OF A DESIGN

Space and Volume

I love the way some new items, such as small appliances, cameras, and calculators come packaged now. I'm referring to the foam boxes that are square outside so they stack well, while the interior is molded to the exact shape of the item so that it's cradled snugly. This is a very righteous idea! It saves space outside and there is not a lot of that to waste anymore. Our homes are like this in a way; they have to sit side by side or stack one upon another because it saves land. But inside the space should cuddle our beings and our lives. We should all have a package that fits us!

Vertical and Horizontal Dimensions and How They Can Affect Us

There are no fixed rules about the effects of different sizes of rooms or their ceiling heights. Some of us are deviates and no matter what some expert has found to be true, that may not be the way we feel. The following is an outline of what is the norm, but if you feel differently, choose whatever makes you feel good.

The standard ceiling height is 8' 0" with some minor variations. As an outgrowth of this, most materials used to construct walls come in 8' 0" lengths. This creates no problem in most situations, but the 8' 0" height isn't always the best.

If a room is very large, it becomes out of proportion if it has an 8-foot ceiling height. The ceiling starts to seem lower than it really is and begins to bear down on you, like the rooms with spikes in the ceiling in horror movies that move down to

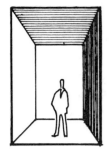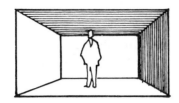

FIGURE 10.   ROOM SHAPES AND
VOLUMES AFFECT US
IN DIFFERENT WAYS

Horizontal dimensions, if they get out of hand, can make spaces that are not only odd but disturbing. A very long and narrow room can make you feel as if you were in a tunnel, and it is not easy to furnish a tunnel! Hallways that are too long will be boring. Hallways should be as short as possible, because it is psychologically better, and long ones take up floor space that you get no real use from.

Making A Space Look Larger Than It Is— Borrowing Space

The open plan, widely used today, allows several uses to share one space instead of each one being contained in separate small rooms. The open plan enables us to borrow visual space from other use areas instead of stopping the flow of space by walls. This has many advantages and some drawbacks. The advantages are that it gives us a big space instead of several cramped, little ones. In the case of the kitchen/family room, it allows for better child supervision and family togetherness. This type of planning is best when you want a feeling of spaciousness but can't afford ample separate rooms. There's one catch to this, though. To work

crush the hero (almost). The ceiling should be higher in a larger room until the proportion feels right again, or more nearly in the proportion of an average room. Conversely, in a very small room, the ceiling should come down a bit so that you will not feel as if you are in an elevator shaft. This, of course, must remain in the limits of how tall people are, because your head shouldn't hit the ceiling either. Usually building codes allow lower ceilings in bathrooms and hallways, or any room that is not a room you *live* in.

Generally, a high ceiling gives the feeling of a more expansive and less protected space. They work best in an area where a lot of people gather or where there is a lot of activity. A lower ceiling feels good in spaces where more intimate or passive activities occur. High ceilings and rooms of large volume aren't conducive to quiet and intimate conversation.

There's a lot of the primitive person still remaining in most of us. We tend to feel really warm and protected in the old cave. A lower ceiling over a conversation area or a fireplace can give this feeling. Larger rooms can be designed with two ceiling heights so that both active and passive activities can be accommodated at the same time—a low ceiling over an intimate conversation area and a higher one for the rest of the room. Conversation and fire pits are popular features in new housing because they too give *cave intimacy*. It is a nice retreat in which to have a quiet conversation away from the noisy part of the party, or will offer a haven if you are reading alone.

FIGURE 11.   VOLUME AFFECTS
VARIOUS ACTIVITIES

well, the big space should have at least as much total floor space as minimal separate rooms would have. In fairness, since the builder is saving the cost of intermediate walls he should offer *more* floor space. If there isn't approximately the same square footage, it is possible that the various uses you plan for the larger multipurpose room won't fit into it. Occasionally the builder has skimped here and since it does fool the eye, one should check the exact dimensions to see exactly what is actually being offered.

The open plan is best for informal living, and if you live more formally, you probably won't be happy with it. Since none of us live all one way or the other, there are several means that will allow you to have it both ways. Temporary walls, such as folding screens, sliding panels, or any other type of movable partition that can be closed or opened between different areas can give you some options. Again, be sure that there is enough total footage in the room to allow for these.

Partial openness from room to room will also borrow space, because it will give an awareness of space continuing beyond. A large opening in a wall, a vertical partition that extends partially across the room, or a horizontal partition that extends above eye level with a view to the ceiling beyond are ways of borrowing space. These partial walls also provide a backdrop for furniture that wouldn't be there in an open plan.

Noise can be a problem in an open plan, so be certain that the uses planned for the space are compatible; watch out for reading versus television, a small child versus teenagers, and other opposing sound sources.

Open planning makes it hard to hide any messes that your family leaves in its wake. You may, if you have an open kitchen, want to shut it off at certain times to keep the dirty dishes out of sight. A movable wall, doors or a horizontal partition high enough to block the view of the kitchen counters would keep the disorder in its place. If you are considering a living-dining room there's the problem of the messy table after a dinner party. If you don't want to look at it you will have to leave your guests to clear it. A partial room divider of the open spindle or shelf type isn't really going to hide the mess for you, only do the job of suggesting a different space. A house that has folding doors or

some similar way to shut the dining room away might let you enjoy your own parties more. Again, What will work for you depends on the way you like to do things.

The tall space or space open to the second floor extends and borrows visual space, and can be very dramatic. If portions of the upper floor open out onto it, these rooms will also gain drama and borrow from the openness of the two-story space. Be aware that this design can lead to noise and heat problems. Hot air rises, and since this type of room is much taller than a normal one it will take more heat to fill. The lower part of the room can be quite chilly, while the top of the room is too warm. If you do choose a tall space be sure it has a radiant or circulating heating system designed to keep the bottom of the room warm. Noise will also tend to reverberate from the rooms below into the upper floor, so if there are bedrooms or other quiet areas opening into the tall space you should determine ahead of time if noise will be a problem.

There's a lot of space outside that we can borrow from, and it's almost free. You are paying for the portion of space around your house or apartment, and you might as well use it in as many ways as you can. A glass wall or sliding glass door will add limitless space while a solid wall with a window stops the flow of space. The illusion of extended space can be increased if the glass leads out to a deck, terrace, or balcony, because this will visually extend the room out beyond the glass. If the flooring material of the room extends beyond the glass, (tile, wood, or slate, for instance,) the continuity will add even more space to your room. It will appear that the room extends to the outer limit of your terrace or deck.

A very narrow room can be brought into visual proportion, or back into square, if it has a large window or glass area on the long wall. If you are faced with a room that needs visual extension, but it faces the street or the neighbor, you can open it up to the outdoors and still retain your privacy by installing a high fence or wall outside enclosing a landscaped area or deck. Even if the space is limited and the fence is as close to the glass as three feet, it will still add that much visual space to your room. If a room is on a second floor or higher, a small balcony beyond glass doors will do the same job.

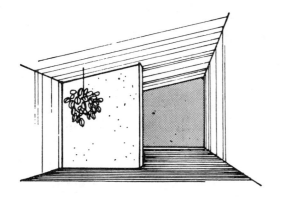 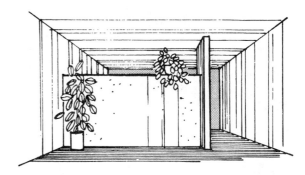

FIGURE 12. PARTIAL WALLS BORROW SPACE

Cheap Tricks to Get More Space

When a room isn't large enough or doesn't appear to be as large as you'd like it, there are several tricks to make it appear larger than it is. The least expensive and easiest way to do this is to paint the room a very light color. The best and lightest, of course, is white. Painting a room a light color seems to make the walls move out beyond their limits. Darker colors bring the walls in and make a room look smaller. Wallpaper or any patterned material works the same way. A lighter and uncomplicated pattern moves the walls out, and a darker, more complicated pattern tends to pull them in. A room with a problem shape can also be corrected with color or patterns. For instance, a long and narrow room can be put in better visual proportion by using dark colors or intricate patterns on the end walls to bring them closer, and a light color on the long walls to push them out. Bookshelves, a cluster of paintings, or any similar *busy* treatment will pull a wall inward.

Mirrors will make a room seem larger. Depending on their size, how many, and where they are located, mirrors can make a room almost appear infinite. One wall of mirror will seemingly double the size of a room, and the and the effect of four walls of mirror has no limits. Another benefit from mirrors is that they reflect the light from windows and will increase the light in a dark room.

FIGURE 13. THE TALL SPACE —
BORROWING SPACE
FROM ABOVE

FIGURE 14. BORROWING SPACE
FROM OUTDOORS

LIGHT WALLS SEEM TO BE FURTHER AWAY AND WILL MAKE A ROOM SEEM LARGER

DARK WALLS SEEM TO COME NEARER AND WILL MAKE A ROOM SEEM SMALLER

FIGURE 15. YOU CAN CHANGE THE SIZE AND SHAPE OF OF A ROOM WITH DARK AND LIGHT COLORS

A house or an apartment will seem larger if the same flooring and wall color are carried through as many of the rooms as possible. This continuity makes rooms seem larger, because the limits of each room aren't absolute in the sense of their being a totally different environment. Most new housing comes with wall-to-wall carpeting, and it's usually one color. If you find a place where they have changed colors from room to room, look to see what the effect is on the space, whether it decreases its apparent size or not. Continuity can be carried to extreme, and it can get boring to have every room the same, but in a small house or apartment, it will buy you the illusion of space.

Spaces appear very different when empty than they will when furniture is added. The seeming size and character of an empty room can be very misleading. Furniture can change the visual size of a room, and a room can change the visual size of furnishings. A very large room needs large-scale furniture. Anything smaller will look as if it is doll furniture, too small for humans to use. This is not usually the problem. We are most often faced with rooms that are too small. Sometimes even a few pieces of average size furniture will crowd the

room and make it appear smaller than it is. If you have furniture that you want to keep, and can't afford to replace, try to determine what it will do visually to the rooms you're considering. Whether or not it will physically fit isn't enough.

Here are a couple of things to think about that will help you visualize or predict how your furniture will fit into the space. Dark furniture in a room with light walls will seem to take up more space than light colors. Light-colored furniture in a dark-walled room will also seem larger than it really is. Another way to help you make a more educated decision is to cut the plan sizes of your furniture out of some heavy paper and take them with you. Lay them out on the floor the way you think you would like your furniture arranged. Keeping in mind the actual height, see if you can easily walk about without stepping on any of your papers. If you have any trouble moving around among the shapes, the odds are that the room will seem overcrowded when the actual furniture is there.

Furniture that is *scaled down* or smaller than standard can help the room to seem larger. Most of this type of furniture is just as comfortable as the standard sizes for average size people, but if there is a football or basketball player in your family you'll need to find other remedies.

Keeping as much floor space clear as possible also makes rooms seem more spacious. If you can't get all the furniture you need into a room without using almost all the floor space, try to get furniture that will do two jobs at once so you can get by with fewer pieces. Some examples would be a dining table that converts to a cabinet when not in use, a coffee table that raises to become a dining table when you need it, or chairs that stack one upon the other when you don't need them. There are many items of this sort on the market, and they will buy back some space.

Space Eaters

Traffic eats space! People need space to move through a room or any part of a home. If these routes are thought of as hallways without walls moving through rooms, it's obvious that they are going to use up huge chunks of space. Later we will learn how to determine where these paths will be so you can plan for them ahead of time. After you know what to look for, you won't be fooled into buying invisible hallways that subtract from the usable size of your rooms.

Doors eat space! My sister and I were looking through some model homes recently. She remarked about the ample size of a master bath in one of the homes. It seemed true at first, but being an architect, and nosy, I took a more critical look. I noticed that the bathroom door had been taken off the hinges. At first, I thought that the reason the builder took the door off was to make it easier for people to look at the room. Then I saw the real reason! The door, when on, would open inward and wouldn't open all the way because it would hit the toilet. To use the toilet, one would have to open the door part way, step past it, and close it before they could sit down. Think of what a nuisance that would be to live with. In addition, the door would have to be kept closed while anyone used the bathroom for any purpose, because half open it would steal the space of a whole corner from the room. These little things are important because they are inconveniences that have to be faced day after day. When househunting, check all the doors to see if they can open fully and lay against the wall without hitting each other or anything else. If they can, they won't steal any space from you!

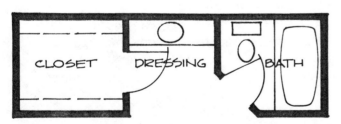

YOU CAN'T DO MUCH IN ANY OF THESE SPACES UNLESS YOU KEEP THE DOORS CLOSED

FIGURE 16. BE SURE TO SEE WHAT THE DOORS WILL DO TO YOUR SANITY

SHAPE—AT HOME IN A DOME?

Living space can be any shape and still house people. Round forms such as teepees, igloos, and yurts have been satisfying their occupants for centuries. But we should, when considering this type of structure, remember that the original occupants lived a very different life than we do. They sat on the floor around a central cooking/heating fire. They had no furniture and therefore the space was totally flexible as to its use. At one particular time the room was the kitchen/dining room and at another the communal sleeping room, play room, or conversation area. Our lives are more complicated, whether they should be or not, and we have many possessions, machines dependent on wires, ducts, and pipes, which makes it difficult for us to be as flexible as our forefathers were. We'll discuss various shapes, their advantages or disadvantages, and some things to think about before deciding what form of home you'll be happiest in.

Rectilinear Housing

This is the form most housing takes. It is an arbitrary shape, but there are many good reasons for it, and it is the one most of us will have to live with. We are able to draw or cut a straight line much easier than a curved one. Most building parts come from the factory in square form. The industry has standardized building components to save money, and this is the standard that has been chosen. Boards, sheets of plywood, and dishwashers come to us in square form. Most furniture is squared also, so in terms of furnishing with standard items, the rectangular house is more efficient. Storage can be tucked into any wall of a rectilinear house while with other shapes it must be put along an interior wall.

Other shapes can be more exciting, but square costs less. It is a wasteful form from some points of view, but in comparison to others I feel a square house is likely to waste the least floor space, and since we can't fly, the floor is what counts! Dome enthusiasts claim that the rectilinear house is less energy efficient because it costs more to heat than a dome of comparable size. This is debatable because there is something the above statement ignores. If you look at Figures 17 and 18, you can see that in the dome, because of its configuration, a lot of space is heated that can't be *used*! Not just the ceiling area, but around the perimeter where the spaces are too low or too curved for an inhabitant to stand up if he wants to. If domes are more energy efficient, chances are, on the average, that they are less space efficient.

A rectangular house, while more common than other shapes and probably more efficient, is usually not as exciting to live in as are houses of other shapes. So again, it's up to you what you trade off to get the thing that means the most to you.

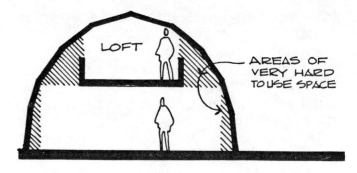

FIGURE 18. AREAS OF SPACE WASTE IN A DOME

Domes

If people aren't square, neither are they round. Domes do present less volume to heat in proportion to floor space. They also let wind glide over them instead of maximizing velocity at the corners as it does around a square house. If you could live as nomads do, you could use all the space. But when you start to divide a dome into rooms and levels and try to furnish it, it soon becomes apparent that in reality it will waste more space than almost any form. The rooms have to be larger to hold the same amount of furniture because it won't fit against the curved walls. Depending on the size of the dome, you often can't stand erect next to exterior walls. In a lot of cases, only the center of space is usable. If the dome is large enough in diameter to allow straight walls to head height, then the ceiling will become very high, and that space will fill up with heat. Many dome designs solve this by building a second level. But since the dome has to curve in sooner or later this gets back to wasting space at the edges again. If you analyze dome space in terms of usable square footage, they are probably not going to be as big as they look.

The acoustics (or sound wave echoes) can be tricky, and can't be predicted without a sound engineer. Domes tend to magnify sound and deliver it to the top, so that if you're considering one large enough to hold a second level, you may find that it's very noisy up there, or that you can hear everyone's whispered secrets.

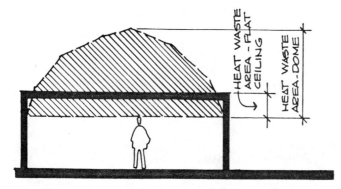

FIGURE 17. HEAT WASTE AT THE CEILING, DOMED AND FLAT

Round Houses and Other Deviate Shapes

Round houses don't have any particular advantages other than their novelty. They don't waste as much space as a dome because the exterior walls are vertical, and you can stand up next to the wall. The wasted space occurs because of the horizontal curve of the walls, and rectilinear furniture cannot be placed flush against it. Furniture must either sit away from the wall, or all be placed against the straight interior dividing walls. Round houses need more square footage than square houses do to hold the same amount of furniture.

A hexagonal house allows for furniture placement, but some weird corners occur that are very hard to use. Hexagonal houses work extremely well when they are designed to include built-in furniture (true with round houses also), but ready-made furniture is somewhat hard to place. In both the round and hexagonal houses, the ability of the designer can solve a lot of problems, but if the designer wasn't really expert, you might regret your choice.

Free Form

Free and natural form is an exciting change from what we always think of as interior space, or exterior for that matter. Its organic qualities can be thrilling! However, it is very difficult to design a free form space so that it is exciting, but works well at the same time. Its sculptural qualities are so important that it really needs to be designed by an especially competent architect or sculptor to be totally successful. If the building isn't an almost perfect piece of sculpture, there is a very great chance that it will look like a cluster of old yogurt cartons. Major furnishings, to a large extent, should be built in so that they become part of the form of the house. Everything must work together smoothly inside and out.

The form should be natural and must work with the landscape. Recently I saw a new free-form house built on a flat site that had been cut into the hillside. This negates everything a free form wants to be. It should be part of the site and grow from it.

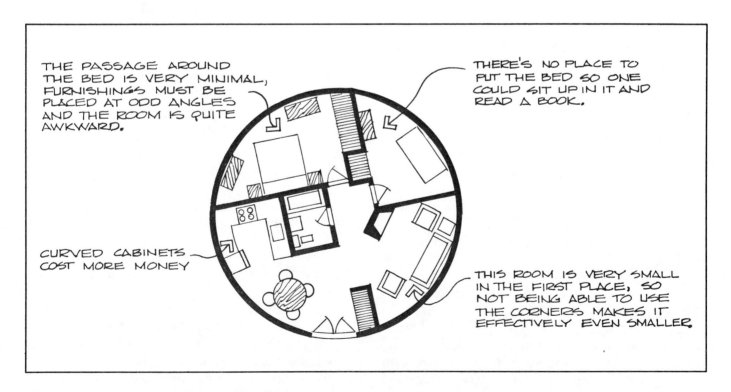

FIGURE 19.   REALLY THINK ABOUT HOW YOU'LL FURNISH ANY GEOMETRIC SHAPE

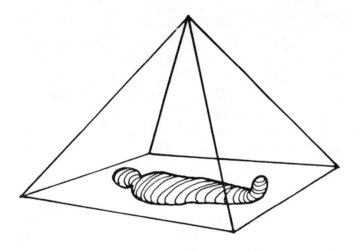

Pyramids

Pyramids are magic or they are scientific phenomena, whichever way one looks at it. It is said that if you orient one to true north, it will attract bio-cosmic energy that will keep razor blades sharp, food from spoiling, give you mystical powers, and even improve your sex life. Architecturally, if you turn to the north you'll lose all of the natural solar gifts, but you can't have everything. Since a pyramid is said to have so many mystical qualities it is hard to predict what will happen to you or for you if you live in one. My advice would be to ask the man who owns one.

A Frames

Because their steep roofs slope to the ground in the shape of the letter A, these can be happily applauded for their incomparable snow-shedding abilities. Laudable also is their simplicity and economy of structure. The interior space is very exciting because of the soaring roof. But again, this allows all the warm air to soar up and away, above the living areas, so they are also very wasteful of heat. The walls slope in, and this again presents some furnishing problems. Most A frames have windowless sides where the roof descends, so if you like a lot of windows, this may not be your ideal home. A frames are worth having if you live in snow country, but they won't do anything particularly useful for you if you don't.

Color

When we were children, somewhere around the second grade, we learned about colors and how to make them. The primary colors of red, yellow, and blue were first, and then by mixing these together we learned to get orange, green, and purple. The water I cleaned my brushes in always turned brown. There are also black and white, which, though they are not technically *colors,* are used as such; and between these is gray.

Colors have a big effect on all of us, and it is especially important in our homes to make sure the effect is a good one. We've seen what the shade of a color can do to make a room seem smaller or larger and to change its shape. Color can do many other things for us if we know what we want it to do and how to use it.

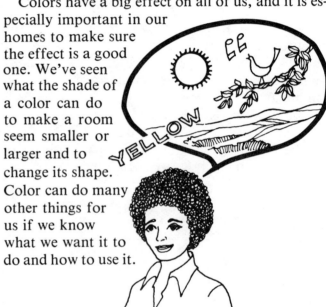

Color Affects Your Head—Psychologically

Everyone has a favorite color or colors. The opposite is true too; most of us have a color we can't stand. Usually there is a good underlying reason for our preferences and for our dislikes. If we thought about it for awhile we would know what it is and probably should if only to achieve more self knowledge. Psychologists have done a lot of work in the area of color and have found general patterns of how one color affects us as compared to another. Since all the experts don't agree and because I don't want to pre-program anyone, we will talk only about our personal reactions. Analyze your own color preferences and try to learn your own feelings about any particular color before accepting it. For again it is how you feel about it that matters.

Frequently I hear myself saying that hot pink is my least favorite color, but that's not really true. I wouldn't wear it or live with it, but I do like to see it on a flag where its strength can shine happily and not intrude too deeply into my own personal space. The color I really detest and can think of no place I would like to see it is *public green*. Not the dark green of park benches, but the pastel green so often used in dreary government and insurance offices. So there is the real reason for my dislike. This green reminds me of closed-in spaces that have a lot of monotonous, and in some cases, troublesome activities occurring within them. I couldn't live anywhere near that color!

The color I love most is yellow. It reminds me of sunshine, flowers, canaries, lemons, and wheat fields. So you can see what living in a public green room instead of a yellow room would do to my happiness and well-being. The thing to do is surround yourself with a color that soothes you and makes you feel as good as possible. The association may be different for everyone—you may have a splendid reason for liking public green, and if so, you should have it.

If you are a family of several, think about colors in terms of all of you. Usually just one family member is delegated the job of decorating. But the decorator should take everyone else into consideration in making color decisions for space that is shared. If someone is going to feel terrible with a certain color, it should be avoided. You can't please everyone, but you can make sure that no one is going to be unhappy. White or a neutral color is the answer if you can't all agree. Each person's private space should be the color of their choice.

Another psychological effect color can have is to make you feel warmer or cooler than you really are. Some very organized people, whom I have always envied, have slipcovers ready to put on their furniture in the summer. This not only keeps perspiration off the real upholstery, but changes the room into a seemingly cooler environment for summer. Colors with short wave lengths, such as green, blue, and violet make you feel cooler, and colors with long wave lengths, such as yellow, orange, and red make you feel warmer. If you live in an extremely cold climate, or have a north fac-

ing room that gets no sun, the space will feel a lot colder than necessary if painted or decorated in a cold color. In hot climates, or in a very sunny room, you will want to use the cool colors. Color won't change a large defect or solve a big design problem, but it can help considerably.

Light Reflectancy

All colors have the ability to reflect light, but in varying degrees. Some whites can reflect eighty to ninety percent of the light striking ceilings or walls back into a room. This reflectivity decreases in proportion to the darkness of the color or shade down through black, which reflects almost no light. If you have a room that gets little daylight, paint it with a high reflectancy color. If you need to absorb light to cut down glare in a room, paint it with a low reflectancy color. Many brands of paint print the reflectivity values of each shade and color on the color chips. You should always look

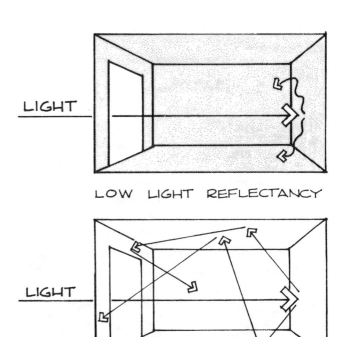

FIGURE 20. GETTING MORE LIGHT

for these when you are selecting paint, even if you have no problem, to make sure you don't get a value that will make your room too dark or too light. One *off white* can vary greatly from another because of the tones that are added to make it *off*. Just picking an off white won't assure that it will have good reflectancy qualities.

LIGHT

How Much Or How Little Light Do We Need?

Here again, it is what makes you feel comfortable personally that counts. The need for light will vary with different activities, and for different persons. There are guidelines which measure these needs in terms of *footcandles*. A footcandle is a "unit of illumination, being the direct illumination of a surface one foot away from a uniform point source of one international candle." I don't know exactly where to buy an international candle or what I'd do with it if I had one. Fortunately, there are easier ways to measure footcandles. If you own or can borrow a photographer's light meter that measures light in terms of footcandles (they don't all do this), take it with you when you are looking at a new home so you can measure the light intensity of various rooms. Use it to check the daylight, and then go back at night to see if the artificial light is adequate. If you can't find such a light meter, call the local power company and ask for one of their engineers or sales staff to come and check it for you with a footcandle meter. However, don't let that person convince you that you should have more lighting than you actually need.

Following are general footcandle needs. If you want to be more exact than this table or have a special need, look in the bibliography for a more detailed source, and more about artificial lighting.

General Lighting:	Footcandles Needed
living rooms, dining rooms, recreation rooms, bedrooms, baths, (except mirrors), and hallways	10

Specific Lighting:
(Also called *task lighting*)

reading	30
study, sewing, crafts	70 and up
kitchen work, surface	50 and up
kitchen work, general	20
makeup mirrors	50

Healthy houseplants need footcandles too, so while you're at it, check to see if there is enough light for the type of plants that you have or want to have. A houseplant book will tell you what they need, so you can include this on your shopping list.

Natural Light

As we saw in Step Two on the natural environment, to maximize the amount of natural light you receive, the orientation of a room and how far the inside wall of a room is from the window is the first consideration. Usually, the best orientation is to the south for the most dependable all-day source of natural light, but another orientation may do a better job for a specific purpose. For example, if you paint or do work that involves color, sun and glare can distort your ability to judge a color or see what it really looks like. So to work with color, a good wide source of indirect daylight is needed, and this may mean a northern orientation. This may also tell us why artists' studios are famous for being cold and drafty.

The location and size of windows is another factor to consider in looking for good, natural lighting. Are they large enough to let in good light, or positioned in such a manner that they will give equal light throughout the room? Windows placed high on a wall pick up more reflected light from the sky and distribute it onto working surfaces better than lower windows do. But that means you can't look out when you are seated, so in that respect, they may not do a good all-around job.

If a room is not getting enough natural light, you can get more light without having to alter the structure. We've discussed painting the walls white or using mirrors but there are other ways too. The

FIGURE 21. TOO MUCH CONTRAST CAN HURT YOUR EYES

First, there is the light bulb, which is called *incandescent*. This contains a wire which is heated by electricity until it is hot enough to glow and furnish light. The second is the fluorescent tube, in which an inside coating is activated (again, by electricity) to glow and to produce light. The fluorescent lamp is the more energy efficient, since it uses about one-fourth of the electricity that an incandescent lamp does. If you put your hand near these lamps, the reason becomes obvious. The difference in the amount of heat generated by each of them is very great. The incandescent gets hot (don't touch it). This allows a lot of heat and, therefore, energy to drain away into the air. This may help heat your rooms in the winter, but conversely it is going to add to heat buildup in the summer when you don't need it. Fluorescent lamps heat up very little, and most of the energy used is for light itself. Fluorescents give off a cold looking light, while incandescents give a more natural and warmer light, similar to the light of the sun. You can buy fluorescent lamps that are called *warm white,* but they will still look *colder* than incandescents. Fluorescent lamps also have an imperceptible flicker that can be unconsciously irritating.

Fluorescents are good when used for task lighting on a specific work surface or work area because they give more light intensity and save more energy per unit. Incandescent light sources are better for general lighting, where high intensity isn't needed, because they look more natural, more subtle, and are more soothing. These two lamp types can be used in many different ways to produce *wide source* general lighting, task lighting, and more.

shades or drapes should draw all of the way back from the window and stack on the wall to keep the total window area clear. Window frames, sills, and sides will reflect more light if they are painted white.

Too much contrast, or variation, between the amount of light inside and the light outside will be disturbing to your eyes. The retina will have to make constant adjustments as your eyes move back and forth to handle the difference. After a while this begins to *hurt*. The contrast can be balanced by lightening the shade of the room, if the outside light is not too extreme. If it is, then a horizontal sunscreen, planting or other similar devices will cut it down. True, the drapes can always be drawn, but that defeats the purpose of your windows and the free light they bring you.

The sun should never shine directly on a work surface. Your eyes will feel the pain this causes immediately. When you shop, always check to make sure the sun won't do this to you. Use the stick trick to check the sun intrusion from the south and your good sun sense to check it from the east and west.

Artificial Light

Artificial light comes from two main lamp types. They both use electricity, but in different ways.

General Lighting

This is wide source lighting. It lights the total room enough to keep you from tripping over the furniture or your friends, and to do some tasks that don't require your eyes to work very hard. Although this type of light usually comes from the ceiling area, general lighting can also be furnished by several sources, working together about a room to distribute light.

There are two types of wide source lighting, direct and indirect. The most common kind of direct lighting is the light fixture in the center of the ceiling, and this is a very poor source. In order to light the total room, the source has to be brighter than is needed at the center to reach the corners, so it causes glare. Also, it is not very flattering to have a shadow cast below your nose, which is what happens with this kind of lighting. A light-diffusing glass shade, or a cover that is frosted or faceted to break up the light rays will give a more uniform light. Still, the central position is not the best. It is always better to have lighting balanced so that shadows, either cast by your body or any other object, don't occur. This can be accomplished by distributing direct light sources such as table or floor lamps about the room. The *luminous* ceiling is a good source of evenly distributed general light. The light comes from many tubes or bulbs arranged evenly over the ceiling and covered with diffusing material of glass or plastic to smooth the light into an even source.

Indirect lighting is very restful, and more interesting because you can't see the source at all. The light is just there! These are designed so that the lamps shine on the ceiling or walls and bounce back evenly throughout the room without glare or shadow. It is also less expensive than the luminous ceilings are, but it generally requires that walls and ceilings be a light color so they have good reflectancy.

Task Lighting

Task lighting, as it implies, is needed for specific jobs, especially those that require extensive use of your eyes. Task lighting should cast a direct and bright light on the work and work surfaces. In almost all cases, task lighting needs to be accompanied by and be an addition to general lighting. If a bright light on your work is the only source of light in the room, there will be too much contrast and that will be hard on your eyes. Eyes need a balance between general light and task light for prolonged work or reading.

Too many kitchens offer only general lighting with which to perform the cooking tasks. At best, they only offer task lighting over the range and/or the sink. The work counter especially needs task lighting so that you can see to read a recipe, measure ingredients, or tell if you got the pots clean last time you did the dishes. The illustrations in Figure 23 show examples of some well-lit working surfaces for kitchens, shop or craft work. You can see that with only general lighting you will be working in your own shadow, but with proper task lighting, the light shines exactly where you need it. Good task lighting is also the most energy efficient, as it allows for lower level general lighting and brighter light only where it is absolutely necessary. There's one other advantage to keeping lower level general lighting. If you're my kind of housekeeper, it means, especially in the kitchen, that you don't have to keep the floor as clean because you can't see it so well.

Mood Lighting

This is low-level lighting designed to enhance a feeling, or mood. Bars, theaters, and restaurants are usually *mood* lit. Mood lighting can make you feel secure, warm, or romantic so you'll surely want some in your own environment. Candles are mood lights. They are romantic, and the light from them makes us all look better than we really do. The soft light from a shaded kerosene lamp will do the same. However, living with kerosene and candles is not always convenient or safe. Low-level lamps in the living room, dining room or bedroom will help you to feel more peaceful, warm, and relaxed.

Most of us need to use our rooms for different purposes at different times, so there should be different systems of lighting within a room to serve these different purposes. If you can have mood, general, and task lighting at various times, you'll get much more use from a room. Lamps with three-way switches can change intensity to suit general, task and mood requirements. A general lighting system with a dimmer switch will also allow you to lower the light intensity when you wish to.

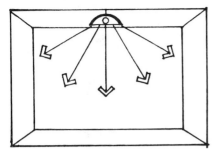

WIDE POINT SOURCE

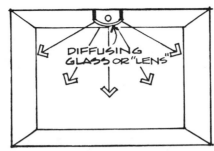

WIDE POINT SOURCE - DIFFUSED

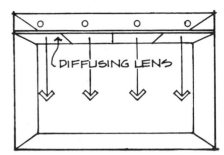

MANY SOURCES - "LUMINOUS" CEILING

GENERAL LIGHTING - DIRECT

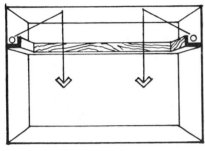

LIGHT TROUGH

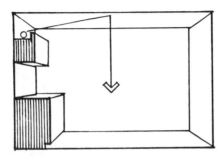

CONCEALED

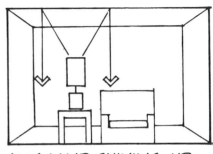

ANY LAMP SHINING UP

GENERAL LIGHTING - INDIRECT

FIGURE 22. GENERAL LIGHTING

CONCEALED

READING LAMP

SUSPENDED

-- BUT NOT THIS!

FIGURE 23. TASK LIGHTING

CANDLES

A VERY DIM LAMP

FIGURE 24. MOOD LIGHTING

SPOTLIGHTS

FIGURE 25. ACCENT LIGHTING

Accent Lighting

This is light that is used to accent or spotlight a particular object. As in art museums, accent lighting can be used in your home to accentuate a particular painting or a sculpture. It can illuminate a collection of pottery, bottles, antique toys, or just about anything that is interesting or fun. A spotlight can also accent a particularly handsome plant or macrame hanging, and it can shine down from the ceiling, or up from the floor, depending on what looks the most dramatic.

Another method of accent light is *backlighting*. In the case of a bottle collection, blown glass, or anything that is transparent, backlighting really brings out the character of the object. This can be accomplished by hiding a light at the back of a shelf or cabinet so that a soft and subtle light will shine through the objects.

Accent lighting can also be used outdoors. It is a way visually use your garden, not only in the daytime but at night, to borrow space and drama. A spotlight on a particularly graceful tree, a flowering shrub, or behind a bank of evergreens will bring a garden to life at night.

SOUND

Sound impact is another intangible factor of a design. Again, there's good sound (harmonious and pleasing) and bad sound (noisy and unpleasant). Step 2, on the natural environment, showed some ways to control outside sound. Now, we'll look at how sound works indoors, its good and bad aspects, and how to get it to work for us, not against us.

The Good Sounds

We want to promote these, because we should get the most of anything that makes us feel good. One good thing sound can do is to make us feel cooler. The sound of running water, or of a breeze rustling through leaves can do this. These sounds can also be relaxing and put you in tune with nature. The sound of birds or of children playing happily out-

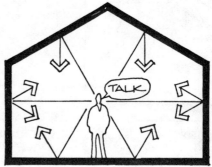

AN EMPTY ROOM WITH NO SOUND ABSORBING SURFACES

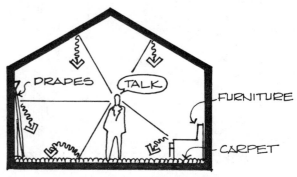

A FURNISHED ROOM WITH A SOUND ABSORBING CEILING

FIGURE 26. SOUND REVERBERATION

side can be cheering. The sound of the sea or a rippling stream can give your environment an undertone of drama and power.

How can you have good sounds if you can't seduce birds up to your highrise apartment, or don't have streams and trees outside or live inland and have no ocean? There are some things that will substitute these sounds. Wind chimes make good sounds. These can range from tiny metal pieces that tinkle and sound like water or birds to heavy steel pieces that give a deep *bong* which can give the same feeling of power as ocean waves breaking on a shore. Clocks that chime give a pleasant feeling of time passing and remind us of it in a quiet way all day. Music is so infinite in variety that it gives us all sounds and evokes many emotions that are even beyond the capacity of natural sounds. Remember when you are shopping to note what the good sounds might be and how you can have them, from the kinds of birds in the area to where the stereo will work well.

Noise

Noise intrusion can have an effect on you that ranges from unconsciously uncomfortable to a jarring din. It can come directly from the source, or from reverberations, echoes bouncing back from interior surfaces. It can come from adjacent rooms through walls and doors or from rooms above and below, through the floors and ceilings. In an open plan or a two-level space it can come directly to you.

We discussed ways that noise coming from the outside can be dulled by using landscaping materials or earth berms. If you haven't room for these, or are renting, you may not be able to correct the situation in this manner. In any case, don't choose a home or apartment that has window openings on the noisy side. If you have to live in a noisy area, find a home with only bathrooms, utility rooms or garages on the noisy side to buffer the sound.

Noise and reverberation occurring within a room will be lessened by interior furnishings, drapes and carpet. All rooms have a lot of sound reverberation when empty, so it is not easy to tell beforehand what the noise patterns will be like after you move in. You can get an ear for differences in individual spaces by talking loudly in each room as you look. Some ceilings have acoustical or sound-absorbing materials in the form of tiles or sprayed acoustical plaster which helps to keep noise from bouncing back down at you. A general rule to keep in mind is that the harder the surfaces the more reverberation you are going to receive. The softer the surface the less reverberation there will be. Plastic paneling will return more sound than real wood paneling and smooth plaster more than gypsum walls. The shape of a ceiling, if it is other than flat, can aim a great amount of noise back down to you and even magnify it. If you encounter a cathedral ceiling, a tall space, or a dome, shout at the ceiling and listen to see if it returns echoes back down to you. The real estate agent may think you are absolutely nuts, but that's better than going crazy from the noise later.

Sound that travels through walls, ceilings, floors, and doors can be minimized by having proper sound insulation. Sounds come from other people, or from machines such as the dishwasher, laundry equipment, stereo, television, or air conditioning system. In another chapter we will show the proper methods to insulate sound and ways to determine if this has been done. Noise is something you harden yourself to after a while, but you are still affected by it. You'll want to know in advance that your body and mind won't be bombarded with noise every day because that can take a lot of your energy.

MATERIALS

The materials used in a design have a lot to do with the feeling we receive from it. There are the materials that are under the floor, in the walls and ceilings and that we cannot see which are called *rough materials*. Rough materials hold the building up and do unseen jobs. The ones that we can see on the surface are *finish materials*.

The visible, finish materials that will surround you should be chosen, as one should choose color, to raise your mood or give you a feeling of comfort. Again, you may find that your preferences are an outgrowth of your childhood memories. It is also important to look at materials in respect to energy and maintenance cost.

Brick, concrete masonry, poured concrete, and even adobe now that *preserving additives* are used, are hard and dense materials. Adobe isn't as stable as the other materials, so it isn't satisfactory for a wet climate. These materials, and the block form, were the first building components man *manufactured!* After the cave, in areas where there were no reeds or trees from which to make shelter, man got into making square mudpies. The feeling masonry gives us in terms of security and substance is probably an emotional one, because masonry is not in itself that structurally trustworthy. Earthquakes or settlement can pull it apart. We only use it today, except in poorer areas, when it is reinforced, braced, and otherwise engineered to be secure and permanent.

Brick has integral color, is what it is, and needs no maintenance. Concrete block usually has grey, tan, or pink (heaven forbid) integral colors. If you can't live with these colors (grey is going to look like prison construction), the block will have to be painted. Adobe is softer and warmer looking than most masonry. Since it is near in character to the earliest masonry, it makes even a new house look warm, lived in, and as if it had a long history.

Poured concrete is rarely used for houses, but it is often used for apartment buildings. If it is left natural it is also reminiscent of prison architecture, cold and depressing. Paint will remove the visual coldness, but the material itself will still be cold to the touch. Concrete is a more institutional material than a human one.

Cement plaster or stucco is the most common exterior skin on buildings in the warm and temperate zones, probably because it is the most inexpensive. Stucco sometimes has integral color and that makes it a low maintenance material. The limiting factor is that these integral colors end up being weak pastel colors or white. There's only a choice of pink, peach, yellow, tan, blue and green. When you see these repeated endlessly from house to house, tract to tract, state to state, you begin to forget where you are and it's boring. I don't get bored when white is repeated. It's not one of nature's colors (except for snow) but it's clean and simple, doesn't clash with the neighboring houses, and is reminiscent of whitewash which has been used for centuries. The all-white villages of the Mediterranean area are delightful to look at, probably because the houses are all one color. Some of the better developers are recognizing this and working mostly with white, tan, or natural wood so the total development has a feeling of oneness.

Wood siding is a warm and natural material. If it's left to weather naturally, it looks at one with nature and most of us feel good with it. If a neighborhood or complex is all of natural wood buildings, it will look as if it had always been there and seem a part of nature. Most likely it won't intrude on its surroundings.

Prostitution isn't the world's oldest profession. Scrubbing the floor of the cave is! Exterior maintenance is only a periodic job, but interior maintenance is *housework*. Materials within a home should give you warmth, excitement, nostalgia or

THIS IS THE WORLD'S OLDEST PROFESSION

whatever other emotions you want to stir up. But always consider how easy or hard they may be to *clean*. I used to forget about this. There was a time when I only thought about how good something looked. I have finally learned this lesson, after flunking painfully several times.

My husband, who is also an architect, had what I thought was a really brilliant idea for redoing our kitchen floor; I forgot about *scrubbing* and agreed to it. The kitchen floor is vinyl tile installed so that it is diagonally striped, white and yellow. If the white is still white ten minutes after it has been washed, it's one of life's miracles. White floors are a natural disaster, and I'm fortunate mine is only half white. I'm in constant envy of a friend who has a kitchen floor of removable duck-board panels above a concrete floor with a drain like they use in commercial kitchens. The dirt falls through the boards and needs cleaning only when you're in the mood for it. The duckboard panels can be taken up and you can flush the dirt down the drain with a hose. If you are a very tidy housekeeper you would probably like the light vinyl floor because you would know immediately if there was some dirt to clean up. Personally, I don't want to know so I'll take the duckboards.

Although great expanses of glass require a lot of cleaning, I wouldn't want to give them up. But be sure that *you* will be able and willing to clean them unless you can afford to hire a window cleaner.

Wood paneling is warm and has a good feeling. If it has a smooth, sanded surface it won't be much trouble. But rough-sawn, pecky or wormy wood paneling will gather dust and cobwebs and although you can vacuum it for a time, eventually it will look as if it came from the inside of a forty-year-old cow barn.

It's possible, of course, to worry so much about maintenance that you get into other problems. Kitchen carpets are a good example of a low maintenance floor, but the problem is that the patterns are designed to hide spills so well that, even when new, they look as if gobs of food had already been spilled on them. I think that defeats the purpose. Your own spots might turn out to be more interesting.

When you choose a home, always analyze the materials and try to project the future ease of maintenance. Then you won't be strapped to constant, painful, and thankless chores like I am to my kitchen stripes. Save yourself!

Machines

Machines and the systems that make them work are the physical lifeblood, circulatory system and functioning organs of a design. The systems and appliances that actively work in your home, their arrangement and location contribute to your convenience and comfort. The jobs they do include carrying energy, such as electricity and gas, water for supply and waste removal, and hot and cool air. There are machines that wash and dry you, your clothes, and your dishes; provide heat to cook with, and make water hot; smash your trash into small cubes; purify water and many smaller chores, from browning your toast to cleaning your teeth.

Since we are talking about choosing ready-made homes, complete with already installed systems and machines, there is no need here to get into how these are planned and located. If you were building your own home, you might not want to install a heating system if you lived in a warm climate and only needed it a few days a year. Or a cooling system if you lived where it was cool most of the time. And if you chose a home that works well with nature you might not need either of these. But since we are talking about ready-built spaces, the decision has already been made by the builder. However, if the presence or absence of any machine is reflected in the cost to you, then you may want to make a choice that will save you money.

In the last step, we'll talk about how you can know if you are getting machines of good quality and if they will do their jobs well and last a reasonable amount of time.

CHECKLIST

How the Design Affects Your Feelings.

Does it give you some feeling of excitement?

Is it possible to create more excitement with landscaping or your own man-made views?

Is it likely that your presence and your personal belongings will enhance that excitement?

If some rooms are depressing, can this be minimized or alleviated by inexpensive interior design or furnishings?

Does it offer you the amount of serenity, that you personally need?

How the Design Functions:

Is the design honest?

Do all the parts of the total design serve a useful purpose?

Is the building in harmony with its surroundings—natural and man-made?

Does the exterior appear organized and in harmony with itself?

Are the rooms in reasonable vertical and horizontal proportion?

If some proportions are awkward can this be altered visually with color or other method?

In an open plan, is the necessary square footage for each separate use really there?

Will the open plan really work with the way your family lives? Or, if it's a closed plan, will that work?

Does the home "borrow" all the space it can? Or will it be fairly easy to do this by remodeling?

Is your furniture the right size and color for the house so that it won't eat space?

Are there few space stealers, such as doors, windows that open inward or hallways in rooms etc.

Some Elements of the Design to Check:

Is its form (shape) going to work for you?

Is it your color or can you change it easily?

Is the color the right one for the room, i.e., warm or cool?

Is the color the right light reflectancy, i.e., a lot for a dark room and very little for a too bright room?

Is the light adequate in all rooms, day and night, for tasks and for general use?

Is the light right for your houseplants?

Is there a possibility of good mood lighting or accent lighting?

Does it have some "good" sounds or can you add some?

Is the building oriented away from noise?

Is the sound reverberation and sound transmission from other sources minimal?

Are the materials of the building psychologically pleasing to you?

Do the materials promise minimal maintenance?

Is the home well sited?

STEP FOUR

People and Their Paths and Places

One of the most important things to look for in a home is almost totally invisible. This is whether it is put together, indoors and out, in a way that will permit a minimum intrusion of one activity upon another, allow an uncongested flow of people and supplies, and connect each use area, according to its needs, to the natural environment.

You can guess whether or not these things will work well, but you may be in for some surprises later and some of them big ones. Here are a few examples that illustrate the type of thing one might not notice. There may be a bottleneck that will cause traffic jams as in the case of the unfortunate "Traffic Cook" in the drawing. A traffic path that you hadn't foreseen may lead directly across a room, and disturb anyone using the room as well as wear a track in the carpet. You may find, when you begin to live in the home, that you overlooked the fact that the bedroom wall of a light sleeper backs the wall of someone who listens to music half the night. Or, that in order to barbecue out on the deck you have to carry the food through the living room. All of these things will cause you disharmony and you don't need that. Fortunately,

there are ways to *prove* in advance how things are going to work. Once you figure out how a space will operate, you'll be able to choose a home that won't cause you little daily madnesses.

Although we will use *house* plans to demonstrate schematic traffic and zoning, the same principles apply to every kind of dwelling. In fact, the smaller the living space the greater the need for good zoning and traffic flow.

The method used to prove how a home will, in reality, work is called a *Schematic Plan Analysis*. In the case of a new home, schematic planning is done before any plan is drawn or the size of any room known, because it is an early step used to determine what the finished design will be. Since we are dealing only with ready-made housing this first step has already been taken, but we need to go back to see if that first step was taken in the right direction. We're going to apply schematic plan analysis to already existing buildings to see if they are well planned and, especially, to see if they are well planned for your particular family.

The first step in analyzing a plan schematically is to start thinking of rooms or spaces not in terms

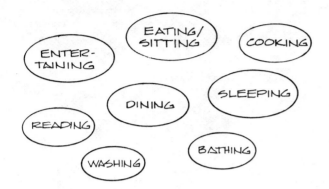

FIGURE I. ABSTRACT THE "ROOMS" INTO "USES"

of a particular shape or size but as abstract, loosely structured shapes such as the circles or ellipses shown in Figure 1. These shapes represent only the use of a space. Later we'll see how to put these *use* shapes together in ways that will show whether or not your new home will function smoothly for you.

ZONING

Spheres of Influence

Zoning a home is the process of arranging rooms with similar activities, so they work well with respect to one another. Again, in ready-built housing the zoning has already been done, but you'll want to analyze it to determine if there are flaws and whether or not you can live with them. If you decide that you can't, how much better to know this ahead of time.

The general rule of zoning is to have all rooms with active uses clustered together and all rooms with passive uses separated from the active, noisy ones. Active uses are social rooms such as a living room, recreation room, or family room. Another type of active room might be a work or hobby room that generates noise. Passive uses are bedrooms, or a study that is really used for study. A den used to watch television should be considered an active room because it will generate sound. Another zone is the cooking-eating group which,

while not clearly active or passive, obviously belong together.

A further zone breakdown, which includes both passive and active uses, is public versus private zones, or the separation of the intimate part of your life from the areas available to your guests.

I am going to demonstrate how to do schematic plan analysis for some example plans. After you see how it works, try practicing on the plan of the house or apartment in which you now live. Besides giving you practice, it will allow you to find what is right or wrong with your present home (you probably already know from experience). You may discover what changes you'd like in a new home or find some ways to make your present home work better.

Figure 2 is an example plan and a drawing of its schematic zoning. The public/private division of this plan is very definite as is the passive/active division. All the bedrooms are clustered together and are separated from the active areas of the house. Another thing this plan does well is to separate areas where daily disorders will occur from areas guests might enter. The study, bedrooms, kitchen, or family room could be in a state of havoc, but a visitor being greeted at the entry or entertained in the living room need never know.

The location of the laundry room is good because it is near the bedrooms and the baths for easy collection and return of clothes and linens. But you must decide for yourself if this would work for the particular way in which you do things. If you spend most of your time in the kitchen or family room, this laundry location will require that you run back and forth to change loads.

You might prefer having the laundry equipment near the kitchen if it would make fewer trips for you and cost you less time. Look at all things that you do and picture yourself doing them so you'll know how the house will work.

The plan in Figure 2 has all the bedrooms together which, while best in most cases, might not be the answer for everyone. The occupants of the master bedroom might want to sleep late on Sunday morning but have children that get up early and make a lot of noise. Perhaps the occupant of Bedroom 2 likes to watch movies on television late at night, and you want to be as far from that as

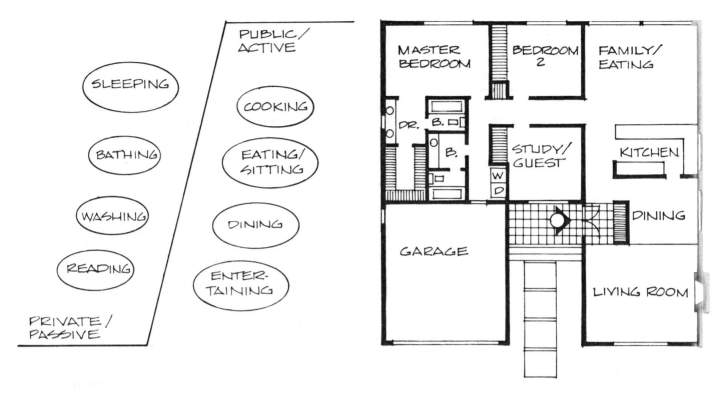

FIGURE 2. SCHEMATIC ZONING

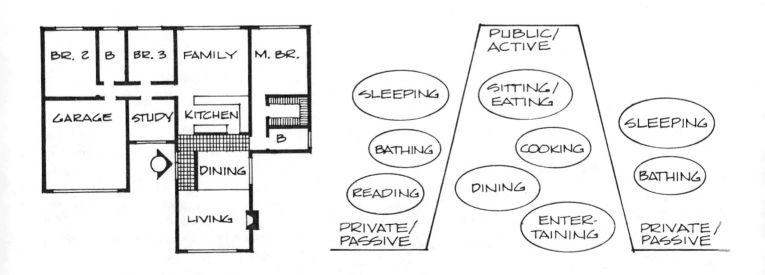

FIGURE 3. A PLAN WITH THREE ZONES

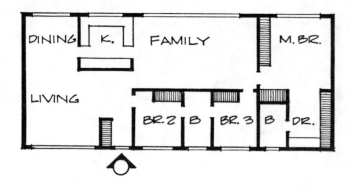

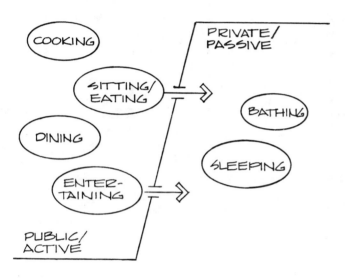

FIGURE 4. A PLAN WITH POOR ZONE SEPERATION

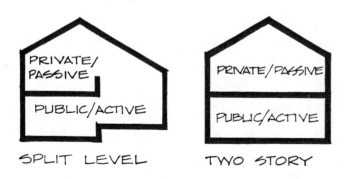

SPLIT LEVEL   TWO STORY

FIGURE 5. ZONING BY LEVEL

possible. Depending on the ages or the noise-making capacity of the person using Bedroom 2 or the habits of the users of the master bedroom, you may want to have two bedroom zones in your home. Figure 3 shows how your schematic zoning might change to accommodate these requirements.

In the plan shown in Figure 3, the master bedroom is located away from the other bedrooms and is positively separated from the active living areas by the bath and closet.

The plan in Figure 4 will not work well because there is no separation between the passive bedrooms and the active areas of the house. This plan would only suit an all-adult household, and then only if all the adults had a similar lifestyle, all did the same things at the same time, or were deaf! An occupant of Bedroom 2 will hear the noise caused by every entrance to and exit from the home, and the use of the living room. The occupants of the master bedroom and Bedroom 3 will hear all the sounds emanating from the family room and kitchen. Although these rooms are separated by walls, it is not a positive separation because the entries from the active rooms to the passive rooms are direct.

Zones of different use can also be separated by a change of level in a two-story or split-level house. Basically, this will work the same as with one level, but the passive/private zone is usually on one level and the active/public zone on another.

The difference between the schematic zoning plan of a one level home and those with two or more levels is that access between them is vertical rather than horizontal.

Recently I saw an example of poor zoning in a two-level home. In fact, it was so bad that you probably won't believe that this house exists! The owners had a good view from the living room and obviously wanted to have the dining room share it, so they located it upstairs on a balcony overlooking the two story high living room. Where was the kitchen? It was on the lower level! Imagine having to carry all the food upstairs and the dirty dishes back down. What a huge amount of work! If the wife was the cook, this couple is probably divorced by now. If they hire a cook, he or she will surely leave after the first dinner party. This is "insanity zoning!" The greatest view in the world could not

80

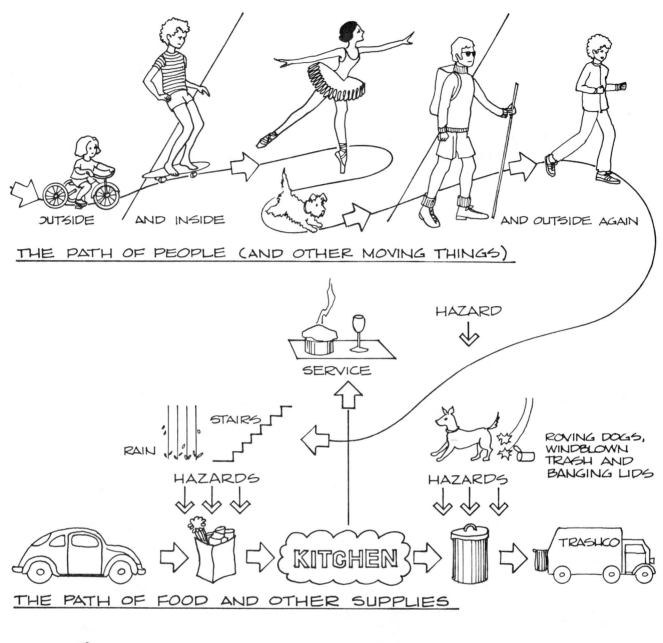

OUTSIDE   AND INSIDE   AND OUTSIDE AGAIN

THE PATH OF PEOPLE (AND OTHER MOVING THINGS)

SERVICE

HAZARD

STAIRS

RAIN

HAZARDS

KITCHEN

HAZARDS

ROVING DOGS,
WINDBLOWN
TRASH AND
BANGING LIDS

TRASHCO

THE PATH OF FOOD AND OTHER SUPPLIES

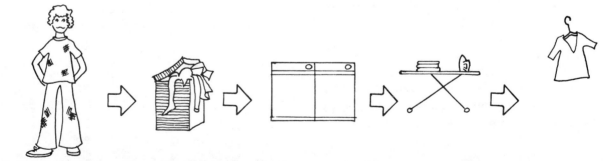

THE PATH OF CLOTHES

FIGURE 6.   EVERY HOME HAS PATHS

be worth all the trouble caused by this arrangement.

Another questionable zoning arrangement is a recreation room located in the basement or on a level lower than the main house. This would work well if you planned to use it as a billiard room, a game room, or for any other boisterous activity that you want separate from the quieter zones of the house. However, if you plan to use such a room for entertaining that includes food service, it won't work well at all! Food and supplies will have to be carried up and down the stairs. Even if there is a kitchenette in the room, you will still have to carry many items from the main kitchen. Even if you completely duplicate everything that you have in the main kitchen, it will still be very inconvenient. As you know, it is impossible to remember everything, so just imagine trying to keep two kitchens perfectly stocked! I have seen too many recreation rooms that are rarely used, and therefore a waste of investment. If you are going to have a recreation room, you may use it much more if it is located on the same level, and adjacent to, your main kitchen. If noise is a problem, there are other ways to solve that.

TRAFFIC

The Beaten Path

Any dwelling has *traffic* on the paths of people and things. If traffic is able to move freely along a path without becoming jammed and without affecting the use of any room, your ease of living in a home is going to be increased. But if the traffic paths encounter obstacles, you will be frustrated every time you try to travel them. Whether or not you will have a good flow of traffic can be proven also. A *Schematic Traffic Flow Analysis,* goes a step further than the zoning analysis and shows where the traffic will move and what effect it will have.

There are several types of paths to consider. First, and most important, are the paths of people as they go about their daily activities, or "people paths." Then there is the "food and supply path," which is the path of goods from the store, through their use in the home and then out to the discard

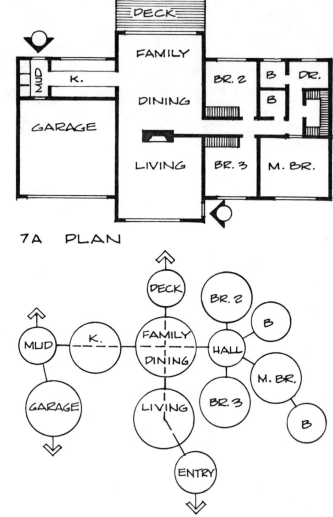

7A PLAN

7B. TRAFFIC FLOW ANALYSIS

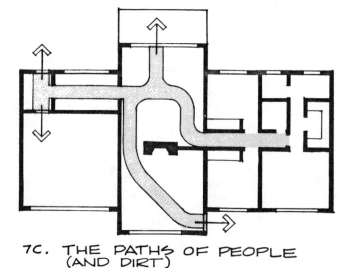

7C. THE PATHS OF PEOPLE (AND DIRT)

FIGURE 7. PLANNING FOR TRAFFIC

area. Another path to consider is the "path of clothes" as they travel from clean to dirty and back to clean again. If you have a particular special activity or hobby that causes another major type of path, be sure to consider that too. Figure 6 shows steps these paths might go through and also some obstacles and hazards that you should take into account if you want traffic to flow freely. These first three paths are invisible to the eye, but the fourth path, "the path of dirt" can make all of the other paths very *visible.*

Since traffic and its paths travel indoors as well as out, the traffic flow analysis should show how the paths enter and exit.

I am going to show an example plan and traffic flow analysis for a home where the paths intrude on the use areas and then another one where they don't, so that you can see how small differences can have a large impact on your usable space, your convenience, and your sanity. We'll still be thinking of rooms as rough forms, and won't worry whether they are arranged exactly as on the plan. The important thing is to determine where the paths are going to be.

Let's make a traffic flow analysis of the plan shown in Figure 7. First, lay out all the uses and their rough relationships, as with the zoning analysis. Show an entry because, although this plan does not have a separate room for an entry hall, it will exist invisibly within the living room. Next connect all the use areas with "path" lines. Right away we see that most of the paths have to travel through use areas to get to other use areas, and this is the first signal of trouble! There is a path through the living room and the kitchen, and an even more heavily traveled path through the family-dining room. It becomes obvious that *all* the paths converge there.

Now that some problems have become apparent, go back and determine just exactly what the problems will be and how they will affect the use of the home. Figure 7C shows the plan with three-foot-wide paths (or invisible hallways) laid out approximately where they will naturally occur. First, there is a diagonal path across the living room which will make it difficult to furnish and deducts a lot of square footage from the usable size of the room. Further, this path leading from the entry will soon show up vividly as a "path of dirt."

There are three paths through the family-dining room. Initially it may have looked very large, but obviously it is not large enough to accommodate all these paths and any decent furniture arrangements at the same time.

This plan has a good "food/supply/waste path" from the garage to the kitchen and back out again. It also has a service area that will work well for a mud room to keep the path of dirt at the rear entrance from entering the house. The kitchen will be a complete disaster! The cooking activities occur in the middle of the path from the garage and backyard. Most of the family traffic in and out of the house will have to pass through the kitchen and around the cook. The cook is an obstacle in the people path, but the pathway itself is an even worse obstacle for the cook! This is a real kitchen, and sadly, there are too many like it. My sister has a kitchen like this! Although she manages to cook some really great food in it, occasionally, she goes berserk and has been known to lock her family out of the house for long periods of time while she cooks.

Figure 8 shows a traffic flow analysis for the plan we looked at first in this chapter, Figure 2. Let's analyze why it works so much better than the plan in Figure 7. You can see immediately that no room has to be intruded upon to get to another. All the paths travel through circulation spaces and

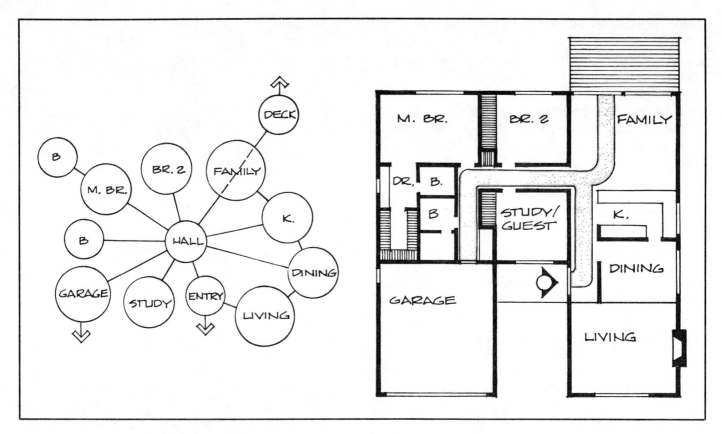

FIGURE 8.   PATHS KEPT IN THEIR PLACES

one can go to any room without passing through another room. The only path that does go through a room is the one to the rear deck, which has to pass through the family room. Since it is probably used less frequently, it will not have as much impact as some others might. Another good feature of this plan is that there are paths from the kitchen to both eating areas (family and dining) that are not crossed by any other path, which eliminates traffic hazards on the "food path." This schematic plan of traffic is obviously cleaner, smoother, and less complicated than in the previous example.

The food/supply/waste path is not good. It is a long way from the garage, and grocery entrance, to the kitchen, and it is not obvious where the trash can go for removal. Either it must travel all the way back through the house to the garage and out or be carried out through the family room. The path of clothes seems to be well planned until you insert the ironing factor into the path if you're one

of those who still iron. The most probable place to do the ironing is in the family room, where the television would most likely be located. Since it's also near the kitchen, it will allow the ironer/cook to do or watch several things at once. The drawback of this ironing location is that it requires carrying clothes from one end of the house to another again. One of the bedrooms could be used to iron in, but you'll need to think of how you want it to be done and how it would work right for you.

The path of dirt is confined to the hallways. Also, the amount of dirt carried in is going to be minimized because most of it will be shed at the hard-surfaced entry or in the garage. The only dirt path will occur where the people path crosses the family room.

On the whole, the traffic paths in this home have been well planned. Almost all of the rooms are entirely usable with a minimum of intrusion, so it will be much easier to live in than the previous plan. The life of our "traffic cook" will be considerably improved if she moves from the first house into this one.

THE SITE

Does It Work With Site and Nature?

Now that we have seen how to prove whether or not the indoors is together, the next thing to do is to find out if it will work with the site and the natural environment. Again, the perfect situation will be hard to find, but the nearer you get to the ideal, the more pleasure and economic value you'll receive from a home.

You are paying for the site, just as you are for the building. In an apartment, if there is a balcony or patio you are paying for it. You wouldn't buy or rent a place that contained rooms you couldn't use, and it's very important to start looking at any prospective site the same way. Ask yourself these questions: Can you use it? How can you use it? Is it convenient to use?

We're not going to guess about this either. We have the zoning and traffic schematic plans for the house, so now we'll take them one step further and add the outdoor uses. Think of the outdoor areas as rooms without walls. There will be rooms you can use physically, such as patios and decks for outdoor living, play yards, gardening work areas, service or utility yards, and parking areas. Examples of outdoor rooms that you may not use physically, but would enhance your interior environment are small fenced or hedged areas that act as buffers to give privacy, stop wind and noise, or hide an ugly view. Small garden yards are sometimes used to create a view where none existed before. This type of land use is especially valuable on small sites where the proximity to neighbors and the streets is very close.

It is as important to do zoning and traffic schematics for the site as it is for the inside of the building. You won't want a noisy play area near adults' bedrooms, or a deck you plan to use for entertaining guests near the baby's room. You'll also want traffic and services to move smoothly in and out of the house.

Following are schematic diagrams which incorporate the site and the home. Using the same plan as in Figures 2 and 8, we'll analyze how the site is going to work with the schematic zoning and traffic drawings.

First consider what outdoor rooms you would like to have. If you want a living-entertaining deck this plan already furnishes it, and it conveniently opens from the family room. Perhaps you'd like a play yard for the children and a place to sunbathe near the master bedroom. If gardening is a hobby, you may want a vegetable garden and a garden work center. Put these items down on a list as needed exterior rooms.

Now let's look for any problems in this plan and its site to determine if they can be solved by sitework or landscaping. As we go through the house, we notice the living room windows look out to the street (and can be looked into from the street). Since the front yard is small the view will probably be of parked cars. To gain privacy for the living room and to create a better view, you may want to consider installing a six-foot-high fence or screen across the front, if there's room within the setback, to form a landscaped entry court. This would make the entrance to this house more dramatic and important, and create a better view from the living room in addition to providing a measure of privacy. The creation of this front yard court will also remove this portion of your site from the public domain and give it to you, exclusively. Write this court down as another needed room.

Next we can see that the only view from the dining room and kitchen is of the small side yard. A landscaped view garden in this side yard would add pleasure and some excitement to these rooms. By "view garden," I mean attractive landscaping. If the foliage is planned to grow higher than the side yard fence it will also add privacy. The master bath has the same problem, a window looking nowhere; so let's add a second view garden here.

And last, we need a place to hide trash cans and hold other miscellaneous and unsavory accessories, so the last "room" needed is a service yard.

Now, add all these needed outdoor rooms to the zoning schematic in the areas where they belong or where you want them. For this hypothetical case, let's put the children's play area near the family room and kitchen so supervision will be easier. You may decide you want your garden work center in this area also, because if you were to put it in the other sensible area, near the garage, it would be too remote from the majority of the yard and from where you'll want to work.

Now, we'll do the traffic schematic. It shows that the plan and site can work well together. There is really only one path problem: The children need a path from the street, and the houses of neighborhood playmates, directly to the play area without going through the house. This kind of in and out traffic brings more noise and dirt than you should have to put up with. The solution is to make a kid path through the landscaped side yard at the kitchen side of the house directly from the street to the play area. Its position will also let you, from your kitchen, know who's coming and going and what they are getting into. A self-closing gate that can be locked at night will solve any security problem. Figure 9 shows how the finished landscape work, fencing, paving, and planting might look to achieve all your needs.

Now that we've got all the activities located and paths directed in ways that will save your sanity, let's see how this house is going to work with the natural environment.

Assigning directional wind and sun arrows to the site we have worked with in Figure 9, let's see what is going to happen when the impact of the natural environment is considered. This should be looked at briefly before you go through all the other exercises to see if there are glaring and unsolvable mistakes in orientation. Since you can't get absolute perfection in a home, don't dismiss one that works really well for you on the inside, just because its orientation to nature isn't perfect. As we saw in Step 2, there are many things you can do to correct minor faults of orientation.

In this situation the winter storms will come from the entry side of the house. How fortunate we added a high fence here that already does two jobs, privacy screening and view enhancement. Now we find it will do a third job—buffering the winter wind! And if the fence is not enough to stop all the wind, there is plenty of room to plant a windbreak of evergreen trees between the fence and the street.

The south sun reaches all of the rear yard and will help heat the family room. Although two of the bedrooms also receive this benefit, the sun would be of more value if it heated the rooms used in the daytime and early evening such as the kitchen, dining and living room. However, since the family room is the most used daytime room, it is the one that should get the most winter sun, so we will be content with that.

The prevailing breeze will cool the rear yard and the family room in the summer, so that will work to your advantage.

The only serious problem here is that the western afternoon sun in the summer will hit all the rooms that it shouldn't—the family, kitchen, dining and living rooms. Since these are all located on the narrow side yard, there is no room for any large and really effective shade trees. The best and only solution there is room for is to plant a tight row of deciduous, tall, skinny trees along the fence. Evergreens would shut out too much valuable light in the winter. The trees will have to be kept well pruned so they won't interfere with the children's path or intrude on the neighbors.

Just for fun, and the exercise, let's turn this plan around 90 degrees on the same lot, as shown in Figure 10. How much better this house would have been if it had been built this way! This illustrates how much a small change in the orientation of any given plan can do. The entry is already private and protected without the cost of adding a fence. All the daytime rooms get good winter sun. More importantly, all the social rooms can share a larger deck and you will have access to it from each of them. The total public zone of the house can now be used as one large entertaining space. With a pass-through, the kitchen can directly serve the deck, so carrying food and dishes in and out is no longer necessary.

The garage now acts as a buffer against the winter wind. It will also block a portion of the heat from the western summer sun from the master bedroom. While getting south sun no longer, the master bedroom will receive morning sun which accommodates happy newspaper reading in bed on Sunday mornings.

The only problem spot left is that the western summer sun still hits the living room. Since now there is open access to the deck on the south, the

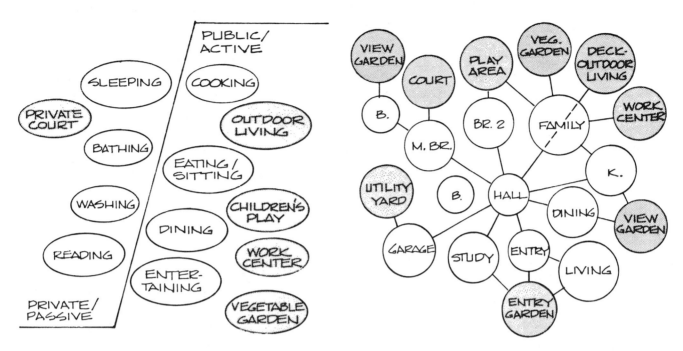

MAKE SURE THE ZONING WORKS

MAKE SURE THE TRAFFIC WORKS

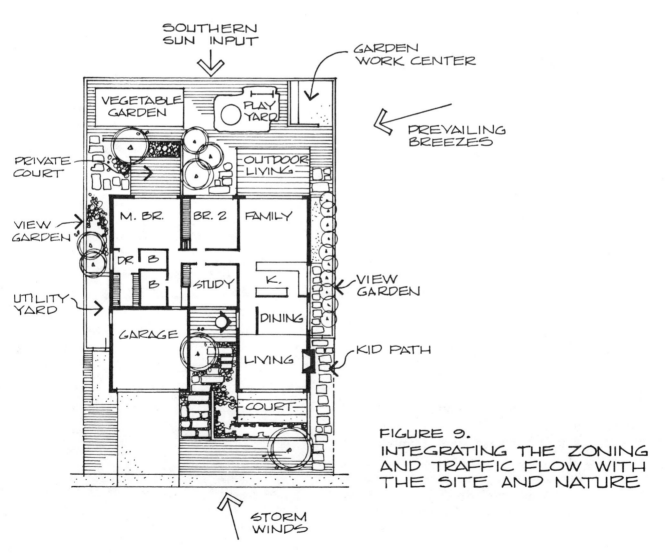

FIGURE 9.
INTEGRATING THE ZONING
AND TRAFFIC FLOW WITH
THE SITE AND NATURE

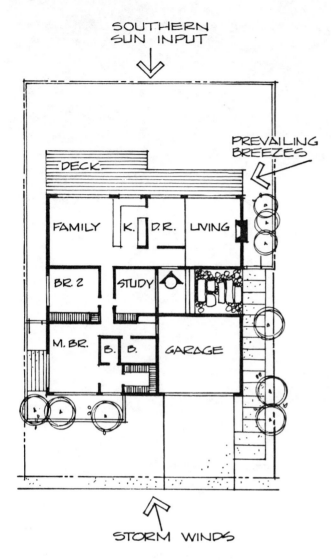

SOUTHERN SUN INPUT

PREVAILING BREEZES

DECK

FAMILY | K. | D.R. | LIVING

BR. 2 | STUDY

M. BR. | B. | B. | GARAGE

STORM WINDS

FIGURE 10. PLAN ORIENTATION CAN CUT COSTLY LANDSCAPING NEEDS

more certain than the person buying a detached home that it works well without corrective landscaping.

CHECKLIST:

Is it zoned well for the needs of your family?

Do all the Paths travel well?

The Path of People
The Food/Supply Path
The Clean/Dirty Clothes Path
Will there be a visible Path of Dirt?

Will there be good Outdoor/Indoor Zoning?

Will the Outdoor/Indoor Paths Work well?

Will the Zoning work well with the Natural Environment?

windows on the western wall of the room are no longer necessary. A solid wall on the west, in addition to the deciduous sunbreak, will make a more effective heat barrier.

Remember, you can judge any dwelling by using the proving diagrams that are shown in this chapter. Everything we have talked about is pertinent to apartments, mobile homes, single family dwellings, clustered homes or townhouses, and even teepees! In the case of apartments and rentals, there will be less you can do to correct problems with the environment, so you'll need to be even

Rooms That Work and Share the Chores Too!

Every room has its own job to do. To get your money's worth and cut housekeeping chores to the minimum, you'll want to make certain that each room you buy or rent will do its job well and be of maximum use to you. You'll want rooms that work well within themselves, are efficient and require minimum upkeep to look clean and appealing.

In this chapter, we'll take a deep look at each type of room and some ways to ensure their cooperation. We'll see which jobs each room can perform and how it will really function. Some of these things are obvious but there may be others we don't normally think about. Traffic of people and things in normal use also occur within rooms themselves, and we'll see how to predict the effects of that. We'll also consider how things within a home fit your body and how your body will work with them. Above all, we're going to scrutinize how hard or easy it will be for you to *clean* things, *cook* things and *stay in command of the clutter generated by everyday life!*

ENTRANCES

At first thought, entrances to a home may not seem important. When you start to think of the jobs they can do and the problems they can solve, however, entrances reveal themselves to be one of the more important areas of the home. Through them funnel all the traffic in and out of your home of people, goods, and services. Entrances are the transition point from the outside climate to the inside climate and from the public world to your private one. There are two main entrance types, family and guest. Some homes have both, but if you're considering a home that has only one, you'll want to be sure that it can handle the jobs of both.

The first thing to look at is how well an entrance handles the transition from outdoors. Entrances that open directly into a room, the living room or kitchen in most cases, can present some problems. Cold air and drafts come in every time someone enters or leaves, making it uncomfortable for anyone in the room. The more traffic there is, the draftier it will be. We've all had to listen to friends (or ourselves) repeatedly scream at children to "shut the door!" This is a predictable result of a direct-access entrance. A separate entrance room or hall will eliminate direct drafts. You may still yell at the children, but less frequently, thereby minimizing another cause of discord in your daily life.

The transition from public to private space is important also. A guest has the psychological need to feel that he is not being *thrown* into a foreign environment. He needs to enter a new territory in gradual stages so there is time to adjust to the surroundings. Cats best illustrate this need for a transition time span. If you move a cat into a new home, he will *freeze!* He may not move a muscle for several minutes (or hours or days). Then gradually, as he sees no danger, he will widen his circle of safety and comfort little by little until he feels secure. Humans, while they make the transition faster, also need some small pause in which to gather themselves together in a new environment. You'll feel better too if guests, especially if they are unexpected, or visiting other members of the family, do not enter directly into a room.

If you find a direct-entry situation, see if there is any way to correct it. Adding a room divider or partially open screen is one solution. This, however, will decrease the usable space within the room.

Unless you're working with a very large room which will accommodate an entry hall, usability of the room itself could very nearly be destroyed.

Figure 1 shows two different 13' x 17' living rooms and the resultant size after the entry and its three foot wide path to other rooms are deducted. Whether or not one screens these entrances from the room itself, the space taken by the entry will be the same. The usable space left in Plan A is 13' x 14' which is fair, but the space left in Plan B is now 10' x 17' which is almost too small in width to furnish. Plan A has 39 square feet cut out of it and Plan B loses 51 square feet, and that's a lot of wasted space.

Entrance of dirt and cold air are not a problem in the case of an apartment which is in a building with a common entry lobby and halls, but the psychological public/private transition is still something you'll have to deal with. If there is considerable hallway traffic you won't want people to be able to look directly into your living room every time you open the door, so you may want a separate entrance area for that reason alone. Security may be another consideration. When you open your door to a stranger, they'll be able to see a large portion of your home. If the stranger happened to be checking it out with burglary in mind, he'd know a lot more about you and the layout than he should. If a separate entry isn't feasible, it will help if the door swings open in a direction that blocks the view of the room.

The main, or guest entrance, should provide some physical conveniences too. The first is a coat closet, in which to hang guests' coats or store their packages, umbrellas, or other goods, so you can greet them and put their things away at the same time. If you have to excuse yourself to go elsewhere, your guests are left standing there waiting. The alternative is to show them to the living room with your arms loaded and ask them to sit down and then excuse yourself. This will make you feel like an awkward beast of burden instead of gracious host. A convenient coat closet will eliminate most of the "ill at ease" aspects of greeting one another, for both yourself and for your guests. It sounds like a small thing, but remember that small things add up!

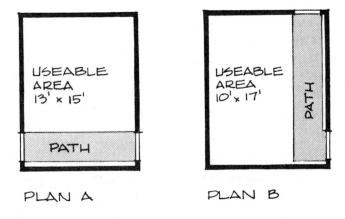

PLAN A   PLAN B

FIGURE I. TWO LIVING ROOMS WITH DIRECT ENTRIES

Another need, and the most important (to me anyway) is a floor in the entry that will handle dirt well or cause the least amount of work and expense. Carpet of a color that won't show soil will do, but since an entrance floor is used more than almost any other room except the kitchen, the carpet will wear out very fast.

An impervious (not capable of penetration) flooring material will offer a better and longer lasting alternative. There are several types of impervious flooring, all of which handle the dirt well, but some have special advantages while others can present some problems. Following is a list of the main types of impervious flooring and their special qualities.

Flooring Material		Good Points	Bad Points
Concrete:	Unwaxed	Not slippery when wet. Lasts forever.	Looks unfinished and can stain
	Waxed	Looks finished. Lasts forever.	Slippery when wet (Best in a dry climate.)
Terrazzo:		Looks expensive (and is).	Slippery when wet.
Hardwood:		Looks expensive (and is). Lasts almost forever	Slippery when wet if polished. Periodic refinishing required. Does not absorb sound, can be noisy.
Vinyl Tile:		Inexpensive.	Can be slippery if not an embossed type. Some need periodic waxing, others have permanent finish.
Impervious Tile: Ceramic and Terra Cotta		Lasts forever.	Can be slippery—needs non-skid surfacing.

One other thing that is often omitted or forgotten in entry halls is natural light. If there is no natural light, the entry will seem like a cave in the daytime. The lights will have to be left on and the es-

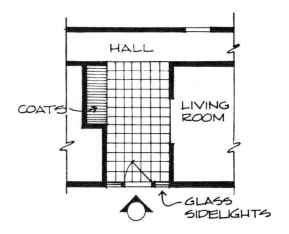

GOOD POINTS TO LOOK FOR:

1. IMPERVIOUS FLOORING
2. COAT STORAGE
3. SOLID WALL OPPOSITE DOOR
4. DOOR SWINGS TO BLOCK VIEW OF LIVING ROOM
5. NATURAL LIGHT

FIGURE 2. THE MAIN ENTRY

thetic result is not as pleasant as it should and could be. Apartment entries almost never have natural light because they usually lead from an interior hallway, and this in most cases has to be lived with. But if you are considering a house, there is really no reason why the entry cannot have natural light. If you are buying a house that has an entry with no light, try to determine if you can modify it easily by adding a small window, sidelight or skylight. For security, it should be unbreakable, wireglass or plexiglass. Most importantly be sure there is a roof or overhang over the door to protect you from the rain while you're unlocking the door.

Figure 2 shows the way a good entry hall should work. A separate entry room, as small as it might be, will be much better than none at all when you consider all the ways it makes your life easier.

Now let's look at the "family," "back door," or "mud room" entrance. Family traffic should be encouraged here, to save both wear and cleaning of the main entrance. The first thing to determine is whether the family entry is more convenient than the guest or main entrance. If it is, it will be used and if not, there will be a continual battle to convince people to use it! Kids, dogs, and everyone for that matter go whatever way is easiest. So be sure the family entry will make a good shortcut, or "path of least resistance." It should be floored with the hardiest and most easily maintained flooring material available. It is where you will, hopefully, stop most of the dirt, mud, leaves, grass, and other debris.

Coat storage is needed here too, and should be able to accommodate wet clothes and muddy boots. Natural light is even more important at this entrance because it will handle most of the daytime traffic. If it doesn't, everyone will have to remember to turn the lights off when they pass through and you'll be annoyed every time someone forgets. So try to avoid this little annoyance and also save on your energy bills.

The family entry should also have space to store items that go in and out with people. Lunch boxes, school books, brief cases and baseball caps will be easier to find, and remember, if a shelf or counter is provided to hold them. Figure 3 shows a rear entry that has all the desirable features.

LIVING ROOMS, INCLUDING FAMILY ROOMS, SITTING ROOMS AND PARLORS

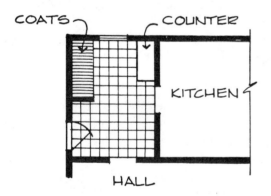

GOOD POINTS TO LOOK FOR:

1. IMPERVIOUS FLOORING
2. COAT STORAGE
3. GOOD ACCESS TO KITCHEN WITH ALTERNATE ROUTE FOR TRAFFIC
4. ENTRY DOOR DOESN'T INTERFERE WITH USE OF ROOM
5. A STAGING COUNTER

FIGURE 3. THE FAMILY ENTRY

These rooms are all basically used for social activity. Although most home and apartment plans divide these rooms into two categories and call them either *living rooms* or *family rooms* these terms don't take into consideration what is actually going to happen in the room. Hopefully your family will be living in all the rooms of your home. It's how you will use these rooms that really matters. Family rooms and parlors are at opposite ends of the "living room" scale by definition. *Family* room implies that the use is informal and mainly by the family. The old term *parlor* implies that the use is very formal and used only to entertain guests *Sitting room* implies that only sitting and reading or talking or knitting is going on, or mainly quiet, passive activity.

Today we don't generally separate these different parts of our lives into such strict compartments. All these uses can be relegated to separate rooms or share the same space as it suits our particular way of life. The only criterion is what activities a family pursues and that will determine what arrangement will work best. Since the primary use of all these rooms involves some sort of "sitting," all considerations and furnishing requirements are similar, so we'll deal with them all together. If you're going to have multiduty rooms, there is an imaginary wall, or walls dividing the areas of different use. Therefore, when you are trying to determine how such a room will work or whether it is possible to get it to work the way you want it to, it has to be broken down into its real parts. Figure 4 shows example plans of multipurpose spaces and ways that the space breaks occur. The most common problem is that there *really* isn't space enough to accommodate all these uses so it's very important to determine this in advance.

A bit later we'll get into the general sizes of any piece or group of furniture and the space it will require to use in estimating how large a prospective room actually is in terms of the use you can get from it. We'll deal with groups for sitting, and groups for eating, sleeping, and other activities.

If a separate *living room* will only be used as a parlor and you have few formal guests, you will not be getting full value for your money. Housing costs per square foot of building are so great that most of us can't afford to waste money on space that isn't used. Similarly, if most of your entertaining is done informally, a home with a minimal family room and a large living room isn't going to accommodate your lifestyle either. You'll get more value if you find a home that joins the same total square footage into a very large family/entertaining room that you will use! The important thing is to judiciously analyze how you use living spaces and buy or rent a home that is patterned to fit the way you live.

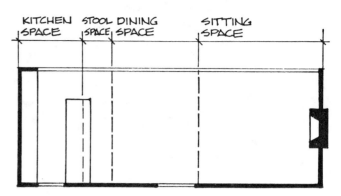

4 USES: KITCHEN/BREAKFAST BAR/DINING/SITTING

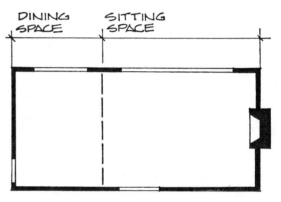

2 USES: DINING/SITTING

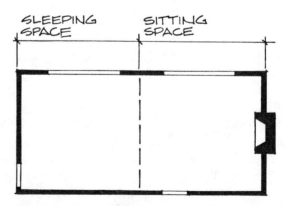

2 USES: BEDROOM/SITTING

FIGURE 4. MULTI-PURPOSE ROOMS MAKE SURE THE VARIOUS USES WILL FIT.

MAKE SURE THE ROOMS ARE
SIZED FOR THE WAY YOU LIVE

Whether living/family or living/parlor or living/sitting, certain activities are common to all. These are:

1. Conversation
2. Television
3. Reading
4. Music
5. Passive play and games
6. Parties
7. Passive hobbies (needlework, etc.)
8. Other (your favorite activity)

Sort out activities your family engages in, to see which are compatible in the same room, and which are not. This way you can begin to picture rooms which will work best for your family. If you don't do this before you commit yourself to a certain home, again, you can come up with some big surprises.

Friends of mine bought a house with a living room and a family room of about equal size. This looked reasonable to them at the time, but after they moved in they discovered that they had a space problem. The husband is a reflective person who likes to spend most of his evenings reading and listening to music. The other three members of the family, the mother and children, all talk a lot and have drop-in friends. These two groups naturally have to divide if he is to have any peace. In this case, he's alone in the living room and all the

rest of the family and their guests are in the family room. He has more space than he needs and the others don't have enough! This imbalance wouldn't have occurred if they had bought a house with a small living room and a large family room. It would have cost no more or less, the area could have been the same, but it would have worked better.

In this case, the living room is at least being used for something. I have other friends who have a home with a huge living room and a very tiny family room. The family room is so small that it can only fairly be called a *television room,* or a sitting alcove. They spend all their time in the small room and since they only entertain a very few close friends and relatives, their guests end up there too. Everyone is crushed into one tiny space while all the area in the living room goes to waste. If they had bought a house with only one good sized social room, their money would have bought something they would *use.* If your budget is limited, it's important to *use* everything you buy.

Regardless of how many sitting type spaces you need for your family, certain rules apply to all of them. How furniture is grouped or arranged can assure that a room will work well. Furniture should be arranged to foster comfortable conversation, not cut it off. It won't matter what style of furniture or what pieces you have if a room won't work for you. So before you select a place be sure it's possible to furnish the rooms in a manner that will promote comfort.

Talking requires physical effort and the more that effort can be kept to the minimum, the more comfortable it will be to hold a conversation. People within five or six feet of one another will be able to talk comfortably. When this distance starts to increase, they will begin to need, or feel that they need, to raise their voices. The ultimate extreme on this scale is feeling the need to shout. If you have guests that do not know each other well, and the seating is more than five feet apart, they will have difficulty starting a conversation or getting to know one another. Physical distance also promotes personal distance!

It is also comfortable to be able to look at the person you are talking to without turning your head. Two people on opposite ends of a sofa can turn their bodies to talk, but three people on a sofa

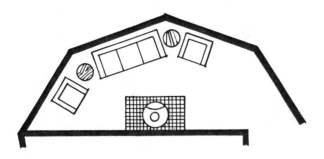

FIGURE 5. THIS ROOM WILL BE FINE IF NO ONE IS ON SPEAKING TERMS

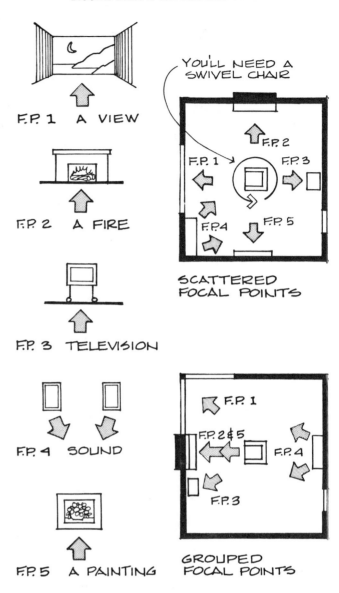

F.P. 1   A VIEW

F.P. 2   A FIRE

F.P. 3   TELEVISION

F.P. 4   SOUND

F.P. 5   A PAINTING

YOU'LL NEED A SWIVEL CHAIR

SCATTERED FOCAL POINTS

GROUPED FOCAL POINTS

FIGURE 6. FOCAL POINTS (F.P.S)

will have to turn their heads, which will lead to strained necks. The peson in the middle may just give up and stare ahead into space. If you're thinking of using a room or portion of one for a conversational grouping, make sure there will be enough space to group the furniture so that seats face each other.

Recently I sent for a booklet of dome house plans because I wanted to analyze how well they worked. The manufacturer showed furniture on the plans and I was amazed to find in almost every case, because of room size and shape, the sitting furniture had to be placed along the outside curved dome wall, in the general fashion shown in Figure 5. Arrangements like this are found at airports and bus stations so you won't have to talk to strangers or look them in the eye. It makes it very difficult for anyone to act like a warm human being.

Another consideration is that a single conversation will usually only be carried by a maximum of five or six people. When the number of people involved is larger than this, the group splits into two or more conversations and then everyone begins to talk louder to compete with other conversations. If you have room for seating more than a small group, it is better to start another arrangement a bit removed from the first.

The next thing to determine is how, or if, the furnishings will work with the "focal points" of a room. Focal points might be a view, a fireplace,

the television set, a painting, or the music source. All of these may occur at once in some rooms while others will have only one or two of them. Naturally, you'll want to be able to arrange furniture groupings to take advantage of and work comfortably with the focal points, so analyze each room to see if it's possible. To get the most from a view, the furniture arrangement should allow you to see it. To be able to feel the warmth of a fire and

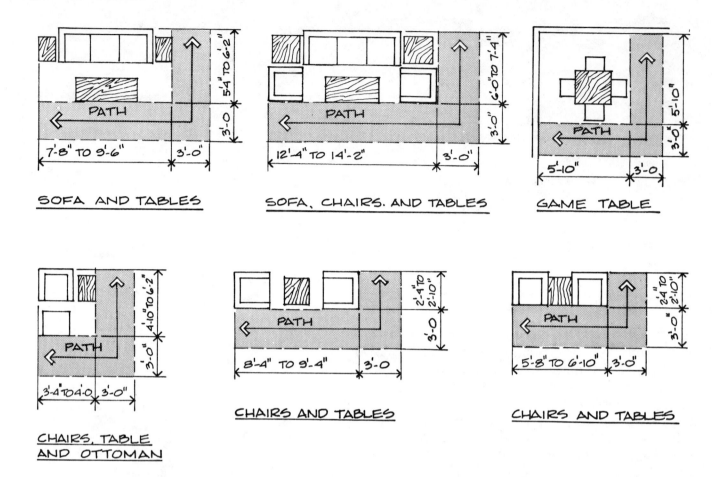

FIGURE 7. BASIC GROUPINGS OF SITTING FURNITURE

to be able to watch the flames, a grouping should allow you to be near it. Seating should also face a television set in a manner that doesn't require heads and necks be turned to watch it. Stereo speakers should be in a place that will allow the sound to reach your ears from opposite directions. If the focal points are all in different directions, it will make furnishing the room very difficult unless you plan to buy a lot of swivel chairs. The closer the focal points are to each other, the easier it is to furnish a room comfortably.

A large room may be easier to work with than a smaller room, because there will be space to have different groupings address different focal points. If your room can only hold one furniture grouping, it may be difficult to get it to work with the focal points. Some rooms are almost impossible to furnish well because of the way the openings are located (doors and windows) and paths that occur within the room. Only very thoughtful planning will ensure that you can focus on all points from one location.

Figure 7 shows some standard furniture arrangements and their approximate dimensions. Use this as a tool to roughly judge if a room is large enough to hold a grouping in such a way that it will accommodate traffic, be comfortable, and address the focal points. If you have furniture you plan to use in your new home, work out your own overall dimensions to use as a guide. Also shown with these arrangements are minimum clearances to walls and minimum dimensions of people paths.

Figure 8 shows three sample rooms, two of which can accommodate a good arrangement fairly well and one that would tax the best interior designer in the world. Perhaps a very practiced person could give a room a quick glance and know whether it will work well or not, but since empty rooms can fool the eye so easily, most of us need to put the room and the furniture down on paper to prove it. However you do it, try to be reasonably certain that you're not choosing a room that, while it looks gorgeous, in reality is hopeless!

If you give large parties, you'll need a living room (or family room) that allows space for groups of people to stand. People don't stand at parties because there is no seating. They do it because they *want* to. They like to stand because they can move about, meet more people, and disappear quickly if someone is boring them. It is much easier to enter or leave a conversation if you're standing than it is to get up and change seats. If you want loose, comfortable and successful parties, there should be standing room. If you have a large room, don't overcrowd it with furniture, and if you have a small room, reduce the amount of seating to provide standing room. And, remember that the standing space should not interfere with your path of serving (drinks or food) to your guests.

Living rooms need storage which is usually not provided by a builder. Most likely you will have to add a piece of furniture or wall storage for this so be certain there is room for it. Living-related items that need storing are books, games, records, magazines and maybe (depending on how the house works otherwise) liquor and glasses. The nuisance factor can be reduced by planning for this ahead of time.

One other consideration in all rooms is the location of heating vents, wall heaters, radiators or similar heat sources and how they will affect the furniture arrangement.

Once you have determined that the furniture, focal points and traffic will work, review the other points we talked about before. Does the path of service of food and drink work well? Is the lighting adequate or if not, are there enough outlets so you can achieve the result you desire? Is it a room that will make you feel good?

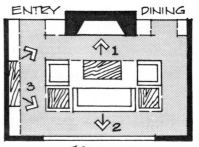

FOCAL POINTS
1. FIREPLACE
2. VIEW
3. STEREO

MOST OF THIS ROOM IS USED UP BY PATHS AND IT TAKES NO ADVANTAGE OF FOCAL POINTS 2 AND 3.

PLAN 1 – POOR

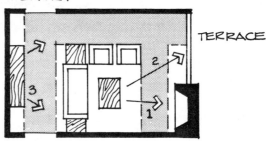

THIS TAKES ADVANTAGE OF THE FOCAL POINTS BUT THE CORNER FIREPLACE IS AWKWARD AND IT LEAVES A LONG UNFURNISHABLE WALL.

PLAN 2 – BETTER

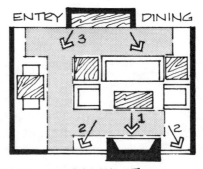

THIS PLAN ALLOWS A SECOND GROUPING OF FURNITURE.

PLAN 3 – BEST

FIGURE 8. THREE 13' BY 20' LIVING ROOMS

Dining Rooms, Dining Areas, Or Any Place That You Eat At A Table

Eating places can be a separate room, such as a breakfast room or a dining room, or they can be in a space shared with another activity. They can be a portion of the living room, share the family room space, or be included with a kitchen in the form of a breakfast alcove or as a part of a large *family* or *country* kitchen. If you intend to use space that is out-of-doors, as an eating area, it should be planned as if it were a room. Be sure the chairs and diners, won't fall off the edge of the deck or terrace! Regardless of the arrangement any dining area consists of the space taken by tables and chairs and an unseen path all around for people. Be sure there really is enough space to seat the number of people you want. If the area shares a room with another activity, is there room for both?

I have a friend who bought a house with a *family-dining* room. When the house was empty, the room looked large enough to accommodate both uses. But later, when she tried to furnish it, she found that after deducting the space taken by

the table and chairs, and the necessary people paths there was no space left for any *family room* furnishings. While the room is too large for just dining, it isn't large enough for anything additional. I've shown this room in Figure 9, so you can see again how much space can be eaten up by traffic paths.

Find out exactly in advance how a room will function. In other words, don't buy a dining room that is too large, and sacrifice the family room you wanted. Or worse, don't buy a family room and have no place to eat except on your laps.

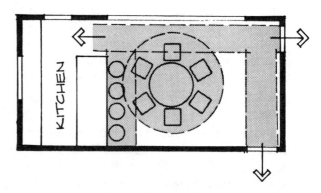

FIGURE 9. A FAMILY - DINING ROOM WITH NO ROOM FOR "FAMILY"

Again, there are general overall dining furniture dimensions and clearances to help you roughly estimate space. These should be used whether you're talking about separate rooms or the square footage needed in a shared room. If you already have furniture you want to keep, use those basic dimensions and add the necessary clearances.

General Rules or Table of Tables and Chairs

1. Two feet of table edge per person, minimum
2. Chairs usually 18 to 20 inches square.
3. Three foot clearance between table and wall or other furniture.
4. Five foot clearance between table and wall or other furniture for service.

Figure 10 shows what this means to you in terms of total square footage taken by a dining arrangement. Both of the situations shown are the absolute minimums. It would be more comfortable to have some additional space. Two and a half feet of table edge per person would be better. The 44″ round table really should seat five at the most. With six, all knees will knock together. The round table gives the visual impression of not taking up as much space as a rectangular one, but physically, as you can see, it uses almost the same space.

Breakfast bars or other similar counter seating also need the same two to two and one-half feet per person along the counter and the same three foot clearance to other furniture, and five foot clearance if there is a path behind them, as shown in Figure 10.

When analyzing any particular dining area or room, check to see if the service path, or path of food, from the kitchen is going to work with the furniture arrangement. Will there be a clear path without hazards? Does the path travel to the table without crossing other paths? Is it convenient to the kitchen?

There are a couple of other things you may want to leave space for in your dining area that will save you steps and other small irritations. A serving station near the hosts' or hostesses' chair to hold warming trays, a coffee pot, or serving dishes

eliminates many of up and down exercises. Storage for napkins and place mats will also save steps. If there is no built-in storage or serving counter near the dining area, and if you need it, make certain that there is enough space for a storage unit, or buffet, in addition to the table, chairs, and the necessary path clearances.

Now consider the lighting. General lighting will be needed of course, but a subdued light level will provide a more pleasant atmosphere at mealtime. But again, you shouldn't ever limit use of any given room. Most of us from time to time use our dining tables for tasks that require a large flat table. We sometimes sew, write letters, wrap Christmas packages, or work jigsaw puzzles on our dining tables. Be sure there will be some good task lighting available for these occasions.

A ceiling fixture will work for general lighting but the best way to provide mood or task lighting is with one that hangs low over the table and shines on it alone. If such a fixture is provided with a dimmer switch, the light intensity can be easily changed from low for mood to high for task. Of course, you can change the bulb from a 40 watt to a 100 watt when you have work to do but the lamp still needs to be over the table.

If a ceiling-hung light doesn't come with the home you're purchasing or renting, or if there is an outlet for one but it is not above the spot where

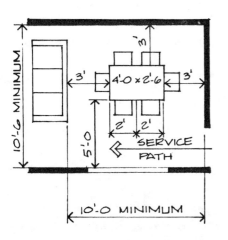 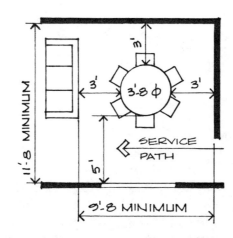 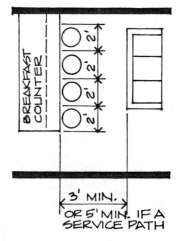

FIGURE 10. MINIMUM DIMENSIONS AND CLEARANCES FOR DINING FURNITURE

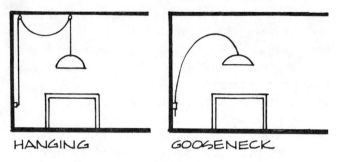

HANGING   GOOSENECK

FIGURE 11. LIGHTING THE TABLE

you want the table, there are alternatives (besides candles) that won't require tearing up the ceiling to rewire it. Figure 11 shows two types of lamps on the market that will plug into a wall outlet and will do this double duty mood/task job for you.

KITCHENS

I doubt anyone has ever had a *perfect* kitchen! It is almost impossible to see ahead of time how a kitchen will really work. Some detail will almost certainly be overlooked or forgotten. Even if you had a kitchen custom designed, neither you nor your designer would be able to cover everything and get it perfectly right.

The kitchen in most homes is the room that gets the heaviest use and is the only room that has to do a manufacturing job. It's a food factory! If you like to cook, your kitchen should help to increase your pleasure. If you don't like to cook, it should minimize your pain. At worst, kitchens can be time wasters, drain the physical and mental energy of the cook, and be hazardous to his health. A good kitchen should be time saving, energy saving and conducive to soundness of mind and body. How do we know if we'll really be happy in the kitchen we choose? There isn't an easy answer so its important to take your time with this room and look at everything.

There are a few established rules for designing a kitchen and there are many books on the subject, a couple of which I have listed in the bibliography. While these books offer a lot of good ideas, mostly they show how model kitchens *look* and offer little in the *how it works* department. I don't feel any of them offer a systematic method of determining in advance how the kitchen will really operate. About half of the things I do in the kitchen are ignored by the books and the rules. And also, I've seen many wonderful exceptions to the *rules!*

THE KITCHEN TEST

With this in mind, I tried to think of a better way to determine ahead of time whether I'd be happy with a particular kitchen. I have devised a *kitchen test* that I think will do this, or at least lead us closer to the *perfect kitchen.* It is a method of scoring a kitchen for workability, efficiency, and contribution to mental happiness. It will enable anyone to score a kitchen according to their individual needs, not in conformance with what an *expert* says is right. If it passes this test fairly well, it will probably be as close to perfect as you can find.

There are five basic categories to score and they are:
1. Appearance
2. Connections
3. Food path
4. Hazards
5. Obstructions

Appearance:

The first test is the easy one. Does the kitchen look good and "feel" good to you? Unhappily many of us don't get beyond this point in choosing a home. A kitchen is too important to be judged only on the basis of looks. This is just the starting place.

Too many of us have married someone that we thought was perfect and that we were in love with; then, later, we found it was impossible to live with the person's hidden flaws. This either leads to divorce or the famous life of "quiet desperation." We need to know whether or not we'll like a kitchen after we've lived with it for awhile. So let's start with the kitchen that *looks* perfect (or possible) and apply the other four tests to see how perfect it really is. If it doesn't pass, you'll know that you should look elsewhere, or at least you will have the option of deciding if it is worth putting up with because you love it. At least you'll be entering the marriage with your eyes open to the hidden flaws.

Connections:

This is how the kitchen relates, or connects, to the rest of the home, the family, and the world. The next decision to be made is how you want it to connect.

Do you want a "closed" kitchen, which has no visual contact with the rest of the house? Do you want an "open" kitchen? If you want an open kitchen, what visual connections would you want it to have?

Kitchens in the past were almost always closed, a separate room used only for cooking. This worked well when a family had a hired cook, wanted privacy, and had no interest in the process of how the food came to be or how it got to the table. Now, most of us do our own cooking and it's not appropriate to shut the cook away. However, some cooks really prefer to cook in private. They may love the solitude, have secret recipes, or prefer not to be seen sweating in the kitchen. There are all kinds of cooks, so be sure you know the kind you are so you get exactly what you want.

I personally feel "left out" in a closed kitchen and can get very peevish about that. Since I am doing all the work, I don't feel good about being left out of what's going on in the rest of the house too. I want to be a part of what the family and guests are doing, and the best way is through visual and vocal contact in some sort of *open* kitchen.

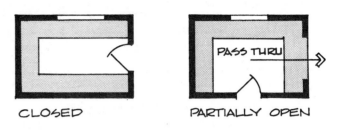

CLOSED   PARTIALLY OPEN

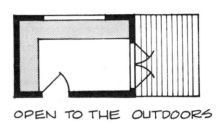

OPEN TO THE OUTDOORS

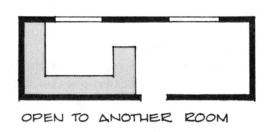

OPEN TO ANOTHER ROOM

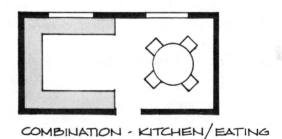

COMBINATION - KITCHEN/EATING

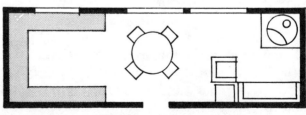

A "COUNTRY" KITCHEN

FIGURE 12.   OPEN AND SHUT KITCHENS

101

A kitchen can be open in several ways. It can open to the family-dining room across a counter-top, or as in many apartments, open to a living-dining room. A *country* kitchen is open, but here the kitchen itself is the room. It is a large room that can accommodate a dining table and some lounging furniture as well. In the country, this worked very well because in the past this was the only room in the house that was heated in winter (by the cookstove). The country kitchen may become a desirable energy-saving necessity again.

A kitchen can be "open" to the outdoors. I don't like to be shut off from nature while I am in the kitchen cooking (this also makes me peevish) and just having a kitchen window doesn't satisfy me. My favorite kind of kitchen would extend to a deck with glass doors I could open when the weather was good. If you plan to have an eating area outdoors, this outdoor connection will be very useful and convenient.

Two problems can arise with an open kitchen. The first is if you don't keep it tidy, you'll have to look at the mess. If that doesn't bother you, fine; if it does, it's going to annoy you. You might want a convertible kitchen you can shut out of sight when you want to, and leave it open when you want to. The other problem with an open kitchen is that if it isn't planned properly, people can wander in and get in your way. Since this can also happen in a closed kitchen, you'll want to be sure to get a plan that will zone noncooks from cooks.

Food Path:

Now for the most important part of the test. That is to determine if the kitchen will help you work efficiently so you can also do it joyfully.

The "work triangle" has been the foremost planning tool to determine kitchen efficiency. This "rule" says that if a triangle is formed from the three points made by the range, the refrigerator and the sink, the sides of which add up to a distance of not less than twelve feet and not more than twenty-two feet, as shown in Figure 13, then this is an efficient kitchen. On the surface that sounds very neat and sensible. But what does this

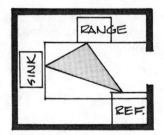 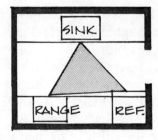

SIDE ONE PLUS SIDE 2 PLUS SIDE 3 SHOULD EQUAL MORE THAN 12 FEET BUT LESS THAN 22 FEET

FIGURE 13. THE "MAGIC" TRIANGLE

really tell us? One, it lets us know that the amount of walking we have to do to travel between these appliances will have a limit placed on it. It also guarantees that the distance won't be so small that there will be the side effect of too little counter space, or none at all. But that is all the triangle can do! There are many other considerations and if they are ignored you may end up with a "Bermuda Triangle" in your kitchen, and with similar results. The reason is that the triangle doesn't tell the whole story. It may show that walking distances are short, but it doesn't indicate how many times you will have to walk that distance. The sink, refrigerator, and the range are only three of the tools used in the total operation of producing meals. Cooking really starts at the grocery store, goes through many stages of preparation, to the service of food, and then clean-up.

Commercial kitchens are the best examples of professional efficiency. Since restaurants are paying wages to their personnel, they have to cook and serve food with the least labor possible. If we modify and use some of their methods, we can also save time and labor. Commercial kitchens are not necessarily warm or happy places, or especially attractive, nor does the food taste like home cooking. I'm not suggesting that their cuisine be imitated, only their methods.

Figure 14 is a flow diagram that is used to program the design of most commercial kitchens. It is an assembly line that works straight through from delivery of food, to preparation and serving, back to washing and storing dishes. Not only is it not triangular, it is obvious that it is another path, a *footpath!* When cooking is seen as a journey through all the operations of food assembly, it becomes apparent we can deal with it in a business-like manner.

Now, let's look at the diagram to analyze the actual physical operation. The food path enters the premises and goes into storage, which is the first thing the trinagle doesn't consider. The restaurant term *dry storage* means anything that doesn't need refrigeration, not that it has to be dry. Vinegar and cooking oil are wet but they are dry storage items, as are flour, beans, canned goods, and crackers. *Cold storage,* of course, means refrigeration and freezing. In restaurants, and in a good kitchen, all stored items are ready and near at hand for the cook when he needs them.

Next, the food path enters the *preparation* stage, which is another major part of cooking not specifically covered by triangular thinking. Preparation of food divides into two categories. *Hot preparation* is any operation that involves heating food. *Cold preparation* includes preparing salads, kneading bread, or cutting up fruit. Cold and hot preparation are twins on the path of food. They both are served by the same storage, cold and dry, and both move on to the assembly stage. Hot preparation needs ranges and ovens. Both hot and cold preparation need a preparation sink. After preparation, both cold and hot food items move along the path to be assembled together on plates or serving dishes, and are served.

After the meal is finished it is *returned.* All the dirty dishes and waste are delivered back to the scullery, or dishwashing area of the kitchen. Then

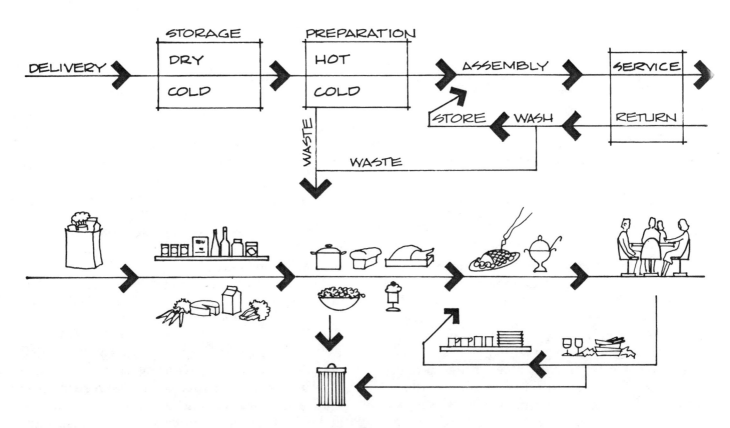

FIGURE 14. FOOD PATH DIAGRAM

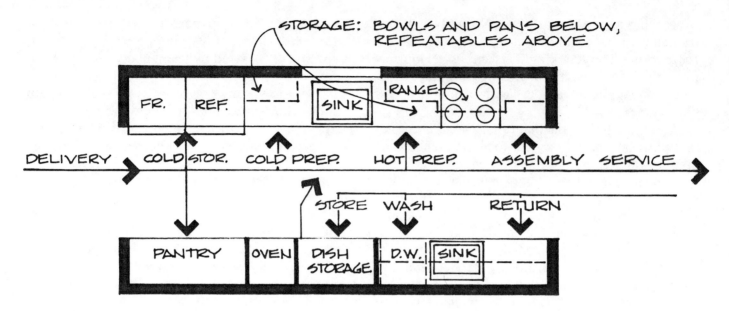

STORAGE: BOWLS AND PANS BELOW, REPEATABLES ABOVE

FIGURE 15. FOOD PATH DIAGRAM APPLIED TO A RESIDENTIAL KITCHEN

the food path continues through washing and finally back to dish storage. The whole process is a matter of progressive order, a very organized and time-saving operation.

A closer look at the path of food would show us that dry storage should work as an in-home market. It should hold things that you use only occasionally. Near the preparation area, very close at hand, there should be a smaller storage facility for the things that you use repeatedly, such as herbs, spices, cooking oils, and other condiments. The refrigerator does double duty; it holds the things you are planning to use soon and the perishables you use frequently such as butter, eggs and milk. The freezer, whether separate or part of the refrigerator, holds things that you use once, but need to hold in storage for a longer period.

If you could find a kitchen designed to produce meals as commercial kitchens do, in accordance with the food path diagram, it would save you many retraced steps, speed your cooking, and allow you to do the work more smoothly. The trouble is that there are very few ready-made kitchens

that are planned this way. At best, they are planned with triangular thinking and at worst with no thinking at all. But don't despair, accidentally or not, some kitchens do follow a food path diagram or come very close to it. By looking for this at least you can discern which ones have very bad paths and which have adequate or good paths. Once you get used to thinking of kitchens this way, it won't be hard to do.

Figure 15 shows a kitchen plan that does adapt to the food path planning method. Let's analyze the way it functions.

This kitchen has dry and cold storage right at the delivery entry. These are near each other so that when a trip is made to gather ingredients, a person doesn't have to go to two or three different places. I show a freezer here, but if you find a kitchen that doesn't have room for one, it could be located elsewhere since trips to it are not as frequent as to the refrigerator. Next, lined up on one wall are hot and cold preparation areas. These are on the same side of the room, so that they can share an adjacent and common sink. The separated preparation counters will also allow two persons to cook at the same time. If a kitchen is very small, the hot and cold preparation can share a counter space and still work well. A side-by-side arrangement such as this will save many trips across the room, from one preparation area to another or to the sink and stove. The oven is located away from this area, but since it is used only occasionally and doesn't generate a lot of trips, that won't be a problem.

Next the path of food reaches assembly. Here there should be counter space on which to fill plates or platters, and enable you to stage everything going to the dining room. Then the path moves out of the kitchen to be served. Then the return operation begins. Here this plan departs from the normal kitchen, but it, as in the illustration, does continue to operate the way a commercial kitchen does, so you can see how well it works. It has a separate clean-up area with another sink and a dishwasher that does not interfere in any way with the preparation sink.

I like this arrangement because when you are preparing food, the dirty mixing bowls, cooking dishes and pots can be stacked here out of the way to be washed later. Another advantage is that the second sink can double for a bar sink before dinner to eliminate any conflict between the bartender and the cook. The path continues then from the dishwasher to dish storage which is immediately adjacent. Now the dishes are all stored where the cook can easily reach them to serve the next meal.

This kitchen would work well even without the second sink. After dinner the preparation sink is free to do the dishes. This is the way most of us will have to do it, but it does have the disadvantage of dirty dishes in the food preparation area.

So the third test that a kitchen must pass is how well it follows the food path. Is there a reasonable progression or does the path double back on itself many times and result in confusion? Walk around a kitchen you are considering and pretend to cook following the path. Or better yet, if you are really interested in a particular house, take a fairly complicated recipe that will involve most of the storage areas and the appliances of a kitchen and walk it through! Watch your movements while you get the ingredients together. This will give you a good indication of whether you'll be going in circles or if you can breeze right on through.

If you don't have time to do the recipe test, draw the plan and superimpose a food path diagram on it. This will show pretty clearly whether it will work well or not.

Figures 16 and 17 show that any plan can have a food path applied to it. The plan in Figure 16 shows that a very neat path can be worked out. The plan in Figure 17 however, can't be diagrammed without a lot of twisting and crossing arrows. In addition, the arrows have to reach a long way to get where they're supposed to go which is an indication that you'll have to reach (or go) a long way too.

While this is no end-all test, if the arrows and their path can be drawn without a lot of crossing and confusion, the kitchen will probably be a lot better than one where the path can't be drawn neatly and looks like a mess. If the paths cross a lot and are confused, it's an indication that you're cooking work will be just as messy and confused as the path.

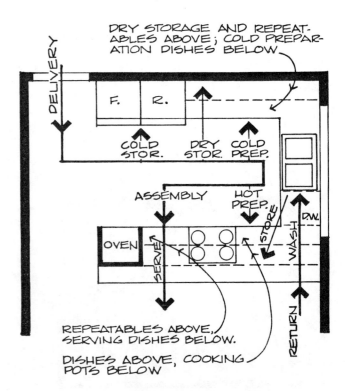

FIGURE 16. FOOD PATH DIAGRAM APPLIED TO AN EFFICIENT KITCHEN

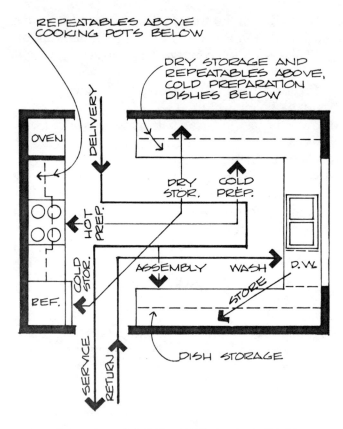

FIGURE 17. FOOD PATH DIAGRAM APPLIED TO AN INEFFICIENT KITCHEN

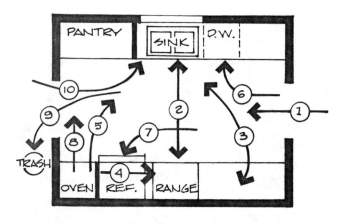

FIGURE 18. THE KITCHEN HAZARDS

Hazards:

The fourth test a kitchen should pass is how many potential accident hazards are present. There are ten major inconveniences and hazards that should be avoided, if at all possible. The more of these the plan avoids, the better the kitchen will be to work in.

The Ten Basic Kitchen Hazards:

1. Through traffic or people paths which can result in collision, spilled grease and burnt children.

2. A range or cooktop across the room from the sink, requiring you to carry hot and heavy pots back and forth. This can result in spilled grease again and burnt feet.

3. A preparation counter not located adjacent to the sink which will require you to do lots of walking.

4. A refrigerator without a countertop next to it which will result in spilled milk.

5. An oven without an adjacent place to put down a hot casserole, which can result in burned hands and broken casseroles. (Note that this hazard exists in the almost perfect kitchen in Figure 15).

6. Having no place to stack dirty dishes except on a preparation counter. This is not very sanitary and might be hazardous to your health.

7. A refrigerator located so that snack seekers interfere with the path of the cook, resulting in collisions again and sticky soft drink spills on the floor.

8. A range or oven near a door where people paths enter (refer to Hazard 1 for the consequences).

9. Trash storage located remotely from the sink where almost all trash is generated. The hazard here will be a trail of garbage.

10. No place to put incoming groceries near the entrance, which can result in broken eggs when the bottom falls out of the grocery sack.

When you score the kitchen, give it a point for each hazard avoided.

Obstructions

The path of food and of the cook can be obstructed by doors. Room doors, cabinet doors, appliance doors, as well as drawers. Here is another call to seemingly mad behavior. Open every drawer, cabinet door, appliance door, or room door all at once, if you can. If you can't, this is the time to find it out. Doors or drawers may hit each other halfway open. The dishwasher may pull out in such a way that a cabinet or bank of drawers will be totally blocked. Or even worse, may open across the sink so that you won't be able to rinse dishes and load the dishwasher at the same time. Perhaps the oven door or the refrigerator door will block the cook's path when open. Especially look to see if the refrigerator door opens toward the work area and not away from it. In the case of a two-door refrigerator/freezer, make certain that it is the refrigerator door that opens to the work area because you'll use that more than the freezer.

Of course, it is unlikely that you would ever need all the doors and drawers open at once, but if you are using items from various cupboards and drawers, conflicts will slow you down, irritate you and cause dents in the cabinets. Make sure that your freezer and refrigerator doors open all the way back to allow you to remove shelves and drawers for cleaning. It's surprising how many builders leave you, the buyer or the tenant, with this problem.

Now, we have five concrete ways to score a kitchen, on a scale of 0 to 10 with 10 being tops:

1. *Appearance*—Does it give visual and emotional satisfaction? _____

2. *Connections*—Does it answer your needs for privacy or family sharing? _____

3. *Food path*—Does it work? _____

4. *Hazards*—How many of the 10 hazards does it avoid? _____

5. *Obstructions*—Is conflict kept to a minimum? _____

_____

The possible high score is 50. The higher the score, the fewer problems are certain to occur later, and by using this test, you know ahead of time what they will be.

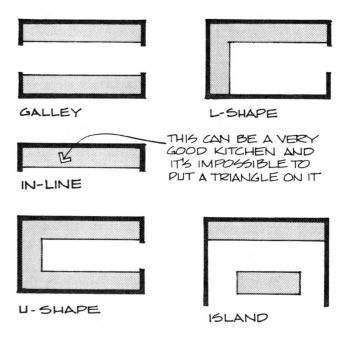

FIGURE 19. KITCHEN TYPES

KITCHEN TYPES

There are five main types of kitchen plans or arrangements. The ones I show are the simple form of these, but there are infinite variations. Some are more conducive than others to a good food path with a minimum of hazards. These plans are shown in Figure 19. Of the five shown, the galley is most susceptible to through traffic problems, while the U-shape absolutely eliminates them. The L-shape and the in-line are best to have where a people path passes through the kitchen, because the work area is all on one side of the room. The cook does not have to cross the traffic path to do any part of the cooking operation. The galley and island kitchens almost assure that you will have to carry things across open floor while the in-line, L-shape and the U-shape eliminate this hazard.

An island kitchen can look very dramatic. They often use more floor space to do the same job as other types of kitchens; but it may be worth it if you enjoy the drama. Island kitchens can have as many hazards as a galley kitchen, if the range is on the island and the sink is across from it on the wall counter. If the sink and the range share the island

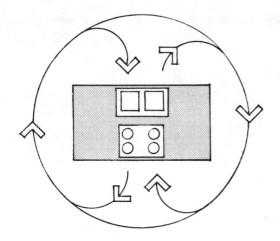

FIGURE 20. THE ENDLESS PATH

so that both hot and cold preparation can take place there, it works much better. I think it works best when the island is used only for cold preparation and serving, with the range and sink placed at the wall counter. A second sink on the island to cut trips and to use also as a bar sink would work even better.

Figure 20 shows an island plan that I have seen used a lot lately. This could only have been designed by someone who doesn't cook, or at least didn't consider the path of food. It doesn't even work with triangles. The only way a cook could operate is in circles. It may look tidy and neatly symmetrical, but get out your roller skates if you choose one like this!

Will It Fit You?

Kitchen dimensions, both vertically and horizontally, are almost uniformly standard. Base cabinets are 3' 0'' high and 2' 0'' deep. Overhead cabinets are approximately 2' 6'' above the counter, are 1' 0'' deep and reach on up toward the ceiling.

The trouble is that we are not all tall enough or short enough to be comfortable with these standards. A tall person can get a backache bending down to use the sink or preparation counter. A very short person will not be able to reach or see into the overhead cabinets. And all of us will have to kneel on the floor to reach to the back of the base cabinets. Unfortunately, there is very little

any of us can do about this. Even if we were able to afford a custom kitchen, we still couldn't change this standard without taking the chance of losing some of the resale value of our home. One company has developed a kitchen cabinet system that adjusts up and down, and in and out, to fit the cook but the odds of finding these in a ready-built home are remote. As it is, the cook is required to do all the adjusting!

While we can't physically change any of this, there are some kitchens that are better than others. Almost none of us can reach any but the bottom shelf in overhead cabinets and the top shelves become dead storage because it takes a ladder to get there! Besides, we already have enough "dead" storage in the back half of the base cabinet. This kind of storage is almost worthless. A kitchen that substitutes a good pantry with reachable storage will do a far better and more useful job for both short cooks and tall cooks. With the wall space freed of overhead cabinet storage, perhaps the builder has offered more windows, or a place to hang some utensils and pots above the counter.

Notice, in Figure 21 that the "reach zone" doesn't really extend to the back of the 2' 0'' counter either. Most of us use only the front half

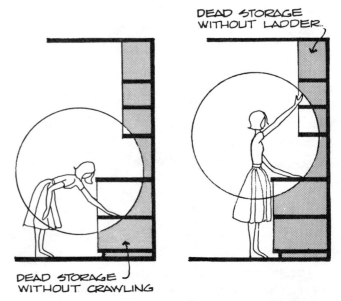

DEAD STORAGE WITHOUT LADDER

DEAD STORAGE WITHOUT CRAWLING

FIGURE 21. YOUR REACH ZONE

of the countertop, where it's comfortable for us. Often the part against the wall is used to place canisters, toasters, and other things we use fairly often. This conglomeration has to be dusted and wiped under frequently. Sine we don't use this piece of countertop to work on anyway, it's possible to gain more storage here. It's a very valuable place to store repeatables because it's so easily accessible, and the cost will be minimal for the added use it will give you. Figure 22 shows two ways to do this, without any alteration to the cabinets or the countertop.

The triangular piece of countertop behind a corner sink is also difficult to reach and clean without getting a stool or climbing onto the countertop. Short bodies should also beware of high ovens. One should *never* have to reach above one's shoulder level to remove something from an oven. A broiler located under the oven of a kitchen range fits no one's body. We all have to kneel on the floor to see what's happening in there.

Kitchen floors are the ones we stand on the most. Therefore, they can be very cruel to feet and legs. Some people are more susceptible to these problems than others. If you are, try to find a kitchen that has a floor of cushioned vinyl which has a foam backing, kitchen carpet, or soft and resilient flooring. The ceramic tile floor may look wonderful, but its your feet that will suffer!

One other physical consideration is the lighting. Both natural and artificial lighting were covered in depth in Chapter 3. Since lighting is so important to the work done in a kitchen, make sure it has both good task and general lighting.

Machines and Other Tools on The Path of Food

There are certain things to look for in ranges, ovens, sinks, refrigerators, freezers, dishwashers, and miscellaneous appliances, large and small, that will eliminate a lot of future trouble and work for you. I am not going to talk about specific brands or types that are available, except to say that they should be nationally recognized so you'll have some idea of how long they might continue to operate. Do turn them on to make sure they work and, if possible, get guarantees.

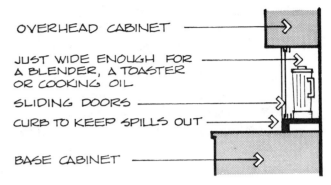

OVERHEAD CABINET
JUST WIDE ENOUGH FOR A BLENDER, A TOASTER OR COOKING OIL
SLIDING DOORS
CURB TO KEEP SPILLS OUT
BASE CABINET

CONCEALED STORAGE

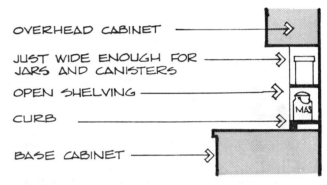

OVERHEAD CABINET
JUST WIDE ENOUGH FOR JARS AND CANISTERS
OPEN SHELVING
CURB
BASE CABINET

OPEN STORAGE

FIGURE 22. A COUPLE OF WAYS TO GET MORE REACHABLE STORAGE

Sinks: Sinks are available as a single or a double unit. Naturally, if you can't have separate sinks for both food preparation and washing, the double sink unit is going to be the next best thing to that.

However, each compartment of a double sink is usually smaller than a single sink, and won't hold items as large as one single would. If you cook in large portions carry the measurements of your largest pots, platters, or baking dishes with you when you are househunting. If you can find a sink that will hold them, that will be one less frustration for you later. Check also to see if the faucet is high enough to allow you to fill your large pots with cooking or soaking water directly. It's a nuisance to have to fill a large kettle with a saucepan.

While you're at the sink, check the garbage disposal. There are two types. The "batch" type has to be filled all at once and won't operate without the *lid locked in place.* The second type is "continuous feed" which operates while you feed it *without the lid on.* If you have children or are forgetful, you'll probably want to have the safer batch type! Next, turn it on to check for noise. Some of them make a horrible racket! There are disposals that are made with sound jackets to deaden the noise. If you're buying a new house, ask the developer to change a noisy one for the sound-jacket model. He most likely will do this for a comparatively small charge or even free, if he wants to sell the house or unit badly enough.

Dishwashers: The first requirement is that it be in a position that will allow you to easily use it and the sink at the same time. Think about how it feels natural to you to load a dishwasher, right handed or left handed. Having a dishwasher located on the "easy" side of the sink will save you another frustration.

Next, check the dishwasher to see how noisy it is. Some dishwashers are very quiet, but others will vibrate noisily. If it is too loud, ask the seller or leasor to change it. If you cannot manage that, ask that sound-reducing pads be placed under the legs or add them yourself later, since they are an inexpensive item.

Ranges and cooktops: The first thing to consider is whether you want gas or electric burners. Every old cook knows which he has to have, but we'll talk about it for the benefit of newer cooks. Electric burners are more energy efficient than gas. Gas burners operate at 40% efficiency (or lose 60% of their heat into the air), while electric burners operate at 75% efficiency. If you want to minimize energy consumption, this should be a consideration when you decide which you want. Personally, I can only cook well with gas, because it can be so finely regulated. I trade off the use of extra fuel by turning the furnace down and wearing a sweater.

Check the spacing and size of the burners with respect to your larger pots and pans. Sometimes they are so close together that you can't use two adjacent burners at the same time.

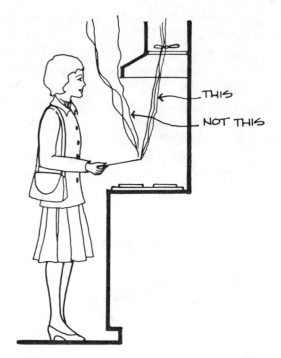

FIGURE 23. CHECKING THE EXHAUST

While at the range or cooktop, see if there is a good exhaust system. This will save you a lot of work later. Grease particles contained in steam and smoke will spread and stick to the walls and ceiling if the exhaust system isn't adequate, requiring more frequent scrubbing or repainting. An exhaust fan mounted in the ceiling won't solve the problem, it will only assure that most of the grease will stick in the vicinity of the fan. An exhaust fan located in a hood above the range lets the hood catch the grease, and that's easier to clean than walls and the ceiling. Some newer model ranges have the exhaust right in the cooktop itself, which pulls the air back down and on to the outside. But the *presence* of a fan and hood or a cooktop exhaust, is not enough. Sometimes the hood is too high or the fan is too weak, which allows some of the smoke to escape into the room. You can test the ability of a fan to draw well by lighting a stick of incense (or a cigarette) and hold it just above the burners (not up under the hood) to see if the smoke is taken up quickly and in a straight stream. Open a window while you are doing this to see if that

110

changes air patterns enough to divert the smoke away from the hood or fan.

While you have the fan on, notice how noisy or quiet it is. Also, find out if there is a screened damper in the duct to keep pests from dropping in for a swim in your stew. A good hood should have a light in it to light the cooking surface, since the hood itself will block any other lighting and cast a shadow on the cooking surface.

Ovens: The main thing to check here is if the height above the floor fits you and your body. Be certain that you are getting an oven that is at a safe height for you. Also, be sure that it is large enough to hold your roasting pans, big braising pots, or the Thanksgiving turkey.

Small Appliances: Toaster ovens, crockpots, blenders and similar appliances all need convenience outlets. You'll want to be sure there are enough to operate the appliances you regularly use. These should be located on the wall at the back of the countertop, so you won't have to have cords strung across the room or have to use multiple sockets. Determine if there will be enough space to store the appliances near where they will be used. Are the overhead cabinets high enough so that the appliances can fit under them? We talked about this not being the most desirable arrangement, but if you use an appliance often, it will be easier than getting it in and out of storage each time you use it.

Refrigerators and freezers: We needn't be as concerned about how these look outside, which is usually good, but with how the inside works. Probably the best method of judging whether a refrigerator will conveniently hold enough for your needs is to examine your present refrigerator so you can compare. For instance, will the refrigerator "tall space" be high enough to store a half gallon of milk, an already opened bottle of white wine with the cork protruding, or your favorite plastic orange juice container? Or is it too high, so that it will waste a lot of space above these items? Check the other shelves to see if they are high enough to take your food storage containers, a soft drink can, a pickle jar or a bottle of soda. Once I got overly thrifty and bought a four pound tub of lard. It wouldn't fit in my refrigerator be-

cause the shelves aren't high enough. If you buy in large quantities, be sure your refrigerator will hold the containers.

Refrigerators will still get messy, but if you check to see if the main items you store fit reasonably well, it will save you a lot of pain later and eliminate the possibility that all this stuff may fall out every time you open the door.

Another useful labor-saving feature of large appliances is rollers, so they can be pulled out easily for cleaning and maintenance. It is embarrassing when a repairman pulls out the refrigerator and exposes an unsanitary pile of dust that has been accumulating under it for years.

Hardware: It's a seemingly small thing, but the type of hardware, or door and drawer pulls, can have a lot to do with raising or lowering your frustration level and the amount of time it will take you to do anything. Door and drawer pulls may look decorative and charming, but what do they mean to you in terms of efficiency?

Cabinet doors will open and close much easier if they have magnetic or "touch" latches. When your hands are full or you have dough all over them, this type of latch only needs to be "touched" by any part of your body to open. Use your elbow for overhead cabinets and your knee

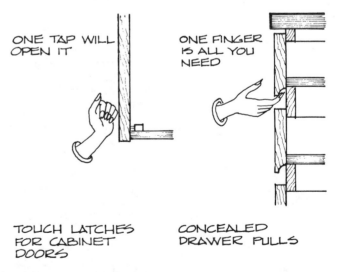

ONE TAP WILL OPEN IT

ONE FINGER IS ALL YOU NEED

TOUCH LATCHES FOR CABINET DOORS

CONCEALED DRAWER PULLS

FIGURE 24. KITCHEN HARDWARE FOR HURRIED COOKS

for those below the counter. Closing a door takes only a slight nudge, and the magnet will take hold again. Some doors have self closing hinges which is helpful, but they have to be pulled open.

Drawers with concealed pulls eliminate the dirty knob problem, visually anyway. They will get dirty, but since they are out of sight, you can clean them when you wish.

Another great convenience is adjustable cabinet shelves. Also, if you find you need more shelves than are furnished, you can add an extra one where you need it.

Sticky kitchen drawers can be another source of frustration. Drawers that slide on wood runners tend to stick. Metal or nylon drawer guides are best, but be sure there is one on both sides. Recently I have seen builders installing only one guide in the middle and this does not work very well at all. Similarly, sliding cabinet doors should be on metal tracks. Wood or fiber tracks, being of softer material, will eventually deteriorate and the doors will stick or come off the track.

The Cleaning Factor

The more you cook the more you have to clean and although cleaning can't be eliminated, it can be minimized.

Flooring was discussed in Chapter 3, so review that before deciding what you can handle. Generally, the smoother and simpler any surface is, the less dirt it will trap and the easier it will be to clean. Natural wall materials such as wood or brick will be harder to keep up than a smooth, painted wall. Drawer pulls with relief designs will be harder to clean than smooth, plain ones. Door faces with surface-applied trim will demand more attention than a one-piece face. The less ornate the kitchen faucet, the less mineral deposits will build up around it. You may want the sometimes "warmer" kitchen that textured materials and psuedo-antique hardware will offer, but it's up to you to decide if that's worth the time you may have to spend later cleaning it with acid and a toothpick.

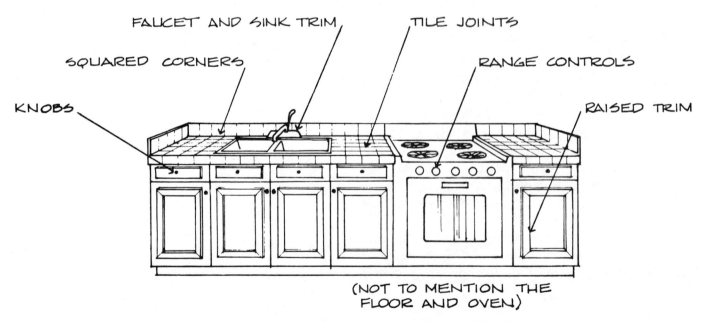

FIGURE 25. COMMON KITCHEN DIRT CATCHERS
(SOME OF WHICH CAN BE AVOIDED)

Tile counters are easy to keep as far as the tile itself is concerned, but the joints can become a disaster. They are little dirt-catching ditches. There are cleaners designed to ream them out but it's still a job that you will need to do often. Some builders install tile with darker colored grout joints. This allows you to clean them less often.

Check all the appliances for simplicity of design which will trap less dirt. All the knobs and controls should be removable so that you can put them in a dishpan and, while they are off, easily clean the surrounding surfaces.

It doesn't matter whether you like to keep a spotless kitchen, or are content with a so-so hygienic situation. The important thing is to know what a kitchen will cost you in labor, so you will know whether or not it's going to ask more of you than you are willing to give.

BEDROOMS

Bedrooms should be private places, where outside influences intrude as little as possible. In fact, in our crowded society a bedroom may be the only place left that is totally your own territory. Even if the room is shared, each person should, within that room, have his own area. It should be quiet so you can keep your own thoughts, or sleep without interruption. It should have visual privacy, so you can behave or look any way you want, and it should be as comfortable as you can possibly make it.

First, check any prospective bedroom for noise level. Take a moment to notice how much exterior noise intrudes. You probably won't know whether a neighbor's dog will bark at night or not, but notice whether an ever present noise, such as traffic of both cars and people can be heard. The noise of automobile traffic cannot be entirely avoided, but a faraway source will even out and be easier to sleep with than the same noise occurring at a closer range. Intermittent noises such as start and stop traffic will be more noticeable and irritating than the smooth, constant noises, if they're not too loud. Avoid a bedroom located above a parking area where people will be coming and going and

slamming car doors at night. Remember also to check the zoning, so you'll be sure that a stereo or a television set won't back up to your bedroom.

Look outside to see if there are street lights, neighboring signs or porchlights that will shine into the room at night. Check the room's orientation to the sunrise. If you are a late sleeper or a daytime sleeper, you'll want a room that faces west or north so the sun won't wake you. If you like to read in bed mornings, you might want a bedroom oriented to catch the early sun. The important thing is, if you remember to think of this, you can get what you'll enjoy the most on purpose, not accidentally.

Will the room allow you privacy? You could get it by keeping the drapes drawn, but wouldn't it be much easier and better if you didn't have to worry about it? Wouldn't it be much more pleasant if you could see out? If you could lie on your bed and look at the trees, the sky and the stars.

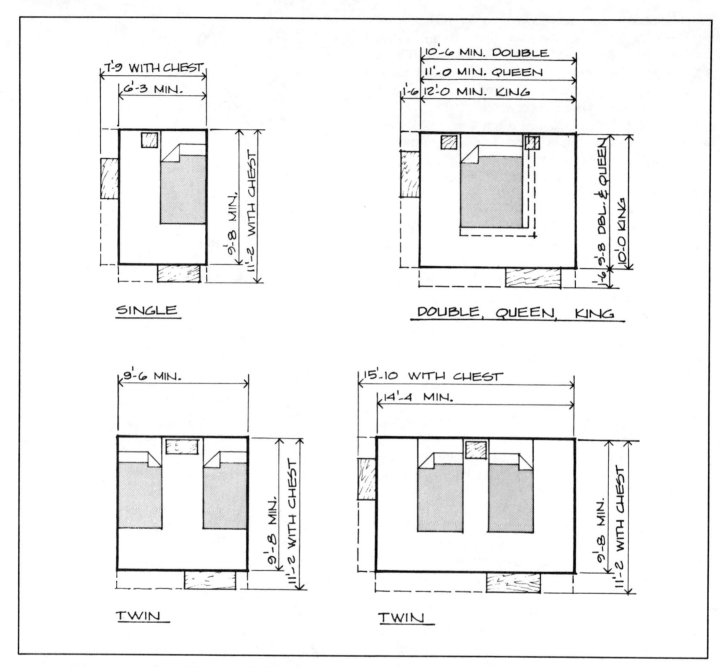

FIGURE 26. MINIMUM BEDROOM FURNISHING GROUP DIMENSIONS

The next thing to find out is how furniture will fit the room. Figure 26 shows some common bedroom furniture arrangements, and the smallest room sizes they require to keep minimum clearances between walls and furniture. A room could be smaller and still hold everything, but if it is, you may bump into the furniture. If you have these dimensions when you look at a room, you'll be able to tell if it can hold the furniture in a somewhat gracious manner.

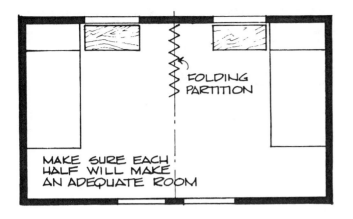

FIGURE 27. DOUBLE BEDROOM

If you plan to have a master bedroom/sitting room, take the dimensions that apply to your situation from Figure 26 and put that together with the dimensions needed by sitting furniture, as shown in Figure 7. Then you'll have the minimum size room needed, just as with any other multipurpose room.

Closet space should measure five linear feet per person as an absolute minimum. I feel that this is only adequate for children, and not for adults. It is a starting place, and the more you can get, the better. Next, each person should have eight linear feet of drawer space, measuring along the front. If drawer storage is not built in, be sure to allow floor space needed to hold chests of drawers. You will probably want a bedside table or nightstand for kleenex, night cream, magazines and books, or pills you have to take before bedtime. The drawing of beds and chests (Figure 26) includes the dimensions needed for these as an addition to the bed space and circulation paths.

Make sure that auxiliary lighting is possible on the bed wall, and that it is switchable from the bed. We talked about the type of general lighting that is provided by an overhead fixture. This type of lighting isn't really functional in a bedroom, so make sure that you'll be able to have task lighting (to read by) and mood lighting (to relax by) instead. Either or both of these will give as much general light as you will need.

Children's bedrooms are a bit more complicated than adult bedrooms. Often, they are actually multi-purpose rooms, used to sleep, play, study, and entertain friends.

All these activities will add a load that a small room can't handle. If you don't want the bulk of this part of your child's life spilling over into the rest of the house, or feel that a child needs his own territory for growth and well being, a 7' 6" x 9' 6" bedroom is not going to be adequate. You can't ask a child to be neat if he has no place to put his toys away, so there should be room for toy and game storage in addition to clothes storage. The remaining free floor space should be large enough to allow a play area for several children to gather around or for a slot-car track. If a child's room is not large enough for all of this, then he'll need somewhere else in the house to call his own.

Double rooms or "Jack and Jill" rooms are bedrooms with a retractable partition dividing them. These have the advantage of allowing two people to share a room, while keeping a sense of their own space. They can have privacy, or a shared play space which would be larger than two separate rooms could provide. The double room does have some disadvantages, so let's look at what they are. If ages and interests aren't compatible, the partition may end up being closed all the time, in which case you might as well have had separate bedrooms in the first place. Sometimes the builder has used this shared room as a device to provide less square footage than he would have had to provide in two separate rooms. This lack of adequate footage could be a problem later when the children are older and do want separation and privacy. So make sure each half of the room is large enough to be a single bedroom.

Guest bedrooms should be just as comfortable as your own. Or they should be if you like your guests. If you don't, then don't worry about this—you'll want them to be uncomfortable! People away from their homes often need a room even more comfortable than their own, to feel good. If you want an extra bedroom to do double duty, to be used as a sewing room or study, for instance, be sure it will hold all the furnishings. If you are working with a guest bedroom that is a minimal size, plan it carefully so it will function well, while not becoming overcrowded.

BATHROOMS

The type of bathroom you will use and need depends on your personal habits. We all have an ideal picture in our heads, such as the gorgeous twenty foot square bathroom, with sunken tubs, dual fixtures, greenhouses and sitting areas that are shown in the plumbing fixture advertisements. Even if we could afford such a bath, it would be worthless if it didn't function well for the way we live. The less than twenty foot square bath that we'll undoubtedly end up with can be a much better one if we make sure that it is planned well for our personal needs.

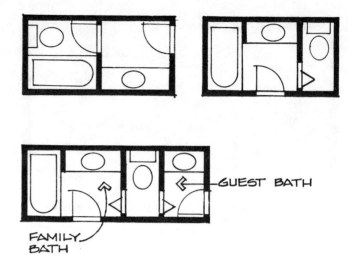

FIGURE 28. COMPARTMENTALIZED OR SHARED BATHS

The first step is to determine just exactly what your ideal bathroom needs. What activities do you pursue there and what do you need to back them up? If you use the bathroom as the reading room, you might need a book or magazine rack and certainly a very comfortable toilet seat. To some, a really long soak in the tub is the only way to truly relax. Others spend long hours in a tub creaming, buffing, tweezing eyebrows, and otherwise beautifying themselves. These activities demand a really comfortable tub that fits your body, storage for creams and beauty tools, or anything else that will

make soaking more comfortable. Some feel only the need for a quick shower and never consider a tub, so a large shower would be better for them. Some turn the wash basin area into a hairdressing and cosmetic salon. Dryers, curlers, hairpins, makeup and nail polish need proper storage. If lighting, electrical outlets, mirrors and work space are available, the salon will work. Analyze your own particular bathroom habits, so you'll know exactly what you need in a new one.

A shared bath will be more versatile if you can find one that is divided or is a "compartmental" bathroom. These offer separate and closeable compartments to house various fixtures and uses. Some of the more common compartmental arrangements are shown in Figure 28.

A shared bath should have enough space and be arranged so that two can use it comfortably. If there are two lavatory basins be sure they are spaced far enough apart so they can be used at the same time.

Regardless of whether the bath is compartmentalized or one open space, there are certain clearance dimensions necessary. if you don't want to bump into the walls or adjacent fixtures. You'll need elbow room! Figure 29 shows some minimum clearances. Bear in mind that these are "absolute" minimums. These baths are very tight and won't be especially comfortable. I'm showing them so you'll know there will be trouble if you accept less, and will try to find a bath that is more ample.

Since we're all different sized persons, check any bath for your personal comfort. Pretend to use all the bathroom fixtures while flapping your elbows to see if you are going to fit. If you plan to use the tub for reclining and soaking, be sure to try it out to see how comfortable it will be. Some tubs have straight backs and are very uncomfortable. If you

like to take baths, try to get an extra long tub. The regular sizes are so short that submersing your shoulders requires that either your knees or your feet be out of the water where they'll get cold!

Check to see if you'll have to walk around a door and close it before you can use a fixture. See if it will open all the way without hitting a fixture or a towel rack, or block the use of some other bathroom accessory.

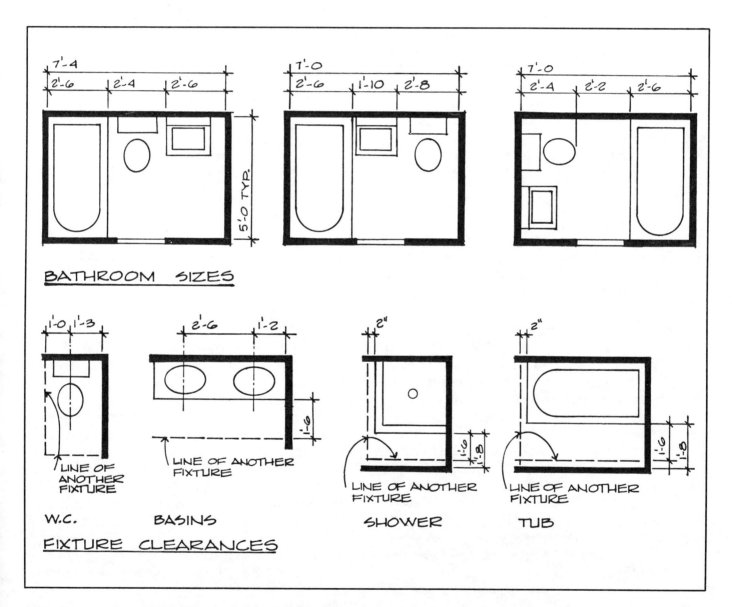

FIGURE 29. ABSOLUTE MINIMUM BATHROOM DIMENSIONS AND FIXTURE CLEARANCES

Good storage makes any bath work better. Each bathroom should provide storage for at least an emergency towel supply.

Tubs and showers should have a place for soap, razors, bath oil, and other things you might need there. This could be a shelf or a recess in the wall or any place closely available, but be sure it is a place where it will stay dry. There should be a towel bar that you can reach from the tub or shower without dripping water onto the floor. Also, it's very important to have a shower that can be turned on without getting you wet. Try it out when you're bathroom shopping. A nonskid surface is an important safety feature in a tub or shower. If you have to add stick-on nonskid materials or use a rubber mat, it will be more difficult to clean.

Water closets need a paper holder and it should be located where it can be reached easily. It should be located on an adjoining side wall at about the same place as your knees will be when you are sitting. It should not be on the wall behind you or any other location that requires bodily contortions.

Again, the more simple the lines of any fixture or faucet are, the easier it will be to clean. Tile joints offer the same dirt catching problems as they did in the kitchen. If you have a tile-lined shower, you can expect soapy dirt to stick in the joints. Molded fiberglass shower enclosures, although they don't look as attractive as tile, are very easy to clean because the corners are molded into curves that won't trap dirt. The metal trim at the edges, corners and joints of plastic laminate shower walls are hard to clean, because the trim edges catch soap scum. Further, this system tends to deteriorate and corrode much sooner than anything else, so it's not a good buy.

Glass tub and shower enclosures will clean easily if they are the type that open on hinges. Sliding glass doors have a track that catches all manner of soap, dirt and unpleasantness, and is just about impossible to clean because you can't get into it with anything but cotton swabs. The doors themselves can't be cleaned on the inside unless you get on the inside too.

My most hated cleaning job is the outside surface of the john! There is no way to clean the base, or behind it, or the floor around it without getting

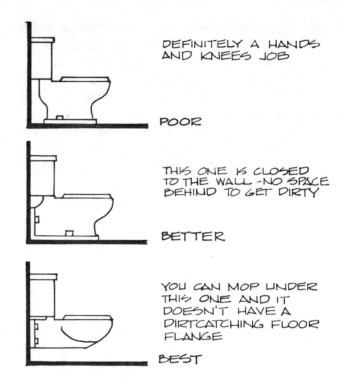

DEFINITELY A HANDS AND KNEES JOB

POOR

THIS ONE IS CLOSED TO THE WALL -NO SPACE BEHIND TO GET DIRTY

BETTER

YOU CAN MOP UNDER THIS ONE AND IT DOESN'T HAVE A DIRTCATCHING FLOOR FLANGE

BEST

FIGURE 30. IF YOU HAVE A CHOICE IN WATER CLOSETS

on your hands and knees. Architects and builders are kinder to janitors. Almost all institutional water closets are hung on the wall so that the floor can be easily cleaned with a mop. Since we civilians usually get the floor-mounted type, all we can do about this is to try to find one that has the simplest design or the fewest dust-catching surfaces possible.

Be sure that there is a good strong heat source that either keeps the bath at a constant temperature or heats it quickly when you need it. Also determine if the room is ventilated with either a window or an exhaust fan, or preferably both. Often the exhaust fan is connected to the light switch and will operate whenever the light is on. Since some fans are noisy and, since it probably isn't necessary that it be on all the time, this not only wastes energy, but can be annoying. A fan on a separate switch will allow you to make your own choices.

Bathroom electrical support systems are very important. A general overhead light source is needed, but sometimes that's all that is provided and it isn't enough. Task lighting is needed at the mirror and, if you read in the bathroom, you'll need localized lighting for that. Finally, be sure there are convenience outlets at the lavatory or mirror areas adequate to run razors, hair dryers, or electrical toothbrushes. A friend who rents an older apartment has no outlets in her bathroom at all, and has to run an extension cord from her kitchen, down the hall and into the bath so that she can use her curling iron in front of the mirror. Don't let this happen to you!

If you give attention to all these little things that make a bathroom easy and comfortable to use, you'll have a "throne" room, even though small, that will treat you like royalty.

HALL AND STAIRWAYS

These "rooms" too deserve your attention. A hallway is a path, and a path should be pleasant. So beware of hallways that are too dark, too narrow, too long, or too dull.

Let's talk about "too dark" first. One fault hallways often have is that there is no natural light source. This might not be noticed when all the doors leading into the hall are open, but when they are closed you may find yourself having to grope in the dark.

A hallway should be at least three feet wide to allow room for persons to pass one another. In addition, less than that will make it very hard to move furniture in and out. Thirty inches is a minimum that most building codes allow, but it isn't enough and will cause you problems. Whether a hallway is "too long" is both a matter of proportion and of dullness. No one would like the feeling of walking down an endless mineshaft. Also, a very long hallway is using a lot of space that might be better used as part of a room. It's possible that such a hallway indicates poor planning, and poor use of space. But, if you do end up with a long hallway because the rest of the house answers your needs, turn it into a gallery for your favorite art, possibly with display lighting to brighten it.

Since a hallway carries traffic, it also carries noise. This can be a problem when it leads past bedrooms or other quiet rooms. In the case of a very busy hallway, carpeting and, even better, a sound-absorbing material on the ceiling will help.

LAUNDRY ROOMS

First make certain it works the way you want it to on the path of clothes. If it is located on a people path, such as a utility or mud room that also carries the family entrance, it won't be too critical because the laundry equipment is only used intermittently. Be sure entry doors can be opened without blocking the equipment however. Storage will be needed for soap and other laundry aids. Storage here for dirty clothes is desirable for some, but others may prefer hampers nearer the source, in the bedrooms or baths. A floor drain is sometimes provided, and can save you from disaster if the machine malfunctions, which you can almost count on at some time.

CLOSETS AND STORAGE

Get as much as you can. You'll need it and use it!

GARAGES

Some people manage to use these rooms as they were intended, as bedrooms for automobiles. It's a rare family, though, that doesn't end up using them for other purposes. Garages become storerooms, shops, laundry rooms, recreation rooms and an infinite number of other things. A car needs a minimum space of 10 x 22 feet, and a minimum size for a two car garage is 21 x 22 feet. Cars are smaller than this, but remember, doors need room to be opened and you need space to walk around. If you face facts, you'll see that if the space is used for other things, it will hold less cars

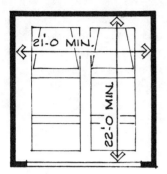

STANDARD TWO CAR GARAGE

THIS IS STANDARD, COMPACTS WOULD TAKE LESS.

TWO CAR WITH EXTRA SIDE SPACE

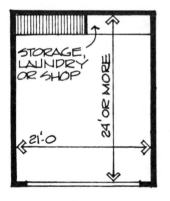

TWO CAR WITH EXTRA LENGTH

FIGURE 31. GARAGES

or none at all and the cars will be exiled to the driveway. If you want a shop, a potting studio, or a storeroom, you'll need a garage that is larger than these minimum dimensions.

Just a few feet extra above the minimum in a two car garage will give you at least 20 feet of wall space that you can use for storage or for a shop bench. If you can find a garage that has extra

length or width it will, in effect, give you an entire extra room for almost the same money, and your car can still have its own room.

This chapter has sounded very picky because I meant to be that way. If you aren't choosy, and don't look at every little thing to see if it works for you instead of against you, you won't wring every cent out of your housing dollar. That's my goal—I want you to be able to stretch your money and get everything you can out of it to make your life better each day!

CHECKLIST

ENTRANCES:

Main Entrance

Does it funnel traffic through without intrusion on another room?

Is coat storage near?

Is flooring low maintenance?

Does door swing stop view into home?

Family Entrance

Is it a "short cut"?

Is coat storage near?

Is flooring low maintenance?

Does it funnel traffic into the home without intrusion on another room?

LIVING ROOMS: (ALL SITTING, FAMILY & PARLORS)

Are they arranged and sized to fit your lifestyle?

Can furniture be arranged to

Allow comfortable conversation?

Take advantage of the focal points?

Allow standing space at parties?

Will the path of food and drink work well, both for family & parties?

Is there adequate storage or room to add some?

Are heat registers, vents, etc. placed so they won't interfere with your use of the room?

Will it have good lighting? (daylight & artificial)

DINING AREAS:

Does the room work for your lifestyle?

Is the space adequate for the arrangement of furniture you desire and the paths around it?

Does the path of food service work well?

Can you have the lighting you want?

KITCHENS:

How well did it score on the kitchen test?

Is the "reachable" storage enough to do the job?

Does it have comfortable, cleanable flooring?

Is the lighting good?

SINKS

Large enough?

Faucet high enough?

Disposer quiet? And the type you want?

Is relationship to dishwasher good?

RANGE

Is it the heat source you want?

Burner spacing adequate for your pots and pans?

Does exhaust work well?

Oven large enough?

REFRIGERATOR/FREEZERS

Will commonly stored items fit?

Will door open far enough to allow removal of shelves and drawers?

Does it have rollers?

SMALL APPLIANCES

Is there convenient place to store them?

Are there enough convenient electrical outlets for them?

HARDWARE

Are door and drawer pulls dirt catchers?

Are shelves adjustable?

Do drawers and sliding doors have metal guides or tracks?

BEDROOMS:

Is the noise level low?

Is the nighttime light level right? (Light or dark, as you prefer)

Is it oriented to sunlight in the way you would like?

Will it allow the furniture placement that you want?

Does it have or will it allow adequate closet space (5 lineal feet per person minimum) and drawer space (8 lineal feet per person minimum)

Will heat registers and vents allow the furniture arrangement you want.

Is lighting and/or outlets adequate for the lighting you desire—general, task or mood?

CHILDREN'S BEDROOMS (ADDITIONALLY)

Good storage for toys and games possible?

Adequate play space?

GUEST BEDROOMS (ADDITIONALLY)

Will it do a double duty job?

BATHROOMS:

Does it allow privacy?

Are the fixtures comfortable? (tub, water closet, etc.)

Is storage where you need it? (towels, toilet tissue, grooming tools, etc.)

Do doors interfere with use of the room?

Does it have convenient towel bars?

Can you turn shower on without getting wet?

Is paper holder in the right place?

Does the water closet seat stay up?

Is it easy to clean?

Does it have good heat and ventilation?

Is the lighting good for both task and general?

Does it have adequate electrical outlets?

HALLWAYS: (AND STAIRWAYS)

Does it have natural light?

Is width adequate? (three feet or more)

Is it too long (wasting square footage)?

Does it have sound absorbing materials or is it otherwise quiet?

LAUNDRY ROOM:

Does it work well on the path of clothes?

Can it be used without interference by a people path or by doors opening?

Is there a surface on which to fold clothes?

Is good storage provided?

Does it have a floor drain?

GARAGES:

Is there room for the car? Cars?

Is there room to allow another use, in addition to car storage?

STEP SIX

High Heeled Wedgies or Motorcycle Boots?

Just as with shoes, the type of home you buy or rent should fit the way you live. If you don't ride motorcycles, you won't need motorcycle boots and, if you do ride them, high-heeled wedgies won't be suitable. The type of housing you choose and the kind of neighborhood it is in should fit your lifestyle, in order to get as much wear out of it as possible. So it's important to look at neighborhood patterns, how the community is planned, and at the various types of developments available. Some will closely fit the way you live and your budget while others will not. You need to know how to distinguish a good development from a poor one, so that for the money you have to spend you can select the best site available in the best neighborhood or development you can afford.

TYPES OF HOUSING

There are trade terms that apply to housing which I want to define before going further, so there is no confusion as to what they mean. These terms identify types of housing, whether owned or rented, and have nothing to do with how the neighborhood is planned.

The first type is *single family,* of which there are two subcategories. The first is *single family detached,* which is a single house on its own separate lot. A mobile or modular home on its own site is considered a single family detached also.

Then there is *single family attached.* This has a few more variations, but the term means that one unit shares a wall with another or is otherwise connected. Single family attached can be a duplex or it

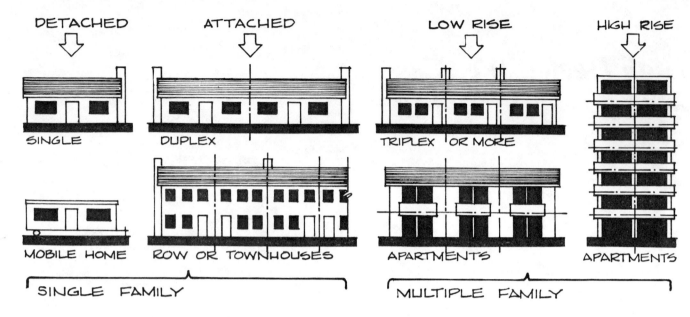

DETACHED   ATTACHED   LOW RISE   HIGH RISE

SINGLE   DUPLEX   TRIPLEX OR MORE

MOBILE HOME   ROW OR TOWNHOUSES   APARTMENTS   APARTMENTS

SINGLE FAMILY   MULTIPLE FAMILY

FIGURE 1. HOUSING TYPES

can be a row of more than two attached dwellings, which are called *row houses* or *town houses*. Row houses or town houses usually have a privately owned front and rear yard and have no other dwelling upstairs or down. In other words, single family attached is only one family deep and one family high.

The term *multiple family* housing means three or more units per building. The minimum amount of units would be three, in which case the building is called a *triplex*. More than three units start being called *apartments,* and as with other unit types, this does not imply ownership or nonownership. In most multifamily housing, there will be other families living above or below you. Multiple family apartment buildings have two other categories. There is *low rise,* which means that the building is no higher than three floors, and *high rise,* which is anything more than three floors.

OWNERSHIP

Any type of housing can be owned or rented. Ownership of a single family detached home and

lot, whether a house or mobile home, used to be pretty straighforward. You owned the lot that the house was on, or rented the site the mobile home was on. Now, there are some new forms of ownership that can apply to any type of housing. Town houses, apartments, and even detached single homes, mobile or not, can be owned as a *cooperative* or a *condominium*. This is often confused, but condominium and cooperative mean types of *ownership* only, not types of buildings.

In a cooperative a group of people hold the total complex in joint ownership. You don't singly own the land your unit is on or the unit itself. You own a share of the cooperative. You are responsible for paying your share of the costs, but are not responsible individually for maintaining any portion of the building or grounds, except within the unit you inhabit. The problem with cooperatives is that since you have a share in the *company,* if one or more persons default, or can't pay their share, all the other shareholders have to make up this difference. It's possible that you'll have to pay a larger share of the taxes, mortgage and maintenance than you counted on to make up for the lack of others doing so. If you can't afford that, and didn't plan for it, you may find you can't afford to keep your share either. In addition, some cooperatives have rules that put restrictions on your choice to sell out, when and to whom you want.

Condominium ownership means that you own and have a deed to your individual unit. If it's a town house unit, your property goes to the centerline of the common walls and face of the outside walls. You may or may not own the land it is on, depending on what the developer offers. If the unit is an apartment in a multistory building, your property lines are at the center of the perimeter walls, the ceiling above and the floor below. If the condominium consists of single family homes, then your property lines could be the same as with single detached ownership. Some mobile home parks are offering condominium ownership also. You own your site and home, and share the costs of the community facilities.

With condominiums, you are responsible only for the taxes and mortgage on your own unit, not the whole complex. If other owners default, it will not affect you or your property. Also, your unit can be sold freely as you would a singly owned home, if and when you desire. In addition to your own unit, you'll own a portion of the community facilities, landscaping or driveways, and, similar to a cooperative, will be responsible for your share of their maintenance. You may or may not be responsible for the exterior maintenance of your own unit, depending on the terms of your deed.

With both these types of ownership, the legalities of agreements and deeds can become complicated. Knowing what you own, how you own it, what services and amenities come with it, and what the rules are, will be very important to you and your pocketbook. The surest way to be absolutely certain that you understand everything would be to retain an attorney to work with you and explain all the ramifications to you before you buy. If you are seriously considering any type of community ownership, *How to Buy A Condominium,* by L. and P. Brooks, will help you to become well informed.

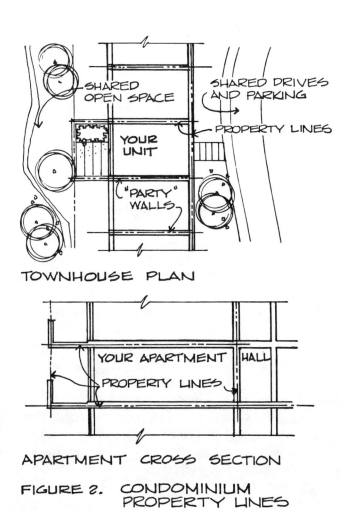

TOWNHOUSE PLAN

APARTMENT CROSS SECTION

FIGURE 2. CONDOMINIUM PROPERTY LINES

THE COMMUNITY OR NEIGHBORHOOD PLAN

The way a community or neighborhood development is planned can greatly influence your peace of mind and the comfort of your soul and body. It will also be a determining factor in the resale of the home later. Good planning is as hard to define as good design, but it's just as important. Community planning is the overall scheme that considers a number of dwellings as a total, organizes the way they relate to one another and the way people and vehicles will circulate. Good planning should increase your personal pleasure of the surroundings and, again, minimize the irritations and inconveniences. Good planning, as with good building design, should encourage contact with nature, and at the same time care for it. It should offer good separation of public/private areas, passive/active areas and the paths of people and automobiles.

Good planning, in physical form, will be attractive, interesting, and offer serenity. It should give you a feeling of privacy, no matter how many others surround you. If a plan does all of this, it obviously will offer you a pleasant place in which to live. This probably sounds vague, but as we examine various factors in depth you'll see there are physical signs which enable you to recognize good planning when you see it.

DENSITIES

Land planners work in terms of density. *Unit density* means the number of dwellings per acre and *population density* is the number of people housed per acre. Single family detached dwellings usually have the least density, which is about six to eight units per acre. Town house developments have a density of approximately fifteen to twenty units per acre, and high-rise apartment buildings can go as high as five hundred units per acre.

There is another insidious density that we have to live with. Each unit has almost two cars that go along with it, so there could be a density of sixteen cars per acre, 40 cars per acre and one thousand cars per acre respectively. These figures do not consider the cars of visitors. Providing parking

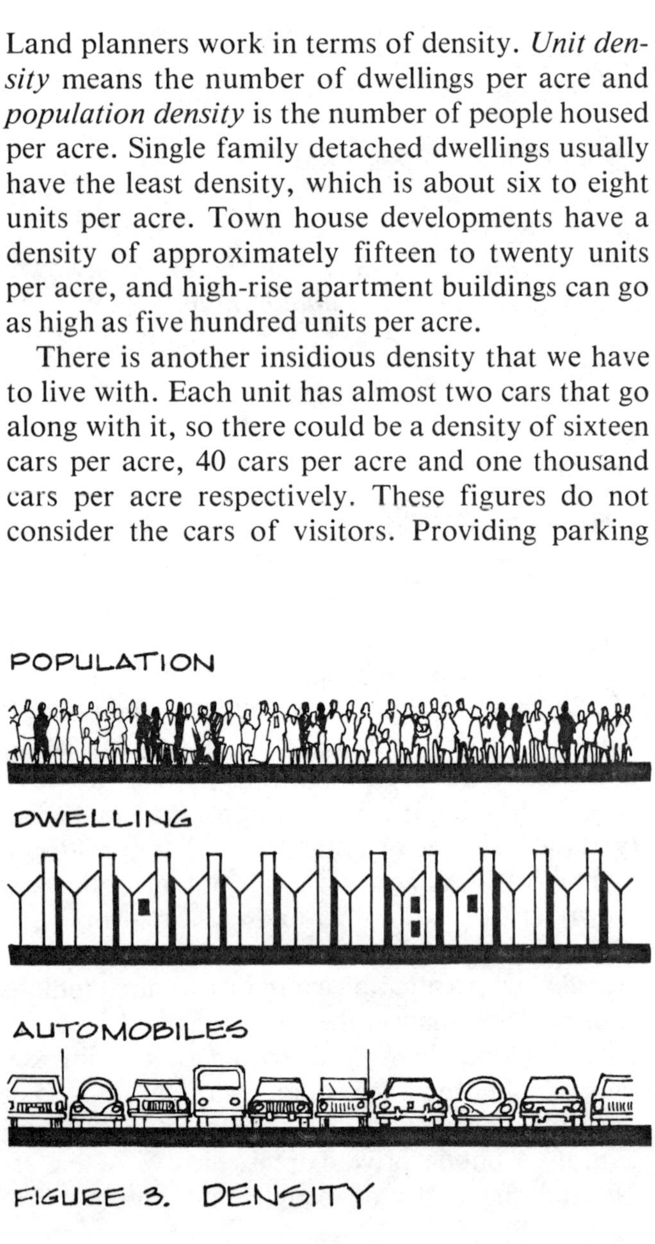

POPULATION

DWELLING

AUTOMOBILES

FIGURE 3. DENSITY

and organizing the traffic flow of all these automobiles is perhaps the most taxing job that a planner has. If any neighborhood is to work well and look uncongested, the consideration of automobiles is of primary importance. A good plan, regardless of density, will assure that the streets and your own yards will not look like a recreation vehicle camp or a used car lot.

GOOD LAND USE

As land becomes more scarce and densities increase, the more vital it becomes to use it well. A good community or neighborhood plan will use all of it to its maximum capacity. By this I don't mean that as many dwellings as possible should be crammed onto it—that's using it poorly. Some environmentalists feel the best use for land is for it just to *be,* and farmers think it is to grow food. But we all have to live on it too, at least until someone invents a good airborne home. So it's important that a neighborhood use every bit of land in a way that is of value. We've done a lot of squandering in the near past and created areas where no one would want to live. In fact, all the places where you wouldn't want to live are probably a direct result of poor planning and squandered land.

Some of our ancestors, even when there were far fewer of them and plenty of land to go around, knew enough to value the land. This, of course, was because the land was needed for hunting, growing food, and grazing animals. When "safety in numbers" became important to stave off the bad guys, the farmers moved into villages or walled towns. They planned them in a way that carefully left all the land possible open for fields and forest. The patterns of early villages and how they related to the land are nearly common, no matter where in the world they were. In approximately the same area that we now use for private yards, blocks and streets, they could have homes for just as many, but had vastly more space left open because they clustered their houses.

This was, and still is, a very thrifty use of land resources. Even though we no longer need a farm

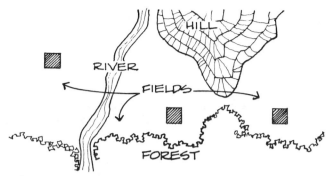

FARMERS WITHOUT ENEMIES
(AND NATURAL PROPERTY LIMITS)

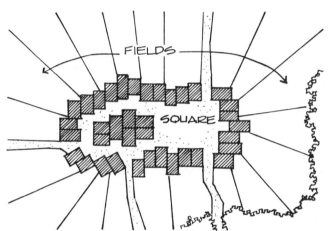

FARMERS WITH ENEMIES
(AND MAN MADE PROPERTY LIMITS)

FIGURE 4. EARLY LAND USE

near our home, open spaces still have a lot to offer. A piece of land left in natural form provides spiritual tranquility, a place where residents can wander, sit or picnic. If neighborhoods use the wasted land in a way we all can share, people won't spend so much time desperately driving around on weekends looking for a piece of country!

We are the culprits who have stolen the free space! In recent times, we almost unanimously chose detached houses, no matter what we planned to do with the land surrounding it. Since there are so many of us, we had to go further and further out, away from the closely clustered small town or city center. Having found our detached home way out there, all of our cars became an absolute necessity in order to get to our job or the market. Our

automobiles required streets, driveways, and parking spaces thereby taking the use of more land away.

Most of us wanted the single detached home because it gave us a clearly marked territory that was ours alone, and we thought it would give us privacy and autonomy. Certainly we all need these things, but are we actually getting them? First, how much of a typical detached home site is really *ours?* Secondly, how much of it is *private?* And third, how much of it can be *used?* Since land is so expensive, it's important to make sure that what we buy will give us what we expect and that none of it will be wasted.

Single lots are now generally so small that the chance of having to look into the neighbor's bathrooms and bedrooms from your kitchen window, and they into yours, is almost a certainty. Front yards aren't private because they are open to all who pass by. Even back yards aren't totally insulated from the neighbors and therefore not totally your own either. When there is a barbecue next door, the neighbor is using his weed trimmer, or his children are having hysterics in their wading pool, you'll quickly learn how much real privacy you have! It's easy to blame the "noisy neighbor" (he probably thinks that you're one too), but actually the fault probably lies in the way the development was planned.

Conventional lots and setback regulations waste a huge amount of land. Most building codes require yard setbacks, which are distances that the front, back and side of a house have to be from the property lines. Setbacks started as a minimum requirement for the purpose of assuring that there would be light and air (for ventilation) between dwellings and to discourage the spread of fire, all commendable goals. This, however, assumes that there is only one way to get light and air into a home or to stop fire from spreading, which is not true. And, as with all else, the minimums soon turned into *standards,* and became the only requirement.

Standard side yard setbacks leave a space of approximately ten feet between any two houses, five feet of which belong to each neighbor. This ends up as two five foot strips with a fence down the middle, and each strip is now too small to use for much else than to store junk or garbage cans. If

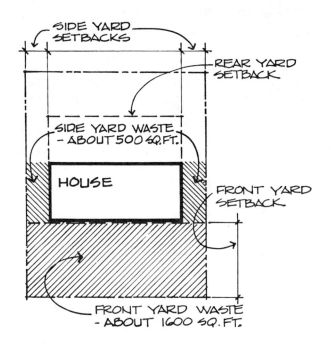

FIGURE 5. LAND WASTED BY SETBACK LIMITS

the side yards on each side of a home are added together, depending on the depth of the house, the waste land per house amounts to about 500 square feet!

Front and rear yard setbacks are commonly twenty to twenty-five feet. This means that we're buying a front yard that will only be used for public viewing of grass we have to mow. This is a wasteland of around 1,600 square feet. That leaves only the rear yard as a piece of land that is usable and more or less private.

When you realize that you're paying for approximately 2,000 square feet of land that isn't usable it becomes apparent that the money you spend for it is being wasted. If this same amount of land was in usable form it would be a much better buy.

An example of better land use is a very old form of *city house* that gives the occupant total use of his property. This is the *atrium house.*. Setbacks weren't a problem because the materials used were not combustible, so closeness wasn't a fire hazard. This type of dwelling turns totally away from the outside world. All the land not used by the building becomes a courtyard, totally usable and private. All rooms face this private court and derive

privacy and space from it, as well as light and air. The outdoor space is totally owned by the residents and not shared in any way, either visually or audibly with outsiders.

The traditional Japanese city house, while not built around a courtyard, retained privacy and the total use of its site in another way. The house and property were surrounded with high walls, or screen fences, that blocked out intruding eyes and most of the outside sounds. This house also captures the space of its yard for the total use of the occupants.

Most present day building regulations prohibit fences or walls over five or six feet in height anywhere within the side and rear setbacks and anything over two or three feet within the front yard setback. If you find a house that does not sit right on the front setback line, but leaves room to construct a high fenced entry court, you can reclaim some of your front yard for your own use. Screening your property with landscaping, a choice mentioned in Step Three is not always a possibility. Sometimes, local laws set height limits and setbacks for plants also. So you can see, in our day it is very difficult to find a way to get your land back for your own use. Codes usually force us into an outward facing mode of living, and ensure the need to keep our drapes drawn to separate ourselves from the street, the neighbors, and the rest of the outside world.

All of this sounds discouraging but there is hope. Recently some changes have been taking place in the thinking concerning setback lines and also about the necessity of having rigid lot lines. Part of the change has been made necessary by lack of cheap land, which forced developers to think of better ways to use it more frugally in order to house more people per acre in a manner that would still be attractive and offer privacy. Planners have gone back to some of the better ideas of our ancestors. They are now getting more esthetic land use to provide better housing for just as many or more people. They are using more natural patterns for neighborhoods, instead of chopping everything up into endless squares. And some localities have finally seen the need to change laws that allow this to happen. Therefore, there are some choices today that we didn't have before.

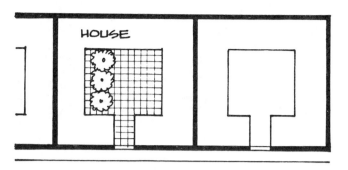

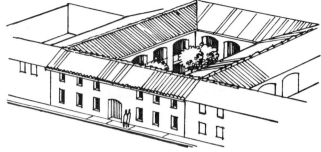

AN ATRIUM OR COURTYARD HOUSE

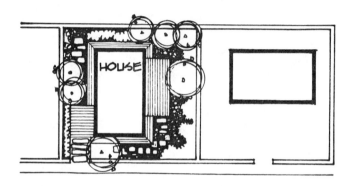

A WALLED HOUSE

FIGURE 6. TWO "OLD FASHIONED" WAYS
TO KEEP YOUR LAND TO YOURSELF

We'll look at all the options available, so you'll be able to decide what type of development will give you the most value, both for your life and yourself and for your pocketbook.

Before going on, I need to mention the type of development that has made it possible for planners to free themselves from the old subdivision (or square system). It is the *Planned Unit Development* or P.U.D., as it is called. This concept allows the developer to plan and build a total neighborhood all at once. While this allows him to build only certain number of homes per acre, it gives him the freedom of placing dwellings closer together. This frees land that used to be wasted for side yards and front yards, so it can be used in better ways for the benefit of each occupant and for everyone in the neighborhood. Although buildings are closer together, they can be carefully arranged in relation to each other to assure more privacy than conventional projects do. The planning of a P.U.D. is usually more sensitive to the land and to the environment. Since the units are all built at one time, with similar materials, by the same builder, and on the same site, with utilities, services and streets grouped, the building costs are usually lower. P.U.D. dwellings usually offer more for the money.

One form P.U.D. developments take is *clusters*. Clustering is a very ancient form of land use, and now many new development are using various forms of it. Cluster developments may be formed of either attached or detached homes. It saves land, because a lot of the paved areas such as the driveways, guest parking and the automobile ac-

129

cess itself, are shared. Attached clusters eliminate the side yards as well, and put all that land into meaningful and usable open space.

Although the main purpose is to keep buildings in closer and better relationship with one another and leave more open land, a good side effect is that outside traffic need not pass through the neighborhood. Clusters also have the advantage any rural or smaller neighborhood has, that since each inhabitant knows who his neighbors are, he also knows who strangers are, and when something unusual is going on. So P.U.D.'s are usually safer and more secure than other types of neighborhoods.

Figure 7 shows sample land plans for both detached and attached cluster development. Cluster mini neighborhoods usually include some form of joint ownership of the shared spaces, such as the community driveway, landscaping and recreational areas to take care of their maintenance.

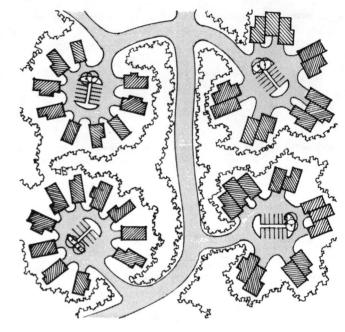

DETACHED   ATTACHED

FIGURE 7.   MODERN CLUSTERS

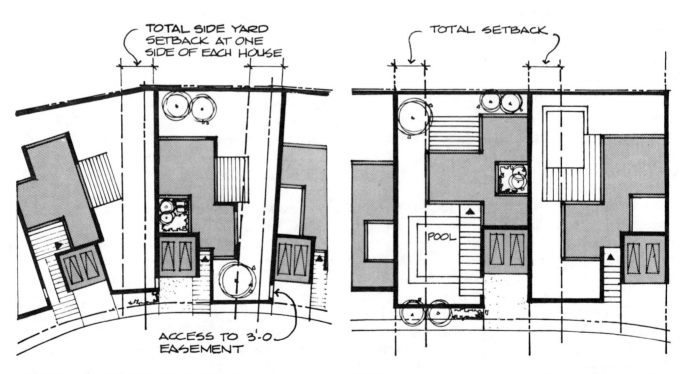

PATIO EASEMENT HOUSE   ZERO LOT LINE OR PATIO HOUSE

FIGURE 8.   MODERN FORMS OF ATRIUM
                OR WALLED HOUSING

WINDOW WALLS
SOLID WALLS

Another ancient idea is coming to the attention of developers and gaining popularity. This one is as old as the Etruscans, but with some minor modifications. P.U.D. also allows the *patio house,* which is, in essence, the same solution that the atrium house offered. Figure 8 shows a *zero lot line house* or patio house and a *patio easement* house. In both cases, the standard side yard setbacks are still there, but now they're one space. Instead of having two five-foot yard setbacks, one on either side of the house, it is now a ten-foot setback, or easement, on only one side of the house. The distance between houses is the same for fire protection, or whatever requirements apply, but now it's a meaningful and usable piece of land. When each house is designed to orient to the larger side yard while presenting a blank wall to the neighbor, all will have an extremely private piece of outdoor space. Since separation between buildings is accomplished to everyone's satisfaction, the garden walls can be as high as in the walled Japanese house, so it is quieter and there is a better screened territory than you would have with standard height fences. Additionally, the front yard setbacks are often allowed to have high walls too, so in most cases you'll get the front yard to use as your own.

In the zero lot line situation, you own the property from the centerline of your house wall to the centerline of the neighbor's house wall. This might present a problem if the neighbor does not properly maintain his side of your wall. The patio easement eliminates this problem, although you may lose a negligible amount of privacy. Even though you have the use of all the land to the face of his wall, he still owns approximately three feet next to his house, so that he can inspect and maintain his wall, just as you can do on your three-foot strip on the other side. While this arrangement does not give you a wholly inviolate yard, as the zero lot line does, you do have the advantage of seeing that your house is in order. Whichever you choose, both give you the maximum privacy and almost total use of your land.

The need for good and nonwasteful use of the land is probably even more important in multiple housing. Multiple unit housing has similar problems, and due to the higher density, there are more

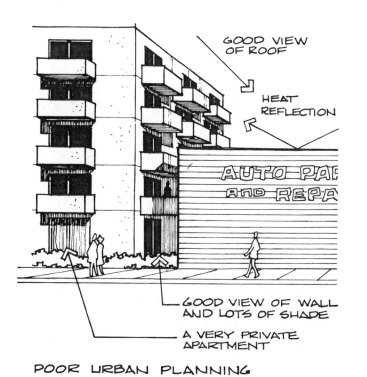

POOR URBAN PLANNING

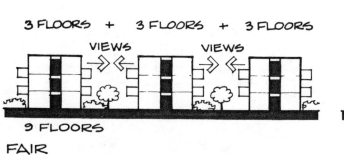

FAIR

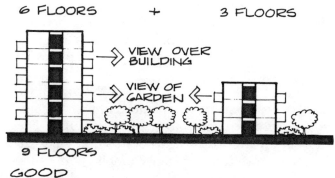

GOOD

FIGURE 9. PLANNING - MULTIPLE HOUSING PROJECTS

131

people to share whatever open space has been left. Apartment buildings have more privacy problems than do single dwellings, and in the quest to get as many units as possible on a piece of land, that is all too often ignored. It is not unusual for apartments to look down on roofs of other buildings, service stations, or parking lots. Sometimes they are face to face with another apartment or another building.

Even in the densest downtown areas, designers have made some thoughtful innovations and improvements in urban housing. Even if they've had to stack units a little higher to maintain the density needed for the project to be financially workable, apartment complexes now offer more freed space and land for landscaping, parks, and recreational facilities. This allows larger distances between buildings giving more privacy and generally offering a more humane environment than some of the old ones did. This type of development is increasingly available because the units sell or rent more easily than poorly planned complexes do, and developers aren't dumb.

While we're on the subject of intelligence, it should be noted that consumers aren't dumb either, nor are any but a few rich. It is a fact that the majority of home sales today in the United States are mobile homes. Since the initial cost of a mobile home is about 55% of that of a conventional single family home, a mobile home is a popular choice. The age group that makes up the majority of these sales is under 35 because, as a group, they have the least money and no equity in a house with which to trade. The other major group of mobile home owners are retired persons who don't wish to keep a large home or yard maintained, or have taken the equity out of a house to invest for income. We'll talk more about mobile homes later when we analyze each type of housing separately, but here I want to talk about land planning as it applies to mobile home parks.

Mobile home parks, just as with any other neighborhood, can be well planned or poorly planned, so there are choices to be made here also. The newer and better ones incorporate good land use and have more to offer. Since mobile home sites are smaller than normal sites, all the problems of single family sites are increased. At best, one can

only achieve a minimum of privacy in a mobile home park. Since there will be very little space that is yours alone, it's absolutely essential to use all that is offered and use it well. Choosing the best site in a good development is more difficult and at the same time more important than with any other type of housing.

The same basic planning principles apply to mobile home parks. Unfortunately, you probably won't find a park that is as well planned as a P.U.D. cluster, but some are better than others. Many are laid out now with open green spaces between groups of units, and parking areas so they don't intrude on the development. Some have community park land and open recreational space. Extra effort to find good planning will be worth the effort.

Street Systems

A neighborhood is governed by its initial planning and the way streets move through it. Streets can intrude on a neighborhood by encouraging through traffic; or they can gently wander through in a natural configuration, and enter the neighborhood only to serve it.

Looking back to ancient times reveals man's natural, if messy, inclinations. Streets and roads

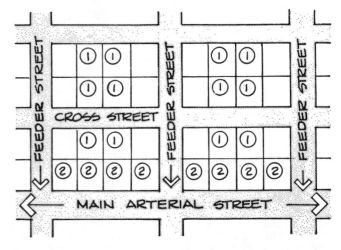

① QUIETEST SITES
② NOISIEST SITES

FIGURE 10. A GRID STREET PATTERN

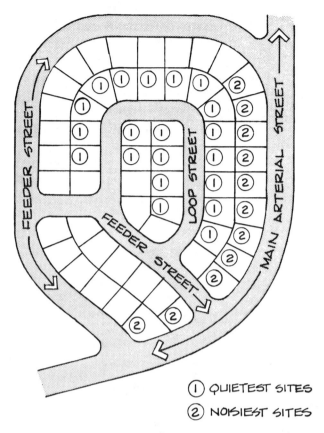

① QUIETEST SITES
② NOISIEST SITES

FIGURE 11. CURVING STREETS

just developed along the easiest and most level way to go. They formed naturally in a pattern that followed the meanderings of man and animal. When people actually began to plan streets and roads it was easier on the brain and hand to draw everything with straight lines, so at this point towns started being laid out with a grid street system. This looks very tidy on paper, but in reality it is unnatural, rigid and boring! In a large subdivision, it also leads to confusion, because it is often hard to tell which is your own block and your own house without checking the numbers. The grid system ignores the contours of the land, and if the site is not level, some streets can become very steep and dangerous. Another drawback of this system is that corners and cross streets occur with great frequency and require cautious driving, or stop signs on every corner. You may become accustomed to it, but why put yourself into a constant state of ap-

prehension? You deserve to relax a little. Straight streets also encourage excessive speeds, and neighborhood streets can become raceways. If you do buy in a grid pattern neighborhood, try to get a house that is off the main traffic *artery* or one of its *feeder streets* but on a *cross street* that will have less traffic.

Streets that follow land contours and curve gently harbor no blind corners and generally offer a lot more interest, serenity, quiet, and safety. The distance between cross streets is usually greater, so there are fewer bad corners. The curves tend to slow traffic which also lessens noise. The further a site is from the major traffic artery, the more noise you'll avoid. If you can find a home in a *dead-end* area, you'll have fewer problems with traffic altogether.

SPECIAL THINGS TO LOOK FOR IN EACH TYPE OF HOUSING

Most of us have a perfectly beautiful picture in mind of the house and neighborhood we want. It may be on a heavily forested site out of view of the neighbors and the world, or on a hill overlooking a green valley. It might be on a tree-lined street, or a penthouse looking out to sea. Since most of us tend to think of ourselves and our families as unique and individual (and we are), we also leave out of our pictures the fact that there are too many people and not enough of the picture places to go around. Unless we are rich, or lucky, the unique home we picture is, in reality, not going to be affordable.

But on the other hand, if you can't have that pictured ideal, you don't have to settle for the opposite, or a very poor picture, either. If you take time, and choose your housing carefully and thoughtfully, you can still get many of the benefits of your perfect picture and eliminate many of the disadvantages of the poor picture. This way you will get the most satisfaction and pleasure from each dollar that you can afford.

I may be a romantic, but I believe it is imperative not to panic and settle for the first place you see that you can afford. You don't choose shoes that way and you shouldn't choose your home that way. You really cannot afford to take less than the proportionate amount of time shopping. Out there, somewhere, if you spend the time looking for it, is a house or apartment that will be your unique environment, and at a price you can handle. I know it's got to be there!

Single Family Detached
(Mobile Homes will be discussed separately)

The choices of single family detached narrow down to an older house in an established neighborhood, or a new house in a new subdivision or cluster neighborhood. There will be a lot of other houses surrounding it which contribute to the total feeling of the environment. Therefore, not only should your home be well designed and look good, but the others around you should too. You're not going to have to live in them, but you will have to *look* at them!

It is important that the neighborhood will wear well, so that you can live there as long as you want and still get the money out of your home when you sell it. In established developments, it is easy to look around and see if the neighborhood is attractive, houses properly maintained, and the yards well kept. This indicates it most likely will remain that way in the future.

If you are buying in a new development, it is harder to project how it's going to look after a few years. If you have determined that the house you want to buy is of good quality and design, and the rest of the houses are by the same builder, then the whole neighborhood will probably wear quite well, and this is about all you have to go on. Another sign that a neighborhood will improve with age is a good amount of landscaping and trees. Architects plant ivy to cover their mistakes, and plants can also make a mediocre neighborhood look better than it is. Planned unit developments usually provide a generous amount of landscaping, so they are a good buy from this standpoint. The normal tract development usually comes with none at all. This means the new owners will have to put it in. Assuming everyone can afford to do so, and are talented enough to do it well, it will still be years be-

fore the landscaping has grown enough to cover the bare look of the neighborhood. Some developers are solving this by offering each buyer a rebate if he gets his front yard landscaped in a specified amount of time. This means you have to do the job right away but so does everyone else. It is to your advantage and that of the neighborhood as well.

If houses in a new development are not built or not yet finished, and the developer is selling from models, be cautious. Often, the models are built

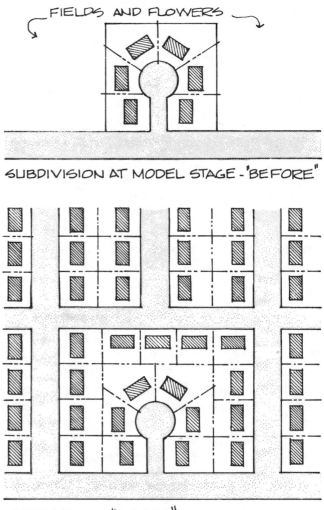

SUBDIVISION AT MODEL STAGE - "BEFORE"

SUBDIVISION "AFTER"

FIGURE 12. IF YOU CHOOSE FROM MODELS, CHECK THE OVERALL LAND PLAN

134

better and are on larger sites than the rest of the houses will be, and are landscaped to make them more attractive. Although the developer has to be totally honest about what he is offering you, you'll just naturally get a better impression from a model than if you were looking at the actual house. Furnished models always look better than they are in reality, because money has been spent just for that very purpose, to *grab you.*

Aside from that there are some advantages to buying in the *presales* condition. You can make small changes in your unit before it is built that will cost you very little money. Also, due to escalating costs the prices will tend to be lower if you buy early. But be sure you're going to get what you expect. Get a guarantee that the quality of your home will be the same as the model. Be sure that your lot will be essentially the same square footage as the one the model is on. Check the developer's street plan carefully to see how your site relates to traffic and to nature. Models are often built in a park-like setting on a peaceful cul-de-sac. Then, the balance of the neighborhood is built with the houses all in rows on straight streets. Don't let models fool you, or better yet, buy one of the models!

Another thing that can make a neighborhood difficult to live in, if not downright ugly, is cars, or the poor planning that did not adequately deal with them. In a subdivision comprised of small lots, the streets and driveways often are totally filled with them. Most developments offer two-car garages, but there is little guarantee that your neighbor will put their cars in them. When houses are too skimpy and don't have adequate storage, the majority of garages will be used as storerooms. When this happens, two cars per house are left out and fill the driveways and the streets. In addition to two cars, some families have campers, boats on trailers, travel trailers, and almost everything else you can think of. If the development hasn't enough space to park these things out of sight the whole neighborhood becomes a parking lot. Some communities now prohibit R.V., boat and trailer parking in residential areas. The owners are required to put them in rental lots elsewhere. So if you find a neighborhood with these restrictions, it will be a better one. Other developments provide

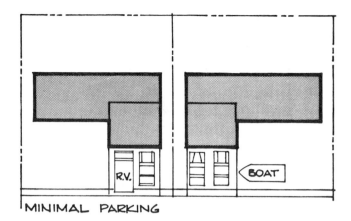

MINIMAL PARKING

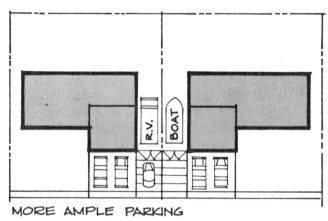

MORE AMPLE PARKING

FIGURE 13. OFF STREET PARKING

sideyards just wide enough to hold a parking space hidden by a fence and gate, as shown in Figure 13, which in addition to hiding the vehicle also gives it some security. A good P.U.D. development should provide a fenced parking area out of sight for these extra vehicles.

It's possible to find a really outstanding site within and among others which are merely ordinary. These are the ones that are well worth looking for. Sites on cul-de-sacs or dead-end streets are better because they will have less traffic and will be quieter. Cul-de-sacs result in oddly shaped lots, so look them over carefully. Some of them may have less square footage than a normal square lot, or they may be of such irregular shape that you won't be able to get good use of the site. On the other hand, sometimes this results in a larger lot which is usually a bonus. Cul-de-sac sites or any site on an inwardly curved street also generally have smaller

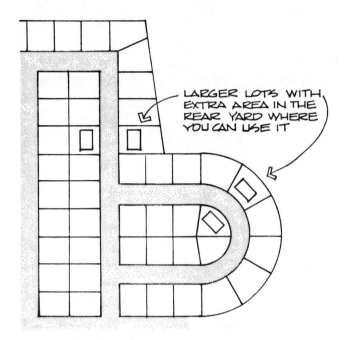

FIGURE 14. LOT SHAPES CAN VARY AND SOME ARE BIGGER THAN OTHERS

LARGER LOTS WITH EXTRA AREA IN THE REAR YARD WHERE YOU CAN USE IT

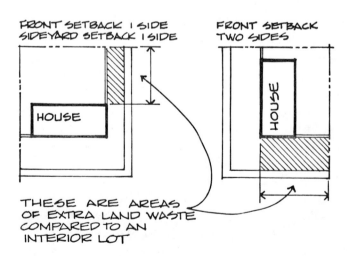

FRONT SETBACK 1 SIDE
SIDEYARD SETBACK 1 SIDE

FRONT SETBACK TWO SIDES

HOUSE

HOUSE

THESE ARE AREAS OF EXTRA LAND WASTE COMPARED TO AN INTERIOR LOT

FIGURE 15. CORNER SITES PUT EVEN MORE LAND WHERE YOU CAN'T USE IT

front yards and larger backyards than normal lots, so they offer more land in your private domain and less in the public. You can see this with the model sites in Figures 12 and 14.

Look for odd corners too. If the original parcel of land was an irregular shape, some sites are often left much larger than others. Usually the cost difference of the house with the larger site is negligible, if it varies at all. If you're fortunate and find that larger lot, it will be a better buy, assuming that all else is equal.

Corner lots, unless very large, are generally *not* a good buy. True, you'll have fewer neighbors, but with exposure on two sides to the street, the noise from traffic will be much greater than on an interior lot. You have two front yards and therefore the amount of usable private land will decrease.

Although single family structures both regular detached and patio houses, are well separated, keep in mind every outside space is a possible party room. Analyze the position of your rooms in relation to the neighbor's rooms and courts, to see if dissimilar uses have good separation, or that the zoning of your home is compatible with his. One problem unique to patio houses is that the surrounding walls are higher than normal fences and can cut the sun out if the house isn't properly oriented or windows are too close to them. So especially sure to check the sun angles to find out whether the sun will be blocked.

Single Family Attached

The value of an attached house, such as a town house or row house, is that it usually costs less money for an equal amount of living space. Depending on the density of the development there may be as much open land as in an ordinary detached situation. But even if not, there are many, if you really seek them out, that are so well planned they offer equivalent value. Usually, except for your private patio area, the land will be in the form of shared open space. In a good project this open space is arranged in a way that gives the feeling of more separation, privacy, and openness than you'll find in a regular neighborhood. In better developments, this shared bonus of land is generously landscaped, and often provides some

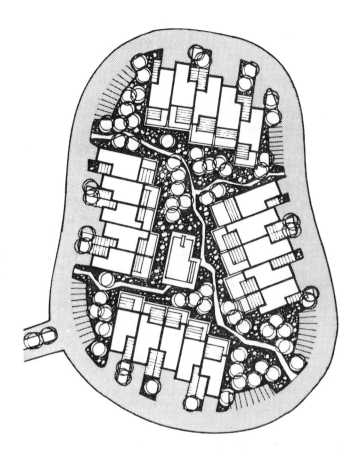

FIGURE 16. CLUSTER TOWNHOUSES WITH SHARED GREEN SPACES AND POOL

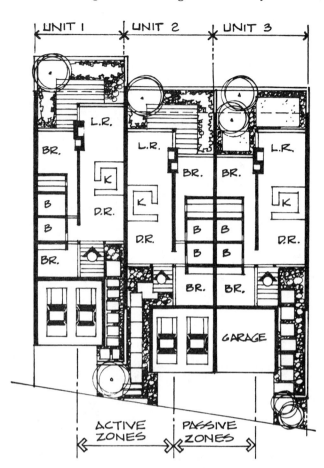

FIGURE 17. ZONING IN ATTACHED HOUSING SHOULD MATCH THE NEIGHBOR'S

community recreational facilities that you couldn't otherwise afford. A well-developed complex of this type, is self-contained and doesn't accommodate any through traffic or cars that do not belong there. Parking spaces for guests are tucked around the project where they will be convenient, but not intrude on the project or anyone's view. The biggest misgiving people have about this kind of housing is that they will lack privacy, but if the development is well planned, there will probably be more privacy and quiet than in many subdivisions. To assure quiet within an individual unit, it is essential that the party wall, or the walls between units, are properly sound insulated. In addition, bedrooms should be back to back and the living

rooms back to back, as shown in Figure 17. Also the units should be offset or turned so that the private outdoor living areas are separated. A completely walled patio, with a wall at least six feet high, will give visual privacy. Units with such a patio tend to have a higher resale value also. But, the patio should be large enough in area to keep it from giving you a boxed-in feeling.

Buildings that are attached to one another, or that share common walls offer more thermal protection than a lone building because the units shelter one another from heat loss and gain and will have fewer exposed outside walls. The important lessons of nature apply just the same so study them well before choosing a unit. If you can choose the unit best protected by neighboring units, you'll be getting an even bigger energy bargain.

Since maintenance of the shared portions of the grounds in this type of housing is done by others, you'll be freed from yard work except for your own deck or patio. You will be concerned, however, with whether the community areas will continue to be properly maintained, so make sure that you have some guarantee of this in your deed.

If you're planning to buy or rent in a development that has community recreational facilities, such as a pool, tennis courts, or a clubhouse, it will be important to determine just how much you'll use them. You'll be paying for the upkeep of these facilities, so be sure you'll want to use them enough to get your money's worth.

Multiple Family Housing

Finding the right place to live becomes even more crucial in multiple housing. Although there may be more to choose from in your price range, the presence of more neighbors in this higher density arrangement is a factor which can make your life infinitely better or infinitely worse.

It's very easy to make friends in a multiple complex, because there are more to choose from, thereby upping the chances that you'll find people you are compatible with. There will be no argument over whose job it is to trim the hedge and other similar suburban neighbor problems. For some, the secure feeling that having a lot of close neighbors can bring will free many worry circuits. But living closely with many neighbors will cause more noise problems than in single family housing, no matter how well the unit is sound insulated. Also, you will have less defense against neighbors you don't want to have as friends.

A good development will be planned so that you all can live together, and interface when you desire to, but still have quiet and a feeling of privacy within your own area. How to tell which developments are well planned, and which will be good as far as your individual needs are concerned, is the key.

Since urban and suburban apartment complexes have some basic differences, let's look at these first.

In an urban area, most apartment buildings have little or no open space around them. There is nothing upsetting about this for a lot of people, and the substitution of a halfway good view satisfies the need for any contact with nature. Others, however, can go stir crazy in the same situation! If you're one of the others, think of what you can substitute for *outdoor* contact, that will alleviate your claustrophobia in a downtown situation. Perhaps a place that has a park nearby will satisfy this need without putting you into the high-rent bracket. Or a place near a landscaped shopping or office mall, that you could use for your outdoors. You'll get more out of your budget if you find an apartment that allows you to borrow space from nature, or space that someone else has paid for. An urban complex that has, through using high-rise buildings, freed some land for a park or outdoor recreation might be worth paying a bit more to live in. We all need to stop a minute and think about what has the most value to us personally. Remember Step 1. Would you rather pay for a good view and no open space, a traffic-free semi-private park, or an apartment near a major park? What exactly will increase your enjoyment of your home?

In urban situations, having a balcony becomes very important. It gives a tiny piece of your very own outdoors. Before you buy or rent it, be sure you can use it or will even want to use it. If its got a good orientation to wind and sun, and large enough to hold a chair and plants, you'll be able to use it. Does it feel comfortable to you? I have a slight case of acrophobia, the fear of high places. If I go out on a balcony that is a certain nebulous height beyond which I feel secure, I panic! I freeze, except for my knees, which gyrate in every direction, refusing to hold me up. I have, on a few occasions, had to crawl inside! If any of you are like me, you'll have to go out there on your hands and knees to water your plants. So be sure you feel secure enough to use it. Closed rails, although they cut the view, give a feeling of more security than open railings. I've seen high-rise apartments with blankets and other such things tied onto open railings either to make them look more solid or possibly to block the sun or the wind. So if you choose a place with a balcony check it out to be sure its comfortable and it will give you an extra measure of enjoyment.

You're not going to escape noise in the city, but you can limit it. Try to find an apartment that faces away from street noise. Remember, since noise travels upward more than down, try to avoid an apartment above a busy street of freeway. If it's on a hill cars and trucks will make twice as much noise shifting gears as they would on a level street. Look to see where the bus line, train line, or any other noisy form of transit is in relation to you. In fact, try to avoid any audible relationship, without getting too far away when you need to use it. Being *on the bus line* may not be synonymous with the best place to be.

An apartment complex in a suburban area should offer more openness and landscaping. Since land costs are usually lower outside urban areas a developer can afford to offer a lower density project with the resulting increase of open space and more privacy per person. Suburban apartment complexes are often called *garden apartments,* but the term doesn't assure that there will be a garden, or that it will be an attractive one if there is. Are there trees and flowers? Or only some bark chips with miniature cypress bushes dotted here and there? A well-tended landscaping job with lots of plants can only look better and better the older it gets. Bark chips will rot and eventually wash away, and untended planting areas will become a haven for cigarette butts and gum wrappers. Are the open spaces interesting? Does it feel pleasant to walk through? Do the building faces and distances between them vary to make interesting spaces? Or is the open space a chunk in the center of straight rows of straight buildings? This will provide as much spiritual pleasure as the exercise yard of a state prison.

Apartments clustered in small groups can give you a feeling of a mini-neighborhood, while straight rows of endless apartments become tedious. People are happier in a more natural setting. The happier people are, the more they will care about keeping the complex attractive and the better neighbors they'll be. At the bottom line, in an insensitive development, there'll be a higher turnover of residents and incidence of vandalism. It's the difference of people caring or not caring.

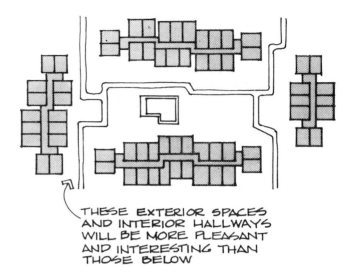

THESE EXTERIOR SPACES AND INTERIOR HALLWAYS WILL BE MORE PLEASANT AND INTERESTING THAN THOSE BELOW

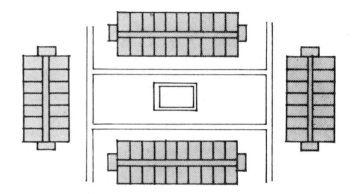

FIGURE 1B. CHOOSE A COURTYARD OVER A PRISON YARD

Just as with single family housing, make sure your apartment and the building it's in are not cheaply constructed of materials that won't wear well. Even though you're renting, and have no direct part in the upkeep, it will still affect you. If the owners don't keep it well maintained or raise your rent so they can afford to, it will affect you. Who wants to live in a rundown place? If you're buying your apartment as a condominium or a cooperative, the extra maintenance is going to come out of your pocket. Step 7 will cover all items that pertain to both exterior and interior longevity and maintenance.

Let's talk about additional ways to assure the maximum privacy, peace and quiet possible. Many people recommend avoiding a building complex with varying age groups in order to live with others of our own age and lifestyle. This could be rather dull and doesn't guarantee that it will be quiet. Some sixty year olds are noisier than children. And some children are quiet. Some singles swing and others are more reserved. I've had neighbors who are in their middle years, hear perfectly, but cannot talk in normal tones. They shout! Their conversations are carried on from outside to inside and from one end of the yard to the other. So it's impossible to tell how quiet or noisy your neighbors may be until you live with them, no matter what age they are. Although you have no guarantee of noise level, you can do a few things to minimize your risk. Choose a unit away from the noise centers, such as the recreation area, the pool, parking lots, and children's play areas (unless you have children yourself and want a unit nearby). Make sure you choose an apartment that is not on the main foot traffic path through the complex or next to the elevator or stairs. Notice where the trash yard or laundry room are. Is the trash yard close enough that you will hear slamming lids and yowling cats? Have a friend go slam some lids while you listen. If you are near a laundry room will you be able to hear the washing machines running? Turn one on and go back to your unit to see if you can hear it. In high-rise apartments that have trash chutes, make sure you don't pick an apartment right next to the chute or you'll have to listen to trash bags thumping down from above. And on the other hand, these facilities should be near enough so that you won't have to carry your trash or laundry long distances.

As discussed previously in any shared wall arrangement noise can be minimized through proper sound insulation. In addition the best apartments are *stacked* with rooms of similar use above and below one another and backed with similar rooms next to each other, as shown in Figure 19. Ask to see the adjacent apartments or the building plans so you will know exactly what is next to you—sideways, above and below.

In a closed hallway situation, the quietest apartments would be those that have kitchens and baths backing to the hallway which will buffer noises to the bedroom and living areas. Some complexes are laid out so you can't avoid one or another of these

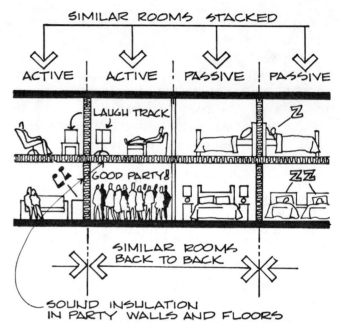

FIGURE 19. GOOD ZONING AND SOUND INSULATION WILL HELP YOU LOVE YOUR NEIGHBOR

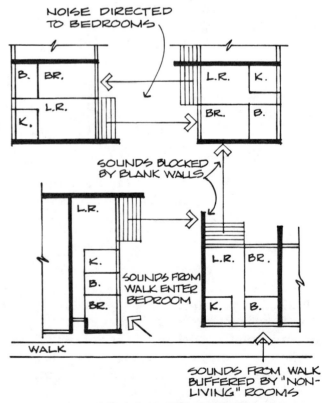

FIGURE 20. CONSIDERATIONS IN FINDING A QUIET PLACE

140

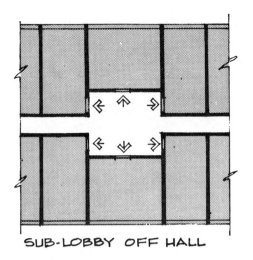

SUB-LOBBY OFF HALL

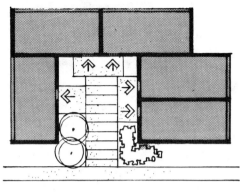

COURTYARD OFF WALKWAY

FIGURE 21   SAFER ENTRANCES

things. Some are so well planned they avoid all of them in most of the units. Other projects just come up with some odd units that work better than others, and these are the ones to seek out.

An end or corner unit will usually give you one less neighbor, and incidentally, more windows and better ventilation. Since landscaping absorbs noise and offers privacy at the same time, an apartment that looks out on well-landscaped shrubs and trees will give you a feeling of more separation than if there is only lawn. A well-designed complex will have parking and storage areas located out of view, or well screened with landscaping.

Security is something else to think about. In some large buildings, the management provides a guard in the lobby. Otherwise, even if the entrance is locked, any stranger could have a key, either by having been a previous tenant or a friend of one. There's a building design feature that tends to cut down burglary and other crimes. It has been found that if a group of six or fewer entry doors are located together in a small sublobby or courtyard, there are fewer incidences of break-in. Neighbors more easily recognize who belongs there and who doesn't. Burglars have no place to hide in the shrubs or around a corner, and have no way of knowing when an adjoining door will open and someone will discover them picking a lock. At least try not to have an entry around a corner and out of

sight of the main hall or other units in a complex, unless you're in shady dealings yourself, in which case you'll need it.

And don't forget to see how the service paths will work for you. Check to see if your carport or parking space is near and is planned so that the hazards on the path of goods and groceries are minimal.

Check the escape routes and exits to see if you can get out easily and quickly in an emergency. In multiple housing situations, since they often are well above the ground, this is more important than with other types of housing. Get a unit as close to the exits as possible. Check it out physically before you commit yourself. If the unit is three stories or less, buy the chain fire ladder that hooks over the window sill. This will give you an extra way out if you're cut off from the hall by fire. You should always have two escape routes and even though the hallway leads to two exits, it is only one exit as far as your apartment is concerned.

And just one more caution: If you're going into a complex for the recreation facilities such as clubhouse, pool, tennis courts, etc., check the rules that govern them. Do the times they can be used fit your schedule? Are they too stringent? If the rules don't fit your schedule or habits the facilities might not be worth the extra money they cost.

141

Mobile Homes and Where to Park Them

Mobile homes cost less than other forms of housing because they are built in factories on an assembly line, almost like a car. Work doesn't have to stop in bad weather, building materials can't be pilfered (which runs up the cost of site-built units), and the whole operation can be run more efficiently, in addition to the fact that the cost of a site is not included. You can in some cases, put them on a site you own, but most mobile homes go into parks.

I think this type of housing can be a good buy, but to be sure you're getting that good buy, you have to know what to look for. Everything that applies to other types of housing applies also to mobile homes, concerning programming, orientation to nature, design, traffic and zoning within the home itself, and how each room works. Here I'll go into the special things that apply to mobile homes and to parks only. If you decide you do want a mobile home, you'll find a book called *The Complete Book of Mobile Home Living* listed in the Bibliography. While it does not include the basic architectural criteria discussed here, it does go deeper into the construction itself and the legalities of buying and owning one.

Parks and What They Offer

With the increased demand for mobile homes comes the resultant scarcity of a good park to move them into. Many communities resist having very many mobile home parks, so at present there really aren't enough to go around. This will probably be your biggest problem. If you can't find a park you'll be happy in, and you should check this in advance, you may not want to buy a mobile home.

Most have the advantage of being a private and secure neighborhood, separated from street activity, unwanted salesmen, and any kind of through traffic. On the other hand, they are so isolated and often so quiet that you can't do á thing without your neighbors knowing all about it. Getting any substantial amount of privacy may be very difficult.

If you can get your home in a good park it can almost guarantee that you will get the best resale value for your unit. Most people agree it's more expensive to rip one out, move it, and reinstall it again than to sell it in place and buy another. This is another reason to be sure you'll be happy in any given park ahead of time. Moving is very expensive!

There are two types of parks, *adult parks* and *children's parks*. Adult Park usually means that no one can live there under the age of eighteen, and sometimes under even older, such as forty or fifty. Children's parks will usually take any age. Children's parks tend to rent sites at lower rates, but only because they generally offer fewer and less opulent community facilities.

In most parks the mobile home site will be rented but increasingly there are parks that work in the form of condominiums. You can own your site and pay a share of the community upkeep. As with any type of housing, whether you own your lot or rent it, you will have to pay your share of the community costs whether you use the facilities or not. So, try to decide if you'll want to use it enough to get your money's worth. If you do want to use community facilities and you're moving into a new park where they haven't been completed (or started), try to get some guarantee that they will be installed and completed, and just exactly what they will offer before you move in.

If rules don't bother you, you'll be very happy in a mobile home park. With everyone living so close together, it is probably the only way to assure order, peace and quiet, and to avoid higher maintenance costs. Be sure you will be able to live with the rules. They often govern how many pets you can have, how many houseguests you can have and how long they can stay, how large or how late your parties can be, where you park, what you park, and how you can park it, as well as when and how you can use the recreation facilities. Get a copy of the rules from every park you look at before you do anything else.

The next decision to make is if you want to be in a lot rental situation or a condominium where you'll own your lot. The rental choice is the one with the least initial expense. But you should also calculate what the real cost will be over many years. One of the most frequent complaints of mobile home owners is that the rents increase often, sometimes severely, and the only option you have is a costly move. Parks that are completely full usually have higher rents. A new park that isn't full yet will have lower rents. The new park may be charging deliberately low rates because they want to attract tenants and fill the park quickly. In some cases, they may have misjudged the cost of operating the park. There's inflation, which can increase the rates at any park, new or old. And last, the scarcity of parks has, and will continue to, push prices upward.

In any case, unless you can get a long-term lease agreement, which are almost nonexistent, you won't know what your monthly costs can accelerate to. If you buy your space in a condominium arrangement, you will have some control over costs and won't be concerned with making a profit, as is the park owner. Condominium parks are obviously going to cost you more initially and require some of your time to watchdog the operation but, in the end, you'll have some say in the way the

park is run, possibly a lower total expenditure and a much higher equity and resale value. While it might appear that a rental park will take less of your own time and effort, it may in actuality take more, if you have to organize tenants' meetings to work out problems with the management.

How any park is managed and maintained should be a factor in your decision. Your home won't have as much resale value in a poorly maintained park. When you're shopping, take note of how neat the grounds are and how healthy the landscaping is. The paving should be in good condition and not full of holes and patches. The park buildings should be well kept, clean and freshly painted. Notice if the other mobile homes are well maintained. The yards of the current residents should be neat and well landscaped. There should be an absence of junk in carports, on porches, or other visible places. Ask as many residents as you can if they are happy with the management and if there are any major complaints. Every manager has a personality that you'll have to live with, so it will be best if you can establish a personal rapport.

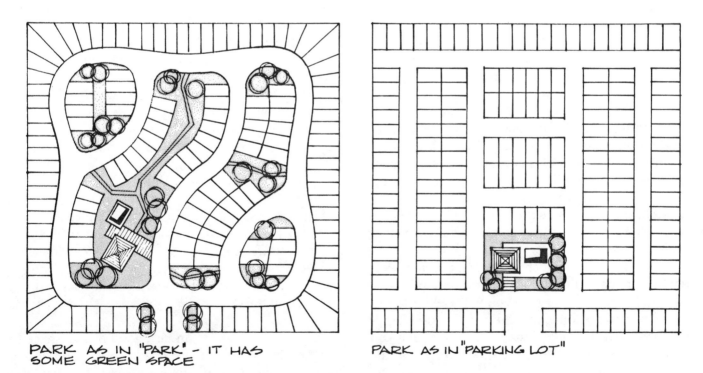

PARK AS IN "PARK" - IT HAS SOME GREEN SPACE

PARK AS IN "PARKING LOT"

FIGURE 22. TWO MOBILE HOME PARK PLANS

The Park Land Plan

The way streets and lots are laid out is just as important as in a conventional neighborhood. Good planning will make a park more pleasant and easier to live in. Find one in which the streets curve a bit and have some variety. Avoid the park that lines every home and lot in straight identical rows on straight unswerving streets. The plan should offer some community green space to interrupt the dwelling frequency. True, the more generously planned park may also have higher rents, but that must balance your own pleasure and the better resale value.

Straight streets allow the developer to lay out every lot so that it is identical in size and shape to every other one. A curved configuration usually leaves some oversized corner lots, some deeper lots, and other shapes that will give you better outdoor spaces to choose from.

Choosing the Space

When you are ready to choose a space or are looking for a home already installed, consider its orientation to sun and wind, to noise and traffic, view, and all other factors, just as you would with any other dwelling. Start putting together in your mind, and then on paper, how nature is affecting that site. If you haven't bought a mobile home yet, get the plan brochure for the one you like best. Get the dimensions and orientation of several sites that are available, and that you think might work well. Then go home and start analyzing all the considerations on paper, as they apply to each site.

Draw your choice of lots to a size that matches the scale of the mobile home plan. Show the direction of north, the directions of storm winds and prevailing breezes. (See Step 2, The Natural Environment.) Now cut out your plan and lay it over the sites, one by one. First of all, see if it will fit. And if it does, how much space will you have left over for landscaping and outdoor living? Will it be enough? You may see that you will need a larger lot or a smaller home, so you can get some landscaping between you and the street or between you and your neighbors. Analyze how nature will affect the mobile home plan if it's installed on the sites you have to choose from.

If you can find an odd lot that will do something extra for you, then that's another way to stretch your money. If you can gain a more private yard or more space in front of your living area windows, and have less next to blank walls where you don't need it, you'll get more use from the site. If you can find a lot next to a green space, that will be another visual extension of your space. Mobile home parks put everyone so close together that *anything* you can do to alleviate that will help.

Don't forget to notice where the nearest freeway is or any other source of outside noise. All parks demand low speed limits and most have traffic bumps in the road at intervals. Cars rattle when they go over them, and all the tools in a pickup truck jump into the air and then crash back down again, so try to avoid a site near one.

The Home Itself

People involved with mobile homes call them *coaches.* Never call them trailers, as they really aren't trailers anymore and it offends mobile home owners. Before you choose which coach to buy apply all the design, traffic, zoning and working room fundamentals just as with any home or apartment. Here we'll cover some special things that apply only to mobile homes.

Mobile homes come in certain standard sizes. The width is governed by what the government allows to be towed down a road, which is a maximum of twelve feet in most states. Thus, mobile homes are usually ten to twelve feet wide. The length can vary; the maximum is about sixty feet. The length expressed includes the trailer hitch, so the home itself is shorter than that. If you are concerned about the square footage it will be something less than the stated length implies. Mobile homes come as *single wide,* the towable width; *double wide,* two towable widths that come separately and are joined together at the site; and *expandable,* which is a single wide with a telescoping section that can be pulled out when it arrives at the site.

Any mobile home can be a good or bad space to live in, but if you choose one keeping good design basics in mind, you'll get a better home. There are two common design flaws that are repeated all too

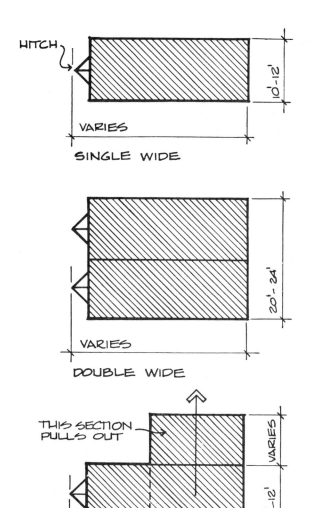

FIGURE 23. TYPES OF COACHES

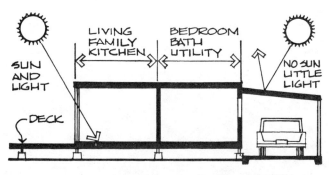

FIGURE 24. DON'T LET CANOPIES
LEAVE YOU IN THE DARK

often. Both of them lead to *darkness!* The first is that to have a carport, the canopy has to be placed along the side of the coach, because that's the only place there's room for it. This requires a wide overhang, which will allow very little light into the rooms along that side. It has to be tolerated, but you should be sure that it will be on the side of the coach where light is least needed. It should be outside guest bedrooms, baths, utility rooms and the like, not outside your kitchen and living areas. Furthermore, many people cover their decks on the living area side in the same manner, thereby shutting out the light from those rooms. If you have a poor orientation to the west, this may be necessary, but it's not needed for any other reason, unless one likes to sit outside when it's raining. A wide overhang stops heat gain when you could use it and may make rooms so dark that the lights will have to be on all day.

Because mobile homes have to be taken down the highway and jolted they can't have plaster or gypsum board walls. Therefore, all mobile homes have some sort of wall facing of a flexible material which is usually wood or imitation wood (plastic). There's not a thing wrong with this except that twenty-one out of twenty-two woods, or wood colors, are *dark* and this is the second design flaw. A dark color doesn't reflect light and therefore makes a room look smaller. If you want a dark interior paneling, at least make sure that the windows and the room are large enough to compensate and that you don't have wide canopies outside blocking all the natural light.

One more warning. Try not to get in a spot among coaches that have light colored aluminum siding even if you have one yourself. They will reflect a large amount of light, heat, and glare back to your home.

Most of Step 7 applies to mobile homes as well as homes built permanently on the land. In addition, there is information that will tell how to know if you are getting a well-built coach and that it is installed properly. If you decide you want to live in a mobile home, you'll want a well-built home that will require a minimum of maintenance, just like any other homeowner.

CHECKLIST

GENERAL: (any type of housing)

Planning of Project or Neighborhood:

Is nature considered, if not nourished?

Are paths of people and autos separated?

Are autos planned out of sight and sound for the most part?

Is the site or unit on a cul-de-sac, dead end street or cross street so that traffic is minimal?

Relationship to other Dwellings:

Will your unit have privacy?

Will your unit have a pleasant view (or can you achieve one easily)?

Are the use areas in your home and in your neighbors homes zoned to work well with each other (active/active and passive/passive)?

Does the neighborhood show signs that it will wear well?

If there are community recreation facilities, will you use them enough to get a return for your money?

SINGLE FAMILY—DETACHED:

If new, are there landscaping incentives?

Does it maximize the amount of land that you can get in your private domain?

SINGLE FAMILY—ATTACHED:

Does the party wall stop sound transmission?

Will your unit be protected from the bad aspects of nature by other units? And not blocked from the good ones?

MULTIPLE:

Does it give the outdoor contact you need—or can you easily substitute some?

Will you be able to use your balcony?

Is the landscaping meaningful and healthy?

Does it offer outdoor spaces that are of varying interest?

Will your unit be located away from the noise generating uses?

Will you have a feeling of privacy?

Will you have a feeling of security?

Are emergency exits adequate and located near your unit?

MOBILE HOMES:

Can you live with the rules?

Do you think you can get along with the manager?

Can you get the coach and the site to work well with each other and with nature?

Handyman's Delight?

We've discussed all the ways a home can help keep our bodies, minds, and souls happy, but all that can be undone by a poorly built or worn out building. So the next thing to do is look at it (forgetting for the moment that it's your dream house) with a cold and critical eye to make sure that it won't fall down around your ears!

This chapter deals with how a home is built, finished, and its state of repair. You need to know how and where to look for flaws so you can avoid the building that will cause you trouble and expense. Although real estate ads sometimes offer a "handyman's delight," I don't think any handyman is ever *delighted* by having to fix old and sometimes nasty problems. Most would rather use their time and skills doing something new and creative rather than digging through a pile of rubble. If you do want the "bargain fixer upper," and feel you can renovate it into something grand, you'd better keep a critical eye also. It's possible that the cost of fixing it, added to the purchase price, will put it out of your budget range, or, if you plan to resell it, make it so expensive that you

won't be able to get your investment back. You'll want to determine before you buy it what the real cost to you will be.

Primarily we'll be discussing conditions that affect houses or apartments that you buy; but a lot of it applies to rentals as well. If something is very wrong with a rental unit you will want the landlord to fix it; but, if he were going to he would probably have done it already. So, it's best to determine such problems in advance. If the flaw is something you can't live with, it will cost you time, money and woe to break the lease and move.

In addition to the building itself there are many other items to look for that concern the site, the utilities, and local laws. It's important to look ahead to see what might happen in the future that will make your home better or worse to live in or to own. If at all possible, do your home hunting in the winter when everything looks its worst and the earth is beset by the elements. In addition, fewer people are thinking of moving then, so you will have less competition and more choices.

GET ALL THE PAPER YOU CAN

First, it's important to obtain the plans and all documents available concerning how the home was built, indicating where everything you can't see is located, and other pertinent information, before you buy. This will not be easy because builders are not used to being asked for them. However, it is to your advantage to give it a good try. This may be even more difficult with older structures, but if the previous owner doesn't have them possibly the local building department will have them on file. In the case of a new home, these should be readily available.

Get a property or land survey. It will show the exact dimensions of the property and the bearings of the property lines. The survey should show the natural topography, or the contours of the site, before any grading or other changes were made. It should show how water originally drained from the site. This information will enable you to see if the natural drainage was disturbed in a way that might cause trouble in a very wet year. It will also show anything which used to exist on the site such as a rock outcropping or an old foundation that might be out of sight be out of sight. The presence of these might become a problem if you want to do any future building expansion or add a pool. The survey will show rights-of-way or easements, if any, that cross portions of the property. Others may own the rights to go over, under, or pass through your property. Normally you can't build on these spaces. The survey will help make sure that there will be no surprises later.

Next, try to obtain the *as-built* drawings, which is what the plans used to build a house are called after it is built. If any changes or deviations were made from the original plans they should be noted on the as-builts. Along with the drawings of the building itself, there should be an as-built site plan. This should show finished grading and indicate how and where water drains from the site, the location of all underground utilities, and the connection to the city sewer, or if not on a sewer the location of the cesspool or septic tank and its leach field.

Find out whether any soil tests have been made and get the results if you can. This information will be needed in the future if you decide to do any more building. Getting them as part of the package when you buy may save you the cost of having new tests made later.

THE SITE

Consider the Future

The rolling hills with the oak trees surrounding your site are so beautiful that they are the main reason you want the house. The question is whether or not they will be there next year. Or if you are buying a house because there is a rental unit included, are you sure you will be allowed to rent it? Don't depend on the builder or realtor in respect to

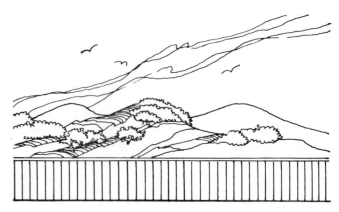

THE VIEW OVER YOUR BACK FENCE
– BEFORE

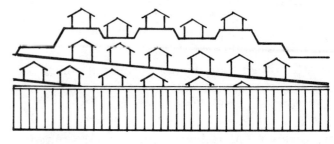

THE VIEW OVER YOUR BACK FENCE
– AFTER

any information about the future. They may be telling the absolute truth but you will be safer if you find out for yourself.

You should make a trip to the local planning and building department to find out what might affect you and the future use of your property. Learn what the zoning is for your property, and the type of use you'll be allowed. Is it single family? If it is you won't be allowed to rent out the apartment. Is it multiple family? In this case your single could soon be surrounded by apartment houses. Perhaps it's not zoned family at all, but commercial, and you might soon have a new car wash next door.

Be sure to check the zoning surrounding your immediate area. Are the rolling hills with the oaks zoned for housing or are they in some form of open land preserve? If they are zoned for housing, find out the lot sizes required and if extensive site grading will be allowed. You might find that soon a large cut and fill tract development will replace the hills you love. In addition to the elimination of your good view, such a development could cause severe water and drainage problems that would affect your site. Check for all types of planned future projects in your area. A steel fabrication plant or a freeway might have been approved but not yet built and you'll want to know about it *before* you buy. Ask what other restrictions affect how you can use the property. Can you or your neighbor cut down existing trees or are you allowed to plant new ones? Some communities restrict these things.

Find out what the setback requirements are, or how close you can build to the property lines. Learn the height limitations of fences and walls within the setbacks. Ask how high you could build if you wanted to add a second story later.

Ask if the home you're considering is in conformance with the local building code. Are there any problems that the city or county might know about that would affect the value of the home or will require that you spend money to correct?

If the house is not on a city sewer go to the health department. Find out whether there have been problems with cesspools or septic tank/leach fields in the area or, in particular, with the home you're considering. If there are no sewers existing, ask if they are planned in the foreseeable future.

Paying for new sewers can cost a lot of money and you'll want to know in advance if you'll be able to afford it. Maybe you'll want to buy a house that is already on a sewer because the cost will be already included in the price and not out of your pocket later.

Now take all this information home. Get out your site plan if you have one, or draw one if you don't. On it put all the invisible property stealers that prohibit future building on any portion of the site. With the setbacks, rights-of-way, easements, septic tank with its leach field, underground utilities, and all else, how much of the property is left? Can you add a pool later or an extra bedroom or a shop? If your plans include expansion and you find there is no room for that perhaps the property is not what you need at all. Probably nothing will be as bad as I show in Figure 2, but if it is you'll want to know about it.

Check the height limitations for buildings and fences and note the areas affected. If you were planning to build up maybe you can't. Or you're thinking of remodeling the garage as a family room, is there room for a new carport? If you need to build a new high fence to give you privacy, will it be allowed?

Outside Things

How does the access for automobiles work? Is the drive wide enough? Is it too steep? Will you have to back past a blind corner onto a busy street? If it is a long drive is there a place to turn around or will you have to back out straight? Try the drive with your car or cars to see how it works. Determine if there is space enough to park your cars or whether you will have to leave them out on the street.

Often today back yards are not accessible by vehicle from the street because the side yards are so small, nor from the rear yard except from the neighboring yard. So again, if you're seriously planning to do any expansion in the rear yard, or to build a sailboat there, try to find a site and building arranged so equipment and trucks can get into it. The cost will probably be prohibitive if you can't get heavy equipment in.

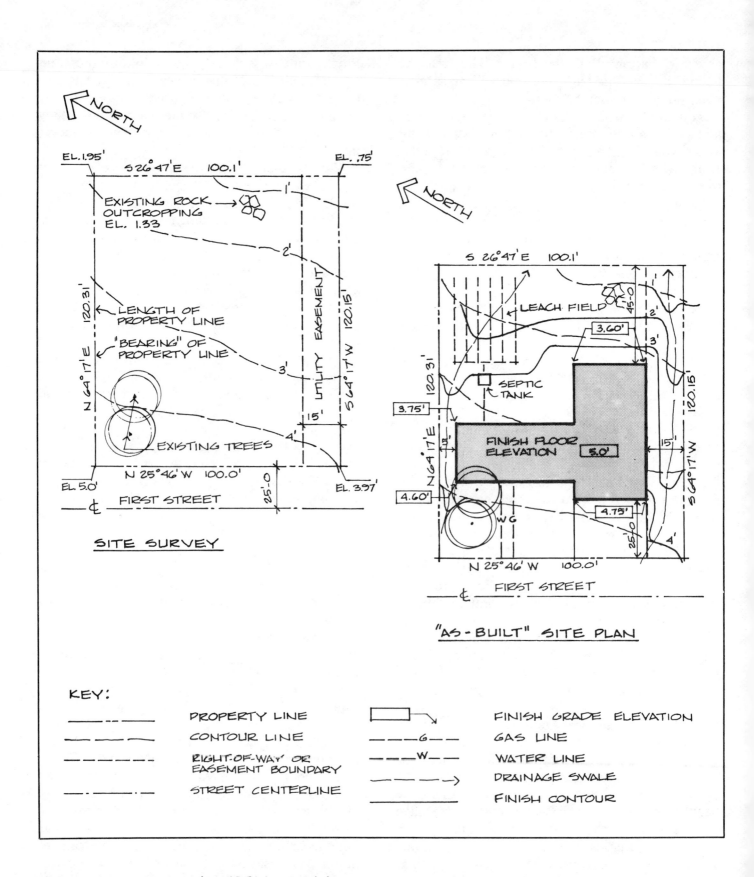

FIGURE 1. SITE INFORMATION

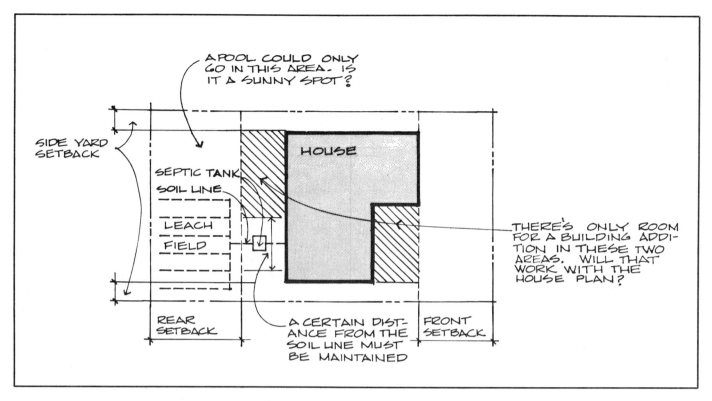

FIGURE 2. HOW MUCH OF THE SITE CAN BE USED FOR FUTURE BUILDING?

The Soil and Down into the Ground

On a flat site the soil and the ground under it most likely will not cause trouble later unless it is in a very low or wet area.

In the case of a house on a hillside site there are a lot of things that can go wrong so start out being very cautious. In a cut and fill situation, the fill has to be compacted or tamped down firmly enough to stay together and in place. If it's not done properly, it may later start to slip down the hill and take the house with it! You need to know if it was *engineered* in accordance with required standards. You can check this with the local building department. A site that has been left in natural condition probably has less of a possibility of causing you trouble. In either case, you cannot trust God to allow you a trouble-free future. He can pull one of His acts at any time!

A very dear friend of mine got "acted" upon. She bought a house on a hillside site that was just mildly cut and filled, nothing drastic. There were some minimal signs of settling, but nothing that looked serious and the house had been there for many years. A few winters later there was rain that would have made Noah happy. About 11:00 one night she called me to report that a sizable fountain of water was gushing out of the ground in her entry court. She asked if I thought this was something that she should worry about.

Although her news panicked me at the time, the situation turned out to be worse than it sounded. I should have told her to get a rowboat and leave. The cause of the new fountain was an underground stream beneath her house. In normal times, it ran well below the ground and did no damage, but in this rainy year, the normal channel was not large enough. The water was escaping not only in the entry court but under half the house as well. By the time the rain stopped several days later, it had washed a great amount of the soil from under the foundations, allowing one wing of the house to drop about a foot, and pulling it away from the rest of the house. As a side result, the plumbing had pulled apart and was gushing more water! Needless to say it cost a lot of money to restore the building to its original height, repair the cracks and plumbing and build a gravel-filled ditch around the house to divert the stream in the future.

This surprise could probably have been avoided if soil tests had been made before purchase. If several borings or test holes had been made, the core samples would have probably shown evidence of the underground stream or of previous slippages. By comparison to the cost of repairs, the cost of tests would have been negligible. I would always recommend that these tests be made on a hillside site. In addition to streams, or bad compaction of soil, sometimes there are layers of clay soil below the surface which act like layers of grease when wet. The slippery layer can allow the soil on top of it to slide and move down the hillside. Soil tests will show the presence of such layers and many other conditions that might possibly cause trouble and cost money later.

Trees on the site can signal that there has been slippage in the past. The trunk will be perpendicular to the hill and the top will be growing straight up again. If you see this, don't pay for soil tests and don't buy it!

Will the soil itself support vegetation? Sometimes the topsoil has all been graded away and the developer has neglected to put any back. Or has put back just enough to cover, but it's not deep enough to grow anything. Dig down a little way to see what's happening. In other cases the site might just have bad soil to begin with.

If you can't determine for yourself whether it's good or bad, take a sample to the Farm Bureau or a local nurseryman for an opinion. If it is not fertile soil it may cost a great deal of money to have adequate topsoil brought in to replace it or to add corrective substances. Even if you don't like to garden, bad soil will assure that even low maintenance planting will just sit there choking to death and eventually die. If you find that the soil is not good, get an estimate of what it will cost to correct it and add that to the cost of the house.

If you plan to make future additions, a pool or building, have soil tests made in the proposed locations to be sure the soil is adequate to support the planned structure.

Site Utilities

Overhead electrical and telephone wires and the poles that accompany them are unsightly. After a time we all get accustomed to them and don't consciously notice their presence. But they are still there blocking views or just looming over our outdoor parties. Viewed across a neighborhood, the wires soon begin to look as if a very untalented spider had been at work! If you can find a neighborhood with underground utilities it will look better and the resale value of the house will be greater. If overhead wires have to be tolerated, try to find a building where the windows and yards face away from them, so at least they'll be out of immediate view.

Check the location of the electrical and gas meters. They also should be out of normal range of sight and in a location where the meter reader won't have to invade your privacy when he comes to read them.

Look to see where the hose bibbs (yard faucets) are located. They should be near the locations where you will want water, and there should be enough of them so you won't have to string hoses together and drag them all about the yard to get your watering done.

Drainage

It is important to know where and how water, either from rain or melting snow, will travel from the time it reaches your roof and site until it leaves the property. Or if it will leave at all! The point is that it should travel and not stay to make puddles, ponds, or cause even more serious problems. The drainage water from the site shouldn't descend on a neighbor or his on you. Examine the site and the roof to determine if water will go away and go where it won't cause anyone any problems.

Start at the roof. Water that strikes the roof should drain from it without causing havoc some-

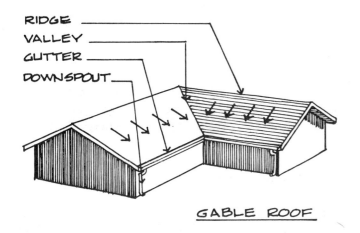

RIDGE
VALLEY
GUTTER
DOWNSPOUT

GABLE ROOF

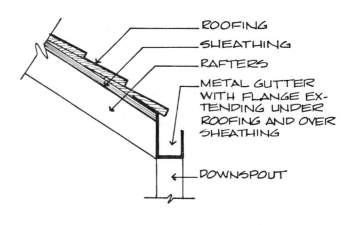

ROOFING
SHEATHING
RAFTERS
METAL GUTTER WITH FLANGE EXTENDING UNDER ROOFING AND OVER SHEATHING
DOWNSPOUT

GABLE OR HIP ROOF AT EDGE

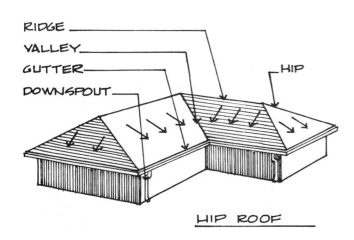

RIDGE
VALLEY
GUTTER
DOWNSPOUT
HIP

HIP ROOF

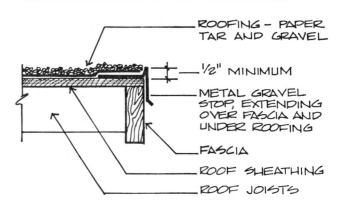

ROOFING – PAPER TAR AND GRAVEL
½" MINIMUM
METAL GRAVEL STOP, EXTENDING OVER FASCIA AND UNDER ROOFING
FASCIA
ROOF SHEATHING
ROOF JOISTS

FLAT ROOF AT EDGE

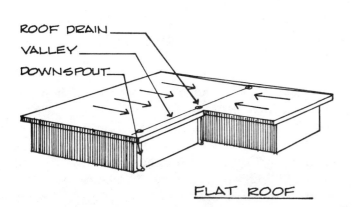

ROOF DRAIN
VALLEY
DOWNSPOUT

FLAT ROOF

FIGURE 3. COMMON ROOF DRAINAGE SYSTEMS

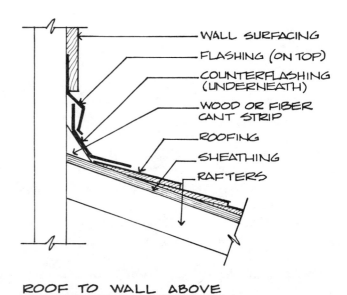

WALL SURFACING
FLASHING (ON TOP)
COUNTERFLASHING (UNDERNEATH)
WOOD OR FIBER CANT STRIP
ROOFING
SHEATHING
RAFTERS

ROOF TO WALL ABOVE

FIGURE 4. ROOF FLASHING, GUTTERS AND GRAVEL STOPS

153

where below. If the roof is sloped make certain that it all slopes to the outside edge or to a valley that slopes to the outside edge. If it slopes inward, or any other direction, there should be a drain at the lowest point that leads to a pipe that will take the water away. In the case of a flat roof, it should slope just enough to let the water drain over the edge or into gutters or drains. It's best that no water is allowed to stand on the roof, although it's possible to get into an argument on this point. In the case of tar and gravel, some believe standing water protects the roofing from deterioration by the sun. I think it's dangerous for the reason that it gives water all the time it needs to find some minute opening to seep through. If you cannot be visually certain all water will drain off, hose water onto the roof to see just exactly how it will behave. Again, I know this may be embarrassing to you. The owner or realtor will at best snicker, or at worst not allow you to do it. I happen to feel that it is necessary to be sure what you're buying really works, before the fact, rather than after. If they won't let you play with the hose, ask for a guarantee that it will drain properly.

The hose test can give you valuable information in addition to whether the water will run off the roof, so it will be worth while to do it if you are allowed.

The water on a sloped roof should run into gutters leading to downspouts that take the water to the ground. Without gutters, water will fall off the roof edge and when driven by wind, run down the walls of the house. This can cause stained and streaked walls at best and leaks around vents, doors, and windows at worst. Even if the overhangs are wide enough to keep the water off the walls, it can still wash out landscaping located below. It is always best when roof water is collected into gutters so that it can be led away without causing any damage.

Watch to see if the water from the hose drains swiftly along the gutters and into the downspouts. If it doesn't disappear into the downspout quickly the gutters are not sloped properly or the downspouts are not large enough. They'll fill up in a big storm, run over the sides and cause the same damage they were put there to avoid. Check to see if the gutters and downspouts are well secured and

the gutters installed in a manner that will catch all the water. If it's a flat roof check to see if the gravel stops are at least one-half inch above the roofing and are firmly attached.

Now, get down off the roof and go look at the base of all downspouts. Did the water get down or was it blocked? If it got down where did it go? What did it do? Was it carried far enough away from the building or into a graveled area, so that it did not splash the walls or walks? Is there a puddle sitting where it landed that is not draining away? One storm is going to drop many times more water than the hose and if the system doesn't work speedily with no problems from your dousing it won't work at all with what nature can apply.

At this point, go into the attic, if there is one, to see if any water got in. If there is no attic you won't know immediately if the roof leaks because it will take longer for the water to build up inside enough to get through the ceiling! We'll discuss later how you can tell about leaks in spaces that have no attics. Inspect it to see if there are old water marks, which are evidence of leaking in prolonged and heavy rains. Look carefully to see if there is any light coming through the roof which can also be evidence that it might leak.

While you're here, take a look to see if the attic is well vented. Venting an attic is necessary to prevent heat gain in the summer and to dry out any moisture that might cause dry rot. Dry rot is a fungus that destroys wood and grows in moist, warm, uncirculated air. All vents should be screened to keep critters out!

If you have the finished site plan, check to see if it indicates how the builder planned water drainage. Figure 5 shows how drainage should work on both a sloped and flat site. A sloped site will be one that has enough change of elevation to show the grade in increments of 1 foot, 2 feet or more. A flat site will probably only show the finish elevations at the building edges and at the corners of the property with arrows to indicate the direction of drainage and where it goes off the property. A sloped site will show what is called a swale, or a continuous low spot similar to a sloped streambed but not as deep. In both cases the grading should be designed to slope away from the house and to divert water around and away from it, leading it to

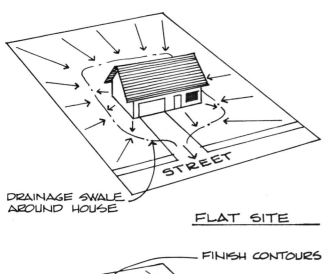

DRAINAGE SWALE
AROUND HOUSE

FLAT SITE

FINISH CONTOURS

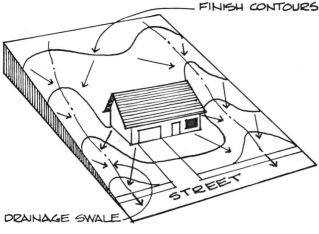

DRAINAGE SWALE

SLOPING SITE

FIGURE 5. DRAINING WATER
FROM A SITE

the street, a culvert or any place it can cause no harm.

A flat site should be graded no less than 2%. This means a 2-foot vertical drop in 100 feet horizontal distance. Another way to look at it is if you have a yard 25 deep, the fall should be .02' x 25' which equals .5 feet or a 6'' drop.

If this information is not on the site plan, or you don't have one, or even if it is just for a check, go back and get the hose! Leave some sprinklers on in critical spots for about an hour to see where the water goes. Put the hose in planting areas at the base of the house to see if the water sinks in, runs off, or just sits there, which is not good. Wash down patios, driveways, and other paved areas to see if the water runs off or leaves puddles. Puddles will dry quickly in the summer and not be a problem, but in the winter you will have to walk around them or wear boots at all times.

With a downslope lot (Figure 6) you'll want to be sure that the curb, gutter and your driveway are elevated enough to keep street water off your property. Use the hose in the gutter this time. The faster the water drains away, along the gutter, the less you need be concerned about a buildup in a heavy storm. Look around any concrete to soil juncture points for evidence of washout. If the

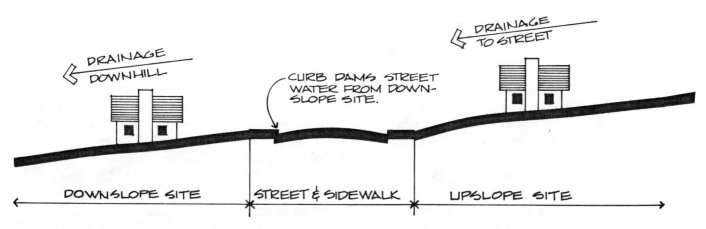

DRAINAGE
DOWNHILL

CURB DAMS STREET
WATER FROM DOWN-
SLOPE SITE.

DRAINAGE
TO STREET

DOWNSLOPE SITE | STREET & SIDEWALK | UPSLOPE SITE

FIGURE 6. SLOPING SITES

street is a city-funded project, or the developer has put in the curbs, gutters and streets to city standards, call the City Engineer for assurance of the adequacy of the design. If neither of these is the case, find out from the neighbors if there have been previous problems.

With an upslope lot, try to figure where the water will come to your property from the neighbor above. Generally, you'll have to guess about this or ask neighbors again. Look for washed out areas in the rear yard around fence posts. If the upslope neighbor has a lot of paving in his yard you can expect to receive more water run off than if there is lawn, ground cover or a lot of landscaping between the houses to absorb the water before it reaches your property.

THE BUILDING

The Builder

The primary concern for all of us is whether a building will last a long time, and require only minimal expenditures for repair and maintenance. The best assurance is if it has been built by an able and honest builder. Unless the home is quite old it shouldn't be difficult to find out who the builder was. If the home is old and still standing you'll know it was well built.

If you are buying new, the builder's name will be easy to obtain. If you are buying a house of fairly recent vintage, say second or third hand, his name will be on the as-built plans or the building department will have the information. The builder should have been in the area for several years, at least, and still be there. He should have been working under the same individual or corporate name the whole time. If not, it might indicate that he had to go out of business for a time, and it might be to your benefit to know the reason. If you can find him, and he is an honest builder he will be happy to provide you with names of people who own or have owned houses that he has built. Get about eight names and call them to see if they've been

satisfied with his product or if they have had significant problems. If he won't give you referrals ask an officer at your bank if they know of him and his reputation, and check with the local Better Business Bureau to see if there have been any complaints filed against him. If you encounter any hesitation about the contractor's ability or reputation (people are sometimes hesitant to criticize) check into it further or pull out. If you get nothing but praise for him, you'll almost certainly know the house is built well!

When purchasing a mobile home, check the reputation of the manufacturer and the local dealer. This information can be obtained from the same sources mentioned above. In addition, The American National Standards Institute has set a minimum standard for mobile home construction and it is called ANSI A119.1. A coach complying with this standard will have a seal that says so. If it does comply, the dealer will eagerly point it out. In addition to this, there are national manufacturing associations that demand their members build to the standard and police them to see that they do. These groups are the Mobile Home Manufactuer's Association and Trailer Coach Association (MHMA/TCA) and the Craftsmen's Guild. A coach bearing the seal of either of these groups is an assurance that it is well constructed. MHMA/TCA also has a consumer action board to help a buyer with any complaints he might have with the manufacturer or the dealer. If you plan to install a mobile home on your own lot, it will be easier to get a permit to do so if it complies with the ANSI A119.1 standard.

Guarantees

A new house, apartment, or mobile home should have a one-year guarantee against all defects! This means that the contractor must correct any defect found within the first year. Get this guarantee in writing before you sign the final papers. FHA and VA loans now require guarantees against major defects for up to four years. If you're getting this type of loan, be sure you know how long the time period is so you can take advantage of it. With other types of loans, you can now buy insurance to guarantee against major defects for similar longer

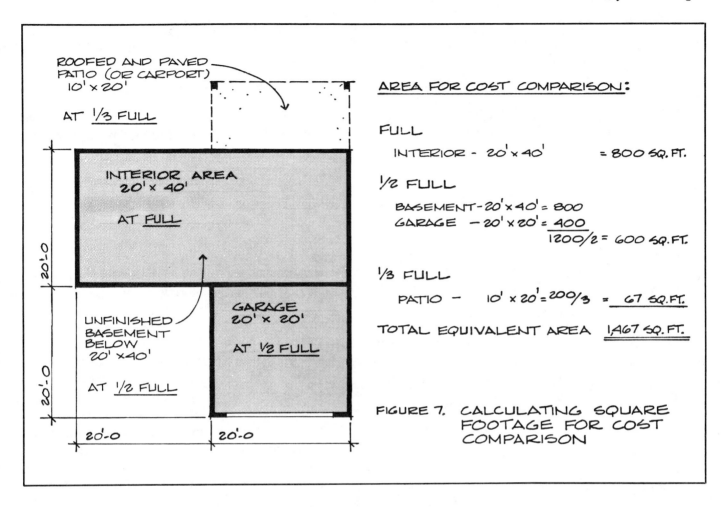

ROOFED AND PAVED PATIO (OR CARPORT) 10' × 20'

AT 1/3 FULL

INTERIOR AREA 20' × 40'

AT FULL

UNFINISHED BASEMENT BELOW 20' × 40'

AT 1/2 FULL

GARAGE 20' × 20'

AT 1/2 FULL

20'-0

20'-0

20'-0

20'-0

AREA FOR COST COMPARISON:

FULL
    INTERIOR - 20' × 40'   = 800 SQ. FT.

1/2 FULL
    BASEMENT - 20' × 40' = 800
    GARAGE   - 20' × 20' = 400
                        1200/2 = 600 SQ. FT.

1/3 FULL
    PATIO -   10' × 20' = 200/3 =   67 SQ. FT.

TOTAL EQUIVALENT AREA   1,467 SQ. FT.

FIGURE 7. CALCULATING SQUARE FOOTAGE FOR COST COMPARISON

time periods. The building industry has recently begun to police its own members and offers a warranty called HOW (Home Owner's Warranty) so the builder may offer this. The program goes as far as insuring against major structural failure for up to ten years. Any guarantee could possibly save you thousands of dollars.

As-Builts

Again, I urge you to obtain these plans if at all possible. Even if you find the builder is above reproach, having the as-built plans can be very valuable. If you need repairs in the future, these plans show (or should show) where everything is located and how it's put together. A repairman will not have to spend his costly time guessing where a cer-

tain pipe or wire is located! If you decide to do any remodeling in the future, these plans will save you or your designer the effort of trying to reconstruct how the building went together initially and show what you will be working with mechanically and structurally.

Square Footage

The size of a house, mobile home, or apartment in total square feet has a direct relation to the cost. Although there are many factors that affect the worth of a home, the bottom line in comparing one against another is the building purchase price per square foot. A 1200 square foot house priced at $35,000 costs $29.00 per square foot. The same size home priced at $50,000 has a square foot cost of $41.67. If the quality is nearly the same for each 1200 square foot house, this price differential per square foot should be a consideration in tthe decision of which to buy! By the same calculation, if you can afford the $50,000 home perhaps you should keep looking for one that offers a better footage price, or more house for the same money.

Measure it yourself, even if it is new, and the sales brochure gives a square foot figure. The printer may have made a mistake. As mentioned earlier, with mobile homes length dimensions include the trailer hitch, so these figures will not give the accurate living area. Measure outside wall to outside wall for the overall figure. Enclosed finished space is counted at full value, garages and other unfinished spaces are figured at one-half value, and unenclosed carports and roofed patios are valued at one-third. The lowered values reflect the fact that partial enclosures and unfinished spaces cost less to build than fully enclosed and finished space. Figure 7 shows how to calculate this.

Physical Inspection

Now, it's time to make a critical, impartial physical inspection of the structure. You can do this yourself or you can hire someone to do it for you. There are home or building inspection consultants who perform this service. A professional inspection will cost very little compared to what it will be worth to you. A home inspector is not an appraiser. An appraiser is only looking at current market values for the same size of house in a similar location, and his job is to put a value on the building. You want a full structural check, and this is what a home inspector does. Another advantage in using a home inspector is that he works for you only. He does not do any of the repair or construction work himself. If you use someone who is in that business to check your house, you won't know whether he's on your side or trying to get some work.

Although this chapter covers what you should look for if you inspect the home yourself, you may feel unsure about your judgment or worry about overlooking a major defect if you're not an expert. A good professional home inspector can do the job more swiftly and with greater wisdom and experience. The inspection firm will give you a written report, but in addition to that, go along and follow the inspector through the house. This way you can get all his comments as he makes the inspection, and can ask questions.

Following is a list of what to look for and where to look for it. Use it if you check the house yourself or to see if your home inspection consultant is thorough. I am going to call this a Punch List, which is an architect's term for the list they make when they check a finished building. Usually a final portion of the money will not be paid until the contractor corrects everything found to be unfinished or poorly done. If you're lucky enough to be buying a new house or mobile home you can demand all flaws be fixed before you move in or pay all the money as a condition of sale. If you expect them to be fixed promptly and cheerily after you pay, you'll probably be very disappointed.

In the case of an older home or apartment, you will probably have to remedy the flaws yourself but you can attempt to get the seller to fix them or use them as a bargaining point to lower the price. The important thing is to know what they are, so you can determine whether you can afford to fix them, have the desire to fix them, or be able to live with them.

No one does *perfect* work, so you can expect to find flaws in any building. Little ones do not affect the structural integrity as a rule, they're just messy; but big flaws could. So in this inspection, it's really only major things that should get you excited, not minor ones. If you find something that looks as if it might be major, and you feel you don't have the background to judge how serious it might be, it will be very good insurance to get an expert to look at it.

Inspecting the house will involve rooting around in dirty crawl spaces under buildings and attics with cobwebs, so wear old clothes and bring something to wrap around your hair. You'll also need some sort of bag in which to carry all your testing tools. Inspecting a house is not good, clean fun!

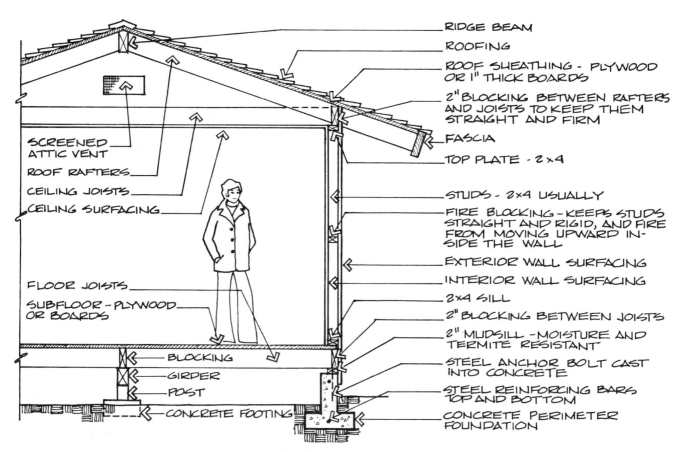

RIDGE BEAM

ROOFING

ROOF SHEATHING - PLYWOOD OR 1" THICK BOARDS

2" BLOCKING BETWEEN RAFTERS AND JOISTS TO KEEP THEM STRAIGHT AND FIRM

FASCIA

TOP PLATE - 2×4

STUDS - 2×4 USUALLY

FIRE BLOCKING - KEEPS STUDS STRAIGHT AND RIGID, AND FIRE FROM MOVING UPWARD INSIDE THE WALL

EXTERIOR WALL SURFACING

INTERIOR WALL SURFACING

2×4 SILL

2" BLOCKING BETWEEN JOISTS

2" MUDSILL - MOISTURE AND TERMITE RESISTANT

STEEL ANCHOR BOLT CAST INTO CONCRETE

STEEL REINFORCING BARS TOP AND BOTTOM

CONCRETE PERIMETER FOUNDATION

SCREENED ATTIC VENT

ROOF RAFTERS

CEILING JOISTS

CEILING SURFACING

FLOOR JOISTS

SUBFLOOR - PLYWOOD OR BOARDS

BLOCKING

GIRDER

POST

CONCRETE FOOTING

A WOOD FRAME BUILDING WITH SLOPING ROOF AND A WOOD FLOOR

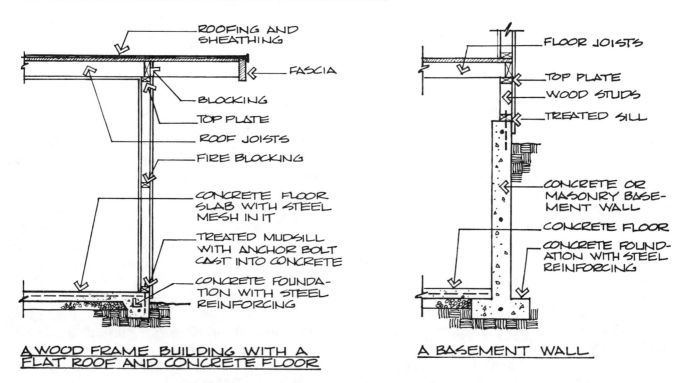

ROOFING AND SHEATHING

FASCIA

BLOCKING

TOP PLATE

ROOF JOISTS

FIRE BLOCKING

CONCRETE FLOOR SLAB WITH STEEL MESH IN IT

TREATED MUDSILL WITH ANCHOR BOLT CAST INTO CONCRETE

CONCRETE FOUNDATION WITH STEEL REINFORCING

A WOOD FRAME BUILDING WITH A FLAT ROOF AND CONCRETE FLOOR

FLOOR JOISTS

TOP PLATE

WOOD STUDS

TREATED SILL

CONCRETE OR MASONRY BASEMENT WALL

CONCRETE FLOOR

CONCRETE FOUNDATION WITH STEEL REINFORCING

A BASEMENT WALL

FIGURE 8.   BASIC FRAMING METHODS AND BUILDING PARTS

159

BUILDING PUNCH LIST

Footings, Foundations and Basement Walls

Concrete Quality: The concrete surface should reveal very little of the aggregate (or the gravel filler) and there should be no large pockets or holes showing. Poke the concrete with a screwdriver at any dubious spot to check for softness or voids. In masonry or block walls, check the mortar joints between the blocks. All in all, concrete or mortar should be smooth, hard, and free from irregularities.

Look for Cracks: Hairline cracks are all right but anything larger may signal excessive settling or poor reinforcing. Concrete should have steel bars cast into it to hold it together and prevent any severe separation.

Is it Level?: If the wall or foundation is properly reinforced it is possible that it could have settled without cracking. To check this, place a hand level or a large marble on the top of the footing or wall to find if it is level. Check in as many places as you can because uneven settlement can cause undulations. The wall may be level one place and not in another. If you can't find a place to put the level or marble, you can check the level of the floors above later. A small amount of settlement and the resulting unevenness is normal, but anything more extreme is a signal that something is amiss. If you're in doubt hire a structural engineer or building inspector to take a look at it.

Infiltration of Water: This is a consideration only in basements, but it is an important one. Look for evidence of water staining on the walls and floor. Look for efflorescence, a powdery white substance that forms on concrete and masonry which indicates that some moisture is entering. A small amount of efflorescence can be expected but if it's extensive that's a sign of rather extreme water problems. If the walls have been newly painted check the floor at the base of the walls for evidence of staining. Deteriorating flooring is another sign of water infiltration. And don't forget your nose! If it smells damp and musty under the house or in the basement, that's a sure sign of a dampness pro-

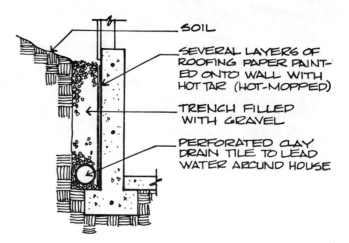

SOIL

SEVERAL LAYERS OF ROOFING PAPER PAINTED ONTO WALL WITH HOT TAR (HOT-MOPPED)

TRENCH FILLED WITH GRAVEL

PERFORATED CLAY DRAIN TILE TO LEAD WATER AROUND HOUSE

FIGURE 9. WATERPROOFED BASEMENT WALL

blem. The foundation should have screened air vents to prevent moist air from being trapped under the house.

Look beneath and around pipes coming from the plumbing fixtures above for signs of leakage. Basements should have a floor drain and a sump pump, or a pump to lift the water through a pipe to deposit it into the main drainage system. Put a hose nozzle right at the drain so you won't get the floor wet and turn on the water and the pump to see if it works.

Moisture and Vapor Barriers: A concrete slab on grade should have plastic sheeting laid beneath the slab. You won't be able to see this but it should be noted on the as-builts. Otherwise, look for efflorescence again. Basement walls below grade, or below ground level, should be coated outside with asphalt or better still have asphalt impregnated felt (as with rolled roofing) layered on the outside, hot mopped (hot melted tar or asphalt coating) in place. This is called as moisture barrier. Get a shovel and dig down to inspect the outside basement wall to be sure it does. If the house is downslope, a gravel filled ditch should be next to the wall, with a drain tile at the bottom to carry the water around the house and away.

Termites and Dry Rot: Termites eat wood, of course, not concrete, but it is around concrete that signs of their presence is revealed. Usually the lender requires that a termite inspection be made before your loan is approved but you should also know how to look for them. Subterranean termites are worms, sometimes called "white ants" but in reality, worms, that live in the ground and travel in tiny mud tunnels through soil to reach wood. Look for evidence of tunnels on the foundations. If you can see concrete all around the house and no tunnels it's probably termite free. If you can't then you won't know. Take a screwdriver and poke it into the wood adjacent to soil or concrete. If there are soft spots it means termites are feeding or dry rot has set in. Neither occurence is auspicious and you'd better call in an expert who can determine how extensive the damages are. While you are checking, see if the sills, or any wood that touches concrete are pressure treated (this will have a greenish, copper color), redwood or other termite and rot resistant wood.

A few words should be said here about professional termite and rot reports. It is general practice for the seller to pay for the report and, depending on the agreement, either the buyer or the seller pays to have the repair work done. Termite inspectors are not impartial agents; they all work for pest control firms that are also in the business of doing the repair work. They are very good at finding everything, even very minor things, which of course you'll want to know about. And since almost every house, even relatively new ones have something wrong, an estimate to repair the damage will be presented, almost without exception.

I want to caution you to not give up a house that might be a supreme bargain and the perfect house for you because the pest report is not totally favorable and the estimate to repair it seems expensive. Find out what the exact damage is and, either by hiring an impartial building inspector or looking at it yourself if you have some aptitude, decide just exactly how serious it is. It's possible that if you hire someone other than the pest company to do the work, or do it yourself, it can be done for much less than the estimate. So don't wash your hands of an otherwise good home until you're absolutely sure that it is too rotten to repair within

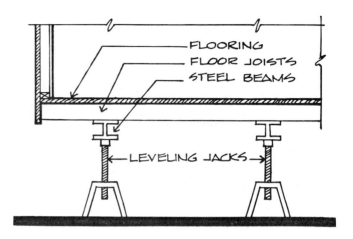

FIGURE 10. MOBILE HOME SUPPORT

your budget or that you'll be spending more than the house is worth to you.

Mobile Home Foundations: These usually aren't permanent foundations. If you're buying one that is installed permanently, then check it as you would a regular house foundation. Most frequently mobile homes are installed on steel leveling jacks placed on bare ground. These jacks can be raised or lowered to level the home and compensate for any grade variation. The other method, in newer parks, is that a level concrete slab is poured to receive the home. In this case the coach rests upon concrete pier blocks placed on the level slab.

If a home is to be located in an area prone to very high winds or earthquakes, this system should be modified to assure that it doesn't tip over or take off. The addition of X-bracing between several pairs of leveling jacks or pier blocks both cross and lengthwise will brace against earthquakes and minor winds. Very high winds can lift a mobile home. This is called uplift and tie downs will be required to avoid it. If you want to be sure that either of these structural modifications will do the job, hire an engineer to calculate exactly what is required. The sizes and weights of coaches vary, as do winds, so that each needs to be looked at individually.

161

Floors

Are They on the Level?: Use the hand level, a ball-bearing or a marble to see if the floors are level. If the floor is carpeted have it pulled up in a few places so you can test for levelness and see the condition of the floor beneath. If it's not level it could indicate foundation settlement. It could also mean that the wood below has severe termite damage and is crunching in because it is soft. It depends again on how much it is out of level. Small differences are natural.

If the subfloor is finished smoothly and evenly with tight joints between boards and no nails protruding, your carpet and finish flooring will not wear out as soon as they will over a rough, poorly finished subfloor.

Are They in Solid?: Does the floor feel spongy under your feet? You shouldn't feel any give at all! Sponginess means that the floors weren't designed to hold the weight required. If they give under the weight of your body, then the weight of furniture will send them into a permanent sag. If a weak floor is upstairs or if there is a finished basement below, eventually the sag and vibrations will cause the ceiling material to crack and fall.

Jump up and down. Does the house vibrate or do the windows and doors rattle? Again, this is a sign of weak construction.

Walls

Outdoors:

Put your hand level on the wall in a vertical position to see if it truly is straight up and down. Do this in many places to see if there are bulges that are not visible. Both of these symptoms could be another sign of building settlement. It could also mean that the builder used wet wood or warped studs, that the plaster isn't of a uniform thickness, or any number of other faults.

Plaster walls: Check for cracks. A few hairline cracks are normal but anything larger is a sign of trouble. Look for cracks at the corners of doors and windows especially. Serious cracking will probably show up at these openings first. Large cracks can mean settlement again or be evidence of a very bad plastering job, in which case it all may eventually fall off the wall!

Turn the hose on exterior plaster walls to see if the water soaks in. If the plaster is painted with a low quality paint or it has integral color with no sealer it will absorb water. Scratch the plaster in an inconspicuous spot to see if the color is surface paint or if it is in the plaster itself. If you're located in a cold climate, cracks allow water to seep into the plaster where it will freeze and then expand and crack the plaster even more. Having a waterproof surface is always best.

Concrete or masonry walls (concrete block, brick, etc.): As for basement walls and foundations look for cracking, efflorescence and the presence of good dense concrete or mortar.

Woodwork: Look at Figure 8 again. It shows the most common method of putting wood structures together. Since we're starting to get into some carpenter terminology which might puzzle you, all the parts are labeled so that you'll know exactly which ones I'm talking about.

Look for any separation of wood from the building itself. Check fascias for warping and gapping. See if they are tightly secured to joist or rafter ends. Check all trim wood especially around windows and doors to see if it's straight, true, well secured and has no rot. All nails used to fasten wood trim should be finish nails, that are counter sunk. (See Figure 11) The nail holes should be filled with wood putty and sealed or painted over. This will keep water from seeping into nail holes and rotting the wood. If you can't see nail holes it's done right, but if you see nails or nail holes it isn't. Look at the exteriors of wood windows. Is the putty holding the glass solid and does it fit

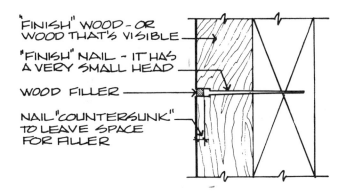

"FINISH" WOOD - OR WOOD THAT'S VISIBLE

"FINISH" NAIL - IT HAS A VERY SMALL HEAD

WOOD FILLER

NAIL "COUNTERSUNK" TO LEAVE SPACE FOR FILLER

FIGURE 11. NAILING AT FINISH WOOD (SIDING AND TRIM)

tightly. If it has chipped away here and there or pulled away from the glass, it is letting water get into the wood frame. Since this can also cause dry rot, poke around the window with your screwdriver to see if there is any soft wood. Even if all seems solid, this condition should be remedied immediately! If you are looking at a home in an area that has severe winters, and it doesn't have double glazed windows or insulating glass, be sure there are storm windows and that they are in good repair.

Paint: Exterior paint, whether on wood or plaster should be a top quality oil base, or a synthetic that is recommended and guaranteed to last outdoors. A good exterior oil based paint will have a glossy and tight textured surface when new and when older, a powdery surface which will rub off on your hand when touched. Accept no blistering, chipping or peeling conditions if you want to avoid stripping and repainting the whole building. Blistering also signals that there may be water in the walls from some source that is working its way out through the paint.

Siding: Taking care of exterior siding can be one of the biggest maintenance jobs you'll have! The types needing the most care are wood, aluminum and anything else that has to be painted. Almost yearly repainting is necessary to keep them looking neat and maintain protection from weather. Wood that has a natural oil based stain or sealer will wear well with little attention. Other long-lasting, low maintenance siding systems are factory finished aluminum; and prefinished plywood or hardboard with vinyl or other impervious coatings designed to last permanently. However, in temperatures less than 20° F. vinyl coatings and sidings have been known to crack. Most reputable manufacturers will give a guarantee of twenty years to factory coated siding if the material is installed in accordance with their recommendations.

There are a few things to mention about siding as it applies to mobile homes. All of them have some form of siding that is flexible and won't be damaged in transit. The majority of mobile homes have factory coated aluminum siding. This type of siding needs almost no maintenance work but it has some faults that should be considered. Many mobile home owners complain that aluminum siding rattles noisily in widstorms, which can be very annoying. Also, because it is thinner than most siding materials and the metal itself is not temperature resistant, it has no insulating value. Even if the wall cavities have insulation, the metal skin won't give additional help. Many mobile homes are now being paneled with wood, or pressboard panels, which do give added insulation. Wood siding makes a coach look more like a conventional house and less like a trailer. A light colored aluminum siding reflects heat in the summer, but don't forget it will also do it in the winter.

In all cases where nails are used, make sure they are rust and corrosion proof types of galvanized steel, stainless steel, or aluminum. They should be counter sunk and the holes filled with material to match the siding. Nails that are not rust resistant will soon make vertical orange streaks all over your walls and eventually rot away. If the siding is secured with screws or other fasteners instead of nails they also should be of noncorrosive materials. Again look for signs of wood decay and to see if metal flashing has been installed at any places where materials change.

Indoors:

Wood Frame Construction: In well-built frame construction the studs should be placed on 16" centers in 2 by 4 stud walls. These will be noted on the as-builts but if you don't have them, or want to see if the builder got sloppy, it's easy to check the spacing without tearing the walls apart. You can buy a "stud finder" for under $2.00 at any hardware or building supply store. Stud finders register a magnetic reaction to the hidden nailing at the stud and tell you exactly where the studs are located. Some walls have wider stud spacing, but if they do, the studs must be deeper than 4" to compensate for the difference in strength. A stud finder will always be useful when you want to know where you can hang a picutre and have solid backing, or hang shelves. Once I was trying to put in some brackets to support shelving. Using the old method of knocking on the wall to see where it sounded solid (a stud) and where it sounded hollow (no stud), I proceeded to drill holes for the screws. This particular wall had no intention of going along with this theory, whether it sounded hollow or solid had nothing to do with where a stud was located. Nor were they, as I found later, on center at 16" but at 14" or 18" or 20½" or whatever struck the builder's fancy. Before I was finished, the wall was riddled with "guess" holes and looked like a pegboard! Now I have a stud finder with me at all times!

Cracks: Look for these inside also and especially around windows and doors. Does all finished wall surfacing have tight joints at the corners, at the ceiling to wall juncture, and floor to wall connection, and around window and door jambs?

Surface Smoothness: Look along walls and ceilings, preferably into the light, to see if any detectable irregularities or bulges occur. A well finished wall or ceiling should look of one piece and be smooth and flat. If a textured finish has been applied it should be uniform all over. It shouldn't look as if it had been slopped on with big hunks in one place and almost bare in another.

The Roof

Inside: Look for any water damage on the ceilings, water spots or blistering plaster or paint.

Outside: Go up on the roof again (if you're an organized person do this when you do the hose test to save a trip). If the roof is sloped with wood or asphalt shingles, or rolled roofing, look for warped edges which are a sign of old age! Has the roofing pulled away from the edges or does it gap away from the flashing? Does the total expanse of shingles or tile look smooth? If not, this could be a sign that the roof structure itself is uneven or that a new roof has been put on over an old uneven one, and will not wear well. With a flat roof, layers of hot mopped felt with a gravel finish is the reliable water proofing method. It should look smooth and whole, not lumpy, bubbled or cracked. Wood shingles should feel firm under your feet, not spongy! Spongy means *old*. Asphalt roofing, whether tile or mopped on, should have a sand or gravel imbedded surface to protect it from the sun. If you see a lot of the black underlayer showing that means old also.

Look at Figure 4 again, which shows good flashing methods for both sloped and flat roofs. The roof could be new and of excellent quality but if it has not been flashed correctly it will leak. Flashing is designed, and should be installed to come from under some materials and cap over others to lead water over and away so it can't come into the house. All materials should be rustproof. Gutters, downspouts and flashing should be made of galvanized iron or other non-corrosive material and should be fastened with galvanized nails or stainless steel screws. If not, they will corrode and have to be replaced. If the metal is coated, try to get a baked on material so you can avoid frequent repainting. A new type made of plastic eliminates maintenance and lasts well.

Materials and Workmanship

Paint: Do the interior painted surfaces, walls, woodwork or cabinets have a washable type of paint? If not, you'll need to repaint them sooner. Take a wet sponge and hold it against the surface for a few seconds, then wipe it dry with a towel. If it leaves a wet spot it is porous paint. It will absorb dirt and grease and will not wash. If you can dry it off, and no dampness remains, it won't let dirt in either, and you can keep it washed for a long time.

Does the paint cover well or is it uneven, perhaps not completely hiding the previous color or the surface beneath? Is the paint applied neatly with no visible brush marks; no roller fuzz or other foreign materials imbedded in it, and is it free of sags and drips? You might find all of these in an older home and if you love the house, you'll probably be willing to correct the problem yourself. If it's a new home, ask the builder to make it right as a condition of sale, because you're theoretically paying for good craftsmanship and you should get it.

Woodwork: All woodwork should look straight and true and have no gaps, hammer dents or any other type of vandalism. All nails should be countersunk and filled; and the wood should be sanded smooth. Usually this has been done where the woodwork is visible but short cuts are often taken where it is not. Feel around with your hand inside all drawers, inside cabinet doors, the cabinet walls and shelves. Roughly finished wood can snag clothes and linens, keep shelf paper from sticking and is impossible to clean. In wardrobes and closets check the shelf and clothes pole for smoothness. Then feel or look inside the door jambs where the wall returns to see if it is smooth or painted; or if wall surfacing has been applied at all. Sometimes this spot is left totally unfinished because no one sees it! The mobile home my parents bought had no wall material on the inside wardrobe jambs at all. They were just left with the open studs. They had already paid all the money when they discovered it and could never get the seller to fix it. Another problem they have is that the manufacturer used plastic instead of wood trim. This was stapled on and pops off frequently. So see if you can get wood trim or be sure the plastic trim is well fastened.

Flooring: Is the flooring a good quality that will last a long time and wear well? In the case of laid flooring (vinyl tile, sheet vinyl, or asphalt tile) try to find out the name of the manufacturer to see if you are getting a name brand. Also find out the thickness of the material if you can. The thicker the better! Sheet flooring and synthetic tiles come in thicknesses from 1/16" to 1/8".

In any case asphalt tile should not be used on top of concrete floors, or in kitchens and baths because it is not water resistant and moisture causes it to crack or buckle. Vinyl or vinyl asbestos will last longer in these areas. With any tile flooring (vinyl, hardwood or ceramic tile) look to see if the surface is smooth and flat, the joints straight and even, and that the tiles themselves have no adhesive or grout smears on them.

With carpeting, make sure that it is laid flat and smooth throughout. If you detect any bumps, either the carpet was not installed well, there is a rough subfloor, or a workman left his lunch under it. In any case, since carpeting will wear quickly over bumps, ask that it be taken up so you can see what the problem is.

Look at all applied bases, whether wood, vinyl, or rubber, to see if they fit against the wall and floor tightly. There should be no gaps at the joints, no nails showing, no hammer marks or splashed adhesive. Vinyl bases should, for ease of cleaning, be "coved" or curved to meet the flooring material. They should also have manufactured outside and inside curved corner pieces. Wood bases should have mitered corners. Don't accept butted corners with any base, wood or synthetic, because the cracks will catch dirt and this will mean more work for you!

Finish Hardware: All finish hardware, door knobs, locks, hinges and pulls should be of solid material throughout rather than just surface plated. Surface plating will wear off and you will have to either replace the hardware or live with it, and it *will* look tacky. The best materials are brass, bronze or aluminum. Scratch hardware with your pocket knife where it won't show, so you can see if the material goes deeper than the surface. Door knobs and locks should not have any holes showing around them that the escutcheon, or "rose" doesn't completely cover. Latch hardware should be set in the jamb neatly and not look like someone

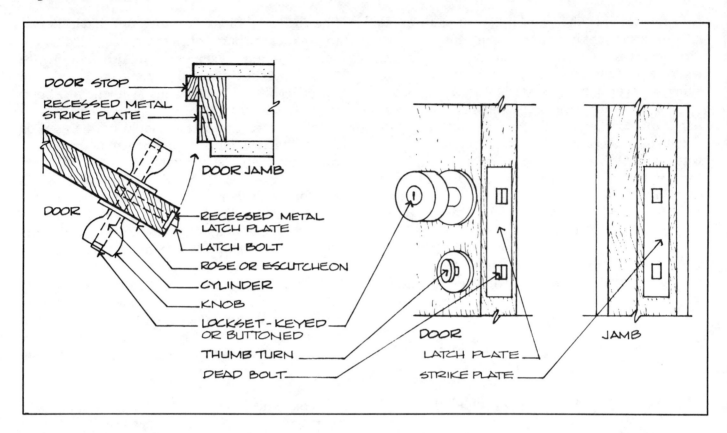

FIGURE 12.   DOOR HARDWARE

did the job with a hatchet. Check all hardware for ease of cleaning; the simpler the design the better.

All exterior doors should have deadbolts or thumb locks that operate only from the inside or are keyed so that only you can open them from the outside. If proper deadbolts are installed it will eliminate the need to add surface bolts inside which are not as strong or as burglar proof. Check every knob, lock and bolt to be sure it works.

Doors and Windows: First of all check to see if all exterior doors have solid cores. You can do this by knocking on them to see whether they sound hollow or not. They should be solid to stop cold air transfer and burglars. Open and close all the doors and windows to be sure they work smoothly. Try the garage door also and if there is a small person in the family see if he or she is strong enough or tall enough to operate it. If doors and windows

stick it could be a sign of building settlement, just too many layers of old paint, a worn out window unit or one of poor quality. Once I rented an apartment (Victorian) and didn't check the eight-foot-high windows. Later, I found that most of them wouldn't open. Besides the lack of ventilation, there was a beautiful Datura lily tree outside and I couldn't smell its fragrance, or touch it!

Tile Showers and Countertops: One method of setting tile is in *mud* or cement plaster with cement grout filling the tile joints! The other method is called *thinset* which is set in mastic, which is like thick glue. The mastic method is not as waterproof as the cement base. This installation method may allow leaking and dry rot problems. Ceramic tile set in mud will be a thicker dimension than thinset as shown in Figure 13. It will also sound solid when you tap it. Plastic or aluminum tile will

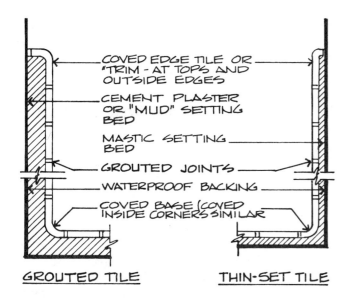

GROUTED TILE   THIN-SET TILE

FIGURE 13.   TILE SETTING
             METHODS

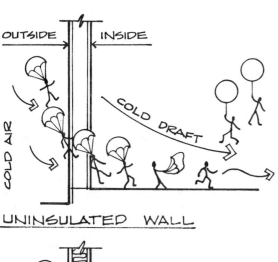

UNINSULATED WALL

INSULATED WALL

FIGURE 14.   DRAFT PHENOMENA

sound hollow, and since these are always set in mastic, avoid them. Also look at the joints to see if they are straight and matching. See if the total surface is smooth and even.

Insulation and Weatherstripping

No one needs to be told about the value of good thermal insulation. We all know its importance as an energy (and therefore money-saving) necessity.

Insulation, besides keeping hot and cold air in or out, works to stop cold drafts. Figure 14 shows how this works. Cold air coming in through a wall sinks to the bottom of a room to replace the lighter hot air. This causes an imperceptible wind which moves along the floor and keeps your feet cold. Good insulation prevents temperature difference between the inside wall surface and the room and eliminates the problem. You should demand proper insulation in a new home. In an older home, if the insulation isn't adequate or is non-existent, there are problems involved in correcting the situation, which we'll discuss later.

R Values: The effectiveness of any insulation is rated with what is called an *R Value*. This is the Resistance Value, a measurement of how hard it is for heat or cold to pass through any material. The higher the R Value the more resistive the material. This resistance works in summer to lower *heat gain* inside and in winter to lower *heat loss* to the outside. If you can keep heat in its place your home will naturally require less energy to heat or to cool. All heat can't be retained or deflected but the standard R Values recommended will do an adequate job.

The Roof: The standard rating requirement for an attic or joist space is R-19. A 6½'' mineral wool blanket installed between the ceiling joists will give this value. Insulation can also be blown into an attic or joist space in a loose form and a depth of 8½'' will also give an R-19 Value.

The Walls: Walls require a rating of R-11 or 3½'' of mineral wool. More would be better of course, but since this is the standard wall thickness, it's all there is room for. Some builders are now building with 6'' studs spaced 2' 0'' apart so that a thicker blanket can be used.

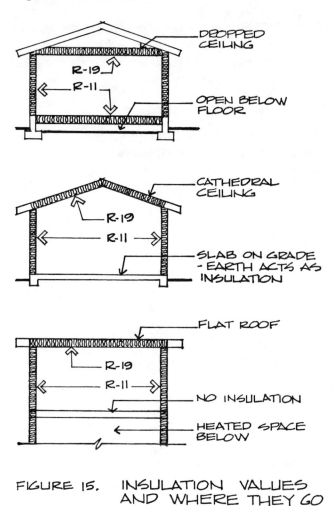

FIGURE 15. INSULATION VALUES AND WHERE THEY GO

The Floor: Floors should have an R-11 rating when they are over a crawl space, half basement or otherwise open to cold air. This can be obtained by stapling glass wool blankets under the floor and between the joists.

Since insulation hopefully is hidden in the walls, the ceiling, and beneath floors, it's not always easy to know if or what is there. The only way to determine what's in a wall is to chop a hole in it. Fortunately you don't have to do that because the electricians have already done it! Remove the cover plates of some electrical outlets or switches with a screw driver and you'll see the holes containing the *J Boxes* (junction boxes that the wiring comes through). Since the hole around the J Box gets covered, usually they are not neatly cut and usually you can see the insulation. It's possible to get the screwdriver into the wall cavity at the outside edge, being certain not to put it into the J Box itself. If you feel soft resistance it's probably insulation. If there's an attic you'll be able to see the insulation but if there's not, unscrew a ceiling fixture and check that similarly. If there's a basement or crawl space, you can look under the floor and if there's no space under the floor, insulation is probably unnecessary.

Older Homes: In older houses adding insulation in attics and crawl spaces is usually easy to do. Installing insulation in the wall cavities or in roof joist spaces in the case of a flat roof, is difficult, and difficult in home repair or construction means *expensive!* Holes have to be bored in the wall or ceiling between the studs or joists and the insulation is blown in by machine. Then all the holes have to be filled or patched. This requires a professional crew, so if you find yourself in this position, get an estimate of the cost, so you can determine whether you can afford to insulate.

Windows: There are always dire warnings about windows causing heat loss or heat gain and admonitions to keep them to a minimum. This is true only when nature has been ignored! If the windows have the right orientation, as discussed in Step 2, they can do more good than harm. Naturally windows on the north side are going to lose heat, and windows on the west are going to gain too much but a house with a lot of glass facing north or west is usually a poor house in the first place. Wood framed windows transfer less heat or cold than metal framed windows and insulating (or double paned) glass will transfer less than single glass. Don't be frightened into buying a house with small or a minimal amount of windows if you're a person that needs contact with outside space. Just be sure they are well oriented to nature.

Sound Insulation: Sound insulation, except the extreme amount used in recording studios, can never eliminate noise completely. If you have managed to avoid a noisy location, the concern now is noise

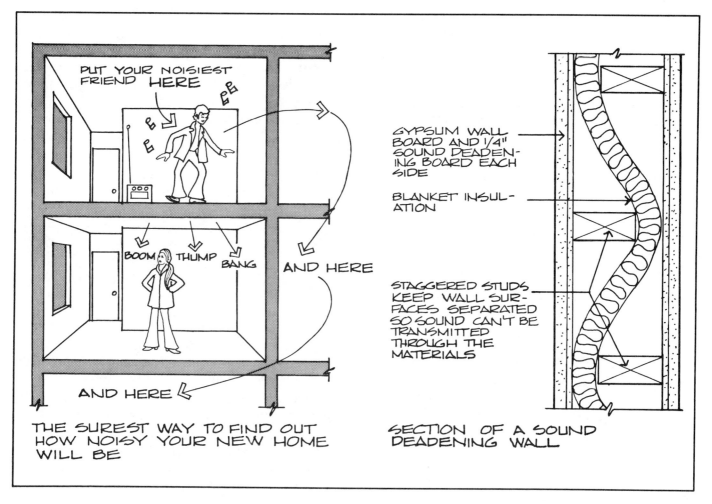

FIGURE 16. SOUND INSULATION

that travels through the walls, ceilings, and floors between rooms. This is an important consideration within a house and between neighboring apartments, above and below. There are many ways to deaden sound in walls but it is really not important to know how they work, but whether they work at all!

The easiest way to tell how much sound will pass through walls and ceilings is to have a friend and a transistor radio with you. Have your helper go into each of the adjacent units, turn the radio on high volume and proceed to stomp around. How much noise can you hear? Decide if you can stand it. If this procedure is not feasible, at least ask the neighbors if they have any problems with noise.

Good sound insulation will assure your future peace.

Weatherstripping: A lot of cold air can enter through cracks, especially around doors and windows. So check this too. A good way to do this is to open a window opposite any closed door or window which will draw air in through cracks. Stand near the door or window you're testing to see if you feel air entering. Light incense and hold it up to the edges of a door or window. If the smoke is disturbed there's air coming in. If there are leaks, try to determine whether they can be stopped with good weatherstripping, or if the gap is too wide to seal!

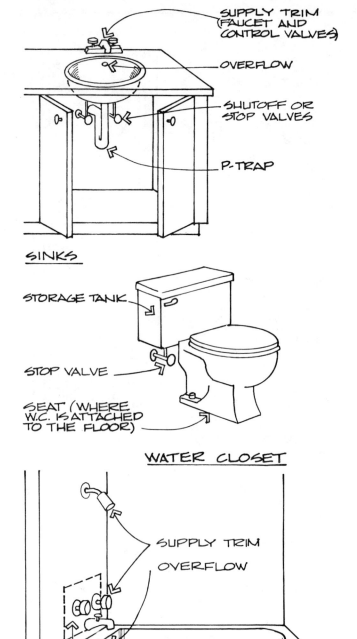

SINKS

WATER CLOSET

FIGURE 17. PLUMBING FIXTURES AND ACCESSORIES

Mechanical Systems

Plumbing: The water supplied to the house should come through a pipe large enough and have enough pressure to allow water to be used simultaneously in several locations without any significant drop in the pressure. The supply pipe should be 3/4" to 1" to do this adequately. Check the pressure by having someone go around the house turning several water sources on and off, including the yard faucets and flushing the toilet, while you watch an open tap to see if there is a decrease in the amount of water flow. If there is not enough pressure, one reason could be that there is not enough pressure in the main, and you can check this with the water company. Another reason might be that the service pipe from the main to the house is too small. And, in an older house, the problem could be that corrosion deposits have built up over the years in the pipes and are shutting off the water supply. If it's the latter it could mean that you might need to replumb the whole house.

Water hammer is an earsplitting annoyance. It is a vibration that can occur in the pipes when a faucet is shut off very abruptly. It is caused by the water pressure reverberating back down the pipes, and it can make a fearful racket and sometimes cause a pipe to burst. There are devices that hold an air pocket, or air chambers, that cushion these vibrations. Check to see if the system will have water hammer by going to all faucets, inside and out and turning the water (hot and cold) on and off rapidly several times. If you hear no noise, the system is installed to prevent it. If you hear the pipes shrieking, you'll need to remedy the situation. Sometimes the air chambers have filled with water so they are not working. Try turning all the water in the house off and drain the system. Then if you open all the faucets to let air in and then turn the water back on you can sometimes refill the chambers with air so they will work. If this doesn't solve the problem check to see what it will cost to have air chambers installed. Water pipes in an older home should be of copper or brass, which are the most non-corrosive materials. Lead, galvanized iron, or galvanized steel corrode. Take a magnet with you to determine what the pipes are made of. If the magnet sticks, the pipes are iron or steel. If it won't stick, the pipes are copper, brass, or lead. To distinguish which of these three materials exist, use your pocket knife and scratch the pipes. Copper or brass will show brightly and lead will be (of course) lead colored.

Plastic pipe which is non-corrosive and long lasting is now being used in almost all new houses. Its only disadvantage is that heat will deteriorate it eventually. For this reason, the pipes from the water heater to the hot water faucets should still be copper.

Now examine the plumbing fixtures. Flush every toilet to determine if they do flush, how long it takes and how noisy they are. A W.C. working silently is a W.C. of quality. Feel around the base of the toilet, or where it is seated, to see if it leaks there. Feel around all the pipes behind and at the shutoff valve for leaks or dampness!

Every water closet, wash basin, and sink should have shutoff valves on both the cold and hot water supply pipes. Shutoff valves allow you to turn off the water if a faucet control fails or a pipe breaks so you can avoid a flood. Tubs and showers don't have outside shutoffs, they are buried in the wall. Occasionally the builder will have put an access panel in a backing wall, when it can be hidden in a wardrobe or other secret place, so check to see if there is access.

Turn on every faucet to see if they leak around the handles or base. Feel around all the pipes underneath for leakage. When you turn on the shower, point the head at the shower door and run the water for a few minutes to see if the door leaks.

Check the tubs and wash basins and the sinks to see if they are of good quality and cast iron. Stamped steel is flexible and enamel will chip off it much easier than with cast iron, so it won't wear well. Steel will ring when you tap it and cast iron will be quiet. The waste or sewage lines should have a *cleanout* on every horizontal run of drainpipe. These look like plugs and can be opened so the rooter man can free clogs. Ask to see where they are located.

Water Heaters: Many forms of energy can be used to fuel water heaters, but gas and electricity are the most common. A gas water heater uses less energy than an electric one, and will heat the water much faster. Good water heaters will have a plate on them that states all its operation and capacity data. As we go on to discuss the requirements of a heater, all the information mentioned should appear on that plate. If it does not, the age or the quality of the heater should be questioned.

A gas heater should have a minimum capacity of forty gallons for a family of four with two bathrooms, a dishwasher and a clothes washer. This is a rough estimate, of course, and the requirements will have to be adjusted to your family size and its capacity to use hot water. A water heater that is designated *rapid recovery* can hold only thirty gallons and do the same job as a forty gallon heater. An electric heater would have to have an eighty gallon capacity for the same family of four. Electric heaters have a very slow recovery rate so more hot water needs to be available in storage. This could be cut to sixty gallons if the heater is *high speed* or *high watt*.

The heater should have a recognizable name brand (Rheem, Night & Day, National, A.O. Smith, etc.) and, in a new house, have at least a ten year guarantee. All water heaters should have a pressure and temperature relief valve. This is designed to blow open if things go wrong, and eliminates any possibility of the heater itself blowing up. This valve should lead to a pipe which leads outside, so your house won't flood if it does blow. There should also be a faucet on the bottom of the heater that will allow you to drain it periodically to get rid of sediment and other buildup so it will have a longer life.

If the heater is an older model, look for rust or corrosion on the heater and around the pipes that lead in and out of it. Open a hot water tap and partially fill a basin or sink. If the water is rust colored, or there are chips of rust present, it is a sign that the water heater is going into the throes of death.

As an energy saving factor, the heater should be close to the fixtures it serves. Long runs of pipe, even if they are insulated, require that some of your energy money will be spent just to keep the pipe hot.

Waste systems: The sewage disposal system and how (or if) it works deserves a thorough checkout before you buy. It can be an expensive commodity. There are three common systems used for sewage removal: the city sewer, the septic tank/leach field, and the cesspool. Connection to a sewer just about eliminates all major problems but the other two can be a source of more problems than you can imagine. Figure 18 shows these two systems. Cesspools will generally be found only with old houses because in most areas they're not legal anymore. The workable lifetimes of cesspools are limited. The drain holes plug up and cease to allow the water to drain or *percolate* out. This means pumping it out often, or replacing it. Septic tank/leach field systems deposit the solid waste in the lower part of the tank to decompose. Only the fluid waste passes on into the perforated pipe of the drain or leach field. Since only liquid matter enters the leach pipes they remain unplugged for a much longer period of time.

Leach fields require a lot of square footage and can use up most of your yard. If the soil is not porous enough to allow the water to soak through, the system won't work. Today the building and health authorities require percolation tests to prove the soil will soak up water adeuately before they will give a permit to build a leach field. In a home built before these tests were required, the soil may not be porous enough. If the authorities won't allow you to use the old system, or replace it this could mean the end of your investment. New or old, it will be safer to check with the local authorities to see if the leach field in question was installed after percolation tests were performed and approved. If there were no tests, find out generally how the soil in the area has been found to percolate. The building or health inspector will also tell you if the system was sized properly in relation to the ability of the soil to absorb water.

Electricity: The way electrical current really works is very complicated except to those who seem to have an aptitude for understanding it. To some it is a matter-of-fact scientific reality. Others believe it's a mystical force with mysterious ways. The rest

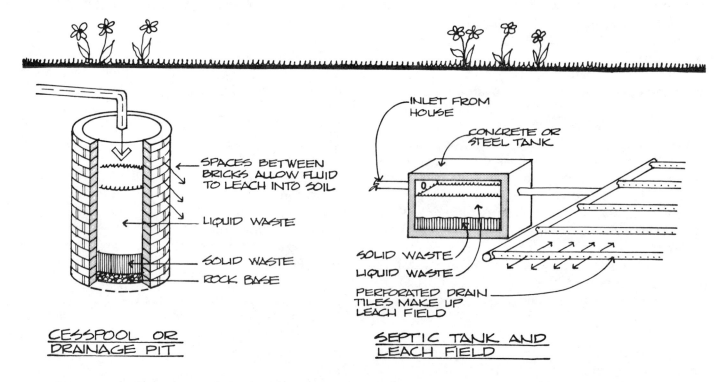

FIGURE 18. WASTE DISPOSAL SYSTEMS

of us just expect it to be there! Here we will go into it just enough to enable you to know what your needs will be and if they will be satisfied in your new home. A complete run-through of the properties and workings of electricity would bore or confuse most of us! I have listed some good sources in the bibliography for those that have more than a passing interest. The important things to know are what's coming to you, where it goes, whether there will be enough, and if it will be safe!

Power companies usually supply two types of current and it comes in terms of Volts. These types are, depending on your local company, 110/220V and 120/240V. Essentially the power provided is the same and this difference is just another electrical confusion! You can find out which you have by calling the company, but its not really necessary to know. What you should know is whether you are getting a *three wire* service. Figure 19 shows how a standard system works from the source to your lightbulb or toaster.

The voltage passes to your house through a *service head,* then through the meter (for accounting purposes) and on to the *main switch*. The main switch allows you to turn everything off in the house and yard quickly in an emergency. Or, it will allow you to make repairs without fear and doubt.

The next stop on the current road is the breaker panel, or the fuse box. A breaker panel is the newer and better type of equipment. It is made up of switches which are heat sensitive. If the wires become overloaded from a short circuit, or having too many lights and appliances on all at once, they will shut off and break the electrical connection before things explode.

Fuses are designed to do the same job. They contain a wire connection that will burn up faster than the wiring itself and break the connection. Fuses are less sensitive than breaker switches and, since they do not repair themselves, require installation of new fuses to get the system working again. Breakers can be turned back on after the problem has been solved without requiring new parts. And too, since fuse boxes are old fashioned, they are a sign that the wiring system is also old fashioned. Their presence indicates that it would be wise to get a home inspector to check the electrical system.

Fuse boxes and breaker panels are sized in terms of amperes (amps, for short). The minimum size breaker panel or fuse box a home should have is 100 amps, increasing to about 220 amps if you have a lot of equipment and appliances. The amperage of the panel or fuse box should be stated right on it. Breaker switches, or fuses, are generally 15 amps each so multiply to find the total amperage if it isn't stated. If you find a panel or fuse box is less than 100 amps, as is common in older homes, the building is not wired for the present day usage. This means that you will have to do without some appliances or rewire the house. Another check you can perform is just as with water pressure, turn on every light, then turn on some major appliances and see if the lights dim, or worse! Each breaker or fuse controls one circuit. A circuit is similar to a string of Christmas tree lights, only it is plugged into the breaker panel and carries not only light bulbs, but plugs (convenience outlets) and lighting fixtures. The panel should have a space next to each breaker switch where a label can be placed to tell where its own particular circuit is located in the house. The labels should be completed so you'll know which one to turn off when the need arises. The sketch of a three wire system in Figure 19 diagrams how the electricity is taken from the panel and travels to the circuits themselves.

Figure 19 shows what items can be supplied by general service circuits, which need a separate circuit and which appliances need 220V or 240V circuits, which amounts to using two circuits at once. Add up the number of circuits you'll need to see if the panel is large enough. In addition, it's always best to have some extra circuits for future use in case you want to build an addition, install an electric kiln or build a swimming pool. Convenience outlets should be located approximately twelve lineal feet apart in each room excluding closets or hallways. This means a cord never has to reach more than six feet. If this spacing isn't adhered to, it's back to extension cords again! If you have an idea how you'll furnish a room, determine if the outlets are in the right place to handle your needs. Check the availability of convenience outlets in the garage or shop. There should be some weatherproof outlets on the exterior of the house so you

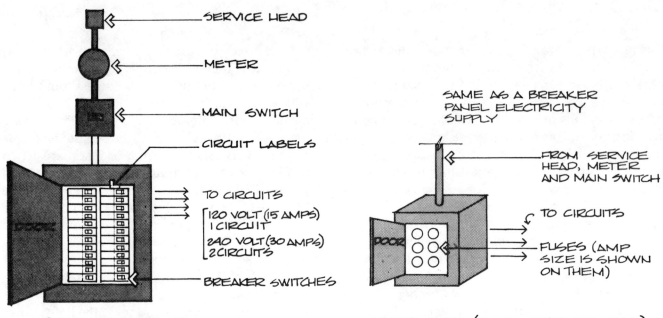

SERVICE HEAD

METER

MAIN SWITCH

CIRCUIT LABELS

TO CIRCUITS

120 VOLT (15 AMPS)
1 CIRCUIT
240 VOLT (30 AMPS)
2 CIRCUITS

BREAKER SWITCHES

BREAKER PANEL

SAME AS A BREAKER PANEL ELECTRICITY SUPPLY

FROM SERVICE HEAD, METER AND MAIN SWITCH

TO CIRCUITS

FUSES (AMP SIZE IS SHOWN ON THEM)

FUSE BOX (IN OLDER HOMES)

HOW ELECTRICITY COMES INTO YOUR HOME

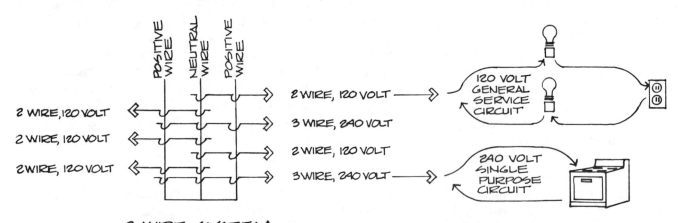

POSITIVE WIRE NEUTRAL WIRE POSITIVE WIRE

2 WIRE, 120 VOLT

2 WIRE, 120 VOLT

2 WIRE, 120 VOLT

2 WIRE, 120 VOLT

3 WIRE, 240 VOLT

2 WIRE, 120 VOLT

3 WIRE, 240 VOLT

120 VOLT GENERAL SERVICE CIRCUIT

240 VOLT SINGLE PURPOSE CIRCUIT

3 WIRE SYSTEM
THIS DRAWING REPRESENTS WIRES INSIDE THE PANEL

NOTE: A TWO WIRE SYSTEM WILL ONLY POWER 120 VOLTS. A THREE WIRE SYSTEM IS NEED TO GET 240 VOLTS FOR MODERN APPLIANCES

HOW ELECTRICITY TRAVELS THROUGH A HOME

GENERAL SERVICE CIRCUITS

CONVENIENCE OUTLETS AND LIGHTS:
1 - 120 VOLT CIRCUIT FOR EVERY 500 SQUARE FEET OF FLOOR AREA.

KITCHEN, SHOP, ETC. SHOULD HAVE A SEPARATE CIRCUIT.

THERE SHOULD BE SEVERAL UNUSED CIRCUITS FOR FUTURE NEEDS.

SEPARATE CIRCUITS

REFRIGERATOR/FREEZER	120 VOLT
DISHWASHER/DISPOSER	120 "
OVEN	240 "
MICROWAVE OVEN	120 "
RANGE/COOKTOP	240 "
WASHER	120 "
DRYER	240 "
ROOM AIR CONDITIONER	240 "

FURNACE, AIR CONDITIONER, ELECTRIC WATER HEATER, ETC. - AS REQUIRED ON LABEL

FIGURE 19. THE LEAST ONE NEEDS TO KNOW ABOUT ELECTRICITY

can run electric equipment out of doors without stringing the cords through the windows.

Most building codes now require that convenience outlets be grounded by a third wire that connects to a metal pipe which is buried in the ground. This takes any loose current safely into the ground thereby preventing shock. It will also ground any overload of electricity caused by lightning or a similar disaster. It is imperative that outlets for major electrical appliances such as a range or the dryer be grounded.

Light switches should be located conveniently, so one needn't wander about in the dark to find them. If possible, try to get touch plates, which are switch plates that turn on and off by touching them. They are preferable to the toggle type switch because they can be operated with any part of your body if your hands are full. Also, they are smooth faced and can be cleaned with one wipe rather than having a lot of grooved detail to catch dirt.

Gas Service: Gas should be delivered through pipes made of black iron, or plastic, which is becoming commonly acceptable. Generally, for a 3 bedroom, 2 bath home a ½" diameter pipe is needed and a 5 bedroom, 3 bath home with fireplace outlets should have a ¾" diameter pipe. Of course the size will also depend on whether or not the appliances are mainly gas. The size could be as large as 1" diameter if you have a swimming pool heater, but in most parts of the country gas is no longer allowed to be used for this purpose. If you want a warm pool you may have to start researching solar energy.

Heating and Air Conditioning: Architects usually hire mechanical engineers to worry about this, so I'm not an expert in this area! If you hire a home inspector make sure he is expert in this so he can assume this responsibility. If you have any cause to doubt the system hire a mechanical engineer to look at it. I don't advise asking a heating or air conditioning contractor since they are in the business of repairing heating and cooling systems or installing new ones. He may be completely honest, but how will you be sure?

There are some general things and a couple of energy-saving features to watch for no matter which type of heating or cooling unit you have.

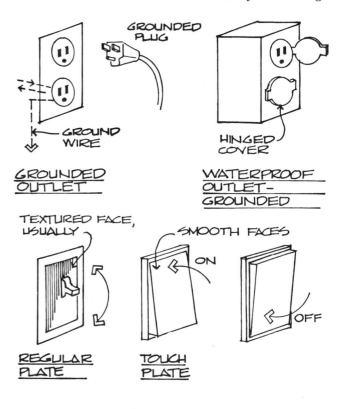

FIGURE 20. OUTLETS AND SWITCH PLATES

First, the closer the unit is to where you want the treated air, hot or cold, the more energy you'll save. Long duct runs lose energy, whether insulated or not, just as with hot water pipes. The newer units have an *energy efficient* rating which will appear on the information plate. Ducts for both heating and cooling should be wrapped with insulation that has moisture-proof outside skin.

A really good system should be *zoned*. This means there are two or more areas or zones of a home equipped for different heat levels. Usually the zoning breaks between living and sleeping areas, and the thermostat for each zone should be located nearby. Separate zoning is usually furnished only in very large homes. Since zoning isn't done for smaller houses or apartments, make sure you can open or close registers in unused rooms to make this adjustment. This is not an ideal situation either because energy will be wasted to heat the unused air in the ducts.

The thermostat should be located in the area of the home that you'll want to keep warmest, on an

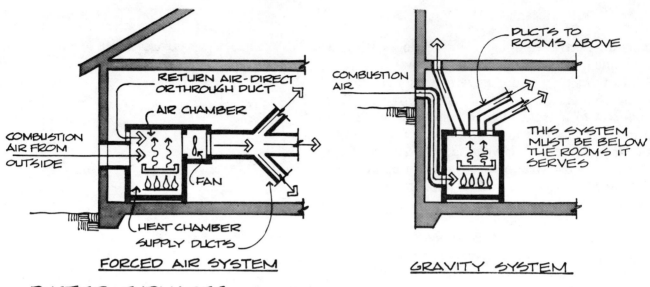

COMBUSTION AIR FROM OUTSIDE

RETURN AIR-DIRECT OR THROUGH DUCT

AIR CHAMBER

FAN

HEAT CHAMBER

SUPPLY DUCTS

FORCED AIR SYSTEM

COMBUSTION AIR

DUCTS TO ROOMS ABOVE

THIS SYSTEM MUST BE BELOW THE ROOMS IT SERVES

GRAVITY SYSTEM

DUCTED FURNACES

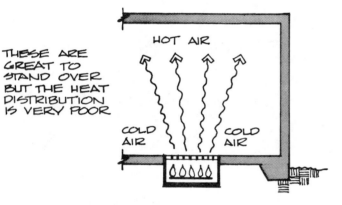

THESE ARE GREAT TO STAND OVER BUT THE HEAT DISTRIBUTION IS VERY POOR

HOT AIR

COLD AIR   COLD AIR

FLOOR FURNACE

WALL FURNACE

DUCTLESS FURNACES

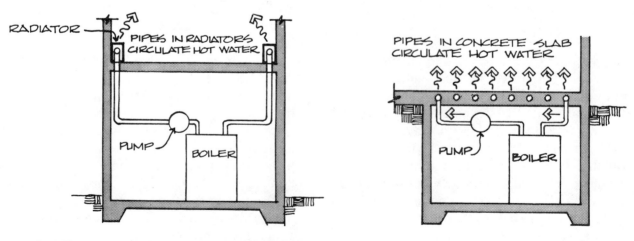

RADIATOR

PIPES IN RADIATORS CIRCULATE HOT WATER

PUMP

BOILER

PIPES IN CONCRETE SLAB CIRCULATE HOT WATER

PUMP

BOILER

RADIANT HEATING SYSTEMS

FIGURE 21. HEATING SYSTEMS

interior wall, away from drafts, out of direct sunlight and away from any source of heat or cold such as a refrigerator or range.

Whatever the type of system, turn it on and let it run while you check the rest of the house or apartment. Is it noisy? Does it cycle, or turn on and off with great frequency? This can be an indication that it is not working properly! Does air whistle when it comes through the ducts and registers? Perhaps this can be stopped by adjusting the register, but make sure that it can. Sometimes a whistle is in the duct itself and can be very difficult to correct. And most importantly, does it heat or cool to the thermostat setting in a reasonable amount of time?

Find the name of the manufacturer of the equipment. All air conditioning units and heaters should have an information plate. Make certain again that it is a known company (Trane, Westinghouse, Carrier, etc.). Get the model number and call around locally to find if parts and service are available.

If you are looking at a second-hand home, ask for copies of gas, oil or electric bills from the previous year or two for the coldest and the hottest months. This way you'll know if you can afford what it costs to be comfortable.

Heating Systems: Forced air heating is a system that uses a fan to force warm air into the living space. Gravity heating means that the furnace is located somewhere below with the hot air rising up naturally through ducts and floor vents. Some systems have boilers and the heat is carried to the rooms by hot water or other fluids. The fluid flows through pipes into radiators or pipes in a concrete floor slab. Both systems are called radiant heating. A wall furnace, while probably cheapest to install, is not as effective because it doesn't distribute heat evenly. Generally, since heat rises, all the best systems are designed for the heat to enter the room somewhere near the floor on an outside wall or in front of windows. This is called perimeter heating.

No system will keep you warm if it isn't sized properly. Look at the information plate again. It should give the size of the furnace in terms of B.T.U.'s (British Thermal Units) per hour. A rule of thumb is that 50 BTU's are needed to heat one square foot of a building, or 70 BTU's in a very

cold climate. Take the number of square feet the house contains and multiply it by 50 BTU's. A house with 1,500 square feet needs a 75,000 BTU furnace. If this output is not listed on the machine itself, try to get a written guarantee from the seller that it will heat the house adequately.

If you are renting there is no assurance that the space will be warm enough. All you can really do is ask other tenants in the building. Sometimes there is one furnance for the whole building and the landlord sets the temperature at his choice! In some cases the furnace is on a timer which turns the heat on only in the evening hours, say from 5:00 to 10:00 and on weekends. I've had to live with this situation. It's cold when you come home from work and when you get up in the morning. If you spend your days at home, or have occasion to stay home sick, you could freeze to death. Fortunately, our apartment faced a south, sun-absorbing orientation, but the people across the hall in the apartment facing north always wore a lot of clothing and looked blue. Humidity is another factor to consider when your home is subject to dry artificial heat all winter. Normally, household cooking and bathing generate enough humidity to keep humans happy. Plants, however, are more sensitive to this because they need more humidity so they may need frequent fogging to be happy.

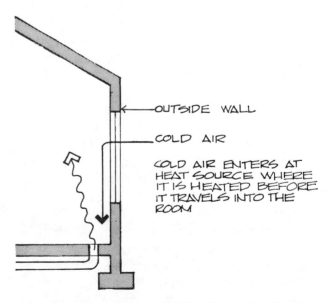

FIGURE 22. PERIMETER HEATING

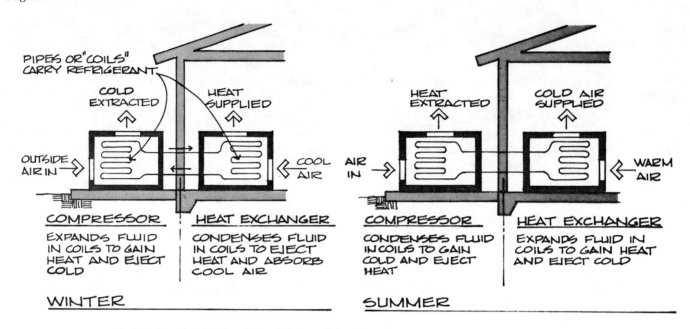

FIGURE 23. HOW HEAT PUMPS WORK

Cooling Systems: These are available as separate refrigeration units or heat pumps. Refrigeration units only cool, while heat pumps can cool in summer and heat in winter. Heat pumps are best in temperate zones where year-round temperature modification is needed because they can do both jobs. In the winter heat pumps absorb the heat out of the cold air and pump it into the house. Both the heat pump and refrigeration unit absorb the heat from the inside air in the summer and pump it outside. Compressors, heat exchangers and mysterious gases are used to do this! Although it sounds complicated it is really very simple. Figure 23 shows in a schematic way how this works.

All cooling systems are sized in terms of *tons.* One ton of cooling equals 12,000 BTU's. The size of the unit depends on extremity of temperature and the insulation, but a general rule is to use 20 BTU's per square foot of house or 1 ton for every 600 square feet. Guarantees that assure 75° with 50% relative humidity are common and obtaining one will free up another worry circuit.

Cooling units should also have an efficiency rating which tells how much it will cool for the energy expended. The plate on the machine will show this rating. If it doesn't you can expect to have high energy bills. It should state the number of cooling units delivered for each watt of electricity expended. Small units should have a rating of 5 or 6 and larger ones 12 to 13. Another money saving feature present on some units is a clock thermostat. This will allow you to leave the unit off when you are away, at work or on a vacation, and set it to turn on at the time you choose so your home will be warm or cool when you arrive. You can be your own miserly landlord.

Solar Heating and Cooling: This is an infant industry and it is impossible to endorse one system or manufacturer over another. Most of them haven't been around long enough to be tested. The fact that most solar type systems are new however, will allow you to ask for and get a binding performance guarantee.

Miscellaneous

Here are just a few more small items that you should notice when you're checking a home.

Stairways: Stairways are permitted to be a minimum of 30" wide in a residence, and since the width of a stairway often poses a problem with getting furniture into the second story look at it carefully. If furniture won't go up the stairway, you'll have to do without or hire equipment (and people) to lift it into the upstairs windows. Further, it means making sure that you can get to the windows, that they are large enough and that the screens are removable. You may save yourself the grief of finding out too late you can't get that over-sized antique into your new home!

Exits: Another factor often overlooked is how your family will get out in case of fire or other emergency. There should be at least two ways out of each floor, either by door or window that is easily opened. A good way out of each room is better yet, and not only out, but to the ground and well away from the building. So look the house or apartment over well to see how escape can be accomplished.

Fireplaces: You'll want to be sure that fireplaces are safely constructed and work well. Any masonry fireplace should be lined with fire brick which is a denser, more highly fired brick than the regular kind. It will not decompose from the heat as will regular masonry. Although it is hard to see when the building is completed, all fireplaces and chimneys should be separated from the structure itself by an air space and by insulation. Check this by looking in the attic, on the as-builts, or ask the building department if they have a record of its construction.

Metal fireplaces are manufactured commercially or are sometimes handcrafted from steel barrels or metal welded into original art forms. The fire box in manufactured fireplaces is usually well insulated and will not transfer enough heat to burn you. Uninsulated custom fireplaces can get extremely hot and are very dangerous, if you have little children. On the other hand, this will transfer more heat into a room, less up the chimney and be more efficient. Even better are metal "circulating" type fireplaces. These heat air in a chamber enclosing the firebox and then, either by gravity or with fans, circulate it back into your living space.

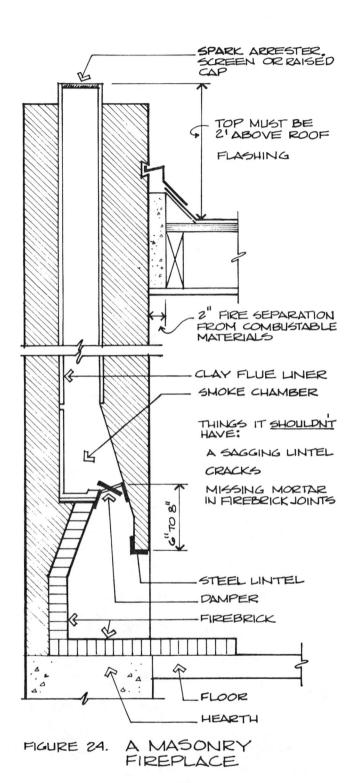

FIGURE 24. A MASONRY FIREPLACE

SPARK ARRESTER, SCREEN OR RAISED CAP

TOP MUST BE 2' ABOVE ROOF

FLASHING

2" FIRE SEPARATION FROM COMBUSTABLE MATERIALS

CLAY FLUE LINER

SMOKE CHAMBER

THINGS IT SHOULDN'T HAVE:

A SAGGING LINTEL

CRACKS

MISSING MORTAR IN FIREBRICK JOINTS

6" TO 8"

STEEL LINTEL

DAMPER

FIREBRICK

FLOOR

HEARTH

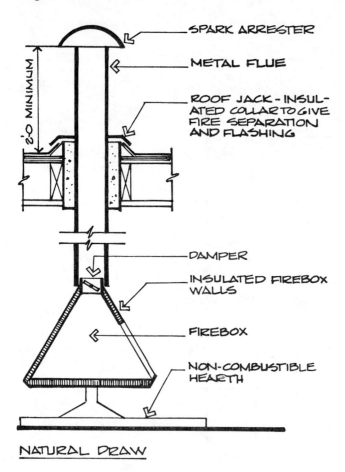

2'-0 MINIMUM

SPARK ARRESTER

METAL FLUE

ROOF JACK - INSUL-
ATED COLLAR TO GIVE
FIRE SEPARATION
AND FLASHING

DAMPER

INSULATED FIREBOX
WALLS

FIREBOX

NON-COMBUSTIBLE
HEARTH

NATURAL DRAW

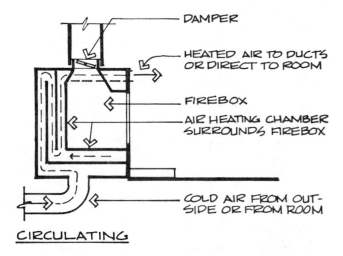

DAMPER

HEATED AIR TO DUCTS
OR DIRECT TO ROOM

FIREBOX

AIR HEATING CHAMBER
SURROUNDS FIREBOX

COLD AIR FROM OUT-
SIDE OR FROM ROOM

CIRCULATING

FIGURE 25. METAL FIREPLACES

Metal fireplaces should be located well away from adjacent walls or other combustible materials. The metal flue of a fireplace or stove should always pass through the roof structure inside a *roof jack*. This is an insulated collar that extends from the ceiling, through the attic or joist space, to above the top of the roof. The elimination of the collar or jack is extremely hazardous, because a hot flue can set fire to the roof.

There are required clearances from combustible materials at the hearth. These generally require that a noncombustible hearth slab (masonry, concrete, tile, etc.) extend outward 18" in front of the fireplace opening, be 12" wider on each side than the opening and be 4" thick. Metal fireplaces or hoods are required to be 18" from any adjacent combustible walls or anything else that is combustible. They must have a hearth the same width and length as required for masonry fireplaces, and be at least $3/8$" thick of an approved, noncombustible material. A damper is a very desirable fireplace feature because it can lower the amount of heat that escapes up the chimney. Dampers will allow the chimney to be closed down to a diameter just large enough to allow it to draw well, and allow no more heat loss than necessary. It can also be closed to eliminate drafts coming down the chimney when you are not using it. A gas connection in the fireplace will enable you to start a fire quickly and easily. It can also save a bundle of kindling and a gallon of starter fluid. Later, if you get tired of building fires and cleaning the fireplace, you may want a gas log installed, so a connection now will save expense later.

Chimneys should extend two feet above any part of the roof or other structure within ten feet of it. This requirement changes with altitude so if you are in the mountains check with the building department to see what is required. Be sure a metal flue or chimney is solidly fastened to the roof, so you won't lose it in a storm. All chimneys should be screened at the top or have a *spark arrester* to stop burning debris from flying onto your roof and the rest of the neighborhood.

The real issue is whether the fireplace will work! Generally, a fireplace with an opening on only one side will draw the best. There is lessening effectiveness as more sides are open. Since any type of

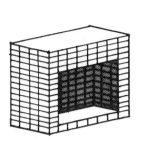

BEST- SINGLE OPENING

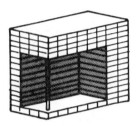

GOOD - OPEN
TWO SIDES

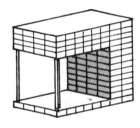

POOR - OPEN
THREE SIDES

BAD - OPEN
ALL SIDES

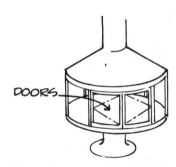

DOORS

ALSO A BEST
- GLASSED
ALL AROUND

FIGURE 26. SOME FIREPLACE
DESIGNS DRAW
BETTER THAN OTHERS

fireplace can smoke, try to find out if it will. In an older house you can look at the firebrick inside to see if the fireplace looks like it had been used a lot. If it does, it's probably worked well. Look for signs of smoke above the opening. In a new house, or an older one with an unused fireplace, ask for permission to light a good size fire (a small paper fire won't be conclusive). See how well it works. Adjust the damper to see what effect it has. Open a door or two and then shut them again to see if this causes the fireplace to smoke. And last, how much warmth does the fireplace seem to project into the room? A lot or almost none? If you're a fireplace freak you'll want it to give you all it can. If you can't light a fire, hold a stick of incense in the fireplace while someone else opens windows and doors, so you can see if that distrubs the smoke and keeps it from going up the flue.

CHECKLIST

PRELIMINARY CHECKS:

Check with local governing body

Property zoning.

Adjacent zoning.

New projects planned.

Height and setback limitations.

Conformance of structure to local laws.

der

Does builder have good references?

Can you get a good guarantee?

Value Comparison

Does price per square foot compare well with other homes?

Drawings

Site survey and topography (Pre-construction).

Site Plan (As-built or post construction).

Soil Test results (if any or if indicated).

As-built building plans (or at least pre-built plans).

SITE CHECKS:

Can you use the property as you wish (for now and future)?

Is rear yard accessible to construction equipment?

Is site stability good (visual evidence and soil tests if uncertain)? Will soil support plants?

Utility posts and wires out of sight?

Hose bibbs adequate and located conveniently?

Water runoff and drainage good—from roof and from site?

BUILDING—OUTSIDE:

Footings, Foundations and Basement Walls (and Concrete or Masonry Walls)

Quality of concrete and/or mortar?

Cracks?

Level?

Water infiltration, dampness and efflorescence?

Moisture barriers if necessary?

Termite or rot evidence?

Sills—rot resistant material?

Mobile Homes: x-bracing and tiedowns?

Walls

Straight and true?

Cracks in plaster?

Is plaster coated with a waterproof material?

Woodwork

Separation of materials, warping, gaps, etc.?

Well secured?

Straight and true?

Nails—rust resistant, countersunk and filled?

Windows—putty integrity, glass held tightly?

Rot around windows and trim?

Paint

Smoothly applied?

Waterproof material?

Blistering, checking or peeling?

Roof

Smooth, uniform surface overall?

Fully covered with sand, gravel or other coating on asphalt-rolled or asphalt shingles?

Firmness of wood shingles with no nail withdrawal or looseness?

No gaps at flashing?

Gutters and downspouts firmly attached with capacity to take runoff adequately and quickly?

Leak evidence (inside at attic or ceiling)?

BUILDING—INSIDE:

Paint

Washable?

Cover well?

Applied smoothly?

Woodwork

Smooth and straight?

Well sanded and with washable paint?

Floors

Level?

Subfloor—smooth and neatly installed?

Floor solid (or not spongy when you jump on it)?

Finish flooring installed neatly and smoothly?

Bases—coved, smooth and tightly fitting?

Hardware

Easy to clean?

Neatly installed?

Good locks and dead bolts?

Windows and Doors

Do they open easily and close tightly?

Weatherstripping good?

Tile

Cement base or thinset?

Even surface and straight joints?

Grout applied neatly?

Insulation

Thermal?

Sound?

Mechanical Systems

PLUMBING

Water supply pressure good?

No water hammer?

Leaks—Fixtures, shower doors, water heaters, hose bibbs, etc.?

Fixture quality good?

WATER HEATER

Adequate capacity and good recovery?

Reliable and recognized manufacturer?

Pressure relief valve and drain?

Corrosion of pipes or rusty water?

Located near fixtures it serves?

Efficiency rating?

WASTE SYSTEMS

Sewer, septic tank or cesspool?

Leach field and soil percolation adequate?

System size adequate?

Is it in accordance with local health and building codes?

ELECTRICITY

Number of circuits adequate (now and for future)?

Outlet locations placed so you can furnish and light the way you want?

Waterproof outlets outside (where you want them)?

Outlets grounded?

Light switches convenient, adequate and easy to clean?

GAS

Supply size adequate?

Pipe of proper materials, or to code?

HEATING AND AIR CONDITIONING

Recognizable trade name and repairable locally?

Adequately sized for heating and cooling?

Quiet operation?

Thermostat location good?

Registers located at outside perimeter of rooms?

Registers located out of the way of furniture?

FIREPLACES

Draws well?

Clearances adequate from combustible materials?

Damper?

Fire separation from roof structure?

Spark arrester?

Chimney height above roof adequate?

Chimney or flue solidly secure at roof?

MISCELLANEOUS

Can you get furniture through stairways and halls?

Are there at least two good exits?

Epilogue

Even though you are probably not yet a home inspection expert, now that you have looked at the mechanics of a structure you know a lot more about what to look for, and what to look out for. You won't be stuck with just "kicking the tires." If you find anything major is wrong, be sure to get estimates of repair costs before you buy. This will give you a bargaining point with the seller, or, if you will have to make the repairs yourself, at least you'll know the amount of money it will take. If you don't want a home that will bankrupt you, you can, and should, be choosy!

That's a lot to remember, isn't it? It's more than a lot, it's too much! Well, don't worry about remembering it all, because you'll be lucky if you find a home that has even half these things right. You know enough now and will remember enough to get the big things right, the little things half right, and the small things whipped into submission, so that they won't drive you mad. That's the best anyone of us could do.

Get your ego up (you know as much as any architect now, don't you?), get your tools and lists together, and get on out there. You're going to find the glass slipper that fits you, and maybe even a prince or princess!

Tools

Things to take with you when home shopping:

1. A bag large enough to hold the following items.
2. Pad and pencil: for comments recording measurements, noting location and looks of each dwelling, etc.
3. Tape recorder (optional): instead of or in addition to pad and pencil, if you feel it will be easier.
4. Instant print camera (optional): this will help you remember what each place *looks* like.
5. 12-foot (or more) measuring tape: preferably with a stop on it so you can measure vertical heights.
6. For the Stick Trick (covered in Step 2): 8" to 12" stick; protractor; play dough, clay or chewing gum; 18" square cardboard; hand level; ruler.
7. Compass.
8. Foot-candle reading light meter (optional).
9. Paper patterns of your furniture (optional).
10. Steel ball bearing or marble.
11. Incense, or anything that makes smoke, to check ventilation, drafts, fans, or any air movement.
12. Flashlight: to look in attics, basements and other dark spaces (if you're a prospective buyer).
13. Transistor radio: to check sound transmission.
14. Screwdriver or pocket knife (if buying): to check for insulation and to scratch pipes.
15. Magnet (if buying): to check pipe material.
16. Stud finder: to find stud spacing.
17. A small sponge and a towel: to check waterproof value of paint.

Bibliography

Dealing with Nature:

Foster, Ruth S. *Landscaping That Saves Energy Dollars.* New York: David McKay Company, Inc. 1978. Includes information on planting for climate control.
Ramsey, Charles G. and Sleeper, Harold R. *Architectural Graphic Standards, Sixth Edition.* New York: John Wiley & Sons, Inc., 1970. Includes additional information about sun angles.

Getting More From Any Interior Space:

Conran, Terence. *The Kitchen Book.* New York: Crown Publishers, 1977.
Liman, Ellen. *The Spacemaker Book.* New York: The Viking Press, 1977.
Naar, Jon and Siple, Molly. *Living In One Room.* New York: Vintage Books, 1976.
St. Marie, Satenig S. *Homes Are For People.* New York: John Wiley & Sons, Inc., 1973.

Special Types of Homes and Ownership:

Brooks, Patricia and Brooks, Lester. *How to Buy A Condominium.* New York: Stein and Day, 1975.
Engel, Lyle K. *Complete Book of Mobile Home Living.* New York: Arco, 1974.

More About How Things Work and Physical Inspection:

Hoffman, George. *How to Inspect A House.* New York: Dell Publishing Co., Inc., 1979.
Complete Do-it-yourself Manual. Pleasantville, NY: The Reader's Digest Association, Inc., 1973.

Financial, Legal and Real Estate Aspects:

Janik, Carolyn. *The House Hunt Game.* New York: MacMillan Publishing Co., Inc., 1979.
Kass, Benny. *Home Buyers Checklist.* (Pamphlet) Washington, D.C.: National Home Buyer's and Home Owner's Association, 1977.

Index

BOOKS OF RELATED INTEREST

CONVERSATIONS: Working Women Talk About Doing A Man's Job, edited by Terry Wetherby, presents frank interviews with women who have succeeded in traditionally male occupations, including chief of police, stuntwoman, tv network vice-president and race car driver. 288 pages, soft cover, $6.95

CRIMES AGAINST WOMEN: The Proceedings of the International Tribunal offers inspiring, dreadful, objective and overwhelmingly moving testimonies. This is a document of extreme importance to every woman. Edited by Diana E. H. Russell and Nicole Van de Ven. 320 pages, soft cover, $6.95

SPECIAL DELIVERY: The Complete Guide to Informed Birth by Rahima Baldwin is a comprehensive, practical guide for couples who want to take greater responsibility for the birth of their babies at home, in a birth center, or in the hospital. More than 80 illustrations and 30 photographs. 192 pages, soft cover, $9.95

EVERYWOMAN'S GUIDE TO TIME MANAGEMENT by Donna Goldfein is a back-to-basics, step-by-step program tailored for the woman who is pressured by routine and wants to take charge of her life. 128 pages, soft cover, $4.95

ALONE: Emotional, Legal and Financial Help for the Widowed or Divorced Woman by Helen Antoniak, Nancy Scott and Nancy Worcester provides complete information to help the woman alone become prepared, realistic and organized. ". . . sensible and practical. . . " *Kirkus Reviews.* 224 pages, soft cover, $6.95

Available at your local book or department store or directly from the publisher.

To order by mail send check or money order to:

Celestial Arts
231 Adrian Road
Millbrae, California 94030

Please include $1.00 for postage and handling. California residents add 6% tax.